MW00816734

THE

MONSTERS

WE

FEED

A LUMINAWORLD STORY

THOMAS HOWARD RILEY

Copyright 2022 by Thomas Howard Riley

Cover art by J Caleb Design

All rights reserved. This book or any portion thereof may not be reproduced or used in any manner whatsoever without the express written permission of the publisher except for the use of brief quotations in a book review.

All characters, locations, and events in this book are fictitious. All resemblance to persons living or dead is coincidental, and not intended by the author.

ISBNs: 978-1-955959-03-2 (hardcover), 978-1-955959-04-9 (paperback), 978-1-955959-05-6 (ebook)

To Allison. To Evan. And to my Mom and Dad.
Special thanks to Rowena, and to Dan for "the challenge"

THE

MONSTERS

WE

FEED

A book is never *just* a story.
It is a collaboration between the author and your imagination.
So every book is a different book depending on who reads it.
A book changes every time it changes hands.
That is truly extraordinary.

CONTENTS

1

Body

EVERYONE'S LIFE CHANGES THE first time they find a dead body.

"I'm sorry, what was that?" Jathan asked.

"Everyone's life changes the first time they find a dead body," Vaen Osper repeated, settling his olive-green magistrate's cape on his shoulders, fiddling with the silver clasps.

Felber Klisp was still busy buckling his swordbelt, on the third try after blundering the job and dropping his rig, scabbard and all, onto the floor twice already. It was not entirely due to clumsiness, Jathan conceded. Felber was a man who possessed an imprecise waist. His droopy eggplant of a torso simply...ended where his legs began.

Vaen was another matter. His body was perfectly proportioned. Lanky, muscles toned more from fucking his way across the west end than for any practice at swordplay. He liked his hair to be trimmed and coifed methodically, but he liked his beard to appear accidental.

Neither of the two had any badges or medals pinned to the breasts of their tunics. Vaen and Felber were not the kind of men who earned medals. They were the kind who did half the work that was expected of them, and then put a soft blanket of lazy deceit over it to make it look like they had done the other half.

Jathan was sure that not all magistrates were like this. Somewhere in one of Amagon's other notable cities there must have been professionals who took pride in a job well done.

But not in the west end of Kolchin. No, this city was run by shiftless, greedy idiots. Jathan was fine with that. He understood corruption, knew how to navigate it. He knew the rules; getting what he wanted was easy.

And what he cherished most was the supplemental income provided by turning in other Kolchans of the abnormal variety, the abominations who dared to have magick. He hated those creatures with magick so much he would have turned them in for free, but Vaen and Felber didn't need to know that. It felt so much better to earn coin while destroying something he loathed. He knew well the Kolcha way; never do what you do for nothing.

"What was that you were saying about dead bodies?" Jathan asked. He realized he had been staring so hard out the window he had no idea how the conversation arrived at that topic.

"That's the moment you realize you are just meat and bone. There is nothing more to you. Everything just ends. You don't even have a chance to know you ended. Realizing that, truly understanding that, reminds you that you have to grab what you can while you can."

Jathan held out his hand, palm up. "That is why I'm here. I want that shiny silver."

Vaen Osper chuckled. "Informing on a magick user isn't a steady enough line of work, and you'll be breaking your back at that secondhand shop in the back room of a winesink until you're a grey, wrinkled old skinsack. You would find easier money marrying off that sister of yours. Eldest male takes a dowry. You stand to make a fortune, what with your parents both dead and gone."

Jathan flinched. He prided himself on keeping a hard shell around himself, fencing off the kind of thoughts that made him feel like sinking into the sea, but that one always seemed to cut its way through his armor.

Felber fumbled his swordbelt again and it plopped in a heap, the hilt clanging on stone.

Vaen laughed harder. "Felber only needs hear mention of your sister and he sprouts a sword in his breeches."

"She is quite lovely," Felber said, reaching down for his scabbard like a man whose trousers were around his ankles, his round cheeks and sagging jowls turning bright pink from even that small exertion.

"She has another lover every season," Vaen laughed.

It's not that many, Jathan thought. *And she is a better person than your tongue deserves to speak of, you shitsack.* He bit back the words, knowing better than to bark at the hand that tosses the scraps...at least until the scraps were in his mouth.

Vaen folded his arms. "Don't give me that look, Jathan. You could have suitors scrambling over each other to throw sacks of gold at you for her hand."

"Her hand is her own to give," Jathan said. He kept his own hand out flat at arm's length, refusing to lower it until five double-silvers landed on his palm. He loved the weight of those coins. Each of them two and a half ounces of shiny wine money. They didn't make any other coins in that size. Just silver, like the silver moon in the night sky.

"What are you paying him already for?" Sau Ruda bleated, clomping into the room as sedulously as his bent leg permitted. "Have you even asked clarifying questions?"

To the furthest hell with you, Sau. Now here was the baseline of what Jathan thought was the lowest form of acceptable magistrate in Amagon. Someone who worked hard, cared at least halfway about what they were doing, and maybe fudged a corner here and there to make sure the lines met. The other two were abundantly below even this sad threshold.

But that was fine for Jathan. He trusted the locals to at least be what they appeared. Anything was better than a damn outsider. Outsiders were all liars, and they were less likely to toss out easy silver. The city of Kolchin was meant for the Kolcha people. If you weren't Kolcha, then you weren't worth the shit on your boots.

Vaen shrugged. "Jathan's eyes are better than most. Why question it?"

Sau grumbled, turned his thick, frequently befuddled brow to Jathan. "What did you see?"

Jathan turned his chin up. "A creature of filthy magick hiding inside a young woman's body. Half my age."

"Five summers old then?" Vaen quipped, laughing himself into oblivion.

"Ten," Jathan corrected, for some reason feeling like he needed to correct the record with Sau present. "I have seen twenty and you know it."

Sau ignored him. "What infernal acts did she perform?"

"She levitated a small stone to amuse some children," Jathan said. "Trying to trick them into thinking she was harmless."

"Are you certain she is not documented?" Sau asked. "Declared legal as a user of magick by the laws of the Lord Protector and the Council of the Nation of Amagon?"

"Oh for fucking's sake. A Kolcha beach dweller with documentation?" Jathan laughed. "You and I both know a wave rat could never afford the fee."

Sau was not convinced. "You are certain it was no sleight of hand? No wire? No other explanation?"

Vaen rolled his eyes. "Who cares, Sau?"

Sau ignored Vaen Osper as well. "Well? Are you certain?"

Jathan clenched teeth and puffed out his chin, trying to hold back a grimace. "I saw a shimmer of blinking lights, a little cloud."

"You see?" Vaen threw his hands up in the air. "He saw afterglow. The telltale of magick being used. With his own eye. That means he was close. Afterglow for something that small would fade to our eyes in moments."

"We should alert one of the Glasseyes," Sau said. "Have them take a look with their tools."

Every hell all at once, Jathan thought. *Not one of them.* To a Kolchin native like Jathan there was no greater blight than an outsider. And the worst kind were the Glasseyes. They acted like they were little princes, coming in from the capital and frightening everyone into obeying them. *We don't need them. Local troubles should have local answers. If you aren't Kolcha, the you aren't worth the shit on your boots.* It was the truest thing his secondparents ever taught him.

Vaen closed his eyes and leaned his head all the way back in irritation. "You want us to go drag one of the Glasseyes out for little wave rat? You know it could take them days of following the little beacher with their fancy crystal monocles before they chance to see her leave afterglow behind."

"And that is after a week of waiting for them to actually answer our call," Felber said, finally doing something useful.

Vaen smiled with half his face, the other half dead-eyed like a killer. "It looks better for our magistracy post if we get the job done without having to bother the high-and-mighties, eh Sau? The less we involve the capital officials the bigger our bonuses are, yes? A better pocket jingle for us."

Jathan smiled wide, ever holding his hand out, palm up, waiting for the pleasant weight of five double-silver coins to plop down upon it.

Sau grimaced, huffed a breath. "Fine. Pay him. Then get to work."

Vaen held one fist aloft in celebration. Felber clapped innanely.

Jathan pocketed the silver he was due and wished them happy hunting. *One less of those foul creatures on the streets of our city. Mine and my sister's streets. My parents' streets.*

"Be careful on your way back to the finestreets, swordless," Vaen said. "The Bowl District and Tenement Lane gangers have been brazen of late, I've heard. Unless your plan is to seduce them."

Jathan needed no reminding he could not afford a sword of his own, but Vaen's last comment confused him. He glanced down at his attire and realized he had momentarily forgotten he already had on his evening clothes, a tight white long-sleeved tunic that left little of his body to the imagination, and snug black trousers that left even less to the imagination. The ensemble had never failed to bring home a sweet thirsty nightbird from a dancehall, sourhouse, or winesink.

He made the sign of the witch at Vaen and stomped happily out the door, heading back to Upper End, the southeastern inland corner of Kolchin, his stomping ground.

He was already halfway down the block heading back to the finestreets by the time Vaen and Felber had wrangled Tylar, Sejassie, and Belo—their greasiest, most alarmingly hideous, lacknamed subordinates—out onto the street, heading north and west, to the dirty coasts where the beach rats lived.

In Amagon a surname came with the possession of property. Even if your family lost everything, they were permitted up to two generations to gain back one bit of land to keep the name.

Only perpetual renters and the lowest wretched scumborn went around without names. Jathan and his sister thankfully did not have to worry about that. Magistrates would not have given as much weight to a lackname. Or they might have offered only one double-silver. Or just a half silver. Or perhaps not even that.

But as much as he loved the uses of the name his parents had blessed him with, he was glad to the hundreds more for the joy they had breathed into his life before they went along to everwonder.

He jiggled the silver around in his pocket with his fingers.

I have found a few little joys on my own to fill the hole now.

He crossed the old Whalebone Bridge over the Kolcha River, where the sandslugs always used to congregate to sip the sweet smoke malagayne, roasting their lungs and their minds on smoldering grey leaves where the magistrates and smokehounds couldn't see.

The Kolcha river stank this close to the beach. Mostly because this tended to be where the facedown bodies usually snagged in the reeds or dragged onto the sandy patches. Everyone in the city called it *the Float* for a reason.

He glanced at the sunset over the sea as he walked, reminding himself he would go back down to the beaches one day and listen to the waves and splash in the surf as he once did. He had whispered that same reminder to himself for seven years, hundreds of times, but the day never seemed to come. He always had somewhere to go, someone to be.

He had already forgotten the promise before he made it a block past the bridge.

He kept to the cobbled road, past the small shops and rows of houses on the sandy shore, through the low end of Bridgetown, and past the butchery road that ran all the way inland to distant Tannery Town, where his parents used to take him and make him stand in its odious aromas when he had been bad.

He trotted his way over the Hillroad Crossing, where the apothecary street and stoneworkers' row intersected perfectly atop a shallow hill. He and his friends had spent the better parts of afternoons betting on which way a marble would roll, then scampering down after it before it dropped through a drain into one of the old Arradian sewers, still functioning five hundred years after Amagon jumped ship from being a colony of that ancient empire.

Jathan hoped the people who kept up the sewers were a more reliable sort than Vaen Osper and Felber Klisp or the whole city would be drowning in shit within a fortnight.

He cut inland at the old fleet road that went down to the abandoned galley docks where a great fleet had once sailed out to join with ships from Ossamport and Ethios to aid in the battle against the Tyrant's armada during the Great War.

The immense fleets of those days had been gone for hundreds of years. The one-two punch of relative peace on a sea lane and the construction of the great port city of Medion up north had turned the jewel of Amagon that Kolchin once was into a dull backwater stone in a shitplugged pond.

He and the ten generations before him never had a chance to know what they had been missing back when Kolchin was a place of abundance. Yet despite none of them having firsthand knowledge, everyone born to Kolchin was born with that same bewildered fear, that same internalized loathing, that same sense of loss.

But while that wide world of promise was no more, Kolchin offered something in its place. It offered peace, calm, and plenty for those who worked hard enough. Kolcha was a way of life. And the Kolcha people would fight to keep it that way.

It was a city where everyone was an insider, whether lushborn or scumborn, whether oozewealth or deservingless, ganger or magistrate, wrinkled grey or newborn pink. It was a place where everyone knew where they stood, and every position had its rules, and if you followed them you would prosper just enough.

It was a place where you were born and you lived and you worked and you stayed and you died. To all the people here, the city of Kolchin was still the jewel of the old days. Jathan assumed everyone else felt the same way. He could not imagine a way that one could not.

The sun was hanging low when he passed the spice exchange, and the smell of the sea vanished in swells of odors from the fish friers, the oileries and salt merchants, and the hay and dung from the corrals of infamous Palatoran horse tamers.

He then descended into the winding maze of streets that most everyone tried to avoid, unless they lived there. The city administrators knew it as the *Tenement District*. To the beachers it was *Tenement Range*, owing to its structures, tall like mountains to the eyes of sandslugs and wave rats. Bowlers called it *the Knot*. People of the East Uppers called it *the Web*. The oozewealths called it *Tenement Stain*, wishing they could wipe it off the city like a drop of spilled oil.

But to everyone else, even the people who lived there, it was called Tenement Lane. It bore that name even though it was actually *hundreds* of narrow streets, all crisscrossing, all intersecting, winding and curving and doubling back, every one hemmed in on both sides by the forty-foot high stone walls of the many hundreds of tenement blocks, pocked with windows for the multitudinous apartments they contained, some constricted by haphazard attempts to build shacks up against the actual tenements...and then more shacks atop the shacks.

Some said there was a mythical perfect route through them that, if followed, would be one unbroken path through the web. Jathan had never tried to find out.

Each tenement was a square block with an open atrium in the center, reached by arched walkways or tunnels. Dull charcoal grey was everywhere, with no deviations in architectural boldness anywhere within the warren, only the shapes and positions and orientations creating any semblance of variety to the space within. Each one was full of winding stairs and long corridors and walkways on every story, and none had their doors in the same places, making even the buildings themselves into labyrinths within a labyrinth.

The stone was everywhere chipped and cracked from a hundred years of weather and hard use, roofs crumpling, windows missing, walkways stained with the contents of unknowable bottles whose shards had long since been kicked away or weathered into colorful beads. The alleys were choked with pools of black water, never drying out, some with planks of wood and blocks of stone forced together into makeshift bridges.

Each block was a tangle, festooned with ropes and cords and wires floating between buildings, many strung through with drying clothes, some made into pully systems to lift possessions to the high floors, and many others that were simply abandoned, nothing more than silent shackles holding the tenements in bondage.

Every atrium boasted a single ancient tree on a small grass plot. Some of the trees flourished, overgrowing until the roots crawled along the ground and the branches climbed onto the walkways or speared through high windows. Other trees had long since died, leaving dry skeletal husks, empty branches reaching solemnly to the sky, begging for their leaves back.

For many who lived in Tenement Lane, these plots would be the only greenery they would ever see. Many worked and toiled and played and lived and loved never knowing there was a horizon, the days only lasting the hour or two it took for the sun to transit the narrow ravines between the mountainous tenements. If his sister hadn't rescued him from his secondparents' apartment in these warrens all those years ago, he would have been one of those people.

It was more than a neighborhood in this way. It was its own little civilization wedged into the heart of Kolchin, where the poorest and the unluckiest and the victimized all shared their lives packed together within the walls, held inside by its own immense gravity. Most were unable to ever escape it.

It was like wandering through an enchanted forest. You were just as likely to make it through to your destination as you were to wander off course into an atrium grotto you had never seen before despite having lived there for decades.

Jathan knew a path through it though. He long ago realized there was a rhythm to the winding of the roads, to the orientations of the buildings. He saw it in his mind, a pattern, a recurring algorithm.

Sometimes when he was drunk, he would wander in to see if it was possible for him to get lost, even for a moment, often egged on by the dares of his friends or his sister after hours of bottom bottling at one of the seedy winesinks or midnight cafes on the street-facing ground floors.

He always knew his way.

Tonight was no different. The double-silvers were burning a wine barrel shaped hole in his pocket. He needed to find Lyra and sand his soles to Winesink Row.

He careened out of Tenement Lane and cut through the deep basin of the Bowl District, where the houses were small and the sewers in disrepair, and the old Arradian hydraulic pumps for running water long since rusted out and left unreplaced. But at least here you could look up and see the sky, watch a sunset or sunrise, and know that the world did in fact go on in all directions.

He threaded between the desperate taverns, mudwaters, and sourhouses of Winesink Row, amazed that simply walking around a corner could bring him to a place of relative plenty when compared to the Bowl. It was like a film existed between them, preventing the different classes from intermingling.   Though he supposed the magistrates who patrolled Winesink Row may have had something to do with it.

At last, he made it through the gate at Fence Post Pike and breathed the pleasant air of the finestreets of the Upper End, where the well-off kept their homes. It was here where their parents' house sat. Modest in size and quality it was, but location was what mattered in Kolchin. It was easier to be poor if you could be poor in the right place, without the very streets around you constantly trying to bleed you dry. That was what his sister had told him, why she fought so hard to bring them back together in that house after their parents were gone to graves. That house meant everything to him.

He came at last to the commerce square everyone called the Promenade, an infinite circular paved walkway, ten strides wide, riddled with tables and chairs, wrapped about a wide plot of green grass and fountains with an oval blotch of a lake in the center just wide enough that he could never quite manage to throw a stone to the other side.

The space was full of stone blocks and statues, studded with benches and sprinkled with carts serving everything from fried lamb and rugged melted cheese toast to honey cinnamon pastries and iced calpas juice served straight out of the rind.

And encircling it all were rows of shops, eateries and taverns, theaters, cafes, tailors, iceries, and spicers, with the only gaps at the corners for people to enter or leave.

Anything could be had at the Promenade. If you wanted an apple from the orchards of Aragol, someone was selling them. If you needed a spur to match a three-hundred-year-old Polonian warboot, you could find it there. If you had to have a Malorese poison portrait, a feathered Biss wargalley cap, or a Halsabadi wood carving commemorating the ongoing thousand-year-long temple war, you could find one...if your money was right.

As soon as he pranced his way onto the grass he knew his sister was near. He felt her energy like the breeze tickling the back of his neck, a tingling in his ears, a subtle pressure behind the eyes. Lyra had a way of projecting her heart and her love and her joy so far outside herself that you were already enjoying her company minutes before she even arrived.

Try as he might to spot her, he was still taken completely unawares when her arms flew over his shoulders and wrapped about his chest, squeezing him in a spritely yet utterly painful hug.

"Oh, my sweet brother, I am so glad to see you!" Lyra sang.

He grabbed one of her arms with each of his hands and lifted them up over his head, twisting himself free and spinning to face her. "You are acting as if you haven't seen me in a lifetime," he complained. "It's been half a day."

"Am I no longer allowed to miss you?" She stood up tall, taller than he, which secretly infuriated him. She frowned melodramatically and puffed out her lower lip in a cruel bloodthirsty pout that always weakened him.

His only defense was to fold his arms and chew the inside of his lip, raising an eyebrow at her. "It was quite dreadful of our parents to saddle me with you," he said.

"I was born first. If anything, they saddled *me* with *you*." She laughed, every perfect tooth visible in a perfect smile. Her nose turned up the way the corners of her eyes turned down. Every limb was long and slender, but strong, the kind of physique that won ridge-climbing competitions at the Academ without its owner really even having to try.

Her sleeveless lavender gown hugged her like a sunset, like she was born within it, as if it grew to fit her as she did. The two lazy magistrates were right. She was better at drawing women than he ever would be. And men...well, men practically fell from the sky around her.

Jathan smirked at her. "You are tall like father and slender and pale like mother. Oh, how many times I tried to use dark alchemy to steal those features from you when we were small."

"Well, you are shorter like mother, but your handsome nose and brow and those tumbling locks of midnight black hair come straight from our father. How many nights I stole into your room and came *this* close to shearing your head and making a wig from it." She held out one elbow-length strand of her silken hair, as thin and straight as a beam of sunlight.

"It is kind of you to try to make me feel better," he said. "Someone told me I should marry you off, you know."

She leaned back and gave a dubious look. "Oh really?"

"Said I could practically name my price for a dowry."

She blushed. "We should do it, then split the money and run off on an adventure."

He laughed. "Not much adventuring to be had around here."

She gave his shoulder a shove. "Not here, silly. Somewhere else. In the wide world."

"The wide world, eh?"

"Distant shores," she said, her voice humming like a song. She skipped twice. "There are so many places in the world to see."

"A fun little idyll," he said carefully. *We are not leaving here for real. You are speaking of fantasy only.*

"Of course we would have to take Nessifer with us," Lyra went on.

He raised an eyebrow. "Oh?"

She wrinkled her nose at him. "I would never seek to part the two of you."

"There is nothing to part. We are not with each other, Nessa and I. We see each other socially." *And I hide the ache I feel when she is near with plenty of wine.*

She squinted at him. "I see through you like a window, brother."

"Am I not sweet any longer?"

"No. You are my sour brother now. But I will still have her accompany us on our adventure."

"So nice of you to consider me."

"Oh, not for your joy, brother. For her. She is my friend, after all. I look out for her, misguided though she may be. It is not her fault she is afflicted with affection for you."

He flattened his mouth. "You may keep that talk to yourself."

"Fine and shine, through brandy and wine. What exotic land shall we head off to first?"

He chuckled. "We are never leaving Kolchin. This is our home. This is where our parents' house is. Where mother and father raised us. All our good memories of them are here. How can we leave?"

She looked away at some children splashing in the little lake. She kept smiling but he thought he saw hurt show itself in the corners of her lips.

I should not have mentioned them. It was the pain of the memory of losing them. It had to be. *She knows. Of course she knows we can never leave here. That we can never abandon the house our parents built.* He should not have brought her back to that memory just now.

"We only still have that house because Aunt Dresa pays the tax and fee on it every month," Lyra said. "Neither of us make anything close to what it would take, even now, all these years later. We cannot get what we are worth here. We spin like wheels in this place."

He raised another eyebrow. "If only we could take a dowry and pay the lifetime fee for our parents' house. Then it would be ours."

She made a face. "I am not marrying a man merely so we can stay here."

He raised both hands. "Easy, easy. Just a joke." He paused, rolling his eyes and grinding his teeth to himself.

She squinted at him quite suddenly. "Where were you anyway? And don't say you were at the cocoa confectioner, because I was there and you were not."

"Nowhere important."

She nudged him with her elbow. "Where were you? I've waited here a half hour outside of Mistine's. You were supposed to be here working your shift." She pointed at *Mistine's Mercantilist and Winesink* sprouting from the ground on stilts where the pavement of the Promenade met the grassy lakeshore. "And now here you come from a different direction entirely."

Shit, fuck, and hell. He was supposed to have been here, not up at Beachside making money selling criminals to their fates for a pocket jingle. He hadn't counted on her coming to look for him so early.

"Well?" she demanded.

He didn't have a decent lie ready. "I...was running a delivery for Mistine. To the East Uppers. I had to sand my soles all the way to the shack at the crossroads. You know, by Inner Valley District. Across from where they have that llama farm." It was believable enough. It was a route he had run deliveries to in the past, but always in the afternoons and always at the end of the month.

She squinted at him, on the verge of believing him. "You are leaving something out. I can see through you like a window, remember?"

Well, shit and shit and shit some more. He should have known she would press him on this. Her curiosity was only matched by her tenacity. "I was in Lower West End," he said. That much was true at least.

But it only made her squint harder. "Beachside? Why? You don't know anyone that far north."

"I know a few people."

"Like who?"

"Not important."

"This is beginning to sound like a secret. Now I *have* to know."

He rolled his eyes, trying to feign annoyance. "It is so unimportant."

"What?" She jabbed him in the ribs with those slender bony fingers, each one as stiff and hard as knife

He sought vainly to block with his elbows. "I was getting us some silver," he finally admitted. "For tonight. Silvers for tonight."

"Silvers?" Now she was deeply suspicious, not in a playful way.

He needed something convincing, to make it look like he would be reluctant to admit it. He was surprised and a little dismayed at how easy a story came to his lips, how easily he lied to his sister. "I...have been skimming the afternoon wares that do not sell and taking them with my deliveries and offering them for a percentage to grovelers and wave rats."

She frowned at him. "You are going to get in trouble. They are going to dismiss you if you are lucky. Fine you or worse if you aren't."

"I know." Fraudulent shame. He was growing too good at this.

"You have to stop," she finally said. "I would hate to have to break you out of a magistrate's prison."

He smiled. "I swear I will never end up in a magistrate's prison."

She eyes him uncertainly. "Alright then."

Jathan changed the subject. "So...did Cristan and Sethleen mention where they wanted to meet?"

"The Bottlebottom," she said.

"The Bottlebottom? In Brandytown? Isn't that a little fancy for them? I would have bet money on the Dripping Bucket or one of the other sourhouses on Winesink Row."

"They don't like it there anymore. Too many people showing up that they do not recognize." She glanced sidelong at him. "Are you worried your brawling won't go over as well in a finestreet winesink in Brandytown?"

"No, that's not it at all." He paused. "If you are talking about that one time at the Sturdy Fundament, I was barely involved."

She rolled her eyes. "You were quite involved. And it was three times. Four more at Stumble With Grace, nine times at the Salty Ham. Oh and fifty times at the Rusty Salvage."

"I had nothing to do with starting those."

She rolled her eyes hard enough that he felt it. "If you say so, sweet brother."

"Brandytown is where the oozewealths go. It is above our means."

"Cristan says he will buy us each a bottle any time we join him there. Now and from now on, he says. Working at the Moneychanger gives him coin aplenty." She appraised his wardrobe, folding her arms the way he did, making an admirable impression of his raised eyebrow. "You will fit right in at the Bottlebottom. You look like a lure at the end of a fishing line. You are bound to hook a trout."

He laughed. "We'll see."

They walked through the Promenade, stopping at the icery for chilled calpas, and taking a wide path around Mistine's.

Finally, they reached the row of shops curving around the north end of the Promenade to say a brief greeting to the bookseller, Harod, who had hired Lyra the year before to work in this very shop. He was in; he always was, much like his grey-streaked mustache was always indistinguishable from either of his eyebrows. They had known him for years and he had never once failed to wear the same many-pocketed canvas vest, or to give them a wave and a smile and to shout, "the more you read the more real you are!"

They waved and hollered promises to come by and see him soon. Which they fully intended to keep, and then the left the Promenade, and segued east along the riverfront, walking against the current for the Float all the way to Brandytown, the neighborhood of misty streets enclosed by walls of two-story stone houses, where the fanciest winesinks were to be found.

Cristan and Sethleen were already there and already swimming in wine, golden hair and pink lips in equal measure. Cristan welcomed them, as he always did, with open arms, a full bottle in either hand, summerwine for Jathan and sweetwine for Lyra. They had a table right inside the door near the exterior wall.

The place was loosely separated into four rooms on the ground, though only *separated* by half walls and strings of Hylamari beads. It opened to a long room with lavatories at one end, and to the right was a wide area of many tables and wedged between them was a dance square with a bar tended by five bartenders.

Two more rooms sat above, in a gallery fashion so that patrons could lean over and holler to those below or spill their drinks on someone and start a brawl. Both were frequent, if one judged by the chips and gouges in the table edges, teak chairs, and ornate rosewood posts holding up the second story and the roof. The tiles on the floor were an imitation marble and looked like they had been replaced at a rate of three every moondance for twenty years.

Fevered smiles were exchanged beneath the red-orange glow of a hundred candles in colored glass bulbs, suspended on enormous candelabras. Pipe and drum wove an ecstatic rhythm while a grinding bass dromba chased a wily twanging zinge through melody after melody.

Sweat-drenched hugs were had all around. By the end of it, Jathan smelled more like Sethleen then he did himself. But he could not exactly say he minded. And her slobbery kisses at his neck while they were engaged in a friendly hug told him she did not mind it either.

The others filtered in one at a time, as they were prone to do.

Ouleem was already dancing when he walked in the door, chasing the beat in an uproarious syncopation of heel and toe. Light from the candles twinkled in his wide eyes. He reached out, muscles almost too large for his shirt, snatching up Lyra in both arms.

She gratefully spun and twisted and twirled in his arms. Her hips leaned hard into a playful yet deliberate mo'amas seven step beat. Even Ouleem struggled to keep up. In the end they collapsed into the polished rosewood chairs—foreheads, cheeks, and chests glowing with sweat.

Branderin trudged in, hands in pockets, always looking as though someone dragged him against his will to the celebration. He wore a slender long coat that was far too warm to wear in a place so packed with the heat of bodies and the fire of dance and thirst. He was thin enough that one might be forgiven for thinking he subsisted solely on sharp tea, sweetbark smoke, and dried kelp. Cristan welcomed him and pulled him aside, placing a full cup in his hand first thing, before he could talk himself out of being there.

Nessifer arrived last, and just in time to provide an excuse for Jathan to stand so he could place some distance between his lap and Sethleen's groping fingers wandering their way into it.

He hugged Nessifer hard, lifting her feet off the ground and swaying them side to side until she giggled. She had a complexion of the darkest olive and slivered emeralds for eyes perched above the highest, rosiest cheeks he had ever seen. It was a pleasure just to see her smile.

"Set me down, Jathan Algevin. Right this minute." She giggled again, and threw her head back, hair red as rubies pouring like a waterfall onto her shoulders.

He was on the fence about putting her down or never putting her down ever again until time ended itself.

"Your feet are far too fine to touch this fetid ground," he told her. But he set her down, arms unwinding, sliding around her sides and brushing against her hips.

She had a bad habit of always looking directly into his eyes. The way she looked through them, it was like she could see some truth inside him that no one else could see.

"You look like you have worked all day." She frowned playfully. "You deserve as much wine as you can handle. What are you drinking tonight? I would be delighted to buy a cup of it for you."

He held up his hands. "You don't have to."

She gave his shin a little kick with her toes. "I know. I choose to. Now quit insulting me and say *yes please*."

"Ouch." He lifted the offended leg off the ground in mock agony. "I'll never walk again."

"Oh no. Now I shall have to buy you two cups."

"No, no, I can walk again. I am cured. Just one is all I need. Save the extra coin."

She winked. "Name the ocean you wish to drown in tonight, good sir."

You are the ocean I want to drown in. "Velvet brandy," he said. "The Lissarian variety."

She smiled and held it just a fraction too long to be simply cordial. "Velvet brandy it shall be then." She turned and trotted off into the next room, past the dancing square and the musician stage to wave down a bartender.

"You forgot to ask what I wanted!" Lyra playfully called after her. "Aragol apple cider." She paused. "The Aragol variety," she added, mocking his choice in her haughty impression of an oozewealth. She chuckled and elbowed Jathan in the one rib she hadn't managed to jab on the walk over.

Jathan elbowed her back and laughed his way through another cup of summerwine.

After starting a little bit of a brawl with a barge captain from the Float, Jathan nursed a swollen rosy cheek with another cup or three of velvet brandy while Cristan bought his foe a bottle of fine whiskey, thereby convincing him not to summon one of the finestreet magistrates.

By then Jathan had already forgotten what the man said that set his fists to flying in the first place. He only knew it had to have been something disrespectful toward his parents. That was how a great many of Jathan's fights began.

As the night went on, Jathan swilled his velvet brandy, Nessifer sang, and Ouleem danced five more times with five more women, including once just after he ate a bucket of spiced roast, narrowly avoiding throwing it all back up on his unfortunate partner.

Lyra wandered around every room on every floor, catching up with friends and striking up conversations with strangers.

Cristan and Sethleen had already had one savage argument, one teary apology, and one aggressive mutual jealousy-fueled slap session, followed by sloppy, grotesque lovemaking behind a tapestry where they thought no one could see, but of course everyone did. Sethleen climaxed just after a song ended, the instruments all going abruptly quiet just in time for everyone from wall to wall and floor to ceiling to hear her trumpet the arrival of the kind of hip-shivering pleasure that can only be had behind a tapestry against a wall at the bottom of your fourth bottle of wine.

Lyra laughed so hard she shrieked, sweetwine spraying out her nose.

Jathan pounded the table with his fist, pointing at her with his other hand. "I am remembering this moment forever," he proclaimed.

Lyra kept laughing, then paused drinking, suddenly determined to get a smile out of Branderin. "My mission is your smile," she brazenly declared.

He shrugged. "I am just in a worry," he admitted. "My sister did not come home from Winesink Row last night and my parents are full of stress."

"I'm sure she will turn up," Lyra said, squeezing his shoulder with one hand. "Women sometimes get caught up in a moment and then they can't get out of it, even though the moment is over."

"She has never done anything like that before," Branderin said.

"She likely went home with someone she regrets and isn't ready to face up to it yet," Jathan said.

"Or perhaps she is caught up in something so good it hides the passage of time. I once ended up in the bed of a man who made me have doe eyes whenever he spoke."

"I am not hearing this," Jathan said. He plugged each of his ears with a finger. "I hear nothing."

Lyra rolled her eyes. "I was so caught up in his energy that I forgot what time it was. I forgot what day it was. It took me three days before I remembered that I had a home to go to."

"All we are saying is that it is probably something normal," Jathan said.

"Yes," Lyra said. "You said she had never done anything like that before. We never do anything we haven't done until the first time we do it. I want to see the world and when a man seems like he can take me there it is so easy to follow. It was a long time before I realized he never truly planned to. We all have to make our mistakes and learn our lessons."

"You are right of course," Branderin said. "I am a worrier."

"Winesink Row is fairly safe," Jathan said. "The magistrates patrol down there most nights. Officers with swords. Local street patrols with spears. More than enough to scare off the scumborn and the smokehounds and any other deservingless sandfoot beachers. Not many sword carriers down there since the ban, other than those magistrates."

"Swords keep the peace," Branderin agreed. "No one would try anything with armed magistrates around. Even the gangers from Tenement Lane and the Bowl District stay away from magistrates."

"Exactly," Jathan said, clapping his shoulder. "It's as safe as Brandytown is.   There may not be as many oozewealths there with gold on their fingers, but the criminal deservingless would steer well around it."

Lyra spent another half hour reassuring him, before Jathan finally had to drag her out the door into the cool night. He waved a half-drunken farewell to Ouleem and gave a sharp salute to Branderin and the warmest of his smiles to Nessifer.

Cristan was already passed out, his head lolling over the backrest of his chair, arms dangling like dead vines, his yawning mouth grunting each breath. Sethleen was also passed out, her head and one arm draped over a spare latrine bucket which she had half-filled with a revisited version of her entire dinner and at least half of a lunch.

Jathan barely kept his own stomach in control at the sight.

He dragged Lyra out by the cuffs of the coat Branderin had let her borrow once she became too cold, as she always did. She did not struggle or argue as he towed her along though.

In truth, Lyra wanted to go home, needed to. She just couldn't ever seem to make herself stop, like a marble rolling down a slope of the Hilltop Crossing. And like the crossing, she had four paths she could suffer that fateful inertia down—art, romance, drink, and literature.

She had always been better at everything. Everything except changing course. She always needed Jathan to pull her back from moments of mania. And he never asked anything of her for it. She was family. You help family.

From Brandytown the fastest way home was through Tenement Lane. For most it was a place to steer well clear of late at night. But that was because most did not know where they were going.

Jathan knew which paths were well-lit, which taverns served clean cups, and which alleys dead-ended. He knew where the smoke slaves went to buy their grey malagayne leaves, and where the magistrates went to take their share of the profits to look the other way. He knew which tenements were placid, well-guarded, and which were run by the warren gangers. He knew where you could find a prostitute who used to be a sacred lady at a

Pleasure House in Ethios, and another who swore that she was, but was lying.

Lyra was still giggling at some half-remembered joke of Cristan's when they rambled into that enormous labyrinth. Lyra would have been hopelessly lost within the first five steps. But Jathan could find his way here drunk and in the dark. Which was good. Because tonight the circumstances were both present.

"Take me to a fairytale," Lyra asked him. "Show me something pretty."

He rolled his eyes. But he did as she asked.

He took her up to the Garden Walk, lined with tall iron lampposts where the lamps were always lit. It rose high above the street level of Tenement Lane, where people could look down on the morass of hulking buildings and winding streets, with a forty-foot-high retaining wall built to keep rain from collapsing the hill into the streets below, and, more importantly, to keep the lowers in Tenement Lane from climbing up to enjoy the view of their own warren. It was one more place they were not permitted to enjoy.

The walkway along the edge of the hill followed parallel and above perhaps one of the only long, straight, unbroken tenement streets in existence. The nearside abutted the retaining wall, and the opposite side went on in one long line of four-story tenement blocks, each separated by a narrow perpendicular street full of shadows, a straight line where two worlds met.

At least the parallel street was well lit, the tenements' ground floors boasting numerous vacant sourhouses and midnight cafes, all drenched in lamplight. This made Lyra happy. The Garden Walk wasn't much of a garden, boasting boring grass and unremarkable willow trees, but to a drunk Lyra it was a mythical paradise.

From this height, it was easy to look down on the streets below, and, more importantly to Lyra, onto the people who traveled them. The only thing that ever seemed to calm her down was watching people be people. It mattered not what they did. Just seeing them living was enough for her.

And her being happy was enough for Jathan.

She stopped to watch two lovers kissing, and then to watch a boy steal a pastry from the last basket of a cafe, and then to watch two cooks from a fish frier toss their garbage down a chute to the sewer running riverlike beneath the ground. They closed off the chute with the slam of a square iron grate, so loud it made Jathan blink. But Lyra thought it was hilarious for some reason. He had to drag her away from watching the two pass a bottle back and forth and gossip about their customers.

It was all the same to Jathan. Since trudging up the Garden Walk, they had already passed a dozen tenements, and the streets and alleyways that ran between and through them. He had been here so many times before, sat and watched any number of people do all of those things and better or worse. It was fun and lively to her, but to him it was dull, suffocating sameness that even a bottle of summerwine did not have the power to breathe air into. Maybe two bottles. But certainly not one.

The path followed the slope of a hill for fifty more paces until the hill ended somewhere ahead, dropping down a series of dog-legged streets into the Bowl District, like the descent from an ancient ziggurat temple from Adumbar.

He left her for a final few moments, walking a ways ahead to relieve himself on a lamppost between two ferns. He was far enough ahead that the side of the current tenement across the street below ended, with a view down the shadowy cross street between it and the high wall of the next tenement ahead.

It was poorly lit, most of the light coming from the last glowing lamp on the main street, and the canopy of a gnarled, forgotten old tree blocked half the light from the lamps up on the Garden Walk.

But as Jathan held himself in his hands, not sure if he wished to test his distance or his accuracy or both, he noticed something peculiar.

Around the corner, not more than ten quick strides down the cross street, was something that looked very much like the body of a man. Flat on his back. Arms splayed out. One leg bent back. Cloak heaped atop him.

Jathan stared at it, flies buzzing in his ears, the syrupy splash of a bottle's worth of wine-brewed piss winding down to a trickle and then to a drip and then to nothing.

He could not stop staring at it long after he was finished.

His mind worked itself into a frenzy trying to rationalize what he saw. A drunkard. An exhausted pauper. A man with a condition. But drunkards don't fall like that. And paupers don't have such fine coats. And those with conditions knew better than to wander Tenement Lane after the sun had set.

There was something wrong about it.

Lyra wandered up beside him. "Put that away. I'm your sister."

Jathan felt sense shaken back into himself. He placed himself back in his trousers, but his eyes never left the man in the street. "Something is there."

Lyra looked. "What? Where?" Her eyes widened. "Is he...?"

"I don't know."

"Well, let us be away then. Better for someone else to find out."

"What if he needs help?"

She gave him a dubious look. "You? Care about some stranger? If you want me to swallow a load of shit, best serve it in spicier soup than that."

"I need to see it closer," Jathan said. But he could not say why. Not even to himself. He climbed up over the railing and lowered himself down the other side.

Lyra's eyes were as wide as the twin moons above. "You stupid fool. Have you lost the one last wit you might have had? You are going to break your neck."

"I can make it," he assured her. He backed his legs over the edge, sliding until only his arms were above the hill's edge. "There is a ledge on the retaining wall, only a stride below my feet. I can land it easily. And if I hang off it, it is only a ten-foot drop. I can tuck and roll. Like when we were children."

"You always hurt yourself when we were children," she reminded him.

He flashed a grimace at her. "Thank you for reminding me how much better an acrobat you always were then me. I have lived my whole life knowing this."

"Yes, and I would not be doing what you are doing." She folded her arms.

He smirked at her. "That is why I'm doing it."

With that, he let go. His feet touched down on the ledge. He nearly lost his balance and tipped over backward, but a half-dozen aggressive arm swings stabilized him. He was glad Lyra had been too far from the edge to see that part.

He eased himself down over the side of the ledge, methodically, until he held on with fingers alone.

Lyra's head poked out above him. "This is foolish. He's gone to grave for certain."

"I have to know for sure."

She shook her head.

He let go. The ground rushed up to meet his feet. He twisted one ankle straightaway but did a passable job of bending his knees and leaning into his shoulder and rolling over.

He looked each way. The street was quiet. He sprang up and danced his way to the man, trying to play off the sprain as if he had not hurt himself at all. *I will not have a week's worth of 'I told you so's over this.*

He crept in close. He was still two strides away when he knew for certain the man was dead. His eyes were wide open, staring at nothing, chest not moving. A part of his scalp had been flattened beneath his hair. It looked rank and purple, wet with a slow trickle of blood.

That is not a wound from a slip and tumble.

Someone cracked his skull.

Jathan crawled the final distance, eyes scanning everything, hands diving into every fold of cloak. He did not have a sword, or even a knife. No coinpurse. Odd. His pockets were all empty.

All save one.

He wore a vest over his silk tunic. On the inside by his left breast was a hidden pocket. Within was a palm-sized bronze oval with a hinge at one end. He flipped its cover open and realized it was the frame for an oval lens of some strange silvery-white crystal mineral. Along with the cover were four more separate lenses of different colors also swiveling away from the crystal. He found that he could slide each of them over the main lens one at a time, or all at once.

He slid it closed until the cover clicked.

Behind it was a heavy parchment, some variety that was part cloth. It folded but he was unable to rip it. On the inside it had a series of symbol markers and a name.

Izimer Kohp.

The name meant nothing to him.

Then he noticed a little metal badge pinned on his tunic. It came loose and tumbled out, ringing as it touched down on the street. It came to rest at his feet. A circle, with five prongs extending off the upper right quadrant, like half an eyelash.

He knew what that symbol meant.

Render Tracer.

Glasseye.

The ones who hunted the magi. The all-seeing eyes who tracked the scum of the earth.

Jathan felt a pit open up in his stomach.

This is a Glasseye.

This man should not be dead.

Did a sorcerer kill him with magick?

Were they still nearby?

That was the moment he noticed the other bodies.

He saw the bootheels of one poking out of the deep shadow near the tenement wall. He saw the hand of another three paces further down. As his eyes followed from one to the next, he saw more, and still more. He held a hand over his eyes to block the lamplight.

There were at least eight all told, half wearing matching blue trousers and vests over ivory tunics, sleeves rolled up, the other half dressed in long-sleeved olive-green coats, hanging down to their knees.

Ganger colors. These were picked men. Fighting each other. He knew blue vests were the sign of Vorlo Wauska's crew. Olive coats seemed like the colors of Soreb Qleen's gangers. Two of the most notorious of the ganger bosses.

Neither of which ran this territory. Wauska Land and Qleen Town were each more than a mile from here. None of them should have been here. What could they have been doing?

Killed each other off, looks like. That much is certain.

He was afraid to move.

The odds of this dead body and those other dead bodies being unrelated at this proximity is very low.

He looked back and forth, his glance moving half as fast as a worm, as if he feared his eyes might be heard somehow.

A hand reached from behind and slapped his mouth shut. He felt a weight on his back. He dropped onto his knees. Pain set fire to his legs. He squealed. He tried to shake himself free until he heard the whisper in his ear.

"That is why I covered your mouth." It was Lyra.

He shook his mouth free of her palm, still sticky with spilled sweetwine. "What the fuck are you doing down here?"

She pinched his cheek and pointed up the main street. "Because they are coming back."

Shit.

They.

He saw men silhouetted by the streetlamps and the distant midnight cafes. The blue-vested Wauska gangers must have won, chased off the rest. Five were returning, pulling one of the green coats along by his ear, hands tied behind his back. Captured.

Lyra pulled Jathan up and dragged him away from the wall, first into the shadow of the tall tree to obscure them, then across the main street, backed up against the same retaining wall they climbed down, flattening themselves behind a stack of unused crates piled against the base of the wall.

There they watched the five drag their captive back around the corner into the shadows. They forced him to his knees among the corpses, two men hovering over him, each with a hand on his shoulder.

Another set to rifling through the cloak of lifeless Izimer Kohp. His movements increased in both speed and hostility, until by the end it appeared he was attacking the coat in order to exact some form of revenge upon it.

"Where is it?!" he screamed. He turned to the captive. Smacked him across the face with the back of one hand. "Where is it? What did you do with it?"

Jathan did not hear the answer. But he was fairly certain he knew what *it* was. And he was fairly certain he knew where it went.

He felt Lyra's heart thudding against his back. He did not even feel his own. It was either beating too fast to tell, or too slow. Every breath rattled him, sounding like pans smashing together in his ears. He was so sure the men would hear him.

But they did not. They scattered, looking into the shadows, while one continued to beat the captive.

Jathan heard a whistle. And then he saw an arrow sticking out of one of them. He tipped backward into the shadow, only his boots showing.

An ambush of the ambush.

More arrows flew, and then six men rushed in, some with truncheons, some with rusty shortswords. None of them were wearing green coats, or matching trousers and vests. That was in line with what real tenement gangers were likely to wear. This had to be their territory.

What the fuck did we stumble into?

Men were screaming and groaning. Batons met skulls, swords met bellies. He knew one thing about weapons. Steel didn't change when it struck flesh. Only the flesh did.

"We have to get the fuck out of here," he said.

"Oh," Lyra said. "The place neither of us should have been in the first place?"

He shrugged, eyeing the ledge he had used to climb down. It was high above, but out in the open, visible. But there was no other way. If they didn't run, whoever won here would be searching about. *And if we bolt down the street we will be noticed for certain.*

He looked back. The ganger in the green coat was speeding across the street, hands still bound, coming right toward them.

"What do we do?" she asked. "Run? Climb? Hide? What?"

"Up," he said.

"Up?"

"Up, up, up." He sprang around the crates, running on the toes of his boots. He saw the green coat disappear into the shadow cast by the tree. Two gangers in blue vests were on his heels.

Jathan turned to look over his other shoulder to see how far behind him Lyra was, but of course she was already passing him. By the time he turned to the fore, she was waiting for him under the ledge.

"You go first," she said.

"Me? No. You."

She gave him a look. "Whoever ends up on the ledge first will have to pull the other of us up. Your arms are stronger." She locked her fingers and held her hands out for him to step up on. She wobbled. He stamped one foot down on her shoulder. Pushed off. Felt the lip of the ledge. Fingers locked around it. Hoisted himself up until he was belly-down on it.

Jathan draped an arm over the side and reached. He felt Lyra's hand lock around his wrist. He took hers in turn. He pulled her up until she had the edge. Once she did, she was somehow up on her feet above him in an instant.

He stumbled upright somehow. From here there were handholds at least, missing mortar, roots of trees up on the hill growing out through the stone retention wall.

He worked his way up. Lyra danced from handhold to handhold, like she was practically floating up to the top of the hill. He had never before experienced a moment of jealously that eclipsed the fear of being beaten half to death by angry men. This was the very first time.

He rolled himself up to the top, Lyra reaching for him.

His hand slipped on cracked mortar, and he slid over the edge, dragging her off balance to the edge. She kept him from falling to his death, but she went over the edge in his place.

He cried out in his mind, hollowing out, blood vanishing from his face. He looked down, fully expecting to see her flat on her back on the pavement below, but somehow, by the grace of her acrobatic talent alone, she was on her feet on the ledge, swaying.

Jathan reached down, slipped, smacked his face against the hilltop, saw bright flashes of light in his eyes, felt the wind gust out of him. He cried out. Stinging eyes wide, dry mouth hanging open, watching her begin to go over backwards.

She waved her arms at the ledge. He was so sure she was going to go over, but somehow, she didn't fall.

He kept seeing flashes, shaking his head, still reaching.

Lyra bounded up the sheer face of the retention wall, her hands jumping from hold to hold, her limbs moving in fluid perfection. She seemed to dance on air, until her hand found his and he lifted her up onto the hilltop, tossing her onto the Garden Walk.

All he could do was laugh.

He lurched onto his side and looked over the edge.

The battle was still raging above the corpses.

Jathan glanced down at the crates he had been hiding behind.

The green coat was looking back at him. Hiding in the same place he had been. The other gangers hadn't found him. He was quiet and still. He stared directly at Jathan. Looked him right in the eyes.

Fuck. He saw us.

Everyone's life changes the first time they find a dead body.

2

What The Eye Can See

TRYING TO ACT LIKE your life is normal after something extraordinary happens is impossible.

Jathan spent most of the morning with his hand in his trouser pocket, twiddling the oval lens between his fingers. Every once in a while, he plucked it out, clicked it open and spread out each of the colored lenses on the hinge. Every time he held the lens up, almost, just about, not quite to his eyes...and then yanked it away, closed it up, and stuffed it back into his pocket.

This is the tool of the Glasseyes. This is how they track the rogue magi. This is how they hunt sorcerers.

He was finding it twice as tedious to finish out his shift in the mercantile surplus storeroom behind the winesink that Mistine ran with her son by law, who Jathan was convinced was also her lover. Mistine's was one of the few permanent structures in the grass at the center of the Promenade. The grass was mostly occupied by transitory things, wheeled food carts and chairs and tables. He wasn't sure how she had managed to get her hands on this place. There were many who felt it blighted the aesthetic of the lake, but enough people frequented it, that no one could manage to get rid of her.

The front half was a stilted tavern, seating twenty at least if packed tightly, and the back was split into the fresh cafe on the street side, and the surplus storeroom on the lake side, nothing more than a tiny warehouse with a lakeside window to make sales through.

Mistine didn't trust him enough around her whiskey to let him work the tavern, so he worked back in the storeroom instead. Every evening the waremongers and caravaners from the great merchant markets who had extra stock to sell before they went on circuit back south, and who thought it not worth the cost to transport the leftovers, would sell to her for coppers on the silver.

Jathan's job was to clean the trinkets and treasures, put them on shelves, and handle transactions for whoever wandered by the window with silver to toss around. He never left the storeroom, and he liked it that way.

Despite this, by midmorning the two front end bartenders he nursed crushes on knew something was wrong. By noontime, the bartender he hated and the deliveryman knew. And by midafternoon his employer, Mistine, knew it, too.

"Your mind is so far up your own ass that if you yawn, I might be able to see it," Mistine said, twisting the top off another jar of vinegar. She had arms as thick as his, and her eyes and her ass were all twenty years younger than the rest of her and she wasn't afraid to say so.

Jathan tried to ignore her, looking out the seller window, across the grass, watching children playing on the banks of the little lake. At least three quarters of his worry was that Lyra had not come around yet. It was unlike her to miss her own schedule—coffee drinks at dawn, morning freework as the librarian's apprentice, and afternoon paywork for Harod the bookseller. They were her favorite things in the world to do...other than drink sweetwine.

"You need to put your head on straight," Mistine went on. "You nearly gave a copperheart one of the Traladari teacups at half price because you somehow forgot how to count."

"It's nothing," he assured her. "I just had a rough night."

She stared at him in that way where it was like she was rolling her eyes at him, despite her eyes not actually rolling. But she left him alone in the storeroom to do his work. Thankfully he was able to keep from fouling up any additional sales.

Ouleem began his shift late. Unsurprising considering the amount of brandy he gulped the night before. But he seemed downright cheerful. He stormed into the room, encumbered by a double armload of hazy glass jars and bottles in mellow greens and violets and greys, each one plugged with a cork. Some held powders and some held liquids, and it was at least a three-god miracle that none of them tumbled or spilled.

"Careful," Jathan said. "If I have to clean the fucking floor again because of you..."

"Shit, fuck, and hell, Mister Algevin. High and mighty this morning, I see."

"Not high and mighty. Just a head full of pain and ears full of Mistine's screaming."

"I heard that!" Mistine shrieked from the other room.

He expected her to.

Ouleem leaned in to whisper. "They are one and the same, if you ask me." He winked and carefully unloaded his cargo onto an empty shelf.

"What's that you have there?" Jathan asked.

"This? The bottles?"

"Those smoky colors of glass look very familiar, like ones my parents used to have. Grey and violet and green like that. Might even still have some in the house from back then. Do you know what they are?"

"Nah," Ouleem said. "Leftovers from some shop that was raided by the magistrates."

"Raided?"

"Some kind of violation. Taxes maybe?" He shrugged. "Anyway, the vendor was taken away, so Mistine sent me over to grab up what I could that hadn't already been taken." He paused. "How did you not know what your parents used them for?"

"I can't exactly go ask them now, can I?"

"No, come on. You know what I mean."

"They just always had them to spread about, anointing things and whatnot, like a ritual. They were into some hazy weird religion. And when I was ten, I could not have possibly cared less about that sort of thing."

"Wine and women are my religion," Ouleem declared. "And I worship at the altar nightly."

Jathan laughed and it hurt. He cradled his head.

Ouleem worked quietly with an ear up as if expecting him to say something else. "You are too quiet," he finally said after only two minutes of stocking Sephalonian statuettes on the shelves. "The Jathan I know would have jabbered my ear clean off and then carried it away to the next room just to be able to keep talking."

"And you are too cheery. Where is quiet, reserved Ouleem? They one who needs three coffee drinks just to open his eyes before noon?"

Ouleem wore his toothiest grin. "Hibernated in the bed of one of those dancers from Ethios. Didn't come up for air until morning. She had the most edible of fundaments. You couldn't make me frown today if you paid me a fistful of gold coins."

Jathan snickered. "Alright, fair enough."

"I haven't seen Lyra all morning. Does she have a new lover? Someone from the finestreets?"

The words stung Jathan, even though he knew that wasn't the reason. She fell into her lovers the way she fell into everything else, lost in a storm until someone pulled her free. It was hard to have her completely disappear from his life for months at a time, and harder still to go through the effort to pull her to safety when she finally came to beg him to do so.

He closed his eyes and sighed.

"Is she not allowed to have a lover?" Ouleem asked, half-joking.

"Of course she is allowed. I do not command her. She makes her own choices."

"Where is she then?"

A part of him wondered if she indeed did have a new lover. Not someone she picked up at the Bottlebottom, but someone she had already met who finally came calling on her only just this morning. He shook his head. *None of my business. Until it is, anyway.* "We had a long night."

Ouleem shrugged, polishing a set of goldenwood Mua dog carvings and shelving them. "Have you seen that Glasseye about?"

Jathan turned to stone.

Glasseye.

What?

What do you mean?

What do you mean by that?

"What do you mean by that?" Jathan finally said out loud.

Ouleem's eyes went wide. "Want some varnish for your face? You've gone whiter than ash."

"What Glasseye?"

"Been sitting around the Lazy Steward." He pointed Jathan's attention out the window and across the lake.

The Lazy Steward was a shop half the size of Mistine's, but with a patio ten times the size, full of high white tables and tall white chairs, all beneath the comforting embrace of massive awnings atop high white posts, blanketing them from the sun like a fleet of heavy sailing ships.

They specialized in hot savory breakfasts and the widest variety of Samartanian and Calabari coffee drinks in all Kolchin. Jathan would have stopped there every morning if the wine would ever let him wake up early enough to circle the lake before his shift was due to start.

"What the fuck is he doing here?" Jathan asked. *Does he know what I did?*

"Nessifer said she spotted him at dawn. I went by to see for myself, and he was still there—just sitting, all day, flipping through his leather folders at all manner of papers and occasionally staring at the crowds on the Promenade, or out by the lake. And I'm telling you he looks the way you would think one of them would look. A man who has lived thirty summers at most, but whose eyes have seen ninety."

Jathan's fingers tightened about the lens in his pocket. The glass eye of a Glasseye. *He must be after this. They must know what happened to their man, Izimer.* How could word of such a momentous murder not spread on every tongue?

"To the furthest hell with him. I don't trust Glasseyes. I don't trust Inner Guard spies. I don't trust anyone from the capital. I trust our local magistrates and that's all. They know what it's like to walk the streets in Kolchin. What could a Glasseye know? They think they are such amazing shit just because they follow that scum around."

Now I could follow them myself, if I wanted to.

Jathan spent the next hour in a stupor, visions of dead Glasseyes and tenement gangers hanging on every nerve.

"Are you going to vomit all over my Mua dogs?" Mistine demanded.

Jathan blinked awake. "No. Me? What?"

"You are done back here for the day," she said.

"I am telling you it was just a rough night. I swear to you I'm fine."

"The last time you swore you only had a rough night you ended up punching one of my customers in the ear."

"He cursed my mother," Jathan explained.

"You are going now. You know where the door is. I'm going to get my broom to shoo you like a rodent."

"You don't need customers like that. It's better I sent him walking away."

"It was the pocket jingle walking away I care about. You chased away a sack of silver coins that should have been in my hands."

Ouleem snickered. "I remember him. Come on, Mistine, if anyone ever deserved knuckles to the head it was him."

Mistine didn't care. She sent Jathan off to run her errands to keep him from either kicking a customer to death or accidentally giving every trinket and every bottle of wine away for free. It was only three errands, each one quicker than the last. She was effectively sending him off early without docking him pay.

She secretly likes having me around.

He swaggered his way across the green, around the lake and up onto the opposite side of the Promenade ring. He slipped into Harod's bookseller shop, making sure to tap his finger to ring the bell that was supposed to ring on its own but never did.

Harod sat at his counter, at the far end of two eight-foot-tall shelves stuffed with books, files, folios, and volumes. The man himself peeked out from behind a stack of leatherbound tomes atop his counter. As always, he was wrapped in his many-pocketed canvas vest. "Early this afternoon?"

Jathan shrugged, eyes drawn to the wild variety of books on the shelves, like exotic animals. He ran his fingers across the spines and tapped the pages. "Is Lyra here?"

"Of course she is," Harod said. "Why wouldn't she be?"

Thank every god. At least this meant she wasn't lost in the arms of another lover. Or kidnapped by warren gangers for that matter. "No one saw her all morning."

"Had her nose in my new batch of books since dawn. Hasn't left once." He snapped at his book boy, Beni. The lad hopped off a stool and assiduously sprinted to the backroom and down the stairs to the basement to fetch her.

Jathan leaned on the counter. "Can I ask you something?"

Harod paused. He didn't say no.

Jathan held up the bronze lens. "Ever seen one?"

Harod's face went more ashen than either his mustache or his eyebrows. "Why do you have that?"

Jathan shrugged. "Do you know about them?"

Harod leaned back, expression severe. He looked down his nose disapprovingly. "I know enough. I know that no one like you or I should be walking around with one."

"What is it?"

"It is called a Jecker monocle. The principal tool of the Glasseyes, the Render Tracers. It is how they see things that a man's eyes should not see."

"How does it work?" It was a single oval disc, but it was large enough to look through with both eyes. "Wide to be called a *monocle.*"

"If you want to know about it then go see Trabius Sorca."

"We know Trabius. A good friend of our parents. Trabius knows about these?"

"He knows more than I would about them. And would be willing to say more to you that he did know than I would as well."

Jathan smiled, widened his eyebrows in acquiescence. "All right then." He pulled the monocle back and slipped it into his pocket.

Lyra loped up the stairs and squealed when she saw him. "Hurray, brother of mine. You are free a bit early."

"Are you ready to go?" Jathan asked. "No one has seen you around all day."

"I just want to go home," she said.

She waved goodbye to Harod.

"The more you read the more real you are!" he called out.

Lyra clapped in agreement.

He held out his arm and she took it and together they strolled out onto the Promenade. She hummed her favorite Norian tune, her voice like savage honey.

"You remember that Glasseye?" he asked.

Her tune shriveled. "The dead one?"

"His name was Izimer Kohp. It was written on a special kind of paper I took from his pocket."

"The pocket of the corpse you looted," she clarified.

"Will you ever let that go?"

"Will you ever put that awful shit back where you found it?"

He flattened his mouth.

"Then *no*," she said.

He let about twenty steps go by before he spoke again. "I was wondering if Izimer was perhaps one of the Render Tracers assigned to our parents'..."

Lyra cut him off. "Have you heard from Branderin? How is his sister?"

Jathan allowed her to change the subject without objection. "I haven't seen him. He should be back at the Bottlebottom tomorrow I think."

"Okay."

"I want to stop by to see Trabius," Jathan said. "I want to show him something."

"What now? Some other trinket from Mistine's that you are *absolutely certain* is a priceless treasure that someone accidentally dumped on her for a handful of copper?"

"One of these," he said, holding up the bronze oval lens.

Lyra recoiled. "What? When did you...? Where did you...?" Her eyes turned dark and squinted. "Did you take that off that dead Glasseye?"

He shrugged, grinning.

"Look at you, then. More sheepish than a shepherd. Think you are so clever. That thing is a complication."

He flicked the cover open and swiveled the colored lenses away. He lifted it up nearly to his eye, pointing it at her.

She ducked back and shoved his hand aside with one of her own. "Ugh, don't point that thing at me. Disgusting."

"You scared little mouse. Why? Because I stole it from a dead body?"

She blinked at him. Paused. "Of *course* because you stole it from a dead body!" Her voice echoed off the shops on the Promenade and back across the lake. People stopped what they were doing, looked up.

He clicked the cover back on and slipped it in his pocket. "Okay, okay. Fine. It's away now, See?"

She threw her head back and sighed, turned it into an exasperated growl. "Well?"

"Well, what?"

"Lead the way. Show off your scavenged loot, vulture." She folded her arms and left them folded all the way across the Promenade.

Trabius Sorca lived in his shop, one street off the northeast outlet of the Promenade. His front door had once belonged in a castle that he had somehow smuggled out and installed here. It was meant to be a residence, but the front room had been repurposed for the sale of...something or other.

Jathan never could find any rhyme or reason to what it was Trabius trafficked in. There were more things hanging from the ceiling than there were on the ground—drooping plants, jars of saturnine glow slugs, strings of phrenetic beads, censers issuing redolent tendrils of smoke, sacks of vitreous crystals. Windows and doors had been covered over with enormous tapestries, none of them originating from the same culture.

Trabius himself wore shoes from Valarna, stone-fringed trousers from Calabar, and a tunic from Olbaran. He loved the idea of dogs, but hated actual dogs, so he dressed up an armada of cats in dog costumes he had designed. They pranced about in very undoglike ways, but Trabius demanded they be referred to as hounds.

"Aha!" he said as they entered, as though he had been expecting them all along. He clapped as the door clicked shut behind them. "Lyra and Jathan Algevin. How good to see you both."

"Trabius!" Lyra sang. She embraced him.

The old man sized Jathan up. "Ah, Jathan. What a man the world has made of you. Your parents would have been so proud."

Jathan nodded. "Trabius."

"Dain Algevin was one of the best men to ever walk the streets of Kolchin. And lovely Vela Tracontis, muse of sculptors from Ethios to Medion, master of seventeen languages. Our world was better to have had them both in it."

Lyra smiled so bright. "Thank you, Trabius."

"So fine and shine to see you both," Trabius said. "That is twice this month. I hope it is the beginning of a trend. You know, your parents used to stop by all time to chat, even on days when they were not needing me to import anything for them."

"I'm sure we would love to hear all about that," Lyra said. "But I am tired, and Jathan has a specific query for you."

Jathan nodded, rolling his eyes. "I don't need to know about meal preparation or any practices of a religious—"

Trabius must not have heard either of them. "Oh yes, sephar spices, ranum crystal powder, sedgewood smoke bundles, fine Borean talcum powder, granulum salt soaps, obsidian sand, Samartanian bone brushes, bristled with the coarse hair of sky giant apes from Chashreel..."

Lyra gave him a stern glare. "Jathan has a specific question for you, Trabius, and then we must be off."

He went on unperturbed. "You know, your mother was said to have read every book in the—"

Jathan coughed into his closed fist. "Ahem, Trabius."

"Ah yes, of course. You young ones have so much to do. No time for stories." He dragged them both into his home. "Here. Sit." He gestured to a pair of small cushioned seats, low to the ground, before a jet-black table. It was smooth and reflective like obsidian.

"I want to know more about this," Jathan said. He placed the monocle on the table and slid it across.

Trabius picked it up and turned it over and over in his hands. "You know what this is, I presume."

Jathan nodded.

"And he knows he is not supposed to have it," Lyra added, unsolicited.

Jathan flashed a sharp expression at her. "I know it is a Jecker monocle." He felt Lyra's elbow jab him in the ribs. "And I'm not supposed to have it."

"But do you know *why* you are not supposed to have it?" Trabius raised his eyebrows excitedly.

Jathan exchanged a glance with Lyra. "Perhaps I don't."

Trabius regarded him, chin pinched between thumb and forefinger. "Aside from what it *does*, and who it belongs to, there is another factor to consider. This object is worth more than if the frame was made of gold and the lenses made of diamond glass."

Jathan's chin might have left a crater in the floor. "This?"

"What you are holding is worth a small fortune," Trabius said.

"We...are rich?" Jathan couldn't believe it.

"If you can find someone willing to buy it," Trabius said. "And I would be careful who I showed that to if I were you. It is like walking around with a sack of gold on your back."

"The kind of thing men are willing to kill for," Lyra said.

"Means they weren't scavenging last night," Jathan said. "They followed him, ambushed him. Found out too late they had wandered into the wrong territory."

"It means there are men willing to kill for this," Lyra warned. "You should get rid of it."

He held it out away from her to signal he had no such inclination. "Do you know anyone?" he asked, imagining how easily they could pay off the house and be out from under their aunt's thumb. "Who might buy it?"

Trabius shook his head. "I don't know the kind of people who would be willing to buy that in an underground market."

"Tell me how it works then," Jathan suggested. "Until I can find a buyer, can I use it?"

"Ugh," Lyra complained. "You're not going to keep that thing, are you?"

Jathan ignored her. "Can you tell me what it does?"

"It is a window into another world," Trabius said. "The world of magick."

"All I have to do is...look through it?"

"That is all. If you want to see your reflection, you look in a mirror, yes? All you are doing is looking, and the mirror does all the work of turning your image back to itself. This lens is no different. Merely looking through it exposes you to the world it unlocks."

"Incredible," Jathan said. He still had not even tried to glance through it. He was afraid if he did, he might never want to stop. To be privy to a secret world was quite alluring. He felt like he had cotton in his mouth. His eyes were watering. He quite suddenly could not wait to hold it up to his eye, to see this secret world transposed atop his own.

"Every time a magick user performs magick it creates a residual effect called afterglow, like a flash of light, a glittering cloud of color, a subtle strobing wave in the air, stains like paint smears on surfaces. They have been described as all of these things. The smaller the magick, the smaller the amount of afterglow. The larger, well..."

"I know what afterglow is. I have seen it before, with my own eyes. When my parents were...it was everywhere. Left by the one who had..." He didn't finish the thought. He never did. Still all these years later and he couldn't say the words.

"Every magick performed makes some afterglow visible to our eyes," Trabius said. "Again, relative the size or power of the effect—the *render*. They render it into reality, and the Glasseyes call the effect itself a *render*, too. They render a render, so to speak, heh."

He paused waiting for someone else to chuckle at his joke. When no one did, he scrunched his lip and went on. "The primary crystal lens on the monocle reacts to the residual afterglow of magick. It allows the one looking through it to see the invisible afterglow, the part our eyes cannot see, and there is much more we *cannot* see with the naked eye than we can. By a factor of fifty to one at least."

"You mean to tell me there could be clouds of this...stuff floating around us all the time?" Jathan felt bile rise in his throat.

Trabius shrugged. "It depends on how many magi are where you are, and how often they, well, *use magick*.'

"We could be walking through this every day and have no idea." Jathan was going to be sick.

"It is possible," Trabius said.

Jathan rubbed his palms together furiously. "What happens if we get it on our skin?"

"To you? Nothing. It has no effect on you or anything else. If a cloud of it wafts against you it will rub off on you, or your hair, or your clothes. If you touch a patch of it on a doorknob it will transfer to your fingers like paint. There it will remain as it slowly fades."

"Fades?"

"Like an odor." He hitched up one cheek off his stool and released a ludicrous fart.

Jathan leaned back, and Lyra waved her hand in front of her.

"After a time that odor will fade. If you are too close to the origin of the odor, it might cling to you for a time, until it fades. It could be helped along by air flow or water or some other real substance. But even locked in a room, all afterglow eventually fades."

"Was that truly necessary?" Lyra asked.

"Will you forget the information now?" Trabius asked.

They both shook their heads *no*.

Trabius smiled triumphantly. "Depending on the strength of the afterglow it might last a longer or shorter time before it fades. As little as minutes, as long as hours, or if completely sealed in a container, perhaps days, I would imagine."

"You're sure there is no way it can affect my skin?" Jathan asked.

"Do you feel like my passed wind is affecting your skin?" Trabius asked.

Jathan was too offended to answer by that point.

Trabius turned to Lyra. "Anything you want to know about it?"

She shook her head instantly. "I think I know enough." She tugged on Jathan's elbow. "May we go now?"

Jathan wanted to say no. He wanted to stay and learn what the rest of the colored lenses did. He wanted every detail. He wanted to know. He wanted it all. He wanted....

But he relented. "Fine, sweet sister." He pocketed the Jecker monocle and held one of her shoulders in each hand. He gave her a little shake. "We go." He glanced back at Trabius. "May I come back to see you another time? I would like to know more about how this works."

"But of course, my boy. But of course." He paused, wagging a finger warningly. "Now remember what I said."

"Don't show anyone. Don't tell anyone. Keep it hidden."

"That's the style, my boy. Now off with you both. I have to unshutter my windows to clear the air in here a bit."

Lyra laughed, but she still pinched her nose on the way out the door.

Outside again it was already night. A cool wind sailed in, and the stars twinkled overhead. *Is that what it looks like? Is it little stars in the air?* He wanted to look through it. He wanted to see what was supposed to be a secret.

"Please tell me you are not keeping that thing," Lyra said.

"I might sell it."

"I have a feeling the kind of people who would be willing to buy it are the very same people who would opt to kill you and take it instead."

"Keep it. Or sell it. What else am I to do with it?"

"Put it back."

"Put it back?" His eyes were wide enough to swallow the world. "Take it back to Tenement Lane and hope the dead Glasseye is still on the ground?"

She held her arms and shivered. "Or go up on the Garden Walk and huck it over the edge for all I care."

"You can't be serious. This is like a miracle."

"It is a curse. It came from death. You heard what Trabius said. If someone sees you with that.... Our Glasseyes are supposed to be untouchable. They are the most well-protected agents in all of Amagon. Our Lord Protector would trade a hundred of his finest magistrates for just one Glasseye. If those gangers were willing to kill a Glasseye for *that* monocle, what else would they be willing to do?"

He bit his lip. "Let me think on it. I'll meet you at home."

"Where are you going?"

"Back to Tenement Lane. I'll decide what to do along the way."

She squinted at him a long time in the golden triangle of light from the lamppost high above. She nodded and trotted down the street.

Put it back.

Not a chance.

He walked back to Tenement Lane, and he skimmed the very edge of its maze, and made his way up the Garden Walk.

The further he went, the larger became the voice in his head telling him to put it back.

No. I can't give up this chance.

But then he thought of the complications it would bring.

I really shouldn't.

But then he thought of the unquenchable curiosity he now had about the secret world behind his own.

I must see it.

Lyra will be so angry with me if I don't.

I will be so angry with myself if I do.

He could not decide. He needed a sign.

If everything is as I left it, I will put it back. That will be the sign to give it up.

He reached his destination and stumbled to the edge overlooking the shadowy corner where he had been one night ago.

He was prepared to look down at the body of Izimer Kohp and hurl his Jecker monocle back to him. He wondered if he could land a hit on the corpse from here. Lyra would think that a disgusting thought, but Lyra wasn't here.

But that did not mean Jathan was alone.

The body was still there. But it had just been found. An entire squadron of the city guard milled around, making a loose cordon of yellow sashes, steel cuirasses and tall spears. A dozen magistrates wandered the site, moving from blood stain to blood stain. The gangers had removed the bodies of their fellows so there was no trace of them except the blood pools where they died.

And then there were the Glasseyes.

Three of them.

None of them hailed from Kolchin.

They each wore their hair long, pulled back and pinned with green moon emblems. And their swordbelts had green sashes interwoven with the straps. That was a northern Amagon practice.

Outsiders. Scum from the capital. Stepping where they don't belong.

These men were from the capital, Vithos, or possibly Medion. They were important. They came a long way to be here.

That meant Izimer Kohp was important too.

Jathan knew he should have put it back.

But this was his sign.

The universe was telling him to keep it.

He turned back for home.

As he went, he clicked the cover free.

He slowly lifted the lens to his eyes, and he looked through it.

3

The Killer

"AWAY FROM MY WINDOW!"

Mistine hollered two more times from the other room, but the way her voice scratched the air she might as well have been standing in their ears.

Jathan hopped but went back to dusting the shelves quickly enough. She hadn't meant him, after all. She was referring to Cristan and Branderin who were hanging in the seller window, frightening off prospective customers with buffoonery of the most elite quality. Neither of them was intoxicated, and when these fools were sober they tended to bounce off the walls.

But as unruly as they were, they were not the reason he was distracted.

He could not stop thinking about the lens, the crystal treasure, the Jecker monocle. He had walked home the night before with it practically adhered to his face. He had seen nothing for a long time.

And then he had seen something. A dab on the corner of a shuttered bakery, like paint slapped on with a brush. It was silver and slight, and it shivered against his eyes. He had been so excited he didn't know what to do. He had just stared at it until it faded away.

He had found another one soon after, a little twinkling cloud of silver and green, right out on the Promenade at midnight. He didn't know what it meant. He didn't know how to make sense of what he saw. Only that one of them had been there, a magus, walking among the people, taking their steps in the same places as everyone else.

I need to see Trabius again. I need to know more about what I am seeing.

He saw no more after that, despite walking up and down the empty Promenade, his only company the twin moons, blue and silver, Anularia and Silistin. They reminded him of the glowing colors. He wanted more. Much more. But he had found nothing. Discouraged, he had passed out at home, Lyra already pleasantly snoring in her room.

When he woke, the monocle was all he thought about. But he had been late for his shift. And so, he threw his tunic and trousers on, slipped it into his pocket and jogged here. He had not had a moment to look through it without anyone seeing.

I would be careful who I showed that to if I were you.

But he wanted to look through it. He wanted to see. He wanted to know. He *needed* to know where magick had been. He needed to be aware. The urge was an itching, prickling, burning, like thornbrush under his skin. His knuckles were white, his belt had craters in it from his fingers tapping.

He needed to get out of here. He needed to leave. He needed to see.

"Tell us truly," Cristan said. "Does Lyra have another lover?"

"For the last time, no."

"She was gone all day yesterday," Branderin said. "She hasn't disappeared like that since she was with Aroush."

"No, Aroush was the one before the last," Cristan said. "*Kevander* was the last of her lovers. The one who claimed to be one of the ten thousand princes of Samartania, remember?"

"I would truly rather you not talk about my sister's lovers," Jathan pleaded. "Or that she ever had any, or that there was any such thing at all." He shivered, disgusted.

"She was in Kevander's bed so often we thought she had been woven into his sheets. Aroush said he would teach her the arts of the Pleasure Houses of Ethios."

"I've stopped listening." Jathan winced. "I also hate both of you." It was bad enough that he had to listen to that kind of talk. But there was something more. They said *lover*, but what he heard was *obsession*. Each one was the name of another obsession he had been required to save Lyra from when she finally broke down and admitted she couldn't save herself.

"At least neither of them was as pompous as that Xork Xorka fellow," Cristan said. "Remember him? Spent more time preening himself than a Hylamari rhythmancer climbing into a fifteen-layer featherdress. He swore he had his own galley ship and would sail her to Arragandis and show her the wonders of Arradan."

"She is back today," Jathan said. "She was prancing about the south Promenade with Nessifer all morning. I am telling you, there is no new man."

"Fine, fine," Cristan said. "On to more important matters. Are the two of you coming out with us tonight? We are going to be bottom bottling at the Rusty Salvage."

"The one on Winesink Row? Where the sailors always start a brawl?"

"The same!" Cristan cheered. "What better way to cheer your sorry self up than to find an aching little nightbird to salvage your manhood for a night?"

I have to go hunting tonight. "No, we are calling it early today. Both of us."

"Oh, come on," Cristan said. "Sethleen has been practically begging me to get you back out to a winesink."

I bet she has. "Another time."

"Ugh!" Cristan threw his hands up, barely avoiding slapping Branderin in the face.

"Oh," Jathan changed the subject. "We have been meaning to ask. Any word on your sister, Brand? Did she stumble in yet?"

Branderin seemed to turn quieter when speaking than he had in silence. "No."

"No?" Jathan was surprised. "It's been three days."

"Seems Lyra isn't the only one to fall into a trance for a man." Cristan laughed inanely, jabbing an elbow into Branderin's ribs. But Jathan saw real concern on his face.

"Three days is not outlandish," Jathan said. "Not enough to worry yet."

"A neighbor's friend told me his mother went missing from Beachside in the same way last month," Branderin said. "Not far from where my sister was the other night."

"Oh, well, then it has happened before." Jathan smiled. "When did his mother turn up?"

"She never did," Branderin said.

Jathan felt the answer like a punch to the gut. The smile curdled on his lips.

Cristan opened his mouth, thought better of it, leaving it hanging open for three whole seconds, looking down. He gave his head a little shake. "Anyway, come out with us. We've been dying to have you. Next time you come to the Bottlebottom, everything is on me."

"You don't have to." Jathan waved his hands.

"I insist," Cristan said. "You haven't smiled in days. I want you at the bottom of a bottle and busy up to your balls in a steamy hot nightbird."

"No really, I—"

Cristan shrugged. "Too late. It's done. Come out. Doesn't matter the day."

Jathan acquiesced. "All right. Soon."

Mistine came back and swung a broom at them until they beat a hasty retreat.

Jathan was left there with little to say.

She never did.

A horrible thought.

What could have happened to her? It was odd. Jathan knew the Beachside magistrates. And even as ruthlessly careless as Vaen Osper and Felber Klisp were, he thought they would have at least mentioned finding the bodies of women from their district in casual conversation. It was precisely the kind of morbid, unsettling thing they loved to talk about.

Unless...they didn't know. Because the women were taken somewhere else.

By a sorcerer.

Jathan's mind fixated on the weight of the monocle in his pocket. He was no longer solely captivated with the idea of peering into their world. He now felt that he might have a reason to.

When his shift ended, he floated out of Mistine's like a fog, the monocle already palmed in his hand. Lyra was already waiting for him, half smile, half disapproving smirk.

She figured out I haven't gotten rid of it.

He did not bother trying to hide it from her.

"Find any secret magick today?' she asked in a demeaning sing-song tone.

"Haven't had a chance," he grumbled.

"Well, I wish you luck," she said.

He turned it toward her, raising it almost to his eyes.

She swatted his hand away. "Do *not* point that thing at me."

"Wouldn't you want to know if you have any of it on you?"

She shivered. "Ugh. No, I think I would rather not."

He shrugged. "Suit yourself."

Lyra's eyes turned across the walkway. She suddenly jumped, tore into a run, hands high above her head, dress fluttering in her wake. "Nessa!" She shrieked, holding the 'A' sound for an eternity. People across the damn lake were turning to look.

Nessifer was running the other way, albeit with a slightly pared back display of enthusiasm, ruffled sunset golden summer dress rippling in the breeze. When they collided, Lyra nearly bowled her over. She had to lean over to steady the poor girl. Good thing Lyra was tall enough to do that, or Nessa would have had to see a physician.

"Lyra, I've missed you." Nessa had a habit of closing her eyes and wrinkling her nose when greeting everyone. Jathan had managed to not lose his taste for seeing her do that yet.

She turned to him, eyed him up and down, and gave a wry smile. "Jathan, how's the leg?"

"The what?"

"The other night. The one I kicked. You claimed you'd never walk again." Her mouth slipped into a smile.

"You remembered that?"

"I did."

"It's better. And many thanks for keeping my terrible injury in your thoughts."

"Ouleem told me he thought for certain it had to have been a severe blow to render you as useless at work as you have been the past few days."

Jathan's eyes widened. "Ouleem is quite a funny fellow. It must be that. You know just where to hit."

"He said it has only compounded your other obvious injury," Nessifer said.

Jathan raised an eyebrow. "Oh really? And I suppose he told you to tell me what that other injury might be?"

She nodded. "He gave me very careful instructions on where it was."

Jathan felt like he was already laughing before the words were out.

She pointed one delicate finger at his nose and then made a circle about his entire face. "That one."

Ouleem, you shitsack. But he broke into laughter anyway.

Nessifer didn't laugh, keeping her mouth carefully crafted in that same smile as she looked up at him.

Jathan looked into her eyes and his gaze felt locked there, imprisoned within them, no matter that the rest of his senses told him the sun was shining and he was free to move wherever he wanted.

Nessifer not laughing at Ouleem's joke was made up for by the fact that Lyra guffawed, and then released a series of shrill giggles as aftershocks. By the seventh burst, even Nessifer was beginning to become alarmed.

"I told him I quite like this other terrible injury of yours."

His eyes widened on their own. He tried to keep his face from flushing red. But all Nessa did was smile at him until he grudgingly agreed to smile back.

By that point, Lyra blessedly pulled her aside and went to work learning the gossip she missed out on from the night before.

They dissected numerous social interactions, trying to search the subtext for clues like fanatical conversational archeologists. It went on for what seemed an eternity to Jathan, but in actuality was only minutes. He kept track of the hour by counting how many times they swatted each other's elbows in shock at the latest twist in the relationship of this friend or that one, which of their alleged friends wore the most scandalous dress to Winesink Row, and which of their friends wore the tamest but was secretly seeing six men at once.

They yammered about Lyra's work at the bookseller, and Nessa's transcribing work as understudy to the Historian, how many texts she completed since the last twin moon, and how she was outpacing most of her peers by a factor of three.

Jathan needed no proof of that last part. Nessifer was nothing if not the smartest, most dedicated woman he had ever met. And that was when they were only ten years old. She had only driven herself harder in the ten years since.

When Lyra finally allowed her to go on her way, she gave her a slap of a hug and touched one cheek to hers.

Then she smiled and threw her arms around Jathan's waist, tossing her head against his chest as if listening for a heartbeat. He felt the press of her against him, her dress thin as a breath.

When his arms didn't settle on her shoulders quickly enough, she shook him and rolled her head about. "Hug me!" She chimed in a faux petulance that he found endearing no matter how hard he tried to be annoyed by it. He gave her a hurried double squeeze of his arms and then pulled back.

Her arms unfurled but then her hands each caught in his belt, and she held him there looking into his eyes with a smile. "May the sun shine on your day, Jay."

He tried not to smile and failed. "And may the moons light your way in the night, Nessa." How he wanted to drown in the scent of her hair, her perfume exquisite and inevitable.

She gave a stealthy tug on his belt and then released him. He landed on his heels and only then realized she had brought him onto his toes without him noticing it.

He waved, but she had already turned around and was gone into the crowd.

Lyra stood there with him for a moment, watching the amoebic void of churning bodies swallow her.

Lyra folded her arms and looked over at him, squinting above a smile. "You need to stop pretending you're not in love with her."

He didn't look at her. "You need to stop pretending you know every goddamn thing there is to know."

"I'm not pretending, sweet brother." She wasn't laughing.

But her surety broke him. He laughed. "Fine, but I don't have to do what you tell me."

"You mean like keeping your hands off my closest friends?" She raised an eyebrow.

For a brief moment he panicked and thought she had found out about that one warm night where Nessa's sweetwine and his summerwine had collided and left both of them tangled in the same set of sheets and snoring away by morning.

But one quick look in her eyes told him she was just jabbing him with her wit. For now, anyway. "I will if you stop trying to set me up with them." The way things had ended with the last two of her friends was the reason she was so skeptical of the concept in the first place. To say things had gone poorly would be to gloss over the fact that neither of them were on speaking terms with him, *nor with Lyra herself* anymore.

"You should try not to be such an asshole."

"They like me because I'm an asshole."

"They think they do."

"At least I let them learn how incorrigible I am quickly."

"Is that a jab at me?" she asked.

"No," he said, thinking of those awful shitsacks she always couldn't quite seem to help but complicate her life with. "You aren't incorrigible. You're the exact the opposite. You're too sweet. You're too forgiving. That's the damned problem." He was becoming agitated without meaning to. He couldn't even joke about it without remembered all the pain they had put her through. That she had *allowed* them to put her through.

She could read even the slightest change in his tone, and she clearly decided to just let the conversation die out.

She started walking again and he raced to catch up. Moving far down the Promenade, away from the crowds he hoped. He desperately wanted a chance to look through the crystal lens.

"Do you ever wonder what it must be like?" she asked. "To have magick powers?"

"That question is out of the blue. And no, I do not wonder that at all."

"I do. I think about it all the time. It reminds me of the fairy tales we were told as children, of beautiful gods and sweet angels and mischievous demons, and heroes and quests and adventures. I always thought it sounded so exciting."

Her smile beamed in a way that made Jathan uncomfortable.

"Stop trying to romanticize them," he said.

"I'm not. I was just remembering the stories. They filled me with such wonder."

"And how does it feel now?" He hadn't meant the question to have so much...connotation to it.

But it did. It made her frown. "It seems less wonderful now."

"Let us just walk," he said. "You may wonder all you wish, but I will look for what is real."

"Real." She chuckled.

"What?"

She pointed at the Jecker monocle. "You do realize you are trying to see the residue of unreality. It is the least real thing there ever could be."

He smirked and waved her off, walking beside her in silence.

He did not feel his feet touching the ground. All he felt was the monocle in his hand. Every few steps along the Promenade he would drop to one knee and pretend to fiddle with one of his boots so that he could scan the area through the crystal lens. It was clear yet it made everything seem greyed out, like the world was submerged in a sea of thick fog. Yet he saw objects at a distance just as clear as those close by.

At first, he saw nothing. Only the endless parade of people down the Promenade, talking and laughing, shouting and playing, children splashing on the banks of the little lake. The sun disappeared in clouds of slow white marble, and Jathan secretly reveled. The world settled into a thick blanket of calm, muting the light, submerging everyone into a mass intimacy.

Then, at last, he saw it.

It was only a little twinkle. A sparkle of golden light, so small, so easy to mistake for the glint of sunlight off a metal cart handle. But there was no direct sunlight to account for it.

Jathan's eyes passed over it at first, and he nearly broke his own neck trying to turn back to it. Trabius had been right—it glittered and sparkled and glowed, it looked like individual particles, but somehow also radiated light as one.

This was not a cloud. It was a handprint. A place some awful user of magick had touched with residue-marked hands. It was a smear, adhering to the cart handle like honey paste made of stars.

Jathan felt Lyra's knee nudge him and he yanked the monocle away from his eyes and palmed it. He glanced up in time to see someone passing by.

"You need to be careful," she scolded.

"I saw something."

Her eyes widened and her face drained of color. "Here? Now?"

He nodded. "Right over there."

"What did you see?" she asked nervously.

He could not blame her. Learning that some of the people you walked past every day were abominations wasn't easy. It was easier for him. He knew they were here. He had turned in two dozen in the past year to Vaen and Felber so the lazy magistrates could go collect them. "It must be a shock to know how close those creatures are to us all the time."

"Creatures." She made a sour face.

"Magick users. The same abominations who—"

"Stop mentioning that," Lyra said. She had acid in her voice. Her eyes watered, but she managed not to cry.

"Sorry."

And a part of him was sorry. But only a small part. The rest of him was already holding the monocle up to his eyes again. He fit it into the curvature of his right hand, so that he could make it appear he was shading his eyes from the white glare of the clouds, when in truth he was hunting for afterglow.

He saw another. This time it was green, fringed blue, but the same ethereal sparkle, the same subtle glow. It was a cloud this time, a little patch of semi-translucent vapor, but with a tiny galaxy of sparkling lights inside it.

Someone walked past it and the air in their wake sucked in the afterglow as if it was a bit of steam, swirling, wafting. It reacted to things around it as if it was quite real. But when he pulled the monocle away from his face, it disappeared. When he held it up again, it returned.

He was not sure what the different colors of afterglow meant. What had they done here in the Promenade? Or what had they done elsewhere and then brought with them? He needed to know what they were all doing. He couldn't stand not knowing. He would have to ask Trabius. But that would come later. Right now, he was too fascinated with finding them to bother stopping.

He glanced left and right as he walked to make sure no one was looking too closely at him. Then he returned the monocle to his eyes and hunted again. They were nearly past the lake when he saw the next one, shiny silver, like a cloud splashed across pavement and the wheel of a fried lamb vendor.

The color reminded him of that terrible night. When he had seen his mother and father both for the last time.

He never stared at anything so hard in his life as this sparkling silver afterglow. His lips pulled back. His teeth clenched. His palms slickened and his eyes watered.

What does that color mean?

He was shaken out of his trance by an abrupt impact. Something smacked him hard in the shoulder and hip. His arms flailed. The monocle nearly dropped but he held on just barely.

His eyes snapped back into the real world, and he saw a man staggering, barely keeping his feet, turning to look back at him.

"Watch where you step you little shit," the man said. His head made no sense. His reddish-brown hair was long in some places, cleanly shaved away in others. Wide, suppurating eyes. A dyed banana-colored beard wreathing thick pink lips. He may have had thirty teeth, but Jathan could not see his way past the bilithic monument comprising the front two for confirmation.

Jathan stuffed the monocle back in his pocket. "Fuck you, you clumsy dogshit."

The words were already out of his mouth before his eyes registered the matching blue trousers and vest the man wore over his white tunic. Before he realized this was a street enforcer from Vorlo Wauska's tenement gang. Before he noticed that he had three friends with him. He thought he recognized some of them from the night he found the monocle. These were the men who started a turf war in Tenement Lane by murdering a Glasseye for his treasure.

Causing all those problems for the prize that Jathan now possessed.

Shit, fuck, and hell. This was not normal. Gangers never came to the finestreets. The risk of attracting endless attention and repercussions from the magistrates who served to oozewealth goldfingers who shopped for wares here was far too high.

So what the fuck were they doing here?

"Knock his teeth in, Ressic," one of them said.

"Smash his eyes," another said.

Ressic appraised Jathan and opted to fulfill one or the other of their requests. He lurched forward, a boulder of a fist swinging.

Jathan stepped back and turned. He felt the hair on the back of Ressic's hand swish aganst his cheek, a gust of air behind it.

Jathan slapped his open palms against the passing shoulder and shoved Ressic aside, sending him tumbling into a fisherman's cart, splintering one wheel with the weight of his body, tipping unctuous oils all down his face and shirt.

Some in the crowd laughed. But the laughs died quick.

Ressic's three friends were quick to avenge his humiliation. They each reached for him, thick fingers taking fistfuls of his tunic, shoving him back even as they grabbed.

Jathan danced backward, trying to pull away. Just backing up was enough for one of them to step short, and then his own hand tangled up in Jathan's clothes, pulling him off balance. He toppled.

But the other two were on him, swinging hard, fists falling like hammers. He collapsed to one knee, reached for one, missed. He threw his arms up, desperate to keep the strikes from mashing his face. His head and shoulders felt like a drumhead beneath their punches.

He felt hands grab at his throat. He swatted them away, but received a smack to the eye in return, and the hands came right back, lifting and choking. He saw stars blinking in his eyes, and his body felt so tired. He wanted to fight, but so many blows to the head had rendered him exhausted.

Then he felt a cold splash of water across his face. The hands vanished. He wiped his eyes clear and looked up.

Lyra had dumped a fisherman's bait bucket over both their heads. They both shrieked and squirmed as worms and finger minnows slid down the backs of their tunics and into their trousers.

They reached after Lyra but she leaned back.

Ressic was now back on his feet. So was the one who tripped. They both froze. Their eyes narrowed. They could not have known her face. It was impossible.

But they were transfixed.

Oh, fuck.

"She looks like the one," Ressic grunted. "Go get her!" The men with him raced to be the first to obey his command.

No! Leave her alone!

Jathan opened his mouth to scream a warning, but he gasped in drops of water and choked out what was left of his air.

But Lyra heard them coming. She lunged away, raced toward a cheese frier's high-top wagon, her silvery white gown trailing after her. She leapt once, and that leap was higher than any jump Jathan ever could have made. Her toes touched the top of the wagon wheel, and for a moment she seemed still, a sculpture wreathed in linen. He watched her in wonder through the spasming lights in his eyes.

And then she sprang up off one foot and hurtled into the air, landing palms and knees on the roof of the wagon. Two of the gangers reached up after her ankles, but she somersaulted forward out of their reach. She slid to a halt on the other side, gave a quick victorious look over her shoulder at them, and then jumped off the roof.

She hurtled through the air like a bird in flight. For a moment she became a sunbeam in the sky, floating, unresponsive to the pull of the earth, just another cloud drifting across the sky.

Then the arc of her leap bent down and she landed in the grass, kicking off her slippered shoes and dashing across the Promenade, darting between the multitude of pedestrians.

The four gangers, Ressic included, had forgotten all about Jathan. They tore through the crowd on Lyra's tail. But, of course, they would not catch her. Jathan could outrun, outclimb, and outjump almost anyone alive. And Lyra on her worst day could outrun, outclimb, and outjump Jathan.

Jathan smiled. They would never ever catch up to her. He had tried too many times over too many years. They would never even vaguely keep up with her. There was no finer acrobat in Kolchin.

He brushed the water from his face and pulled his hair back. He dared not take out the Jecker monocle again, as every eye for a hundred paces was on him. He worked his way the opposite direction Lyra had led the gangers, past the bookseller, slipping out the egress, then moving three streets over before curling around and moving parallel to the path Lyra had taken, off toward home, where he knew Lyra would already be.

But when he reached the intersection of the Trenchroad and Fencepost Pike he paused. He told his feet to keep walking home. But they disobeyed. Some stronger part of his mind told him to turn down past Winesink Row and on toward Tenement Lane, to walk through the dark of night with the crystal eye open wide to the presence of the creatures he hated, ready to plunder their secrets.

I could find them.

I could hunt them all.

I could tell Vaen and Felber where they are. With this I can find three a week. I can cleanse them all from this city myself.

He stopped in for a pair of bottles of sour ale from the Dripping Bucket, nursed them as he sauntered his way along, then stopped in for two slightly-less-sour ones from the Rusty Salvage. He took leisurely steps, waiting for the sun to dip and dip and dip some more and finally slip below the horizon. He took his time. He wanted to do this the real way. He wanted the darkness.

He stood at the mouth of the first street leading into the maze, on the very border of Tenement Lane, until the light had all drained from the sky. Then he crossed that final boundary that would have separated him from what he was before and what he had become now.

He stalked through the tenements, through tunnels and alleys, atriums and bridges, hooks and loops, stairwells and switchbacks and doglegs. His eyes were staring through the ghostly grey of the monocle most of the way.

It was not long before he found what he was looking for.

Terrifying tiny clouds that shined. Glittering gold and purple floating through each other and combining yet remaining distinct. They floated near the entrance to a dark alley, so that he would have had to duck to pass them without getting any of it on himself.

Through his eyes alone, it was nothing. A black shadowy alleyway, pocked with pools of black water. Yet through the lens there existed an effulgent ethereal glow. Though through the monocle there was no reflection in the water.

What was it? What had been done here? What action did this aftereffect belong to? He had to know. But there was no way. He did not understand what the colors meant, nor what the quality of the shimmering lights signified. All he knew for sure was that one of them had been here.

He reached out to touch it. He took one step closer. Then another.

He heard voices. Footsteps. The very idea of him being discovered here made him feel ill. He flattened himself into an inset doorway until the voices subsided, the boots turning from nearby sounds to distant echoes. They did not see him. They moved on and disappeared. He was alone once more. Alone with the afterglow of magick.

He went on to find a smear of deep orange glow in the back of a wooden bench two streets over. It shimmered and shined. It slithered and crawled. It wafted and smoked. His mind began to spiral out of control trying to imagine what each of the living patches of color meant. What crimes had he been only a little too late to witness? The longer he let it go on, the more awful and horrific the possibilities floating into his thoughts. He began with thieving and pranks, and quickly escalated to savage maniacal atrocities.

How many different sorcerers live in this place?

He thought the unnatural qualities of the light, and the twisted thoughts they gave him would be enough to awe and terrify him.

But there was one more bit of afterglow he noticed. One that drew him in far more than any of the others. It captivated him, and his eyes found themselves compelled to look at it, his feet drawn to it. This one was silver.

Silver sparkling afterglow. A smudge of it on the back of a stone bench.

Silver.

The same color as the one who....

He found another, nearly a full handprint on a lamppost.

A sorcerer. A magick user. He leaned right here. This is where his hand was.

Jathan tried to think back to what Trabius had said. It would fade in a few hours, even when using the monocle.

That means he was here today. Recently.

It seemed very bright, and very *present.*

This evening. Perhaps minutes ago.

He kept going until he found a cloud of it hanging in the air. Near a stairwell beside a back alley between two tenements. Barely lit, one dim streetlamp at either end. Both buildings had walkways wrapping all around them at each of their four stories, with a waist-high wall rimming each.

Jathan heard grunting.

He took to the stairs. He moved so slowly, he could not tell if he was even breathing. He climbed two stories high and then followed one of the walkways around, turned a corner, and then another.

The grunting grew louder and louder.

Jathan stopped. He leaned the edge of his face over the wall, peeking down at the alley below, ten paces wide and thirty long. It had a tree growing in a little plot off to one side, but the ground was all pavement otherwise. The tree itself was scrawny and drooping compared to the sturdy branches and lush green leaves of the big atrium trees he was used to in this place.

The alley opened right off the street Jathan just came from, with nothing but a vine-wrapped hedge to screen what went on in here from the outside. There was a ground level tunnel in the center of the tenement across from Jathan, and there must have been one in the building he stood upon as well, three stories down.

As the monocle rose further and further, his eyes gravitating behind it, he became abruptly aware of what the sound was.

He saw a man below. Standing upright. Facing off to the right. His hands twinkled silver. A woman bent over before him, her long dress heaped up onto her shoulders, her backside white as chalk. The shining silver color smeared from his hands onto the cheeks of her ass like paint wherever he grabbed hold of her.

Jathan's mouth fell open.

It's him.

Jathan thought he heard the snap of a footstep behind him, but when he turned to look, he saw nothing. He turned back to look at what was happening below.

The man pumped his hips into her over and over, skin colliding in wet smacks. He wore a fine coat, with a thick cloak over it that had fallen off his shoulders down to his elbows. His trousers were still on, so he must have let himself out between the strings.

She turned up to look at him, reaching back one hand and raking fingernails down his chest with a growl. His pace quickened. She shook, gasping and moaning a song through gritted teeth. He sucked in a breath and let out a long groan, his hips tight to her backside.

The thoughts swirling within Jathan's mind were threatening to overwhelm him in the chaos, implications flying at him. He had come out here to be the hunter, to find sorcerers, magi, men and women who could wield magick, creatures who deserved to be destroyed. He knew the moment he stepped into Tenement Lane that he might stumble upon one of them. But now that he had, he realized with great clarity that he had no plan at all for what to do next.

What do I do? Who do I tell? Does he live here? How do I find him again?

As if in answer to his question, he heard sudden shouting below.

He panicked, almost pissed himself, nearly dropped the monocle over the side. He all but asphyxiated on his own sharp gasp.

"Seber Geddakur!" one of them shouted. "We're here to take you in!"

The man who was Seber Geddakur casually glanced over his shoulder, then looked down as he tucked himself back into his trousers. The woman seemed much more concerned than he, scampering into a passageway at the far end and disappearing.

Jathan turned his head, careful not to move so fast they would notice him. He saw five men, coming into the alley from the same street Jathan had. If they had taken the stairs instead of staying on the ground, they would have been standing precisely where he was.

They were each dressed in magistrate garb, blue tunics with olive capes, swords sheathed in shiny polished rigs. The tunics were clean, the capes pressed, and their chests littered with silver badges.

Definitely not Vaen and Felber and their team then. That much was certain. If someone ever gave Vaen Osper a medal, he wouldn't have even been able to figure out how to pin it on himself.

"Seber Geddakur!" the magistrate shouted again. "Drop to your knees. We have a writ for your arrest."

The man turned slowly, meticulously, to look at them, his face hidden the way the shadows played. "Lambs," he said. "Lambs to the slaughter."

"On your knees! Do it now!"

Seber raised his arms.

The magistrates drew their swords.

Jathan felt a rising fear, like hands climbing up his throat from somewhere deep inside him.

They don't know what he is. Oh, gods. They don't know he is a sorcerer.

Jathan watched the air ripple in the alley. He could not see what was happening, but it was distorting his vision.

Invisible objects slammed into the magistrates, puncturing their bodies with wet, pulpy slaps. Bones cracked, blood spilled, and one by one they all fell.

A glittering silver light flushed around Seber's hands, slithering in and around his fingers, shedding off them into the air. It quickly began to fade.

Without thinking, Jathan raised the monocle to his eyes again and gazed through the ethereal grey of its crystal world. He saw a mighty plume of silver light, rippling and folding in on itself, writhing in the air. Long strands connected it to his hands, each giving off pulses of silver light like sparkling steam.

Jathan fell out of himself. He could not look away. It was beautiful and terrible. *You are just meat and bone. There is nothing more to you. No bright light. No everwonder waiting to take you home. Everything just ends for you.*

Seber turned and walked away. He never did see Jathan there. No one did. Now he was alone. Seber and the woman gone. His only company now was a set of five corpses, freshly murder-dead, little bubbles of steaming silver hissing from each of their wounds.

Jathan heard a loud thud, like a door slamming somewhere in the tenement. The sound jolted him back into himself. He turned and ran.

He ran down the stairs. He ran through the maze of Tenement Lane. He ran along Winesink Row to Brandytown and onto the finestreets. He ran all the way home.

He was drenched in sweat by the time he made it, but he was too terrified and exhausted to bathe.

Lyra was already in her room, safe and gently snoring.

Jathan sighed. He had nearly forgotten to be relieved.

He freed a bottle from the high cabinet in the dining room, where they kept their drink, same as their parents had, all hidden among a sea of bottles, a rainbow of gold and violet and green and red and grey, for every spice and salt and oil and soap.

All those bottles hadn't been enough to hide the wine from him when he was ten summers old and had to stand on a chair to reach the cabinet door. They surely were not enough to hide it from him now. He reached in without looking, his fingertips navigating the shapes, slender, short, narrow, or bulbous, in endless combination, until he found a fat one with a long slender top.

He had to be careful though. There was still an old whiskey bottle in here, one his parents had opened that night ten years ago. He couldn't drink that one.

Luckily the one he pulled out was wine. He sighed with relief to see it, ready to embrace it like an old friend, to tongue the rim like the lips of a long-lost paramour, to swallow it all like a greedy lover.

Before long he found himself at the bottom of that bottle. Not a moment later he collapsed face-first into his bed and plunged toward sleep.

4

Is It Better To Know

SOMEONE SLAMMED A FOOD cart door shut on the Promenade and Jathan jumped like a cat. He let out a sigh and cradled his head while Ouleem dusted the Mua dog carvings again.

Vaen Osper and Felber Klisp stood outside in the grass, dangling their arms in through the lip of the seller window, their filthy magistrate tunics torn, their cloaks one minute from being rubbish, their three lackeys milling around out in the grass behind them.

Their man, Sejassie, was casually kicking over the little white chairs clustered around the lake.

"Could you ask him to stop that?" Jathan asked. The last thing he needed was more grief from Mistine.

Felber shrugged.

Vaen glanced over his shoulder. "Sejassie. Stop making a nuisance of yourself."

Sejassie complied, though unwillingly.

Tylar and Belo were not being overtly annoying, though between Tylar's nose and Belo's eyes, they were doing their fair share of driving customers away from the window, too.

So far Mistine had left them alone.

"Gods great and small, you need to relax," Vaen said.

"You jump like a bunny," Felber said.

"Fuck you both," Jathan said.

"Ungrateful," Vaen said, chuckling.

"Get away from my window!" Mistine hollered from the other room.

Well, it was inevitable. Jathan cradled his head again.

"The big one with the yellow beard who took a swing at you was Ressic Wauska," Vaen said.

"Oh gods high and low," Jathan said. "Vorlo's son?"

"Step-son," Felber said.

"Almost as bad," Jathan said, holding a wet cloth over his bruised eye.

"Bad news is he's known for having a terrible temper," Vaen said. "Good news is he's known for having a terrible memory."

"Best lay low for a while," Felber suggested. "Keep your head down, don't lollygag on the Promenade, and definitely stay away from Tenement Lane."

Shit, fuck, and hell. How could he stay away now that he had seen the true extent of the immaculate darkness there. He wanted more of it. He already wanted to go again tonight.

Vaen clasped his hands together, elbows on the windowsill. "Give it a few weeks and he will forget all about you. He could look in your eyes and not know he'd ever met you before."

"As for the others..." Felber flipped open a pad of parchment. "Torp, a gutter mouse from Beachside; Pranji, a Hylamari who worked as a hand in dockland for a year, now breaks skulls for old Vorlo; and lastly, we aren't certain from the description, but we assume the other one was Graekor, a big Kolkothan brute that Vorlo probably bought from some Borean pirate."

"So, I am still fucked," Jathan said.

Vaen laughed. "Well, they may have better memories, but not great eyesight. I think you and your sister will be just fine. They haven't been back here since. People would talk quite a lot if any gangers began showing regular on the Promenade. Any time a ganger is seen on the finestreets the marshall triples the city patrols and every ganger knows it. I doubt they would risk coming back here. Do what Felber said—keep your head down. Watch where you are walking. Steer clear of their territories for a couple weeks and it'll be like it never happened."

"Great," Jathan said. "Many thanks."

"We can't let our informants dry up," Vaen said. "It would be bad for business. Especially one as reliable as you. You're an extra payday for us all by yourself turning them in no questions asked the way you do." The corner of his lips broke into a smile. "Speaking of which, any new leads for us?"

"Not yet," Jathan said. "But I'm working on something. It could be big. I'll let you know as soon as I know."

"Very well," Vaen said. He eyed Jathan for a moment, eyes sharpened, suspicious with a hint of anger. "Be seeing you."

That was odd. Did I really just see that?

Felber waved inanely.

Jathan didn't bother.

Tylar, Belo, and Sejassie plundered the tray of drink one of Mistine's widesink girls was taking out to some patrons. When she complained to them, Sejassie shoved her, and Belo kicked one foot out and tripped her. They let her fall flat on her ass in the lake.

"Oh for fucking's sake!" Jathan shouted. "Can you get your dogs out of here?"

The girl flew to her feet, barking an angry diatribe at them. They were a bit intimidated.

"Vaen! I can't have them doing that shit around here."

Vaen swatted each of them across the head as they all walked away. They all stumbled along, cradling their heads.

Jathan fumed. "Fucking hell, they are so fucking stupid."

"You all right?" Ouleem asked, once they were gone.

"Those damn magistrates are just a barrel full of trouble. I wonder if they are worth knowing sometimes."

"Never liked any of them."

"One day I am going to have to stomp the shit out of them."

"If you ask me, they are lucky they left before Dalya let them have her boot heel."

Jathan closed his eyes and took a deep breath. "Very true."

"You need to sit down for a spell? You look more tired than usual."

"I just had a hell of a rough night."

"You've been having a hell of a lot of those lately. What's going on with you?"

"A lot of things landed on me all at once," Jathan said. "I can handle it. I just need to get it all sorted out."

"If you say so."

"I'm fine, Ouleem. Really, I am."

"Anything to do with Lyra?"

Jathan dropped his hands and turned to look up at him. "Why do you ask?"

Ouleem shrugged. "She wasn't around again today."

"She wasn't?"

"She has had the same routine every morning for four years—grabs a coffee drink with Nessifer at the Lazy Steward at dawn, then walks around the lake with Branderin, then chats with Cristan before he has to begin his morning counts at the Moneychanger, then she interns with the librarian, then she has lunch at either the Willow Hut or the Lakebreeze, and then goes to work her shift for Harod."

"You memorized all that?"

He shugged again. "It's not exactly hard to remember. She does it every morning...well, except this morning. And that other morning. And..."

"I get it. I get it."

"Did she perhaps have a rough night, too?"

Jathan shook his head. "She was out cold before I even made it home."

"Cristan is convinced she has a new lover."

"Is he?" Jathan raised a skeptical eyebrow. Yet even he was beginning to have suspicions. She had disappeared too many days in a row. He wanted to ask her. But he couldn't ask her. Not again. He didn't want to have another one of *those* fights.

"Oh, and another thing. That Glasseye is back."

Shit. "Same one?"

"Same fellow. Every time he sits at the Lazy Steward. Same high chair on the patio, beneath the shades. If someone is already in that chair when he gets there, he stands three feet away and stares into their eyes until they leave."

"Was he asking about me?"

"I think so. A friend told me he said the name Algevin. That's you."

"What else could land on my plate right now?" Jathan tossed his hands in the air.

"I'll pray to my gods and yours," Ouleem said. "I would like to live my whole life without a Glasseye ever setting foot in it. I don't trust them."

Tell me about it.

He finished out his shift in a daze. When he was finally freed for the evening, he staggered across the Promenade. He kept his head down and went straight to see Trabius. He did not run into any of Vorlo Wauska's thugs. He took it as a win. A small win, but a win all the same.

"Aha!" Trabius said when Jathan pounded on his door.

Jathan charged in, nearly bowling him over.

"You are in quite a rush today," Trabius noted, closing the door.

Jathan stood in darkness. "Do you live like this all the time? Fetch a light, would you?"

"Ha, demanding," Trabius said, striking a fire stick and lighting a series of slender reed candles against two of the walls.

"What do the colors mean?" Jathan asked almost right away. "The sparkles, the different colored afterglow. Are they different for everyone?"

"Yes and no," Trabius said. He gestured for Jathan to sit in a cushioned chair. Trabius himself sat on the floor. "Through the primary lens the colors are usually associated with which type of physical forces are being created or affected by the one altering reality. The Render Tracers train to notice all manner of things about those colored clouds of afterglow. Some of these sorcerers, wizards, magick users, magi, or whatever you want to call them, will have only one color to what they do. Some with have several. And many may have the same ones."

"I see." Jathan's shoulders sagged. *So just because they are silver doesn't mean they are the same as the silver ones I saw that night so many years ago.*

"However, there are some of the other lenses when slid into place over the primary one that can show many things. They have ways of identifying one of them to a degree of near certainty."

Jathan's eyes perked up. "An easy way?"

"Are you entertaining the idea of becoming a Render Tracer?"

"No. I just want to know what I have been seeing. I want to know what it means."

"I am not sure I should continue with this," Trabius said. "It is not safe to follow the people who leave these traces behind. Render Tracers train extensively and have enormous structures of support to do what they do. You cannot simply pick up a Jecker monocle and decide to be one."

Jathan leaned in close. "Please Trabius, tell me."

Trabius paused a long time, regarding him, like he was inspecting the work of a carpenter for flaws. "Of the four other lenses, *filters* they are called, that can be swiveled over the primary lens, only two of them might be of immediate interest to you—the blue and the green. Especially the blue. It is essential. The rosy red filter and the milky white filter look for details that only extensive training would allow you to know what you were looking at, let alone what to do with the information they presented you."

Jathan swiveled the green filter on the hinge until it clicked softly into place over the lens. Trabius' face was bathed in green, as was the light of the reed candles. But it was not like looking through green glass. It was as if the image of every object itself *became* green. He did not understand how the lenses did what they did, but it was fascinating. "What does this one do?"

"The effects these magi render may be of many varieties. They rewrite the physical laws of our universe very briefly. Some can alter the mass of an object, or change how porous a material is, or change the rate at which heat flows through a metal, or simply remove something from being able to transfer a force. Some users can do many things, some can only do many variations of one type of thing, and some can only do one thing over and over again. But nearly all things that are rendered have some things in common—they must all have a *shape*, a *position*, and, if they are set in motion, a *direction*."

"What about invisible things? Things that could hurt people."

"Some can make their own objects—shapes or force fields—out of thin air. I have been told many have the ability to make objects that they can then move about this way and that."

"These objects they can make, how fast can they move?"

Trabius pinched his chin. "Well, from the slowest speed you can imagine to the fastest you can imagine. The magick user is only limited by their strength, their experience, and their physical constitution. Weak means slower speed, less mass, smaller ability to effectuate change on the way heat works, or stress, or gravity. Inexperience means less options, slower reaction time, poor concentration. And if even the most powerful sorcerer simply has not had a healthy enough breakfast, they may pass out from exertion after trying their smallest render."

"So, to make one of these objects go fast enough to kill someone...would mean fairly powerful or experienced."

Trabius nodded.

"And if they could make many such things at once, that would indicate power as well, true?"

"The concentration to render multiple things at once would need to be high, certainly." Trabius squinted. "These questions are oddly specific."

"Curiosity, I swear."

Trabius tapped his chin. "Where was I?"

"Shape, position, and direction."

"Ah yes. This filter, the green one, allows you to see the positions that forces existed in, or the precise locations where a law of nature was temporarily changed creating an unnatural effect. It will show the shape of an unreal object and the path of its travel. It will show the dimensions of an unreal wall. It will show where a blast of flame was sent through the air. It will show where they reduced the effect of friction on someone's boots so that they slipped and fell. It will show where they levitated the largest boulder or the smallest pebble. And it will show you *how*."

Jathan was salivating. He could not wait to go back out to see what more he would see with this new filter. "And the other one? You said one of the other three is useful?"

"Ah, yes. The blue one. It is often called the most versatile of all. It—"

Trabius was cut off by a sudden pounding on his front door.

Jathan shot upright. The noise took him by such surprise he very nearly voided his bowels right there on the floor.

"Open the door!" someone shouted.

Jathan remembered the voice. It was the same one that had suggested Jathan have his teeth knocked in the day before.

"Send him out!"

Shit, fuck, and hell. They saw me on the Promenade. They must have followed me here.

"Friends of yours?" Trabius asked.

Jathan tip-toed to the door. With one finger he pulled the tapestry blocking out the front window back a smidgen. He saw Pranji and Torp, two of the enormous thugs who had been with Ressic Wauska.

It's only the two of them.

Okay.

I can handle just two.

"Do you have a back door?" Jathan said.

"I would just as soon not have these two at my door all night," Trabius said.

"I'll draw them away."

Trabius led him down a short hallway, into a corner with a door that only came up to his shoulders. "Back door." He shrugged and pulled it open.

Jathan sprinted out and around the corner. He worked his way along the opposite side of the street. The twice-stupid gangers kept pounding on the front door all the while, oblivious.

Jathan crossed another street to the edge of the Promenade, where he found a cart stacked high with ripe calpas fruit. He purchased two, holding one golden rind in each hand. They were nice and soft.

He squinted, reared back, and let one fly. It followed a high, lazy trajectory, and dropped with unerring accuracy on Torp. It exploded on the back of his head, forcing his face into Trabius' front door.

He hurled the other one as Pranji turned around. The timing was such that the second calpas smashed down directly into his face, splattering sweet pink fruit all across his vest.

Jathan waited until they had wiped their eyes clean, and then he waved at them, smiling.

They both roared and came after him. But they were bulky and slow, and Jathan had more than enough of a head start to lose them in the crowd and then work his way around and off the Promenade.

He headed straightaway to meet the others at the Bottlebottom, trusting everyone would be too drunk to care he was wearing his work clothes. Lyra would certainly be there, and Cristan had offered to pay.

But when he arrived Lyra was nowhere to be seen.

Where in all the hells is she?

The flickering candle flames cast writhing red shadows through the imperfections in the ruby glass. The drums were thumping and the zinges were thrumming and twanging. Bodies hurtled across the dance square, narrowly avoiding the griffon-carved posts. Dancers flopped exhausted into creaking wooden chairs and dumped substantial amounts of wine down gasping wide-open mouths. Cristan was throwing silver around like it was nothing, buying bottle after bottle for the table.

Sethleen greeted him with a tortuous, groping hug, her mouth nearly swallowing his ear. He could smell the sweetwine sweating out of her skin more than he could smell it in his own cup. "Come dance with me," she said, over and over again. "Come dance with me, Jathan."

But he would not. He could tell from the way her hands squeezed his buttocks and the way her tongue searched into his ear that if he went with her to dance, she would not let him come back to the table until they fucked right in the dance square.

She grabbed a convenient stranger walking past and took him out instead. Cristan noticed with a glance, but he was leaning back, arms draped over the chairs to either side of him, half-empty bottle of sharpwine in one hand. He would wait until she came back. And whether she came back full of a stranger's seed or not, he would still take her over the table. It was all the same to him.

Nessifer and Branderin were there, though Nessifer was spending all of her time consoling Branderin. She gave Jathan a sympathetic look from across the table as she patted poor Branderin on the back.

Jathan nodded to her. *I would love to sit with you close tonight. But I understand.*

She kept Branderin busy, and even made him crack a smile more than once. Eventually Cristan plopped himself down in the chair on the other side and began to rattle off another of his endless stories in Branderin's ear, freeing Nessa to lean over the table to snag Jathan's.

"Where is Lyra?" she asked him, half-shouting above the din of the music. Her red bangs were shorter than before. She didn't have to part them anymore. Now they rested evenly on her eyebrows, the rest of her ruby red locks thrashed together into an approximation of a ponytail. She had squeezed herself into one of her slimmer sister's dresses again, and the bodice was generous when it came to letting her chest breathe.

"Don't you know?" Jathan asked. *Damn it.* He had been hoping to find her here to tell her to keep an eye out for any of Wauska's bluevests on the Promenade.

"I haven't seen her," Nessifer said. She shrugged. "But if I know her, she is likely trying to buy passage on the ten fastest ships out of here."

"Ha ha," Jathan said, sarcasm in full flow.

"You don't think she would fly away from here if she could?" Nessifer asked. Her expression was so serious that Jathan for a moment thought she actually meant it.

"Nessa, everyone has dreams and big ideas of leaving where they are to go out there somewhere. But they are always dreams. Out there is a lie. The wide world is a mirage. No matter where you go, the grass is always greener somewhere else."

Nessifer seemed skeptical. "Surely she has spoken with you about it."

"Well, of course she has." Jathan's skin flushed in irritation. He tugged at the collar of his tunic with a lethargic finger. "But we talked about it. We decided that we would stay here."

"We? Or *you?*"

"We both agreed. To keep the house, we needed Aunt Dresa's stipend. And she would only agree to give the stipend if we both stayed here. In Kolchin. Together. To honor our parents. To keep whole the one part of them we still had left."

"Okay, okay. I believe you. Fucking gods, Jathan, you get so damn intense. I swear your blood only runs one temperature—molten." The way she spoke it sounded like a criticism, but the way her lip curled in as her eyes wandered over him told him there was another meaning within her words.

His face flushed. He smiled. "I've yet to hear you complain."

She smiled. "Because riding that volcano didn't disappoint. Fucking you was like fucking a river of magma."

He smiled wider. He forgot his irritation. "We were both swimming in wine that night." He kept smiling. He didn't want to say that the wine had stolen most of his memory of that night. But it was not exactly a lie. What images and sensations and sounds and smells he did remember were among his favorite memories. It was a hazy cloud of flashing impressions, but every time he thought of them it was like an ascent to touch the stars.

Her face went suddenly serious. "I swear to you, you had better not tell Lyra about that either."

He held up his hands innocently. "When have I ever?"

They had decided the morning after that it should not be something they do again. Their lives had been complicated then. Still were. And he thought it would not have been fair to Lyra. He had not known how he felt about her then, and worried endlessly over them having a spat and Lyra being forced to choose between them. It was a childish thought. But it had consumed him at the time.

And now it was too late.

She slid out of her chair and swayed off to the bartender to refill Branderin's cup for him. "Just...give her a break, would you?"

"Fine." He didn't have to promise.

Ouleem showed up late with a woman in tow, a quiet girl who kept glancing at the door. Jathan tried talking to her, but her answers to his questions flew right past his head.

All that was in his mind was the monocle. He nursed his wine, checking the lens whenever he thought no one was looking. He never saw any afterglow.

He was surprised to find he was...disappointed.

With the monocle in his hand, he *wanted* to find afterglow with it. He *deserved* to find afterglow. And when he was in a place that had none, he felt cheated, cheated of the secret world that he was supposed to now have access to.

He pocketed it with a curse.

"What is it?" Branderin asked. He was drunk enough to slur his words, and also barely enough to drown the heartsickness he was feeling.

Jathan felt a quick fear, as if he had been caught with a hand in the cookie jar. "Oh, nothing. I am just having a rough day."

"Seems like you say that every day."

"Lately, I cannot deny it."

"I am also having a difficult time. My sister still has not been found."

"Still? This does sound like it is more than simple forgetfulness."

"That is the difficult thing we are coming to realize. We have gone looking. We have offered rewards. We do not know what else to do."

"Did you hear anything from the magistrates from your district?" Jathan asked.

Branderin put his head in his hands. "They can do nothing, they say. They practically shooed us away."

"Oh, gods high and low," Jathan said. "I'm so sorry."

"My father is beside himself. We don't know what to do."

"I know a few magistrates," Jathan said. "They are from Beachside. Near enough to where she was last seen. They might know something. Ask for Vaen Osper or Felber Klisp. They might be able to help. They can check the city gate logs. They may be able to talk to the right people."

Branderin nodded. "I will give that a try."

"Do it," Jathan said. "Tap every resource."

Nessa spent much of what remained of the night consoling Branderin, Cristan spent much of his time either watching Sethleen fuck men on the dance square or fucking her himself, and Ouleem was putty in the hands of the woman he brought, doting painfully upon her.

Jathan was forced to sit idle, wishing he could be putty in the hands of the woman seated across the table from him. Wishing he could dote on her.

But Nessa was in consolation mode, and whenever she was, she became the high priestess of the group, an ear for them to spill their worries to. When she was the high priestess, she could not be steered away from someone in the throes of depression.

Jathan felt his interest in joviality passing as quick as a pluck of the string on the zinge. He left his cup half-full on the table, twisted out of his chair, and walked out of the Bottlebottom.

He did not say goodbye. Not that he needed to. They were all too distracted to notice anyway.

A man brushed past him outside the door and hurled an insult over his shoulder. Jathan called him a farod, the worst of the old Arradian insults. After that, Jathan intended to let it go, but the man had a long reach and swung a fist into his ear.

The impact set all the summerwine in his head to sloshing. The pain staggered him into a wall. But somehow he brought his forearm up in time to deflect a second swing, and brought his other fist up under the jaw, knuckles cracking on bone, setting those teeth all to rattling. He shoved the man against the wall and gut punched him until his belly split, leaving him in a soup of his own piss and vomit.

The man hadn't insulted his mother or father, so Jathan opted to stop there, walking away without kicking him fifty or a hundred more times. By the time he made it a few blocks he forgot what the man even looked like.

Jathan had intended to stumble his way home, but that was not where his feet took him. He spent a thousand and more steps staring down at his boots and by the time he looked up he was standing in front of the south arch entrance to Tenement Lane.

What am I doing here?

But even as he asked himself the question, he was already walking under the arch, taking the first steps into the maze, night raging all around him, the moons up, but precious little of their light making it into these slender defiles. The buildings were mountains, the streets and alleys narrow ravines.

The streets were choked with abandoned objects, scraps of food in puddles of water, broken crates, clothes too torn to wear. None of them lasted long. Every scrap was soon absorbed by this place, reused, repurposed. It was an endless renewal.

The streetlamps were sparse, and those that were lit even less common, oil stolen years ago, wicks stolen decades ago. What few pale silver and blue beams from the moons that penetrated this far were all he had to light his way. Only the atriums within each tenement were lit in any meaningful way, the lamps cared for by the inhabitants. But their care did not often reach through the tunnels to the outside.

He found a space between two tenements that abutted one another at an odd angle. Instead of a narrow alley between them, he saw a wide triangular space. He stood at its base, narrowing to a point the further it stretched away from him.

He thought he saw a faint glow high up one of the walls, on a dress dangling from a wire. Neither building on the long sides of the triangle had walkways, but the tenement behind him did on the upper stories. He turned into a stairwell and climbed to the third floor, navigated the walkway until he was once more at the base of the triangular space, only this time looking down upon it.

He stared through the Jecker monocle, and the glow on the dress was much more pronounced. That meant it truly was afterglow. It was real. *Users of magick. Users. Magi. Abominations. One lives here, or at least nearby.* It was too far to see clearly, but it was a silvery-white shimmer.

He was about to head back down when he heard a sound. Tiny footsteps pattering in the dark. Wheezing breaths. A whistle and a whine.

It was a child.

Jathan dropped low behind the railing, his eyes peeking over the top.

He saw a young girl run out one of the alleys below, and go flying across the triangle, threading two benches and a rusted iron rail, heading for a slender tunnel on the far side, near the sharpest point of the triangle.

Her clothes had been made of the pieces of other clothes. Every bit of trouser was of a different fabric in a different color than any of the others. She wore a slim tunic made of a different front and back sewn together, and over it a coat of heavy fur, ten sizes too big, fluttering off her shoulders like a cape.

She was halfway across the triangle and Jathan saw who was coming behind her.

He recognized him immediately.

Seber Geddakur. The sorcerer. The murderer. The same man who had slaughtered a whole team of armed magistrates the other night.

He wore the same trim coat, fitted, dark. He took every step deliberately, as if the soles of his feet were hammers and every step was the precise location of a nail. He was stalking the child, his path changing course specifically to follow hers.

Something about the way he moved made Jathan freeze in place. His eyes watered uncontrollably, fogging his vision, draining out the corners of both eyes, running down his face. He was unable to look away.

The child flew into the bleak shadow of escape down the tunnel. Disappeared from view.

The sorcerer followed effortlessly. He never increased his pace, and yet it felt like he was soaring across the open space as quick as a shout.

He neared the tunnel entrance. But he stopped.

A woman stepped out of the tunnel. Hair dark. Trousers of bright soupy leather, with patches of different colors down the legs. And then patched-in holes on those patches. She wore a leather vest, sucking to her torso like skin. She wore a heavy belt with full pouches, and a black baton.

Seber did not appear surprised. "Lamb," he said.

She raised her arms out in front of her as if to push him back.

Seber did what Jathan had seen him do before. He lifted his hands and invisible projectiles flew from them.

The woman stood her ground. Jathan heard the snap and pop as the missiles struck some obstruction, an invisible wall in front of her.

Did she have a shield? She must.

None of the objects reached her.

She is one of the magi.

Seber Geddakur sent more spheres, stronger this time. They rippled the air. Jathan saw air distorting around them, like reality itself shaking in terrified anguish in their presence.

The missiles struck. They sounded different this time. They sounded like they were not being blocked or deflected like before. This time they cracked and pitted the invisible shield, breaking it, cracking it open, splitting it apart.

Jathan could not believe the woman still stood there. She did not even try to run away.

She must be protecting that child. What?

She faced down the sorcerer, chin up, defiant, even as her shield began to rip. Even as the deadly projectiles tore through. Jathan heard them smack into the tenement wall behind her, sending splinters of stone in all directions, showering her with sharp grey dust.

He made out little of her expression, but he could see her eyes. They were wide and glowing with tears. She was terrified. She knew it was hopeless, but she did not run.

Her shield fell apart. Her lips pulled back, baring bright moonlit teeth. Effulgent yellow beams of energy extended from her hands, like swords made of fragments of the sun. She screamed in rage and despair, and she charged the sorcerer.

Seber leaned back. But he did not step away.

Her legs churned, her arms chopping the air with those radiant swords.

Seber flicked his wrist. An object flew through her. It ripped through her belly, and shot out her back, liquifying any organs in between, blasting her vertebrae against the wall like shrapnel.

Her legs ran three more steps, then they turned to jelly. The golden beams of energy winked out. She smacked face-down, but her momentum rolled her onto her side so that her eyes were looking up at Jathan. For a moment she seemed to see him even though he was so far from her. Then her eyes turned to glass, and there was no more life to be had from them.

Jathan didn't know what to think. He was looking at a dead magick user. A magick-wielder gone to grave should have made him happy. Them killing each other more so. His rational mind could think of no more just and natural thing.

And yet he did not feel joy. He did not even feel neutral. He felt horrible. He felt a sickness of sorrow holding him in its grasp, tightening around his throat, as if he had been weeping alone for hours. He did not understand why he was feeling this way. Something about the way she sacrificed herself overcame him, and the anxious watering of his eyes became actual tears.

Seber calmly stepped over the body, and entered the tunnel, but by now that little girl could have been across the Bowl all the way to the East Uppers if she had kept running. Unless she hit a dead end, she was safe at least.

The space was quiet once more.

Jathan took calm breaths, trying to steady himself, summoning everything he had to keep his legs upright.

He turned to his right and someone was standing there.

"Shit." His heart leapt out his chest and flew off the balcony. His arms and legs felt a jolt that stiffened them.

He saw a body bathed in darkness, heels planted on the railing, squatting over it as if preparing to jump below.

Jathan squinted.

It was a woman. Black hair, long enough on one side of her head to swoop down and cover her face like the wing of a raven and shaved to nothing on the other. Her eyes were each as wide as the moons. He saw tears glisten, running down high narrow cheeks. Her tiny mouth never opened. She only stared at him, weeping. She wore two different boots, patched leather trousers, and a sleeveless tunic beneath a tight shiny leather coat.

She never said anything.

Only stared at him with watery eyes.

Jathan was certain more than ten seconds went by in silence. Then she hopped down, turned, and fled around a corner.

Jathan was so startled that he merely stood there, staring at the empty space where she had been.

I need to go.

His legs did not move.

I need to get out of here!

He finally forced himself to take small steps, though each one felt impossible. He needed to go home so very badly. He needed the safety of its familiarity. He needed it to wrap its walls around him.

He needed to get out of Tenement Lane.

He unwound the path that he had just wound to come here, and Tenement Lane spit him back out into the Bowl. From the nearside it was only a hop and a jump to Winesink Row, and thence to the finestreets beyond.

Jathan staggered home, to the house his parents had built, in the safest neighborhood of all the finestreets, tucked into a quiet little corner in a row of small houses astride the always silent government square, always well-guarded, always well lit. So different from where he had just been, what he had just seen. Wide streets, quiet, calm, protected, safe.

It was a part of the city that people would have killed to live in. His parents had made sure they had a piece of it. For him. And for Lyra. And he honored them by keeping it the way it was.

He never wanted to leave this house. As long as he was here, he had a part of them still in his life, his mother and father still existing around him. It made him smile every time he saw it. It was large enough that it did not feel cramped but small enough that it felt cozy. It was perfect.

They had nearly lost it after it happened. With no one to pay the fees, he and Lyra had been forcibly separated and sent to different secondparents, forced to live in Tenement Lane.

But Aunt Dresa had stepped in at Lyra's request, paid the fees up to date so that when Lyra gained her majority at sixteen years, she could petition to have Jathan released from the alternate parent service of Amagon, and returned to live with her even though he was still all of eleven summers old at the time.

And Dresa was happy to keep paying as long as they both remained together, brother and sister, under the roof their parents established for them, making the fee payments herself all the way from then to now, and here it was, nearly paid off, nearly theirs at last.

He loved this place, this perfect little house. He could live with everything that happened out there in the world, as long as he was safe here, in this little fortress. All the drinking and fighting, all the hunting and spying, all the murderers and the murdered.

He needed it tonight more than he had in a long time. He could not get the image of the dead woman down out of his head, how casually she died right before his eyes. All her energy, all her strength, all her emotions, rendered to nothing in an instant.

You are just meat and bone. There is nothing more to you. Everything just ends. You don't even have a chance to know you ended.

He had never needed to be home more than he did at this very moment.

Most nights he just smiled, turned his key in the lock, and slipped inside.

But tonight, after what he had seen, he was possessed by a sudden thought.

He slipped out the monocle.

He held it to his eye, laughing.

He thought it was a silly little lark.

He peered into the grey gloom of the crystal lens.

His heart stopped.

His blood became stone.

His bones shattered and his organs burst.

He thought he had died.

He looked through the lens and he saw something.

A glittering silver light.

On the doorknob.

Of his own front door.

A hole had been punched through that armor he had relied upon for his sanity since the day his parents had died.

One of them had been here.

Jathan tested the knob. The door was still locked. He inserted his key and turned it. The lock clicked. He pulled the door open. Inside was silence, except for the faint little rumble of Lyra snoring in her bed down the hall, deep in a peaceful sleep.

Jathan was exhausted, but he checked every inch of the house for more afterglow, even the insides of cabinets. He found none. The house was clean.

But someone had been here. Someone had touched that door.

He felt his stomach rise. Could Seber Geddakur have seen him? Followed him? Found out who he was? Had he come for Jathan? Or was he here for Lyra?

Jathan shuddered.

You scum. You will never touch her. I will see to it that you are caught. My whole life will be to do this. Now and from now on, I swear. I will find out where you go, and I will have them capture you and send you to burn.

He plundered a wine bottle from the high cabinet in the dining room, scooting all the short, slim bottles of old oils and salts out of the way until he had one full of summerwine that could help him douse this flame.

He thought of the steps of his new plan, and how to go about achieving each one. He fell asleep smiling, happy in the knowledge that he would bring about the end of a powerful magus.

He would save his sister. He would save the day. It was easy to dream when his eyes finally closed.

5

You Little Fucking Liar

WHERE WERE YOU?

Jathan had asked the question silently a dozen times, glancing at the side of his sister's face as they walked. She was in her lavender silks, skin-thin and shiny, rolling off her shoulders like water, trailing behind her like flags in a breeze. Her hair was wrapped tight and pinned behind her head today, as if she was trying her hardest to not look like herself.

Jathan trudged along in his old emerald green tunic with the little hole at one shoulder. Dull black trousers, not fitted to him, with a torn seam. Muddy old riverboots. It was the ensemble that felt the most like his mood.

There were few people on the Promenade this early, leaving them to sip their warm coffee drinks and drift their way down to the grass and around the edge of the little lake.

He eyed a pair of city guards with yellow sashes and ruby red scabbards for their broadswords. They ate calpas and laughed at stories about recent fights they broke up on the overnight watch by Winesink Row.

Lyra ignored them entirely. She kept glancing over at the Lazy Steward, its stools and high shaded tables empty. But if she had been thinking of going over there for breakfast this was the wrong path to take.

His sister had been absent nearly every morning since the night he saw that magick-wielding woman killed in Tenement Lane. Three straight days of avoiding him, and then avoiding answering him when he asked where she was. That or outright lying to him.

Nessa asked me to give you a break, and I did. Everyone thought you had a new lover, and I have been defending you, telling them it's not happening again, that you are not lost once more in the self-inflicted saga of some doomed romance.

And then for her to break her routines, to hide from him the reason she was not coming out during the day. What other secret reason could there be than that she was dodging her life for the sake of sharing a bottle and a bed with some beau all day?

Where were you?

Running around with someone new was one thing. But in order to hide it, from Jathan and Nessa and everyone, she was forced to go outside her routines, outside her normal boundaries. Instead of dining in Brandytown or Winesink Row where she belonged, she was going to out of the way places where she wouldn't be caught. Places where she shouldn't be. Dark places. Seedy places. The kind where monsters lurked. Places where some abomination saw her, followed her home, and touched the door to their house. And who knew how long it would be before they came back?

Branderin's sister had disappeared from those unfamiliar streets. So had a great many young women of late. There were killers in Tenement Lane, gangers on the Promenade looking for her, and magi all over. Now was not the time to walk unfamiliar alleys and visit strange sourhouses to hide a love affair. *Don't you have any idea how dangerous this is?* He wanted to shake her, make her see sense.

It made him furious that she kept lying to him when the stakes had become so high. Yet at the same time he couldn't tell what he knew. It would terrify her. How could he burden her with the knowledge that the gangers were looking for her, that one of them had seen her face? How could he plague her with the knowledge that invincible sorcerers prowled the streets, stalking women, killing magistrates? She would faint. She would never sleep again.

He had to protect her as much from knowing what the world really was as he needed to protect her from the danger. It was important that she hide nothing from him, so that he could keep her safe. But it was equally important that he hide everything from her.

To keep her safe.

He didn't have time to explain the logical rationale to himself. He only knew it was there somehow.

Just tell me the truth. Please.

He tried to ask her his question again but was too slow.

Where were you?

Lyra happened to turn away, looking across the water. She smiled at the little children and their mothers gathering there beside the mummer stage where they performed weekly singsong puppeteering sagas.

But Jathan did not see the smile as a smile. It existed now as a subterfuge, something to be suspicious of, something to question.

How many of your smiles have been lies?

Jathan saw everything and nothing. His mind could not focus on what he saw or heard or felt. He barely saw where his feet would take their next steps. Everything became greyed out, the way the world looked through the Jecker monocle. Subduing everything except the glittering bright thought in his head. The same question. Many variations. But all the same question.

Where were you? Where have you been going?

"You are quiet this morning," Lyra observed.

He almost tripped over his own feet at the sound of her voice, momentarily panicked, as if his thoughts had been overheard. "I was—"

"Obsessing over your stolen treasure," she surmised.

"No. Well, not exactly."

She sighed. "When are you going to give it up? It has been a week. You have not even looked for a buyer. You said you wanted to make a profit from it, yet here you are."

"I am looking into options."

"If I didn't know any better, I would say you were playing pretend that you yourself are a Glasseye."

His blood became ice. "I...I am just looking through it while I happen to have it. It's not the same thing."

She turned and gave him a brief look before continuing. "You act like I don't know you at all. It makes me sad."

He felt hurt, but also angry. How dare she stand there and pretend like she did not have something going on? "What kind of things have *you* been up to lately?"

"Things?"

"Ouleem says you have not been around at your usual routines."

Her eyes momentarily widened. She glanced sheepishly at him. "I do not need to do things the same every single day.

Except that you always do, save for when you are about to tumble down a manic pit with a man who will rip your heart to shreds and leave you as nothing but a puddle of tears. "I noticed you were not at the Bottlebottom last night."

"You went?" She seemed surprised.

"I did. Everyone was there. But not you."

"I was at home."

"Were you?"

She squinted at him, her lips pinching and tightening. "This feels like an accusation disguised as a question."

He shrugged. "Well?"

"In that case, I have a question for you."

He looked at her oddly, but he chuckled. *Trying to turn it back on me, are you? Hoping I'll forget about your mystery lover? Good luck.* "Ask away."

"Where have *you* been going?" she asked.

"You can't just ask my question back at me like it isn't—"

"Seven days ago, you said you were in the East Uppers doing a delivery for Mistine to the merchant shack at the old crossroads near the edge of Inner Valley District. But you weren't. I was talking to one of their porters at the Wineforge the other day and they said they hadn't seen you in a fortnight. So I checked with Mistine. She said you had that morning off, released from any and all duties."

"I was..."

Lyra stared through him. "You are going to try to lie to me. Before you do, know that I have also heard some things from Ouleem."

"You heard *what* from Ouleem?" He set his hands on his hips and chewed his lip.

"He said some magistrates from Beachside came around. He said they looked into something for you as a favor. Why would a couple of sandfoot magistrates feel like they owed some kind of favor to *you* of all people?"

He was not chuckling any longer. "I..."

"Why would a couple of Beachsiders know you at all? Unless you have been going there to see them. And so, I asked myself, why would you do that?"

"I can explain."

"And then I remembered the extra silvers you suddenly seemed to have every other week. And I remembered Ouleem saying the two of them asked you if you had anything else for them. Any *what* else?"

The crowds were really beginning to fill in now. Close enough that some of them brushed against his shoulder.

"Can we talk about this later?"

"Now works just fine for me."

"I have been informing," Jathan said.

"Informing about what? What kind of trouble are you mixed up in?"

"No trouble. See? I knew you wouldn't understand. I'm giving them the names of magi, you know, sorcerers, magick users."

Her skin turned to ice, her eyes deadened. "You *what?*"

He knew she wouldn't like it, but he had deeply underestimated how upset she was. "It is nothing that will ever be traced back to me, to us."

"How long were you going to keep doing that without telling me?"

He shrugged. "I was going to tell you eventually."

She looked up at him, red eyes wet with tears. "Our secrets and lies are the monsters we feed. You should know that. Every time you tell a lie you are giving it a little piece of your soul to eat. The older the lie the bigger the piece. Then one day you have nothing left. Then the lies eat you."

"Well congratulations are in order," he said flippantly. "You slew this monster. Now I won't become a soulless husk."

"You are still selling people for silver."

"To the magistrates. To the *law*. How much more righteous a thing can I do?"

She turned away from him. "I can't believe you are doing this. I can't believe this." She put her head in her hands.

The more upset she became the more his defenses thickened. "I help take those scum off the streets. I know you think working with magistrates is unseemly considering how the city governors nearly split us up all those years ago. But things are different now. I'm different now. I help cleanse our streets and I get paid silver to do it."

She pulled her hands away from her eyes and he saw there were tears spilling down her face. "How can you do this? How can you stand there and want me to be *proud* of you for doing this? I thought you were my brother."

His mouth twisted into a grimace. He felt tightness in his chest. The way she stood in smug judgment over him was infuriating. He had not meant to bring it up so early in the day, but now his mouth was beyond all control.

"Oh yeah? Well, are you going to tell me about your new lover then?" The question was already out before his mind could reason with itself why it was not a good time to ask.

Her expression disintegrated. She stormed across the Promenade, forcing him to scramble to keep up, which made him even more angry.

"Do you have a new lover or not?" he asked.

She did not even look at him. She just kept walking. "It is none of your business, but no, I do not."

He clenched his teeth. "Do not lie to me, Lyra. Do not do that. If you have one, you had better tell me."

"I am not lying to you," she said.

"Why would you hide it?"

"I am not hiding anything. But I can think of more than a few reasons why I might hide something from you." She spat the words bitterly at him. They smacked like pebbles against the side of his face.

He recoiled. "What is that supposed to mean?"

"You are so angry," she said. "All the time. You hide it, but it is always there. You get ideas in your head, and you won't let them go. You build your whole life around them and you violently attack anything that tries to get between you and the world you want to make, even if the world only exists inside your own head."

The words came at him in a dizzying barrage. He had a response on the tip of his tongue for one of her accusations, but before he got one syllable out, she added another thing that rendered his response useless. Finally, he had to shake his head from side to side to get his thoughts in line.

"You say I obsess? I do? How many times have I had to come save you from your toxic infatuations? How many times have you begged me to come pull you away from a terrible man who you clung to even though you knew you shouldn't? How many times? Kevander, Aroush, goddamned Xork Xorka for fucking's sake!"

She did not answer. Her mouth went flat.

"You have no response because you know I am right."

"I have no response because you are angry. Because I am not going to let you bait me into provoking you. Because I know how you get."

"Must be nice. To stand there and render judgment on me. Because you were always the tallest, the fastest, the one who could leap mountains while I had to scrape and scramble to keep up. You think you know what I have been going through?"

Finally she did stop and turn to face him. This time she did not speak, she screamed. "I lost my parents, too!"

Jathan almost tipped over backwards. "I didn't—"

"You did. You always do. You always act like it only happened to you. But it happened to me too."

"At least I do not hide from it. I do not run from it."

"You have no idea what you are talking about."

"I know who my parents were."

She laughed. "You don't. You have heard nothing I have said. You think you know but you don't. You were a little boy back then. You didn't understand. There were things you have no idea about. You *decided* that you knew. And what you decided became your reality. You don't know all about our parents. You know all about a *version* of our parents that a ten-year-old boy saw, and you made up the rest in your own head."

Jathan no longer felt his face. His skin felt cold, but inside every tissue of his body was inflamed, raging, scratching, biting, trying to tear its way out of his skin to attack her. "I know one thing. I know what kind of abomination killed them. I do know that."

"You don't know anything."

"I do. I saw the glittering silver. I did not make that up. That was not a figment of my imagination. I saw it all around them. I remember the kitchen was in shambles. I remember the little jar of thyme was overturned. I remember scooping it back in so it would not go to waste. I remember holding it in my hand when I looked up and saw the blood on the floor. I do remember that. I did not invent that. The afterglow was there. I know who killed them. It was one of them. It was a sorcerer. It was a user. It was an abomination. It was a *magus*."

He noticed the tears raining down her face.

She hid her eyes from him. "I want to stop arguing with you. Please stop."

Her plea diffused him. He suddenly felt absurd, atrocious, barbaric. He realized he had been shouting at her, had made her cry, had focused every eye in the Promenade on her. "I'm sorry."

"I'm sorry, too."

But even as the heat of his rage subsided, the ice-cold suspicion wound even tighter inside him. *Why are you lying to me about having a lover?* There was no other reason for her to disappear during the day. It had to be that. It always had been that every time this happened before.

People have patterns. Patterns don't change.

He smiled warmly at her. But his expression was fraudulent. Inside he was thinking of ways to catch her in the lie, to force her to confront the truth she was hiding from him.

I will protect you. I will protect you from whoever it is. I will protect you from your patterns. I will save you from yourself.

But before he thought of where to begin, there was a shout and a commotion across the Promenade.

They both turned to look at it. The pavement was choked with people, like an unstoppable river flow, but a tiny island had formed within it, where two city guards dragged an old man in a black robe out of his shop of wares. Some people paused to look, but most simply diverted around it.

Behind them came a knot of magistrates, none whom Jathan recognized. One of them carried a stack of three old leatherbound books.

"I want to go," Lyra said, tugging at his sleeve.

The magistrate dumped the books in a heap right there on the Promenade. He then unstoppered a bottle of liquid and poured it on them.

Indexed books. Illegal ones. They had to be. The kind with dangerous knowledge, the encoding of the fundamental laws of the universe. *Good. Get that shit off our streets. One less thing for a filthy magus to get their hands on and do something inhuman with.*

"I don't like this," Lyra said. "Please, can we go?"

Jathan started to walk away with her but could not tear his eyes away. Behind the old man, a group of magistrates were smashing their way through his shop, dumping out wares and overturning containers and spilling velvet pouches, until the floor inside was a series of hills of glittering crystalline powders, with rivers of opalescent soaps and gels flowing like creamy pearl honey between them.

This was a finestreet shop through and through. The kind of place Jathan would have to work a month to afford only one jar of powder, one vial of scent, one bottle of lather. The cost of the soaps they were smashing and ruining must have been astronomical.

Each of them was easily as fancy as the kind his parents had always used so sparingly in their religious practices. They had been better off than most and even they could afford to use pinches and daubs. He could not fathom being wealthy enough to be able to use this kind of thing in a full amount on a daily basis. *Someday maybe I will though, if I can hand in enough magi pelts to Vaen and Felber...and then keep myself from immediately drinking the profits.*

The magistrate struck a spark from a flint, and it snapped Jathan's focus to his hands, eyes fixed on the little flickering flame held between thumb and forefinger. The liquid he poured on the books must have been some sort of flammable oil. The books went up in flames immediately. The old man began to weep. The magistrates snapped their batons on his head once, twice, three times, then he went limp and the city guards dragged him away.

"Did you see that?' Jathan asked. "That was madness. I've never seen that happen right out on the street like that. What was that?"

Lyra did not answer. She was walking away through the crowd, not even waiting for him. He raced to catch up.

But the faster he walked, the more a new thought loitered in his mind. *What if the user of magick who touched our front door wasn't there because of me?* What if it was someone following Lyra? Women had gone missing in Beachside. And soon after the same happened to Branderin's sister on Winesink Row. It was only the throw of a couple stones from there to the Promenade.

Jathan became convinced that it was Seber Geddakur stalking her.

Who else could it have been?

The man had laughed as he slaughtered magistrates right before his eyes. The kind of man who could do that was the kind of man who could pull women off the streets and do who knew what with them.

Jathan shuddered.

Abductor of women.

He remembered what he had seen magick do to human bodies.

But how could that monster have ever even seen Lyra?

He had been trying to think of how the abomination had found the house. He must have followed her home from wherever she was having her little trysts.

Jathan had never seen him around the Promenade before. Not in all his years. No one he had described Seber to could recall having seen anyone of the sort. Neither had any of his friends who frequented Winesink Row or Brandytown.

Did the man ever leave Tenement Lane? The place was a labyrinth. If one was trying to hide from the magistrates, or anyone else for that matter, Jathan could think of no better place than Tenement Lane.

Then how could he have known Lyra? How could he have known about the house? She never went to Tenement Lane, but for that one night she was with him. The night he found the dead Glasseye.

Jathan nearly reached her side once again, but he pulled back at the last moment, letting her walk on alone.

He noticed something odd in the crowd.

A man was passing by. A man in an olive-green coat. The man glanced at Lyra. Then doubled his take. Then stared at her, head turning to track her as she went by.

What are you...?

Jathan recognized him.

He was the ganger who had seen Lyra's face the night he stole the Jecker monocle from the dead Glasseye.

The greencoat ganger eyed Lyra, glanced over his shoulder at the cluster of magistrates moving up the street, fresh from beating the old man. Looked back at Lyra. Looked back at the magistrates.

Damn all the gods at once.

The greencoat blazed toward the magistrates.

Jathan left Lyra's side and jogged after the ganger, trying to reach him before he caught up to the magistrates, while also trying not to cause a commotion that would bring the magistrates back that way. He finally caught up to the man, got a hand around his collar and yanked him aside.

He turned to Jathan, eyes wide in recognition. "What do you want from me?"

Jathan had imagined it would be more of a struggle. The man appeared like the lanky, wiry type, but he was pitifully weak.

He is terrified. "Get over here."

Jathan dragged him by the collar of his coat, pulled him into a slender gap between a bakery and a silk merchant on the outer edge of the paved walkway. It was barely wide enough for the two of them to stand facing each other, a calm space mere steps away from the flow of people around the Promenade.

The man kept squirming, holding his empty hands up. "I have done nothing."

"Really? Where were you headed just now then?"

"I was...I was..."

"Going to fetch those magistrates?"

The man shrank back, expecting a fist, no doubt. "I wasn't supposed to be there."

"The other night, yes? When that Glasseye was killed in Tenement Lane, yes?"

He nodded. "I saw...I saw a girl that night."

My sister, you little shit. "So? So what?"

"The magistrates who caught me, they told me..."

"They told you what?"

"They told me if I saw any of those faces again, the ones I saw that night, that I had to tell a magistrate."

"Well, you need to forget one face. Hers."

"But if they find out that I..."

"If they find out? How are they going to find out if you never tell them?"

"They were there. They knew who I was."

"Of course they knew who you were. You work for Sor Qleen. Everyone knows the gangers of Tenement Lane. The magistrates there keep track of who is who."

"Not them. The others. The other gangers. They made me tell who I saw."

"What other gangers?"

"Wauska's."

"Vorlo Wauska's gangers made you?"

"I had to tell them about the girl. I saw her on the Promenade two days later. I had to tell. They were going to kill me."

So that is the reason Ressic's crew was on the Promenade that day. "You piece of shit. You told a rival, and now you're going to tell the magistrates?"

"If Ressic tells them I gave information to him but not to them, they will put me face-down in the Float."

"Wauska's people aren't friendly with magistrates."

"They are when they need to be. I just don't want anything else to come back on me. That's all. The magistrates have gone mad. They found five of their number piled up like scrap in a smithy. They have lost their minds because of it. They will beat anyone for anything now."

I know what happened to them. Seber Geddakur must have moved the bodies somehow. "Just keep your mouth shut."

"I don't even know you. This could be a test. You are testing me. You are a magistrate, and you are testing me to make sure I am doing what I'm supposed to."

"I am not a magistrate," Jathan said. "This is not a test. This is just me telling you to forget it."

"I don't believe you. I don't believe you. My wife, my sister, their children. I don't want them to be hurt anymore. I told them I would tell what I know. I swore it. I'll do it, I swear. I'll tell them. Please. I passed your test."

"Well, now you need to swear to me," Jathan said. "I don't care about your family. I don't care about you. But I care about my family. So, tell them whatever you want. Just don't tell them you saw that girl. Forget her face. Forget you ever saw her."

"I...can't. If they find out she was there, and that I didn't tell them..."

"You have to let it go."

"I didn't mean for this to happen."

Jathan shook him against the wall.

His head smacked against the bricks with a pop. He winced and cried. A spigot of watery mucus opened within his nose and it ran down his chin.

"Don't say anything." Jathan wore his fiercest expression.

"I...don't want any of this."

"You shouldn't have become a ganger then. You shouldn't have killed that Glasseye."

"Please let me go."

Jathan shook him. "Swear to me you will forget her face. Swear it!"

"I...I can't."

Jathan felt the skin of his face pull back taut. His teeth bared themselves. His brow narrowed. He opened his mouth, and a scream came out. "Forget! Everything!"

Jathan threw the greencoat with both hands deeper into the narrow space. His head and shoulder scraped the wall. He spun, stumbled. He reached out for the wall on the other side. Foot slipped. He staggered two steps. His heel kicked a broken-off piece of pipe near the base of one wall. His arms flew up. He tipped over backwards.

The greencoat's head cracked on the stone.

Jathan froze.

He is okay. He must be okay. Just stunned. He will get up. He is okay.

But he did not get up. Blood ran out from under his head like a tide coming in, reaching farther with each pulse, unspooling his life unto the ground.

Just meat and bone.

Jathan's mouth fell open. He put one hand up to cover it, fingers holding his jaw and chin as if he was afraid his face would break apart at the sight of it.

Get up.

He already knew there would be no getting up for the ganger. Jathan lifted both hands over his head and held the back of his neck, pacing in the tiny space. Finally, he reached down and felt for the monocle.

Still there.

Feeling it there focused all his attention.

Leave.

Leave now.

He ran. He fled out the back into the street beyond the Promenade. He ran to Winesink Row and hid in a sourhouse called the Sturdy Fundament until the sun fell from the sky. He paced and drank whiskey and milled around there all afternoon, and the better part of the evening as well. He did not dare return to the government square until nightfall.

And even then, he felt the pull of Tenement Lane. He crossed the Bowl again and entered the maze. He wandered its back alleys for hours, not seeing any afterglow, not even sure what he was looking for.

Afterglow. Just afterglow. He did not care its origin. He needed to see it. Now that he knew it was out there, he wanted to see it all, every day, every place. He needed to know where magick was being used. He could not stop himself from looking for it.

He took a different route than he ever had before, cutting through tunnel after tunnel, atrium after atrium, only stepping on the actual streets long enough to cross them to the next tunnel, or the next arch.

The moons were rising but there was silence. Jathan did not understand it. The people who lived in the Bowl flowed into the streets and played pipes and drums, ate feasts lit by bonfires, and played crabatz in the streets until the midnight hour.

Why not here?

Every street was empty. Every paved court, tunnel, bridge, and atrium was vacant. The windows never seemed to have any lights coming from them, either snuffing every candle out or covering the windows from the inside.

It didn't make sense.

It felt like Tenement Lane was haunted. A ghost town after sunset.

After a while he did hear little things here and there. A quick shuffle of boots, a patter of slippered feet, the snap of a twig, the creak of an old door, the rustling of a pile of debris, the splash of a puddle. He heard them all more than once in different places. He received the distinct impression that there were people moving about in the labyrinth, but in secret, as if they were hiding from something.

Jathan paid closer attention to the sound of his own passage, stepping toe-heel, peeking around corners, sticking to the shadows. He heard an echo from above on one of the walkways, but when he looked up, he saw nothing.

After that he slipped out of his boots and carried them, relying on the silence of bare feet. No matter how many times he checked, he found no afterglow of magick anywhere. He felt blind. It infuriated him. He could finally see magick traces, and he expected the city to provide them. Now that it hadn't, he felt cheated.

The quieter he made himself the more desperate he became to follow the sounds he heard to their sources. Most were too far away, or had their location masked by the echoes. But those that were close, he followed. Down tunnels and through alleys, and into atriums.

He thought he heard a sound to his right. He turned into an atrium with a large overgrown tree, a thick net of thornbrush around it. He crept slowly up to the tree. Whoever had been here was gone, he heard the sound of their steps down a far tunnel.

But before he could move in after it, he heard more footsteps *behind* him. They weren't stealthy, but confident, thick with purpose.

Jathan scurried behind the thornbrush, ducked low in a spot drenched in shadow, hugging his boots to his chest.

Who is it? Who is coming?

He already knew the answer.

Seber Geddakur strode into the atrium. He paused and looked all around. Listened. His eyes were deconstructing everything he looked at, as if his gaze was challenging their very existence.

He stared at every corner of the atrium in turn. He must not have seen anything. He continued on his way.

Jathan thought he could finally breathe again.

But the sudden lurching back into motion must have panicked someone else hiding in this atrium.

A young girl leapt from behind a stone bench beneath a low-hanging branch. She was at least twice as old as the girl from the night before, but still half as old as Jathan. She had swift legs, and she flew across the atrium, across Seber's path, around a corner just in time.

The sorcerer raised a hand, walking after her. He was stalking her. Same as the little girl the other night.

Jathan's heart fell into the earth. His feet joined with the mud and soil below and he was unable to move them.

Do something.

There is nothing I can do.

There is something you can do.

What can I do?

Think.

Jathan looked down. He saw a scattering of dried out leaves and pebbles among the roots.

Think!

He dropped to his knees, felt around in the dark with one hand. Pulled up the largest pebble he found. He took aim. Threw it.

It landed in between Seber's boots, rattling off one first and then the other. A lucky shot.

Seber froze. He stared ahead endlessly. Then, at last, he cast a caustic knowing gaze all around the atrium, staring everywhere. Staring through Jathan. His hideous gaze made Jathan want to stand up and say he was sorry and beg forgiveness. But try as he might, Seber was unable to tell the origin of the pebble, no matter how many times he appeared to turn it over in his head.

Jathan held his breath until his blood froze and his lungs turned to stone. *Please don't see me. Please don't see me. Please don't come over here.* There was nowhere to run. If he made the slightest sound his life would end. Here. Now. Tonight.

Finally, glacially, Seber stepped toward the tunnel the girl had fled down. But he was too late to catch someone with such a head start. He kept going, looking for someone else to follow next.

Jathan didn't move until he heard the distant whine of a gate as Seber passed out the remote end of the tunnel and moved on to another area.

He had no breath left to exhale. When he tried to pull air in, it choked him and he nearly passed out. He crept out from behind the tree. The atrium was silent once more.

He looked up at the walled walkways running around the upper floors of the tenement. He saw the white moon, Silistin, begin a quiet transit across the brief patch of sky, lighting the atrium like a flair.

He noticed motion in the corner of his eyes and glanced at the second story walkway above him. He saw someone there. The same young woman as the night before. Same erratic hair. Same defiance.

She gave a barely perceptible nod.

Jathan nodded in reply.

Then she was gone. He never even heard her footsteps. She was like a wraith.

Jathan took his time leaving Tenement Lane this night. He went the opposite direction the sorcerer took, yet one could never be too careful in here. The streets were full of curves and cross-tunnels and switchbacks. So, he checked carefully around every corner before he continued on.

By the time he made it back to the finestreets, it felt like another lifetime back when he had shoved the greencoat on the Promenade. Whenever Jathan was in the maze of Tenement Lane it was as if he was in another realm, another time, another life. The things that happened to him in the mundane world felt so infinitely distant they might as well never have existed.

But that was all dispelled the moment he stepped free of it. Now everything came rushing back. The tightness in his gut was as sharp and twisting as if he had only just walked away from the body a moment ago. The rush with which the emotion came back startled him. He was nearly home before he even remembered to put his boots back on.

The closer he came to being home the more the stress and fear unwrapped him, until he reached the front door. He was being strangled by thoughts of the dead man in the Promenade, the one they would find by morning, the one he had killed, the one he had murdered.

He turned the key.

He coasted through the door. Closed it. Locked it.

Being in the house brought him instant peace. He felt safe. His mind began to calm itself. Shedding the fear, he became almost weightless.

Lyra was already in bed, sound asleep. The house was clean.

Jathan breathed a sigh of profound relief. He shed his tunic and trousers, bunched them up and tossed them into a pile in his bedroom. He roamed nude into the kitchen to carve himself a hunk of bread and cheese. His stomach suddenly burned, and no sleep would come until he fed it.

He dug his fingers into the bread and tore a chunk free. He collapsed into the wooden chair, took one bite of bread and set the rest on the table. As he lifted the next bite into his mouth, he realized he had set the Jecker monocle down on the dining table. He poured himself some stale summerwine from a bottle he had forgotten to drink last month. He took a sip and raised the monocle to his eye.

He spit the wine all over the floor, and the table, and himself.

He nearly lost the bread.

He nearly lost everything his stomach contained.

Afterglow.

Smears and smudges of glittering silver everywhere. Anywhere a finger or thumb may have touched.

On the edge of his dishes, on the handles of his spoons, on the backrests of his chairs. On the carpet. On the walls. The inside of his house was covered in it, as though a sorcerer had stopped in for dinner.

Jathan followed it.

Down the hallway.

To Lyra's door.

He saw it on her doorknob. He touched his knuckles to the door and pushed it slowly open. She was asleep. Alone. Whoever else had been here they were gone already.

He saw a handprint on the edge of her bed. He saw it on her dress discarded on the floor. He saw it in her underclothes on the floor beside it.

He saw silver strands of it in her hair.

You little fucking liar.

You do have a lover after all.

And it's one of them.

It explained everything.

Small wonder she had been romanticizing magick like a simpleton the other day. She had let one of them into her bed. She had slept with him right here.

In our parents' house.

How could you? Sweet sister of mine, how could you? After what their kind did to us.

He looked at everything again through the green filter. He saw no shapes, no lines, no arcs. No nothing. *At least he didn't use his foul magick within these walls. There is that at least.*

Jathan spent all night pacing a trench into the commonroom floor. He took bottle after bottle from the high cabinet, fingers swimming between all the old green and gold bottles of oils and salts, pushing hard past the grey and violet bottles of spices and powders, demanding something more in harmony with his racing mind. Something full of alcohol.

He was lucky Lyra had stocked the cabinet since the last time he had gone all night like this. Otherwise, he would have had nothing but rotten brown-bottle wine and a glass rainbow of whatever old soaps and oils and crystals and spices they had managed to keep still after all these years.

That and the ancient whiskey bottle that had been open since the night they lost everything ten years ago. He had never touched that one. But he was so furious and wild that he thought he might have if there hadn't been something else to intercept his hand.

Luckily, she had bought him some velvet brandy. Perfect. It lubricated the friction of his grinding thoughts. He swallowed mouthful after mouthful, walking in circles around the dining table until his feet blistered.

What do I do? What do I do? How can I fix this? How can I stop this?

Just before he drifted into slumber face down on the dining table, he thought of his answer.

I will save her from herself. I will save her from her magus lover.

I will save her. I will hunt him. I will find him. And I will see him burn.

6

I Am The Hunter Now

HE THOUGHT THEY WOULD have given up by now.

The very idea that a tenement ganger like Ressic would pull his entire crew from their regular duties over one man and a little fish oil was absurd. It had to be about the stolen monocle. Didn't it? Maybe a bit of both.

He would have normally laid low for the two weeks, like Vaen Osper had recommended. But that was before he saw what Lyra had let into their parents' house. That was before he knew the very real danger of Seber Geddakur wandering the streets at night. Now time was of the essence. Now he needed to find Seber Geddakur at the quick and track every step he took in Tenement Lane. And to do that most efficiently, he needed to know what the blue filter on the Jecker monocle could do.

It is essential, Trabius had said. If he was to do this fast, that was the knowledge he needed. The danger of Ressic's gangers didn't matter. He simply had to speak with Trabius. What he saw last night made his decision for him.

But if he had known they were still actively watching Trabius' house, he might have been more careful.

As it was, Jathan never even made it to the door. As soon as he set foot outside the Promenade, he felt the hand clamp down on his shoulder. His foot tried to take another step and he nearly fell.

He tried to twist free, but a foot caught the back of his opposite knee and his leg buckled. He flopped on his side. It happened so fast he was still not certain how many of them attacked him.

But based on the quantity and frequency of kicks, he quickly surmised it was all four of them. He caught glimpses of them hovering over him as he bucked and shook under the assault, keeping both arms up over his head and face.

He found that Graekor kicked the hardest, but the toes of Torp's boots were just pointy enough that they hurt worse. Ressic himself did mostly heel work, going for the ribs, hitting his mark unfortunately often.

Of all of them, Pranji seemed to be the one most interested in waiting for his preferred strike, which happened to be a hard stomp onto the ball of Jathan's heel. The other hits had brought forth varying degrees of grunts and groans from him, but that one made him scream like a rabbit.

Jathan had been in his share of brawls, from the time he was a child. After what had happened to his parents, he had been quick to snap a nose or crack a jaw, and he never felt bad about starting confrontations, even when he lost more often than he won. He learned how to take a beating well before he learned how to fight.

After a century, the kicks stopped, and two pairs of hands fastened to his arms and lifted him to his feet. His ankle did not want to allow him to remain upright, so they had to hold him by bending his arms back by the shoulders. That was its own kind of pain, a stretching, twisting kind, the kind that promised to pop the shoulders from their sockets in the not-too-distant future.

Pranji held one arm. His hands were as big as Jathan's head, arms as thick as Jathan's legs, fat muscles cocooned in slick reddish skin. He may have been Hylamari, but he smelled like a Borean buffalo's asshole.

The other arm was in the vise grip of Graekor. The hefty Kolkothan's fingers felt like steel, his stare like a predator. Every exhale came out through his nose, like the hissing belch of blacksmith's furnace. His face was so unblemished it looked like he was wearing a mask.

"You should watch your step, little rat." Ressic's voice was like gargling sandpaper and lemon pulp. Seeing him up close for an extended period of time was its own special torture. Jathan couldn't tell if he was cross-eyed or if he was only imagining things. His reddish-brown hair was shaved flat on one side of the head, like a ham with one round side carved away. He had a nose that began with one trajectory in mind and ended somewhere entirely different. And Jathan remembered those mammoth front teeth, tusks that could have blocked a sword strike all on their own.

A little voice told Jathan to stay calm and not antagonize them. But, as he often did, he told that little voice to go fuck itself. "You should try being less ugly."

Ressic was less than pleased. "If you tell us who the girl is, we'll spare you half the pain and take it out of her instead."

"No thanks," Jathan said. "I like my chances."

"What is her name?"

"Why do you care?"

Bad memory. Bad eyesight. No, these people remembered him. They remembered his sister. They knew something. They had to. This couldn't just be a random grudge. They were in the Promenade that day looking for the person who ruined their payday. They were looking for the monocle. That damned greencoat sent them here before Jathan made him gone to grave. That had to be it.

I killed him only a few days too late.

"There are rules to everything," Ressic said. "Especially for us. Break the rules and you may get your head broken in. But sometimes a prize comes along that is worth enough to take the risk. Something that will make up for the extra attention it brings. And when we take a risk and find the prize taken out from under our noses, well..."

"Sounds to me like you're bad at gambling. Best steer clear of the hippodromes then."

"You seem to like risk," Ressic said. "You are taking a powerful one every time you open your mouth."

"How does it affect my odds if I tell you to go fuck yourself?"

Ressi ground his teeth together. "A man told me he saw a girl there, where our prize was supposed to be. He said he saw her again here on the

Promenade. He pointed her out to us. And just when we are about to grab her to give her the question, you show up."

Jathan smiled. "Was it the fish oil? I've heard seawater does marvels for the smell."

Ressic snarled. "Just give me her name and we don't have to break anything today."

Jathan didn't give them her name.

Torp stood before him, thin, wired with tight cords of muscle, strings of hair stretched over a bald head, bulbous eyes as painful to look at as his kicks were to feel. With a nod from Ressic, he went to work with his fists. He weakened ribs, and loosened teeth and knocked the wind out of Jathan so many times he thought he would drown in the air.

Ressic smiled. "Who is she?"

"Never seen her before," Jathan spat.

That earned a half dozen more bruises form Torp.

"Anything to say?"

Jathan rolled his head around until Ressic's face orbited into his vision. He smiled. "No."

"You had best gain wisdom at the quick," Ressic said. "Or you'll meet your gods."

"You can't kill me," Jathan said. "You're betting that I wouldn't know that."

"I'm a Wauska, you little scumborn shit. No one tells a Wauska what to do. I'll kill you if I like."

Jathan leaned over and his mouth heaved another splat of blood onto the pavement. "You can say you can do it all you want. I'm saying that you're not going to. If you were, you wouldn't have jumped me just off the Promenade in broad daylight."

"I do what I want, when I want," Ressic said. "I'm a Wauska. No one tells a man with that name what to do."

Jathan expelled a long drool of bloody spit. "You would have taken me off one of the backstreets, at night. You would have had me done up with a garrote or a knife. No, you want me alive. Because you think if I'm alive it means you can keep hurting me, keep scaring me. But it's not going to work. Because you can't scare me. And you could never hurt me as bad as any four runts at the gutter orphanage already have."

Ressic frowned. "Say a name, you shit. Say you're sorry for ever getting in my way. Say it!" He took two more swings. The first was a belly shot but it missed, glanced off to the side. The second hit, but Jathan had time to clench his abdomen for it and kept it from doing much in the way of pain.

"Wait," Jathan said. "I have something to say."

Ressic stopped, leaned back, surprised. "Speak."

"I am most definitely not sorry," Jathan said.

Ressic's face dissolved into a soup of radiant fury. He charged in, punching, kicking, slapping. Most of the hits were utterly ineffective. But one good one landed on his mouth and split his lip.

But by then Ressic had already exhausted himself. He backed away, gasping, while Jathan sagged in the grip of the two thugs.

Jathan spat blood at their feet. "You look like you need a nap, little brat."

Ressic ordered Torp to hit him again. Which he did. Jathan took a solid fist to the head, then knuckles to the eye. He felt it swelling before Torp had even recoiled.

By then Jathan heard some voices, many sounding very alarmed.

Jathan laughed. "This is the part where you let me go."

Ressic had a look of frustrated rage seared onto his face.

Jathan smiled the color of bruises. "If the finestreet magistrates catch you, your father may be able to buy you out of a cell, but then you would have to explain to him why you pulled your entire crew from their drops and collections for a whole week just to have a face to face with some nobody."

"I wouldn't have to explain anything to him if I have that little treasure. It's worth its weight in diamonds. That much money will cure my father of whatever aggrieves him about the things I've done."

The little treasure that is sitting in my pocket right now if you all weren't too stupid to live. "I don't have it."

"But you're going to tell us who does."

"How the fuck would I know?"

"Because you knew that girl. No soft girl from the finestreets would ever raise a hand to the four of us to help some shit like you if she didn't know him."

Fair enough. "I don't know her."

"I'm going to break you apart," Ressic said.

"I bet you want to avoid having that conversation with dear old Dada Vorlo more than you want to do anything to me."

Ressic growled and his men dropped Jathan onto his belly. They all beat a hasty retreat.

Jathan lay there for a long time, feeling pain blossoming all over his body. *I'm going to be feeling this for a while.*

But at least he knew that they had no idea who Lyra was.

A stranger knelt over him to see if he was dead.

Jathan raised a finger and pointed at Trabius' front door. "Can you knock on the door for me?"

Trabius and a kindly neighbor tried three different ways of lifting him before they managed to heave Jathan into Trabius' commonroom. The tapestries were all up, and when Trabius closed the door, if bathed him in darkness. It was a mercy for the headache he was nursing.

Trabius, being Trabius, had an endless compliment of salves and substances—skunkweed and blackroot for the pain, tannamine powder and berrynickle seed for the swelling, and a little horocaine powder just for the fun of it. That was still not enough to keep Jathan together enough to make it through bandaging without a bottle of sharpwine and a flotilla of wet rags to cover his legion of swollen wounds.

Jathan ended up on his belly, on a rug that smelled like it was made of feet, his body covered in salves and rags.

"What were you thinking?" Trabius asked.

"I thought they would have given up by now."

"What are you doing back here so soon anyway? You and Lyra visit me once every phase of the moon, if that. Now twice in one week?"

"I need to know the rest. I need to know how it works."

"The monocle? Are you still on about that? I thought you were going to sell it."

"I am. But not yet. I need it first."

"*You* need it?"

"For one little thing. But I need to know how it works. I need to use it. I need to right now."

"What could possibly be so urgent that you could not wait?"

"The blue filter. You said it was important. Why? What does it do?"

"Are you sure you wouldn't rather...heal first?"

Jathan lifted himself enough to turn his head over to face Trabius, ripping a long, whistling groan out of himself, until he dropped his head back onto the rug. "Knowing what it does will heal me better than any exotic ointment you could possibly have."

Trabius blinked at him. He seemed reticent. But in the end, he relented. "So you want to know about the blue filter." He paced the length of the room and back, head narrowly passing between two ferns, potted and swinging from iron chains, his legion of cats dressed as dogs supervising his progress. "The blue filter is what you want to know about." He paced again. "The filter you want to know about is the blue one."

"Trabius! Get on with it."

"The blue hides the colors that the other filters show you."

Jathan squinted, shifted his head on the floor. "That doesn't make any sense at all. Why wouldn't you want to see the colors? The colors tell what magick was done. Isn't that the whole point?"

"Yes. But the other filters show the colors that can be used to identify which forces or energies or matter were manipulated, how they were manipulated, where they were manipulated. Some even show the patterns of the pieces of altered reality each magick user binds together to render their result. They show you everything a wizard or wizardress can *do*."

"And the blue?"

"It shows you *who they are*."

Jathan grinned. His eyes glazed over, imagining the sweet murder he would deliver unto this creature who had seduced his sister, who had preyed upon her, who had tricked her into forgetting herself. "How?"

"It removes all those other colors and leaves you with one color. Just one. The color specific to that sorcerer. Every twinkle of every particle of every glowing cloud of afterglow will be this color. Every glittering smear of sensitized fluorescence on an object or other person will be this color. And within this color is a pattern. The Glasseyes are trained how to read these patterns, to match them to one magick user, to be able to even differentiate between two with the same color if the need arose."

"I don't have any training. But I can look at colors. That part almost seems too easy."

"There is another thing that the blue filter can do."

"Go on."

"When a sorcerer leaves the scene of their magick, they are not free of their afterglow. It haunts them until it fades."

Jathan squinted. "How do you mean?"

"This color you can see with the blue filter, it...changes with the movements of their creator. If you look closely, the edges will turn blue if they are moving closer to their afterglow, or red if they are moving away. The closer or the father, the more the glow."

"So, I can tell how close they are."

And whether they are moving closer or farther away. Not with any great certainty. But in a vague general sort of way."

Useful, but still far from perfect. *Even that will do me little good in a maze like Tenement Lane.* But being able to match the colors would be of great use.

"Disappointed?"

"I was hoping for a something a little grander. You set my expectations high."

"I wasn't finished."

"Oh, well then, by all means."

"There is more to that red and blue color shifting. It works when the afterglow moves closer to the sorcerer as well."

"How do you make clouds move one direction?

"Not the clouds of afterglow, but objects sensitized by it."

"Meaning?"

"Meaning anything the clouds come in contact with. A wall, a door, a cloth, a wooden spoon."

Jathan nearly drove himself cross-eyed thinking of the possibilities. "If I had even a bit of it in my hand, I could move it from side to side and watch the glow."

"And if you had two samples of the same type collected at the same time and held them apart, you could triangulate the sorcerer's location by judging the differences in the color shift between the two. That is the very thing that the Glasseyes prefer to do if they can."

"So, you would need to find some of it first, before you can try to find the one who made it."

Trabius nodded. "That follows, yes."

"But you said it fades so quickly," Jathan said. "Within hours, you said."

"Unless you seal it in something. A cup with a tight lid, a wine bottle, and the like. A non-opaque glass vial with a properly sized stopper of cork would be ideal."

Jathan raised an eyebrow. "Do you have such vials?"

Trabius laughed. "Oh, I have plenty."

Jathan heaved himself onto his elbows, cold rags and poultices sliding off him onto the floor.

"What do you think you are doing?" Trabius asked.

"I have to get home. I have to check on Lyra."

Trabius pursed his lips. "You had better go straight home."

Jathan climbed to his feet. The sour ache in his chest ripped a groan from his lips. He gestured at himself. "Do you honestly think I'm going to go anywhere in this condition? I need a bed. I need to sleep for a thousand years."

Trabius nodded and led him to the door. Waited for him to check around every corner for signs of Ressic's thugs. When the way looked clear, he left, his face and direction hidden among moonlight and shadows. Trabius closed the door gently behind him.

The Promenade was too well lit at night, with lampposts the height of three men standing on each other's shoulders, oiled and lit nightly by lamplighters with poles long enough to scale a castle with.

There were still people about, though most of the shops and cafes had closed down, so that their proprietors and staff could sleep, or be with their families, or head down to Winesink Row to swim the swells of brandy and sour grapes. So, Jathan walked in the back alley behind one side, where the shadows were thicker. He did not want to be seen, or worse, recognized.

Trabius believed him when he said he was going home.

Jathan said it so convincingly he almost believed it himself.

But there was no way he was going home. Not now. Not when he finally knew what he needed to know. Not when he had a chance to try the blue filter.

He walked the streets alone. He crossed the street to avoid anyone coming his way. He turned corners and doubled back twice when he thought he was being followed by someone, but both times it turned out to be a coincidence, just old men stumbling home in the dark.

He flowed into the labyrinth of Tenement Lane, taking turns and switchbacks that no magistrate would ever take, slicing through back alleys that even some of the locals weren't aware of, and cutting through atriums no one outside their surrounding buildings had ever seen before.

All the while he used the Jecker monocle. He peered through it at every street, around every corner, seeing everything in a foggy crystal world. He held it up to his eyes so often he once forgot to pull it away and stumbled into three people coming the other way.

The look they gave him chilled his bones.

It was a look of fear.

They are afraid of me.

Good.

He hoped Seber Geddakur would come to fear him as well. Jathan would make sure he knew who sent him to the fires before he burned.

I will find him, sweet sister. I won't allow this creature to bewitch you. I will figure out where he goes, and I will hand him to Vaen and Felber. So you can see him for what he is before it goes too far. So you can pull yourself away before you get too wrapped up in him to swim to safety. It won't be like last time. Or all the other times.

I will set you free of the chains he has cast about you.

I will protect you the way you always protected me when we were children.

Now and from now on, I swear it.

He hid twice around corners and once behind a cluster of bushes beside a shuttered tavern, to keep out of sight of packs of Soreb Qleen's tenement gangers, or Zim's, or even Vorlo Wauska's, though thankfully not any of Ressic's people.

He was not seen. They had missions of their own, goals to achieve, money to make, skulls to bash in. They likely would not have bothered with him even if they saw him, but he was unwilling to take chances with something as valuable as the Jecker monocle in his pocket. Not with the beating his body had already taken today.

By the time he stumbled through the seventh undiscovered atrium, beneath a broad oak tree, his ribs were giving him sharp reminders that he should not have been on his feet. His head was beginning to throb again, and a hissing sound was strobing in his ears.

And still he had seen nothing.

He was on the verge of giving up for the night when he finally saw something. A shiny silver sparkle on the back of a stone bench. He stopped. Knelt. Stared at it through the monocle. It was shimmering, distorting, shivering light at him.

There you are.

He levitated to it.

He flipped the blue filter into place. The grey world became a blue world, full of shadows, the outlines of shapes and surfaces barely visible. But the afterglow, the afterglow was even more pronounced. The silver winked into nothing, still there, but in the background, like an echo of visibility. The silver smear had been replaced with a vibrant green smear, moonlight through colored glass.

He suddenly felt very vulnerable, conspicuous. As if he had found a pile of abandoned gold coins and wondered if anyone else was watching him. But the night was quiet. He was alone. He was the only one who could have seen it. He was the only one who knew. Even the man who had created this little stain of color could not see it. It was something only Jathan would ever know.

He remembered what Trabius had told him. He looked closely at the glowing roiling color, and he noticed the fringes of it turning a distinct red.

He is moving away from this, but slowly. Jathan rubbed his finger against it until it rubbed off on his skin. He held two fingers up in front of the monocle and stared at the glittering color coating his fingertips like oil, like paint.

He walked to each of the exits of the atrium. When moving toward three of them the color on his fingers became more red. But when he approached the last, it began to shade blue at the edges. *I am bringing it closer to him when I walk this direction.*

He kept walking.

He passed many and more signs of afterglow, different colors, and new obvious powers. But none of them were those ones he was here to find. He fell into the role of the hunter, seeking the telltale signs of a certain prey, excluding all others.

He let the color choose his path, taking turns and passing through tunnels and under awnings, up stairs and over the canal. Every time, he only moved the way that made the colors bluer. It was as if he was walking with a guide, a navigator blazing the trail for him, pointing him true. The afterglow made a better partner than any person could have.

Please be his. Let me find him tonight. Let me follow where he goes. If he was lucky, he could give Vaen and Felber his location by morning.

His energy was renewed by excitement, the anticipation of finding that terrible danger once again filling him with strength. His feet flowed like water. His eyes sharpened, tearing at everything like talons, ripping apart every detail.

He thought of Lyra and what she had done. He knew it wasn't her fault. He was angry, sure. He hated when she lied to him. He hated it more than he hated standing shoeless on burning coals. And he hated it when she disrespected their parents' memory by letting one of those things into their house. But he wasn't doing this to punish her. He was doing it to protect her.

The afterglow guided him down unlit streets, across back alleys, around hulking tenement blocks, sleeping grey stone giants, resting after swallowing their many inhabitants for the night.

He made some wrong turns. The afterglow proximity to its maker could not account for obstacles that fell in between. He hit terrifying dead ends, high walls and switchbacks. He heard chains swinging, pipes dripping, and dogs pawing at doors, begging for scraps.

He encountered clusters of tenement gangers, standing about hasty fires set in metal buckets, plotting where to score their next whiskey, or sell the next pipeful of malagayne leaves, or find the next head to crack because payment was late.

Or battle to the death over one of these, Jathan thought, running his fingers over the monocle. It was because of the tenement gangs that he had the device at all, he realized. If they hadn't murdered the Glasseye for this prize, Jathan never would have had it, never would have known what was going on all around him, never would have known about Seber Geddakur, never would have known about a magus involved with his sister.

A freak occurrence. And now here he was lurking in shadows at midnight instead of sleeping. Here he was walking in the footsteps of a powerful killer instead of laughing at the Bottlebottom with Lyra and Cristan and the rest.

Everyone's life changes the first time they find a dead body.

He at last found another blotch of opalescent color, half a handprint on the corner of a wall. It glowed much more sharply. *He must have only just been here.*

Jathan peeked around the corner. He saw a brief tunnel running beneath a tenement. Moonlight bathed the other side. Halfway through a man lay propped up against one wall. Drunk. Passed out.

Jathan walked to the end of the tunnel. He held his fingers up and saw blue versions of them with the awesome and terrible colors radiating off of them. They turned more and more blue, crushing the green into a smaller and smaller space. It was as if the whole smear was one thing, but also as if each particle was its own dot of green, turning blue as well. It made no sense and yet it was.

He found Seber Geddakur.

He followed him for hours. Watched him walk the streets. Watched him eat at a midnight cafe. Watched him meet a woman. Watched him take her in a back alley. Watched him stalking through all the narrow spaces of this labyrinth. Watched him disappear into a long tunnel that Jathan dared not follow him through, for the echoes of his steps were sure to be noticed.

Jathan was left hiding behind a tree, staring at the opening, waiting for the sorcerer to come back. Only he never did.

Jathan lost track of how much time he stared at the entrance to the tunnel, yawning wide like the mouth of an enormous beast. He felt it pulling him toward it, some strange gravity urging him onward, nearly lifting his feet. But he fought against it.

After what seemed hours, he finally built up enough determination to make his feet go.

But a hand reached across him, snatched his wrist and bent it back behind him. A face lunged at him from the darkness, eyes like the pools of black water, a face fierce and beautiful. He felt the cold steel of a knife against his throat.

It was the same woman he had seen before. The one who had seen him throw the stone. She smelled of old leather and night air, her tight leather coat and leggings creaking as she shifted her footing. She bent his wrist back further, forcing his head to lean forward, knife cool against skin, at the mercy of her blade.

"Are you one of them?" she asked, her voice sharper than the steel at his throat. "You don't look like one of them."

"Them?"

"A hunter. Are you a hunter?"

"You mean a Glasseye?"

She pressed the knife harder. "Are you?"

"I was just looking," he said. He felt his skin on the verge of giving in to the blade.

"I saw you with it. I saw the glass eye." She twisted his wrist a little further.

Sharp pain streaked up his arm, and for a moment he truly believed she would break it. "It's not what you think. I'm not—"

"I saw you," she stabbed the words into him, a whisper like a razor, lips raking his ear, hot breath on his neck. "You looked through the eye."

"I found it," he said. "I just found it. It's not mine. I just found it."

"Do they know about us?"

He felt the blade scraping against the stubble of his chin, skimming his flesh. "They don't. I mean, I don't know. I don't think so. I don't know them. I just...I stole it." He felt defeated admitting it. He was not some lucky adventurer, destined to receive some powerful artifact and go knocking on the door of the gods. He was just a thief, following a murderer through a twilight realm. He was mundane, so painfully ordinary.

For a brief moment, he felt the pressure of the knife lessen. She pulled back and looked at him. "Where do you come from?"

"I'm from here."

"Here?"

"This is my city."

"If this city belonged to you, you wouldn't be alone in the dark with the knife of a little scumborn girl at your throat."

"I was born in Kolchin. I swear."

"You may be born of the city, but you are not from *this* place. This is Tenement Lane, the land of the lowers. I can smell the finestreets all over you." She sniffed at him for emphasis.

"It's all one city," he said. "I was born into it."

"One city, two worlds, finestreet boy." She pulled the knife away from his throat and tapped his cheek with the blade, the point below his eye, making him blink. "Bad things happen to finestreet boys who wander in here."

"I lived here once," he said.

"I lived here twice," she said, mocking.

"I did. I swear." It was true. When they put him with those secondparents he had lived on the edge of Tenement Lane for almost a year before Lyra was able to get him back.

"Don't you get it, stupid boy? It doesn't matter where you were. It only matters where you are now. And right here, right now, you don't belong."

"I haven't done anything to anyone."

"Get out," she said. "You shouldn't be here."

"I was only..."

"It doesn't matter that you *were only*. It doesn't matter your intentions. Just being here makes things harder. You need to go." She urged him on by shaving an inch of the stubble from his throat.

"I'm not hurting anyone."

"Just by being here you are changing things. You are scaring people. My people. We have worked hard to have our spaces and to know our places. You are fucking up the balance, finestreet boy."

"I swear to every god that I never meant any harm. I was just looking for something."

"You found it. You're looking at it. This is all there is. Lushborn and scumborn. Predator and prey. People who hunt and people who are hunted. You look like a hunter to me, finestreet boy. If I see you in here again, I can't promise I'll let you live."

He heard a sharp step, a boot heel smacking down on the next street. He turned to look out of reflex.

So did she.

By the time he turned eyes to her once again, she was backing away from him, returned to the shadows. The feel of the knife at his throat remained, a phantom sensation of razor-sharp steel. He had to cup one hand around his neck to prove to himself it wasn't still there.

"Wait," he said.

"Run along, stupid boy. Before you can't get out."

She was gone. Vanished like a wraith.

He could still smell her, still feel her breath on his ear, still feel her steel at his throat.

He felt so alive he couldn't stand it.

He finally turned around and left Tenement Lane.

He would have to find his sorcerer again another time.

He did not chance across anyone else, not the whole way home. That was good. He was so distracted he might have walked right into them, started a fight, ended up in a magistrate's jail until dawn.

His head was full of two armies of thoughts, each battling for control. One army was of sorcerers and saving his sister, the other a horde of thoughts of the beautiful scumborn girl who had put a knife to his throat.

He couldn't tell which of the two he wanted more of.

He let himself into the house with his key. He heard Lyra gently snoring, her door a hand-width ajar. He inched the door closed and tiptoed to his room.

His mind was so wound up he nearly forgot to check the rooms through the Jecker monocle. He lifted it to his eye, expecting to see nothing. For how could Seber have left anything here if he was busy up to his balls in another woman?

But he did see afterglow. Sparkling and silver. The same as before.

He was so startled by it he needed five tries clicking the wrong filter into place before finally sliding the blue home. He fully expected to see the verdant green of Seber's core afterglow.

But this afterglow was a lush purple. Deep, relentless, enveloping, paralyzing, beautiful afterglow. So gorgeous that it hurt his heart to look at it. That was confirmation of one thing.

It was good news wrapped in bad.

Seber Geddakur was not his sister's lover.

It was someone else.

He merely had no idea who it could possibly be.

7

We Need To Talk

JATHAN BLINKED AND ANOTHER week had gone by.

His bruises had settled from deep purple to lazy brown. His split lip had gone from dry and stinging to soft and sore. He could breathe without pain once again. He wore fresh clothes, newly bought with the leftover earnings from working for Mistine.

The Jecker monocle was still in his pocket. It was always in his pocket.

He had stalked every district, every neighborhood. He had found afterglow in the most unlikely of places. Class did not matter. Status did not matter. It was equally present among the scumborn in the Bowl as it was in the most oozewealth of the finestreets. He found it among the agehouses of the wrinkled grey, and among nurseries for the newborn pink.

He discovered the glittering clouds of color by the riverside, in the doorways of the god temples, on the crabatz field, in a shitplugged lavatory in a mudwater sourhouse.

He found smears and blotches of sensitized fluorescence on doorknobs, gates, chairs, utensils, longtoss balls, even handprints on windows.

Do none of them know they have it on them? How many were left by little sorcerers who had no idea what they had done left a mark?

He saw it on people, on their clothes, or their hair, where some little shit wizard had wiped it on them, or someone it had been wiped on, wiped it onto someone else. In crowded places like the Promenade, lasting afterglow could spread from person to person until one little cloud became a hundred little glows on hands and clothes.

He once found some on a glass Mistine had served to someone. He had not had a chance to figure out who. He even saw it on a body caught in the weeds of the Float near Whalebone Bridge.

It was everywhere.

He saw a little child of no more than four summers swiping coppers and slices of fresh calpas fruit from a distracted food cart. But Jathan didn't follow him.

He had followed a goldfinger girl who had used it fresh to defraud a merchant, floating her coin back to herself under the counter after she had paid. Then did it again at the icery, and the meatery, and the spicer. Using the same handful of coins each time. He was surprised she didn't just walk into the Moneychanger and rob it blind.

He tried to follow her and catch her name, the easier to turn her in to Vaen Osper and the magistrates, but his eyes had been pulled off the girl by the sudden appearance of Nessifer across the lake. He happened to glance at her chattering with some friends in the shade at the Lazy Steward, and the glance became a look, the look became a stare, and before he knew it the little oozewealth goldfinger was gone in the crowd, her name lost right along with her.

And, of course, there had been a wealth of afterglow within the steep artificial ravines of Tenement Lane. He had been back there every night.

Every night he told himself it would be the last time. Every night he swore he would bring the lead to Vaen Osper and let the magistrates take Seber down. But every morning he made a new excuse for why he needed to follow him just one more time. Every excuse was a lie. He knew it even as he told them. And by the evening he had already talked himself into believing them.

And then he would lie about where he had been. He lied to Nessa, he lied to Cristan, he lied to Branderin. Ouleem was his closest friend, but he lied to him, too. He hadn't seen Lyra once in all that time, but if he had, he would have lied to her about it as well.

Our secrets and lies are the monsters we feed.

But the one thing he had not found any sign of was afterglow with a purple core color when seen through the blue filter. None of these creatures could have been the one who was sneaking into his house, involving themselves in his sister's skirts.

That was the one he truly wanted to find. That was the one he truly wanted to kill. He vowed to stop tracking Seber today if only fate would show him a trail to that one magick user. But his prayer went unanswered.

He had not gone back to see Trabius. He had not wandered the Promenade. He had not gone out to Winesink Row or Brandytown with his friends. He had avoided run ins with Ressic and his crew.

He had not seen hide or hair of Lyra either. Not when she was awake anyway. He always stumbled in well after she was asleep, and she was always gone well before he woke up in the morning, whether she went to work her shifts or disappeared to wherever this mysterious magick-wielding lover lived.

The serial murderer on the other hand had been simple to find. He was the crown jewel of Jathan's obsession. He had found Seber Geddakur there every night but one. Every time he was with a woman. End every time he was near one of the same four landmarks in Tenement Lane. Jathan had the sorcerer's evening routine down already.

Jathan had no idea what horrors the man was up to during the day. He did not know if he held a job, or if he robbed Moneychangers to support his lifestyle. Jathan did not ask around. He did not want anyone, even strangers, to know that he even knew the name Seber Geddakur.

Jathan felt like he was the Glasseye now. He was the one who could see what no one else could see. He was the one who could point the way. Who cared if he did not have any other knowledge or training? It was all in the device. The extra numbers and factors and algorithms were pointless. He did not even know what else a Glasseye did.

Because they did nothing. Nothing except lord themselves over the real Kolcha people, hiding behind books and papers and pompous fraud. All that mattered was that he could find magi and he could track magi. He would prove that all their Glasseye *training* was a sham. Render Tracers were outsiders. They did not belong in Kolchin. Jathan would make sure this was done by locals.

Yet every night he came up with a new reason *not* to bring this information to the magistrates. Each of these reasons, he assured himself, were not mere *excuses*.

This was beginning to cause another problem, however; one Jathan had not foreseen.

Vaen was growing more and more suspicious by the day. This was the longest Jathan had ever gone without bringing him a lead, and he was beginning to think Jathan had worked out a side hustle of some kind. Jathan assured him there was no such thing, and in truth there wasn't. But there was a deep secret. And Vaen could tell.

That was one thing. But Jathan had not been prepared for how angry Vaen would become. His face was no longer friendly, his tone was no longer familiar, his demeanor no longer unthreatening. He even shoved Jathan on his way back to Beachside once.

Lyra still had not admitted to having a new magick-wielding friend. He had backed off her, giving her the chance to come to him and admit the truth, redirecting his anger and anxiety into studying Seber Geddakur. But after two full weeks he was beginning to lose patience with this strategy.

She had been absent more often than she was present, being completely away from the public eye for four of the past five days. No one had seen her on any of those days. Not Cristan. Not Ouleem. Not even Nessifer.

Jathan had checked with Harod every day, but Lyra had not even been showing up to her shifts of work at the bookseller most days. There was no reason he could think of that she would miss a single minute surrounded by her precious books other than being transfixed on a man.

It had to be Kevander again. Jathan always felt that there was something off about him. He seemed to look at everyone and everything like he knew a joke no one else did. He must have been the owner of the purple core afterglow. He must have been the creature Lyra had been tricked into allowing into their parents' home.

As if his sister being absent wasn't enough, the high and mighty cosmopolitan Render Tracer from the capital was there nearly every day as well, always wearing his smug Glasseye condescension, always sitting at the Lazy Steward, always ordering the same meals, and keeping the same shady table on the veranda.

Jathan could think of nothing worse than a snake from the capitol nosing around his home city. All they ever did was ruin things for the people who lived here. He wished he could have asked Vaen Osper to arrest the Glasseye, or disappear him. Anyone from the capital deserved it for the way they ignored and oppressed the people of Kolchin.

The scum would patrol the Promenade thrice daily, as if it belonged to him. Jathan even thought he saw him deftly holding a Jecker monocle to his eye. He would not have noticed it before, but now that he was using the same methods to stealthily hold his own, it stood out like the sun.

Jathan could not control his reflexive sneer every time the Glasseye caught his eye. Mistine nearly slapped him more than once when it happened to coincide with her listing off his duties for the day.

When night finally came, Jathan artfully dodged Ouleem and Cristan and headed to a trusty old sourhouse on Winesink Row where he was sure he wouldn't run into anyone he knew.

There he drank until he was warm, and then a little more. Within a few hours the denizens of Tenement Lane would be off the streets, and he could hunt alone. Then it was back into the labyrinth once more.

He knew Seber's routine well enough now that he could narrow his likely sunset locations to three. He found him at the second one, the tunnels between the slingball courts and the east lowers bridge.

He heard sounds before he even reached the tunnels.

Grunting. Slapping. Moaning. Shoes shifting their grip on the stone ground.

At the far end of the tunnel, there were some stone steps heading up and to the left, opening into a wide court, with markings for people of the tenements to play longtoss. They were all empty at this time of night. All the tenement windows overlooking them were dark.

In the center of them all was a fountain. It was in disrepair, covered in writhing moss and strangled by vines. The stone was chipped and cracked, and the water that should have been a bright spray was no more than a trickle.

Bent over the rim of the fountain was a woman, skirts hitched up, hands holding on for dear life. Behind her, the owner of the afterglow, wearing the same long coat, slapped his hips against her, driving himself into her harder with each thrust. Was it the same woman as the week before? Jathan couldn't be certain.

Jathan tried to back away. But he couldn't. He was frozen, halfway laying across the steps, his eyes peeking over the top step. They were so close, ten paces at most. He could only watch as Seber Geddakur fucked the woman from Tenement Lane halfway to falling into the fountain.

Jathan was looking forward to following the sorcerer around all night, filling in the missing pieces of his map of Seber's movements. Bringing him one step closer to being able to turn him in to Vaen and the magistrates.

But something interrupted those plans.

The sounds of Seber's aggressive fucking were what brought attention from the gangers. Three of them. All belonging to Sorab Qleen's faction—the greencoats—from what he could tell.

Jathan wasn't sure why they were here. This area was nowhere near Qleen Town. They had strayed far from their territory. And now they had made a terrible mistake.

They walked up behind Seber and yelled at him.

Shit.

Jathan might as well have been stone. His heart shuddered. His bowels floated like balloons.

They were going to challenge the sorcerer.

Fools.

They were gone to graves already. They just didn't know it yet.

"Look at the lovers," one of them said.

"Look at the god of love himself," said another.

"Did you save any for us?" the third asked.

Seber did not even look at them. He did not register their presence at all. He certainly did not stop fucking.

The three gangers looked at each other and shrugged. They walked closer.

"You have a problem with your ears?" one of them asked.

"Maybe a little ring of your bell would get your attention," one said, sliding a baton out of his coat.

The sight of it made Jathan's ribs ache. The other two smacking their fists against open palms made his head throb with memory. Every bruise activated at once, and he nearly collapsed.

Jathan found himself having strange thoughts, ones that he could not rationalize. He did not understand what was happening inside his own mind. He found himself rooting for Seber to kill them.

He was still committed to bringing about Seber's demise.

But not quite yet.

He wanted this to happen first.

The three men were within five paces when Seber Geddakur finally finished in his mistress. He let out a long groaning breath and collapsed on her. He pushed himself up and off, then turned to face the gangers. He didn't even bother to put his cock away. He just left it swinging there, slick and pendulous.

"Precious lambs," the sorcerer said.

He swung his fists in a pantomime of fighting, landing imaginary punches, body blows, and roundhouses. He was far too many paces away from them for any of his swings to come close to hitting anyone.

Yet each of the gangers were hit.

Every swing distorted the air, rippled it, connected with flesh and bone. Crushed and broke it.

Jathan did not understand what was doing it. It was invisible. But then he remembered he held the Jecker monocle. He lifted it to his eye. The night turned hazy grey. Except for Seber's fists. They radiated shimmering silver starlight, and exuded strings of pale silver smoke whenever he moved them.

And where the gangers were struck, each hit left a warped splash of particles across their skin and clothes.

Then Jathan remembered the green filter. *It will show you where their forces have been.* He flipped it into place. And sure enough, it did. The world shifted into murky green. The afterglow disappeared and was replaced with sharp white arcs in the air between where each swing had begun and where each hit was landing.

He wasn't truly punching them. *The motion merely helps him focus. He is sending spheres through the air at them.* But larger than before, and slower. Only enough to batter them and maim them.

He is toying with them.

The predator is playing with his food.

Jathan smiled as he watched each of the gangers suffer the way he had suffered on that morning. Even if it wasn't the same ones, it felt good to see them where they were not the most powerful ones in the streets. It lasted until well after they were all on the ground.

When Seber tired of beating and breaking them, he finished each of them with a tiny sphere that appeared at his fingertip, and it shot out at the speed of a shout wherever he pointed. And where he pointed was into each of their heads.

All three died in an instant, holes punching through their foreheads like a snap of the fingers.

Jathan realized his mouth was open, drooling onto his jerkin. It was horrifying and magnificent and he did not want to look away.

When he swapped out the green and added the blue filter back into place, he saw every patch of afterglow, floating in clouds, shedding from fists as they swayed, and hissing like lambent smoke from the holes in every skull.

This was the horror of what they could do. This was the reason they all needed to be destroyed.

Yet Jathan found a part of himself wishing. Wanting. Needing that power. For himself. So he could set right a lifetime of wrongs done to him. So he could mete out justice to those who deserved it. And there were so many who deserved it.

Seber walked away, leaving a trail behind him like a shimmering haze. Jathan dropped the monocle into his pocket. Even without it he saw small amounts of afterglow with his own eyes, but only the dimmest images of it. Nothing at all like the raging luminous bubbles made of twinkling stars he saw through the crystal lens.

Seber turned and conversed with his mistress, and Jathan thought it would be his moment to slip away and return home.

But as he slipped his boots off, and prepared to slink back through the tunnel, he noticed two little children. They were walking down a ramp, walled off on one side with a waist-high wall. Anyone would have been able to see over it and know the sorcerer was still there. But the children were too short to see over it. They were going to walk right out into Seber's line of sight.

Shit, fuck, and hell.

One of them he recognized. He knew the girl. She was the same little child wearing patches over patches and the adult fur coat. She was the same child that woman—that *magi*—had died trying to save.

A fountain and two old willow trees stood between the children's walkway and the sunken stairs where Jathan hid.

Jathan left his boots on the stairs and threw himself up. He snatched a copper coin from his pocket and hurled it high above the sorcerer's head. It landed on the far side, drawing his attention and that of his mistress.

Jathan flew across the pavement, leaping over the fountain, racing under the willows. He snatched up both panic-stricken children and wrapped one in each arm, lifting them and dropping behind the end of the half-wall. He cupped a hand over each of their mouths.

He had meant to listen to the sound of the coin, to judge how much time he had to get them behind cover. But now he heard nothing and could not remember hearing it at all at any point during his sprint.

His heart was screaming out his chest. His head was dripping sweat. He felt like he was drowning in it. He strained his ears but heard nothing. Nothing to tell him whether he was safe, of whether Seber was standing directly above him about to slaughter the three of them.

Finally, blessedly, Seber picked up the conversation with his mistress, and they both wandered away together, their voices slowly fading. Jathan waited there in pulsing terror and silent wonder until they were long gone.

He released both children just as the fist hit him. He felt a sharp pain on the back of his head.

There was suddenly a man there, skin like blue ice in the light of the moons. His head was bald, and he wore a butcher's apron over a tunic that was more stain now than cloth. He somehow managed to scoot both children away and also lift Jathan by the neck and slam him into a tenement wall.

Jathan felt his face tingle and then go to rubber. His skin felt thick and immense. His vision turned dark.

But he saw someone else. A hand reached in and touched the man's chest. The hand lowered Jathan, and the fingers uncoiled.

He saw the same woman, hair half swaying low across her face and half shaved, trousers and coat of patched-over golden-brown leather. She held her hand out to the man, palm outward. She gestured at Jathan and then shook her head, making a horizontal swiping gesture with her flat hand.

The bald man nodded and released him, leaving Jathan gulping air. The man corralled the two children away to a little stone bench beneath a lamp that was still lit despite having been halfway to becoming a bird's nest.

This time the woman didn't leave. "You'll have to forgive Mister Shine," she said. "He doesn't trust strangers. Even ones who help."

Jathan was struck dumb by the combination of her voice and her face both directed at him at once. He looked into her eyes, dark and infinite.

"We need to talk," she said.

8

The Haunted People

THE FIRST WORDS OUT of her mouth were not what Jathan expected.

"What are you doing here?" she asked. She leaned her head back, so that she could look down her nose at him even though he was taller.

"Are we safe here?" he asked.

"My people are watching. They will keep a lookout. Otherwise, they wouldn't still be here." She gestured over her shoulder at the two little children seated halfway on the stone bench, each one scooping fistfulls of powder sprinkled with shards of broken glass from their pockets, arranging them into little piles on the stone. The powders sparkled, some like bright diamond powder, and some like sand made of a starlit night. The bald man, Mister Shine, hovered protectively over them.

She took a step closer to him, so that he could have reached out and touched her. "What are you doing here?"

"I am walking the free city streets," he answered. He smelled the leather she wore. "Kolchin is my city."

She rolled her eyes as hard as anyone but his sister could. "I think you know what I'm asking you. You want to avoid the answer so hard you are going to play games at midnight. That alone gives me a part of the answer." She held a finger in his face. "And I also think you like to believe that because you have walked through these streets once or twice that you know what it's like to live on them."

"I have lived in Tenement Lane before."

"*Before* sounds temporary."

"For a year."

"Before going back to the finestreets where you belong?"

"I lived on the fourth story of a block," he said. "I could look out my secondparents' window and see the Sand Tower."

She chuckled in a way that made it infuriatingly obvious that she was mocking him. "So, you spent all of a year on the outward facing side of the outermost block with a window facing Bowlside the whole time and you think Tenement Lane is a part of *your* city?"

His mouth wrinkled into a grimace, shuddered into a snarl. "What do you think you know about me?"

"I know that you don't really know what you are doing."

"I'm not some fool. I have lived these streets all my life. I—"

"I never said you were stupid, though I also wonder about that. But I don't mean that you don't know because you can't understand the actions you make. I mean that you don't know because you are trying to hide it from yourself."

Jathan almost laughed. "I don't need to hide."

"Yes, you do. You won't even be honest with yourself about that. A man confident in his answer will speak it plain. You do not. You play games. So I ask you again. What are you doing here? Why are you in Tenement Lane every night? Why do I suddenly see this lushborn finestreet boy everywhere in all the places I know, when I have never seen him ever before?"

He stared into her for a long time. He wanted to project the confidence she claimed he lacked, but her eyes opened so wide that they swallowed his subterfuge, like truthsayers, tossing out his fraudulent responses before he even put voice to them. "I don't know why. Maybe I don't have a reason. Maybe I have too many to know which one is real."

"Finally, a truth escapes your lips."

He was not going to admit he had the Jecker monocle within earshot of anyone else, though he figured she must have told others here by now. "I found something," he said. "Something that opened my eyes to a world around me I had never seen. It had always been there, but I was blind to it."

"When our perspective changes it throws us into turmoil," she said. "Because it is unknown territory. The unknown makes us fear. Fear makes us angry."

He was surprised to find himself nodding along with her words. "And now I need to know more. I need to understand it. I can't stand that I didn't see it for so long. It makes me afraid. You are right about that. And I suppose it does make me angry." *They tell me everything makes me angry.*

"And now your fear and your anger have brought you here, to my home."

"It sounds so foolish to say it out loud."

"We hide from our truths because deep down we know they are foolish, and we don't want anyone to see how foolish we are. So we create elaborate lies to conceal ourselves from those we love."

"It is easier to say it to a stranger," Jathan said.

"Because when we walk away, the things we say will not be hanging over our heads. It gives the truth its freedom to breathe."

"How old are you?" he asked. He did not believe she could be older than he by the look of her, but he had never known anyone with hair less grey than Trabius to talk like that.

"How old are you?" she responded.

He let it go. "Point taken."

"Now that I know you can speak truths, I will ask you what your name is." She looked up at him, curious, demanding, daring him to lie.

"My name?" For some reason the question surprised him, despite it being the most normal thing to ask.

"The sounds by which you are called," she clarified.

I deserve that. "Jathan Algevin."

"Well, Jathan Algevin, today is the day you have met Jansi Wake. That is the name that belongs to me."

His eyes squinted uncertainly, one corner of his mouth pulling into a smile. "That is an odd surname to my ears."

"We are not allowed surnames in Tenement Lane. Those who live here have not held land in centuries, or ever. The law says we do not deserve surnames to know our family lines by. So we make our own. We are given one by our parents, and we take another when we cross the threshold of adulthood. I meant it when I told you I'd lived here twice, once as a child and again now that I know who I am and what I'm here for."

"The city governors will never record those names. They would be useless for transferring possessions to the generations. Why bother?"

"I see plainly one of the reasons why you are here, Jathan Algevin. Because you are thick-headed. We have no possessions to pass on. We pay landlords for the privilege to be trapped in this place. No one owns anything in Tenement Lane. All we have is each other."

"I don't understand."

"Of course, you don't. We are from the same city, but we live in two different worlds. We are the lowers. We are the deservingless. They call us scumborn. You call us scumborn. I know you have without ever having to hear it from your lips. You all do. As if our lives were not hard enough lying flat on the ground, you have to grind us into the mud with your boot heels."

He felt suddenly ashamed. He used that world often. Every day of his life. Because it was easier. Easier to think of them as things. Compassion required energy. Objects don't need compassion.

He glanced at the children again, painstakingly scooping the piles of sparkling powder over the edge of the bench into separate little clear jars held by Mister Shine.

"What is that?" he asked. The lamplight refracting made the powders twinkle. The way they glittered was mesmerizing, like something from a half-remembered dream. "It looks familiar. Soaps?"

She chewed her lip. "We may live in tunnels and on rooftops, but believe it or not, we bathe as well. Eat and drink, too, clean up after ourselves, build things and save things, and try to make things better for ourselves. Almost as if we are actual people."

He nodded. "Fair enough."

He watched the children work, saw little bits of broken green and grey glass among the piles of salts and powders. They tried to pinch them out with their tiny fingers wherever they could.

"Bottle shards," he said. "Did you steal those? Did you send children to steal?"

"Where a thing comes from doesn't matter to us."

"Those are expensive. You have fancy taste for tunnel-folk."

She shrugged. "Those are what we need. We get them however we can. We borrow. We steal. Nothing worse than what they do to us."

Jathan nodded, eyeing the man who had nearly choked him to death. "Your friend wanted to end me. Mister bald must respect you to hell and back to let the air back into my lungs without a fight."

"He does. And I saved you once, for saving them." She nodded at the children. "I won't save you from Mister Shine again if you piss him off enough to try to kill you a second time."

"Is he called Mister Shine because of the way the lamplight makes his head glisten?"

"His given name is Benwin. We call him Ben for short. We keep our given names, but each of us must choose our own surname. Some of us keep the name of our parents, if we know who our parents are. Ben's father chose Shine because he is a teacher. He shines light on knowledge for the little ones. Ben follows in his footsteps, though he teaches something different." She pointed at the two children. "He teaches magick to the little ones who are blessed with it like he is."

"Little ones. Children. They are magi?" He felt a revulsion in his mind that did not match what his eyes showed him. His eyes showed him sweet little children, patient and kind, helping each other with their little scoops of stolen soaps. His eyes told them they were innocent. His heart told him they could never be.

Jansi nodded. "At that age they can be very dangerous, mostly to themselves. Without a teacher they would never make it. He shines like his father, lighting the way for them to grow to be safe and wise."

"History and mathematics are a bit different than changing the universe with your mind."

"But he feels that same calling. Some of us find a new calling and make our name from it. We choose our names by what we do that makes us the best version of ourselves, the thing we do that makes us the most proud."

"You don't take names for a legal purpose? You take them for...pride?"

She touched a finger to her nose. "We take these names because we are proud of the people who came before us, and we are hopeful for where we will go in the days to come."

He felt those words. He was proud every day of his life that he was brought into the world by his parents, the greatest people who had ever walked this earth. It made sense to him. At least in part. "Then why are you always hiding? So proud you slink in the shadows at night."

She frowned fiercely. "I think that is another question you know the answer to already."

"Because of him. Because of Seber Geddakur."

She spat at the sound of his name. "He is a demon. He haunts these streets. He will not leave us alone. We can never gather. We can never be together in the night. We cannot comfort each other with songs in the darkness. We are afraid to whisper."

"How long has he been here?"

"Years. A lifetime. And the gangers know it. They know we can't stand together in the night. And so that is when they come to take what little we have and keep our faces in the dirty water."

"Wait a minute now. If you are not safe at night, then how can the gangers be?"

"They have a deal with him. He won't touch men in ganger colors as long as they don't challenge him."

"If they do challenge him?" Jathan asked.

"You've seen what he can do."

"I have," Jathan said. He glanced at the bodies of the three greencoats. "I saw him. The first night I came here."

"I know. I was there watching you every time you saw him kill."

He glanced at her. "Why do you follow him?"

"I am a lookout. We have a network of watchers. We follow him, we signal each other, pass his trail off to the next one of us and the next."

"Why?"

"In case he comes too close to the hiding places of other street dwellers. I run rooftops. I jump down from great heights. I climb walls. I run tunnels. That's why I wear these leathers. I need to not have any fabric on me that could catch or rip or snag. He must never know we are there, watching."

"You do it every night?"

"Most nights. Those of us that do are given food, clothes, tools, knives, soap to wash under the drip pipes. Our people take care of us because it is the most dangerous thing we can do."

"Has he ever seen you?"

"Almost. Once. I've yet to run faster in all my life than I did that day."

"I saw how terrifying his power is. And I felt afraid of that power, but somehow seeing it made me fear this strange world less."

She nodded knowingly. "You are fascinated by it, this power."

He nodded. He was surprised how easy it was to admit. "I...want it. I want the power that he has. Even something like the power he has. I want to be able to do the things they do. I hate that I can't."

She nodded again. "It is so easy to become jealous of them. I have. We all have been at one time or another."

"How do you stand it?"

She shrugged. "My mother used to say that we are all born with a blindness, that eventually we all realize that there is something special about each of us. Our problem is that we can't see how special we are. All we can see is how special everyone else is."

"They are so obviously superior," Jathan said.

"We each have two eyes, and oh the many things they can see. But they can only look outward, never inward, never at ourselves. You could take a hundred different magi with a hundred different skills, and there would still be at least one thing that you can do better than any of them."

"Better than magick though?" He was skeptical.

She rolled her eyes. "You likely know what these skills are. How could you not? They are yours. But because they are yours, you can't see them for what they are. They seem natural. So instead of seeing them as special, you see them as ordinary. The only thing you need to do is step back and realize how special are the skills you already have."

"Do I have to leave a sacrifice in exchange for that wisdom, oh wise oracle?"

"I accept money. Any coin will do." She made that half-smile again.

"Where do you live in this place?"

She eyed him with a suspicious smirk. "Trying to come home with me, lushboy? I bet all your lushborn ladies would have a word to say about you wandering off to bed with a scumborn girl like me."

"You keep calling yourself that. Why?"

"It's what people like you call me. It's what people like you have always called me. When I was little it used to sting. It used to make me cry. Until I realized that it is just another name for where I come from. And I am proud of where I come from. When I hear it now, I hear it with pride. And now no one can hurt me with it anymore."

He wasn't sure what to say to that, so he let a silence float over them. She seemed more than comfortable in it.

"What do we do now?" he asked.

She turned suddenly stern. Her welcoming tone vanished. "Now, you go away. You go and never come back." She said it casually, not angrily. But she was very serious.

His eyes snapped back to her. "What do you mean?"

"This place is my community," she finally said. "And that means I have to protect it. And I do. However I can. From whoever I need to protect it from. Whether that be magick killers, gangers, magistrates. Or you."

"Me?"

"You come here for reasons that I can understand. But that does not mean that I like them."

"I thought we were getting along."

She opened her eyes wide and looked into his. "I think you have a good heart. I would have slit your throat already if I thought you were a fraud. I'm not blind. I've heard your words and seen your actions. But you are putting your good heart to bad use."

"What am I doing that is any different from what you do?"

"You are chasing something that is missing in yourself. You are hoping to find it here. You won't."

"I don't need this place."

"By tomorrow you will already be thinking of coming back. I can see the emptiness inside you. It is pulling in everything around you. A man with that much darkness will only draw more darkness to him."

"I am nothing like that abomination."

She winced at that word. "You will come. And you will think you are doing right. When all you will really be doing is stomping around in a place that doesn't belong to you, making noise, drawing attention, kicking over rocks that should not be upturned. And one of these times, your carelessness will be the cause of great pain."

Jathan was offended. "I do not stomp. I know these streets. I lived here once. I am not what you think I am."

She shook her head sadly. "You are worse. Because you do not even realize that you are."

"I helped you. Your people. I helped them twice now."

"And I and everyone around me is grateful," Jansi said. "And now we are gratefully asking you to go."

He didn't know what to say. What was there to say in the face of that? "I am more than what you think I am. I know what I am."

She stared into him, her eyes cold and deep and complete, a darkness that contained universes. "And someday that will be true."

"You can't just cast me out. There is so much I need to know."

"Go home, Jathan Algevin. Go back where you belong."

He felt a pain behind his eyes. It hurt to hear someone say that to him. He had always felt that this was his city. Every part of it was a part that he knew. Other people were the outsiders. Not him. Never him.

And now to have someone dismiss him the way he dismissed outsiders from the north country, from the immense cities, from the capital. It stung him. And it kept stinging him. For he could never not have this knowledge—that there were very serious, very important things that had been happening in his city all this time *and he had no idea.*

There were people here he had never known about. His lens was cracked. His perspective awry. He felt a horror in his bones. That everywhere he looked he was missing something, seeing what his eyes expected to see but losing out on some vital thread, some piece that was invisible to his eyes because of where he stood when he did the looking. Like the invisible afterglow that had been all around him yet never seen.

Magick users could be children. Of course, they could. Logic dictated that they had to be. But theory was abstract. To see them in practice was something else. You know it by touch and sight. To be this close to it. It became something more. It became real. It was always real, but he could not see it. His perfect vision had a blind spot.

How can I trust my own eyes? How can I trust my own mind?

He began to question everything he thought he knew.

Jansi Wake was gone before he even realized. She vanished as quietly as she had every other time he had seen her, leaving him alone beneath the willows.

Jathan barely remembered stumbling home. His head was so full of thoughts he only obtained awareness of where he was and what he was doing every hundredth step or so. He felt like he was asleep. The world made no sense.

He couldn't think. He couldn't act. He didn't know what to do. He didn't know himself.

The only thing he knew for certain was that he could not stop. He could not give up the monocle. He could not stop hunting for his sister's beau. He could not stop following a brutal murderer through a moonlit maze. He could not bring himself to do any of the things that would save him from the trouble he was in with his magistrate friends, or with the gangers, or with the Glasseye outsider.

This was his obsession.

He simply couldn't stop.

Our lies are not the only monsters that follow us. And every time he fed this one, it made it that much harder to stop the next time. And the next. And the next.

He was walking off a cliff, unable to stop himself.

It wasn't until he made it through his front door that he realized he had forgotten his boots back on the steps in Tenement Lane.

His mind was splitting in two.

A part of him was living a normal life, working on the Promenade, chatting with Harod and Trabius, swimming at the bottom of a bottle with his friends, throwing a few fists at whoever wanted them.

Another part was ducking gangers and Glasseyes by day and wandering an underworld of tragic haunted rogues and bloodthirsty sorcerers by night, saving children and trying to find the creature that had seduced his sister and let its magick-infested hide into his home.

What the fuck am I doing?

He had no answer.

9

Nessa

HOW COULD YOU EVER explain that you had been living a different life by night? How could you ever make them understand? Jathan could not think of a way to do it without even his closest friends looking at him like he had gone mad.

Go and never come back.

He heard those words in his head over and over. Every few minutes. He found that the harder he worked, the less intrusive the thoughts became. So, he threw himself into all of his usual tasks at Mistines's and then many more besides.

So much so that Mistine became suspicious. She spent the better part of the morning either eyeing him or inspecting him for signs of fevered delirium.

Once he had run out of other things to do, he resigned himself to joining Ouleem cleaning and polishing the many trinkets on the shelves—fine silver pendants, feathered coats, Samartanian statuettes, Valarnan gameking figurines, and the last few carved Mua dogs.

"I think that Glasseye is after you," Ouleem said, glancing out the window as he handed a blue glass necklace through it to an Academ student in exchange for ten coppers.

"Why do you say that?" Jathan asked, startled.

"He is coming back this way for the fourth time today. He keeps walking by our window and staring inside."

"How do you know he's not looking for you, Ouleem?" Jathan cracked a sardonic smile.

"Because one of the times I watched him do it from outside while I was picking up the morning pastries. No one else was here but you."

Jathan's sly smirk died a slow terrified death. *He knows. He knows it was me. He is waiting to make his move. Arrest me. Reclaim the monocle. Send me to prison.*

"You look like you just went to hell and back before my eyes, my friend," Ouleem said.

"I...I think it was something I ate."

"Best get right at the quick," Ouleem said. "Your turn to watch the seller window."

"Can't you handle it?" Jathan asked without looking over at the window.

Ouleem raised both eyebrows hard.

"You're right. I owe you."

Ouleem shut the door behind him, leaving Jathan alone among shelves full of the flotsam of failed caravans he was supposed to clean and sell. Brass censers corrupted his reflection, garnets winked slyly at him, and austere wooden Mua dogs stared holes through him.

Ouleem should have been careful what he wished for. Jathan could already hear Mistine barking at him through the door.

Jathan reached for the broom, just to have something in his hands in case she burst through the door, to give himself at least the appearance of being marginally better than useless.

He glimpsed the shape of a woman out in the light of day in his periphery, feet squishing through the dew-covered grass, stepping hesitantly up to the seller window, the way someone did when they were checking if a familiar face was in.

Jathan turned, expecting Nessa, or maybe even Lyra. He turned toward the seller window and was halfway to forming a charming greeting when his eyes fell upon the last person he expected to see.

Jansi Wake.

"What the fuck are you doing here?"

She widened her eyes with half a smile. "What a greeting. No wonder you have so few customers at your window."

"Would you feel better if I held a knife to your throat?" Jathan asked. "I want you to feel at home."

She smiled. She didn't say anything, but he was fairly certain the answer was yes.

"What are you doing here?" he asked.

"So, this is where finestreet boys work." Jansi rested both arms on the windowsill, leaning forward, tapping her fingers on the wood, her eyes looking up and all around at the shelves full of wares.

She wore a three-quarter sleeved tunic of orange, and a yellow skirt hanging down to her knees. Resting on her shoulders like a cape was an oversized wool coat that looked like she had taken it from the garbage behind the finethread tailor's shop and stomped on it and rolled in dirt for a decade or two. He was so used to seeing her in her leathers it surprised him that she even had any other clothes.

He stepped up to the window. "Tell me," he whispered. "What are you doing here? You can't be here. What are you doing here?"

She looked past him at the shiny Mua dog carvings. "This conversation is sounding so familiar to me."

He put his hands on his hips and rolled his eyes. "Fair enough. But seriously now. What do you think you are doing? What if someone sees us talking?"

She shrugged. "So what if they do?" Her eyes were so wide and earnest that he felt like he was falling into the deep sea looking at them.

"Then they'll know...that I...that we..."

Her wandering eyes stopped and fixed their gaze on him, pinning him in place in space and time. "That we...*what?*"

He felt her breath on his skin, a memory from the first night she spoke to him. He couldn't breathe for a moment, not that his lungs ceased to function, but more like he forgot how. "That we...know each other."

"Worried about your reputation, finestreet boy? Worried what the lush ladies from the Promenade will think of you flirting with a little scumborn girl?"

"No, it's not that, it's that..."

"So, you *are* flirting with me then? You're not very good at it."

"No, I..." He stopped. He closed his eyes and settled himself, locking down his thoughts. He leaned in close to the window, arms on the sill directly in front of her, so he could whisper without Mistine or Ouleem hearing through the door. "They don't know I've been going there. To Tenement Lane. They don't know. I don't want them to know."

She seemed puzzled. "So this dangerous thing you are doing, that is taking up your every night, is a secret?"

"If they find out where I've been, they'll start to ask why. And if they ask why, sooner or later they'll get around to asking how." He slipped the Jecker monocle free and flashed it in her eyes before dropping it right back into his pocket.

"That astonishes me. To keep all this turmoil you are going through from the people who care about you the most. That is something that never would have crossed my mind to do."

"Don't you have any secrets?"

She shrugged. "Maybe I should start. Maybe I'll tell my people that I was just out for a walk. Maybe it will make it seem more interesting to make it a secret that I'm just standing in the Upper End talking to some stupid lushborn finestreet boy on the Promenade."

He rolled his eyes. "It's less intense than following a murderer. I'll give you that."

She half-smiled. "You feel the need to justify yourself to everyone, don't you? Maybe even to yourself. You can't just say I do this, this is what I do, and fuck you if you don't like it. You feel the need to explain yourself all the time."

"Except when I'm at the bottom of a bottle," he said. "Then I'll tell them all that with a fist behind it."

She smiled a little wider. "Now I'm starting to like you."

"You weren't before?"

She looked away. "Quite a life you finestreet boys live."

"Why did you come here?" he asked.

She reached down with one and and picked something up off the grass outside. She lifted it up and held it through the window.

It was a pair of boots. His boots.

She gave them a little shake. "You left these in my world when you went home last night."

"Fuck, shit, and hell. On the steps." He remembered. He took them from her and set them down inside. He paused, embarrassed. "Thank you."

"Look at you, little lushboy," she said. "More sheepish than a shepherd."

"Why did you bring them here?"

"Is that an insult brewing?"

"I mean, well, why didn't you just keep them? Why bring them back here at all? Why not give them to one of your people?"

"Not everyone is a thief like you, lushboy."

"Tell me. Why?"

"I didn't want you to think you had to come back again."

He did not have a response to that. For some reason it deflated him to hear her say it.

A strange little silence fell over them. It seemed to last eons.

She broke eye contact and looked around the room again. "Fine little life you've got here."

"Too mundane for you?"

"Don't be an idiot. I would give anything to have a life like this, doing the same thing every day, without having to watch out for a killer around every corner. I start every night knowing my life could be taken at any moment. You think I wouldn't give that up if I could? I would give anything to just be."

"Then leave. Walk away. Get out of Tenement Lane."

She chuckled. "That is lush coming from you, finestreet boy."

"What do you mean?"

"You've been coming to my world for two weeks and you already can't walk away when I hold a knife to your throat and threaten to kill you. You expect me to walk away from my home and the people I've spent my whole life with?"

"Fair enough."

"Are all finestreet boys this thick-headed?"

"You keep calling me that. I may live here, I may walk here. But it takes every coin I earn just to get by. The only thing we have is the house our parents left us."

"Which is more than I will ever have in my whole life," she reminded him. "You truly get mad when I call you that, don't you?

He shook his head. "It's fine." But it was a lie. It did bother him.

She paused. "What's the reason?"

"For what?"

She smirked at him annoyed. "You said you don't want your people to know why you are going out at night. So what is the reason you are coming to my world every time the sun sets?"

He looked away, embarrassed. "I was there because I was trying to find out who my sister is seeing"

"You mean who she is fucking?"

"You really are trying to get under my skin, aren't you?"

"You finally noticed." She seemed proud of herself. "Why are you so worried about her?"

"Because of who she is with. One of them. A user of magick."

She paused for a long time. "You never told me why you hate them so much."

"My parents were killed by magi." He couldn't believe he said it. Out loud. So causally. Like commenting on the weather. It stunned him.

"How old were you?"

"I'd seen ten summers by then."

"I'm sorry."

"Not your fault."

"I'm still sorry. Just because I almost cut your head off once doesn't mean I can't feel for your pain."

For some reason hearing her say the word pain made him suddenly feel it all. He held his breath. It staggered him.

He heard Mistine screaming through the door. "If you don't get your filthy friends away from my seller window, I'll take a broom to their heads! I swear I will!"

Jansi widened her eyes. "I like her."

"You had better go."

"I know."

He was surprised to find that he didn't want her to. "I'll see you again."

She raised an eyebrow. "You think so, eh?"

"I know it."

She backed away from the window, hands clasped at her waist. "Stay out of my world, lushboy. I came here to give you your boots and to tell you not to come back."

He waited until she was too far away to hear. "Try and stop me." His eyes followed her until she joined the crowd and vanished in the swells.

"Who were you talking to?" Ouleem asked over his shoulder.

"Fucking gods!" Jathan jumped so high he nearly smacked his head on the top of the window frame.

"You're wound up like a spring, Jay," Ouleem said.

"Just a neighbor. Brought me back my boots."

Ouleem raised an eyebrow and elbowed his ribs. "Brought you your boots, eh?"

Jathan rolled his eyes. "Don't tell anyone, all right?"

"Your secret is in the vault and nary a soul will hear it."

"Thank you, my friend."

"Looks like you have another suitor." Ouleem pointed over his shoulder, across the grass around the near side of the little lake.

Jathan looked over Ouleem's shoulder, out the window. He saw the Glasseye marching away from his usual table at the Lazy Steward, coming around the lake, his stride confident, purposeful, focused. He was coming to the window. He never adjusted his course for any other pedestrians. They diverted for him, or he bowled them over.

Shit, fuck, and hell.

Jathan glanced to the door. "I have to go."

Ouleem turned to him, annoyed. "Are you serious? Where are you going? What do I tell Mistine?"

"Tell her I saved you both from having to clean these damn trinkets twice by not throwing up all over them. I'm going to be sick."

Ouleem rolled his eyes. "Fine. Goddamn it. You owe me."

"I'll catch your drinks tonight at the Bottlebottom."

Ouleem pointed a sharp finger at him and closed one eye, like he was aiming a nonexistent weapon. "You better."

"I will, I swear." Jathan was already out the door, crossing the wineroom and racing out the door onto the pavement-side. That would put Mistine's between him and the Glasseye. But there was no cover to either side. It would have to be *blend in* or *be caught.* He edged around, his back to the wall, peeked around the corner.

He saw the Glasseye come right up to the window and lean inside.

Just in time.

He waited until the Glasseye selected a direction to walk, and then Jathan went the opposite way, jogging to the nearest cluster of people to slide in among to obscure himself. He looked over his shoulder every third step. The Glasseye was going the other way.

That was too close.

He wondered if he would be able to go to work as long as the Glasseye was hounding him. He tried to think of places he could hide the Jecker monocle during the day.

If they catch me with this....

But he had never let it leave his side. Not since the day he found it. The idea of leaving it anywhere felt like leaving his right hand somewhere. And worse, with Lyra sneaking that creature into their home, he no longer considered it a safe place to store something this important. There was no telling what Lyra's magick lover would do if he chanced across it.

He was still trying to come up with ideas when he rounded the corner by the icery and ran headlong into Vaen Osper.

His shoulder caught the magistrate and it spun Jathan until his back slammed against the side wall of the alley.

"In a very big hurry, I see," Vaen said. He wore his cloak and boots. His sword hilt was polished to a shine. He wore a very slick smirk, as sharp as his longsword. His smile was a far distance from friendly.

He had Felber Klisp with him, radiating dumb menace. "You have been avoiding us, Jathan."

His three stooges—Belo, Tylar, and Sejassie—were just behind. They were all wearing their steel, pulling their soiled olive-green capes aside to show the hilts and scabbards. Belo's cheeks were trying to swallow his eyes, Tylar's nose was trying to dive into his mouth, and Sejassie looked as though he had been purchasing his face in installments and ran out of coin before he could get himself a chin.

"What are you all doing here?" Jathan asked. "You are five districts over from Beachside."

Vaen glanced to Felber with a knowing smirk. "Look who suddenly knows so much about where to find us." He turned back to Jathan with a stare like a hammer to the forehead. "You see, Jathan, Felber was thinking perhaps you forgot how to find us, what with you not coming around all of a sudden."

"No leads in a long time," Felber belched from between the fat mealworms of his lips. "The regional overmagistrate is looking at our capture count and raining down hell."

"This doesn't look good for us," Vaen said. "We need your leads. I know you have some."

"I don't," Jathan said. "I swear. Just a possibility. I'm looking into it. It could be a big one. But I don't have anything precise yet." *I don't want to give up my midnight secrets. I don't want to stop being the only one who knows where he is.*

"You see," Vaen said. "I think you're lying to me."

"I'm not."

"You have been seen going to some interesting places late at night," Vaen said.

Damn it all. "What are you talking about?" *Had they followed me?*

Felber hissed out an exhale. "You seem to be spending an awful lot of time down near Tenement Lane."

"Look, what I get up to at night is just personal. It has nothing to do with you, or with any other magistrates, or with any wizards."

Vaen stared at him. "I think you have a juicy lead, and you are shopping it around to some of the other magistrates form the center districts. I think you are playing us, striking a bidding war for the information on the magick user."

"It's not like that at all," Jathan said. "As soon as I have something, I will be out to see you."

Vaen fingered the hilt of his longsword. He turned and looked back at the others, made eye contact with all four men with him.

Jathan sensed some silent communication between them. He didn't like it. Everything about Vaen and Felber had changed in the last few weeks. Their charming playful demeanor was gone. A yearslong friendship had turned sour in a fortnight.

I thought we were friends.

He knew he should have told them about Seber. He should have given him up and let them go deal with it. He could not even explain to himself why he didn't. Seber was dangerous. He should not have been walking around free in this city. He should not have been allowed to exist. Jathan should have wanted to give him up and have him sent away to burn in the fires of execution.

But he simply was not ready to let his secret go.

"By the end of this week," Jathan said. "I'm sure I will have something by the end of the week."

Vaen did not appear convinced. He made the sinister shared smile with Felber and the other three once more. "End of the week. You sure you aren't going to go running to the East Uppers or the Bowl or Tenement Lane to shop our rightful lead to them tonight?"

Jathan held up both hands. "I'm going to the Bottlebottom tonight. For drinks with friends. I go there all the time. I am not meeting any other magistrates. I don't even know any other magistrates."

Vaen leaned in close to him, hand squeezing the sword hilt. "Have a good time at the Bottlebottom," he said.

Jathan tried to hold his ground, but he couldn't help but lean back submissively. "Thank you."

Vaen turned and strolled away, Felber, Belo, Tylar, and Sejassie following suit, each of them glaring at Jathan before they did.

"And I mean it," Jathan said. "End of the week. I'll come see you. I mean it."

None of them turned around. They left the alley and left the Promenade and left Jathan, and he should have felt relief. But he didn't. He felt fear. A strange fear. A fear that his world was coming apart. That the careful life that he had spent so much time constructing was crumbling. Circumstances were all changing so fast his old life would not be able to bend to fit. It would shatter. In every direction he looked it would collapse.

He needed to save Lyra, needed to pacify Vaen Osper, to get away from the Glasseye, and to do something about Seber Geddakur. Most of all, he needed to get rid of the Jecker monocle.

I need to get out of this. I need to do something.

He made up his mind that he would go to the Bottlebottom, he would have his velvet brandy and summerwine, and he would figure this out. He would force himself to make a decision tonight. He swore it to himself.

He staggered home and found it empty. No Lyra. No afterglow. He sat alone, drinking tea, nursing the pain in his heart, trying to swallow his obsession back down.

He did not realize how much time had passed until he noticed he was sitting in the dark. The sun had long since set. He was late.

He melted across the finestreets, eyes furtive, monocle in hand. Always looking. He saw two distinct varieties of afterglow along the way, blue and gold, red and bright green. He could only guess what they meant.

They were both shifting red around the core colors. Whoever left them here was long gone and moving further away still. Jathan let hem go and went on.

He floated across the city like a ghost, lucky to have his subconscious guiding him, as he had every thought in his head except where he was going. He passed people without seeing them. But his feet delivered him to the Bottlebottom.

Cristan greeted him with a sloppy embrace, bottle in each hand. His breath was half wine and half whiskey, and he slobbered a kiss on his neck and then threw him to Sethleen, who welcomed him by shoving her tongue all the way into his mouth, slathering him with the taste of sweetwine. The sweat behind her ears pattered his neck and her fingers slithered into his trousers and squeezed him until he was agonizingly hard before he managed to guide her back to her seat at the table.

Cristan was taking the bottles so hard he spent most of his time looking at the ceiling, and Sethleen was so inebriated she likely had no idea she had brought him a hairsbreadth away from spilling in her hand. She was already deep in a conversation about cetaceans with a beautiful woman with a tiny nose and umber bangs and a body like a soft pink skeleton. *Cristan and Sethleen will be fighting over who gets to be first to kiss her between her legs before the night is over.*

He didn't see Branderin anywhere, and when he asked Ouleem, he couldn't get a straight answer. He had seen him but couldn't remember which day. Jathan remembered to buy Ouleem his drinks at least.

Jathan was into his second cup of summerwine when thankfully Nessifer stopped in. She was wearing a gown as blood red as her hair, baring her shoulders, with a slick black corset over it. Her smile was virulently jovial, and her eyes shined vulpine in the light of a thousand candles.

Jathan wasn't sure if it was the dress, the lighting, or the fact that Sethleen had just left him hard as stone—or if it was all three combined—but his eyes were stuck like glue to Nessifer's every movement. It had been more than a while since the time she had invited him between her legs, and he suddenly felt every single painful second in between.

She sailed through the door and nearly walked past him. He kicked an empty chair out into her path. He panicked a bit when it looked like it might go past her and strike another woman he did not know, but it came to rest just short.

She stopped in her tracks and turned her head with a slow s̶m̶ almost hit that poor girl."

"I could have blamed it on Cristan."

"Believable." She shrugged. "But then she might have tried to start a fight with him and end up being talked into bed with him."

"You're right," Jathan laughed. "That is even worse than being tripped by a chair." His laughter was mostly forced, and it faded far too soon as a result.

She scooted the chair back with a squeak and a whine and slid herself into it, her knees touching his. Her smile bit its way into his full attention. It was so dynamic and infectious.

He should have been thinking of his problems. He should have been trying to find solutions. He should have been making tough decisions. He had promised himself he would make the decisions tonight.

But instead, he ordered another bottle of summerwine and drowned himself in her smile.

"You forgot to shave your face," she said. "Five days or more by the look of you."

His hand reflexively went to his cheek. She wasn't lying. His fingers found a forest of stubble. He could not remember the last time he had taken any care in his appearance. He looked down at his tunic, unchanged and unwashed now for two days, and then his trousers, now going on their fifth day at least.

He could have dressed in clean clothes. He had some fresh from the washerman two weeks ago. But his routine had devolved to grabbing the closest ones to the door on his way to morning work. And those all too often ended up being the same ones he stripped off while crossing his bedroom the night before.

"I am unkempt," he admitted, swigging a quarter of a bottle in one triple gulp.

She smiled wider. "I like you disheveled," she admitted. "I like you dirty."

ned, and her compliments were making it easier not

ıy you come. But especially how you look right now.

ɔne tonight?"

ɔrow. "Why are you so suddenly interested in the

"I am ᴋᴄ... , rested in monopolizing your attention tonight."

She shrugged playfully. "I am more than capable of having conversation with more than one person at a time."

He narrowed his eyes. "I don't mean that kind of conversation."

Her expression never changed. Her smile never left. "When you talk to me like that I can't think straight."

"When you wear that dress, it makes me want to talk to you that way all night, and again in the morning."

She blushed. "I feel so special to have such a rapt audience from your eyes, Jathan Algevin. You have not showered a woman with this much of your attention in months. Unless you are meeting a secret lover who never sets foot in Brandytown."

"I don't have any such person," he said. His voice started playful but plunged into anger and sadness. *Secret lover. Gods high and low, is there nothing that can keep from reminding me of my sister's thrice-damned lies?*

Her brow narrowed in concern. "Sorry to bring up your cold spell. I am simply astonished that a boy like you with a face like that would have any problems other than fighting all the women off with a stick."

He smiled halfway. "It's other problems. I don't even have the luxury of having a chance to worry about that one."

"How many problems could one boy have?"

"Many."

"What kind of problems could Jathan Algevin have? Of all of us, you seem to have your life the most together."

If you only knew. If only I could tell you. He couldn't tell her about the monocle. He certainly couldn't tell her about following Seber Geddakur around. She was liable to call the magistrates on him for either of those things. He couldn't tell her about informing on the little magick users in

Beachside Kolchin. She would tell Lyra and that would open the wound all over again. So what problem *could* he tell her about?

"I am worried about Lyra," he finally decided.

She looked at him skeptically, leaning her head back. "You seem awfully sour about it. Your sister seems fine. A little anxious of late perhaps. But otherwise, fine."

"I know for a fact she has another lover."

Nessifer pursed her lips. "You sound so sure."

"I know, Nessa."

"Have you caught them in the act? If not, how can you know?"

"I know, all right? I know." *I saw the afterglow.*

She leaned in close to him, washing the smell of her and of her perfume over him. He had to close his eyes for one moment to take it in, otherwise he might tip forward and fall into her and become lost inside her.

"I will preface this by asking you a question," she said.

"By all means."

"Why do you feel the need to concern yourself so deeply in the matter of her love affairs?"

He felt a snap of anger at the question, but he was able to chase it down with another breath of her sweet smell and it calmed him enough not to shout. "Because of how she is. Because of how she gets. You know. You have had to listen to her words and feel the splash of her tears when she weeps over them all."

"Exactly. I do. That is a place for her friends. Let her have that place."

"I can't. You know why. Because she can't leave them on her own. And she always needs to leave them. I don't make her do it. She comes to me in tears, begging me to help her leave them because she falls too deep."

Nessifer nodded. "I know. I have had her tears on my shoulder for every one of them."

"I never compelled her. I swear to you. I never tried to control her. I let her do whatever she wanted. But that was my mistake. She needs boundaries in her life. She is unable to impose her own, and it leads her to disaster. I failed her before *because* I didn't try to stop her from this foolery before it got out of hand."

"There are other ways to approach this. Trying to prevent her from being with someone she is infatuated with, while in the depth of that infatuation, feels like it is too late."

"It is too late even before it starts," he said. "The question is how much later can she afford to have me wait before I step in?"

"Why you?"

"What do you mean *why me?*"

"Why do you have to always assume the burden?"

"Because she comes to me when it all goes wrong. Because we are family. Because when it all is said and done, there is no one else to watch out for her but me."

She flattened her lips and took a long breath. She put one hand on his leg. "I understand. I do. I know you just want to help her. But you know you are not immune from getting carried away with things."

"How do you mean?"

She laughed. "You become obsessed with things just as easily as she. More so even. You get ideas in your head, and they take you over. Remember when you spent a whole year obsessed with trying to save up enough money to buy a sword? Do you remember years ago when you convinced yourself that the reason we couldn't get any calpas fruit in the markets for six months was because of the city tax collector in a conspiracy with officials from the capital, and you could not let anyone argue you out of the idea? And then it turned out that it was just a merchant fleet that was beached by a storm down the coast and it took another one to restock the city's supply? Ring any bells?"

"I don't think it's the same thing," he grumbled.

"You two are cut from the same cloth. You just find your obsessions in different places. Oh, how I would have loved it if a boy like you would obsess over being in my bed the way Lyra does for the men she meets. Oh, how I would have loved it if it had been *you*, Jathan. But it couldn't be. Because you are the way you are. I cried over it when I was younger, but I understand it now, and I don't blame you for it. You can never give that much of yourself to a woman, because you have split so much of yourself off into your many obsessions. There is no room left."

"You seem to cut me an awful lot of slack," he said.

"You knew I had a crush on you years before we fucked. Years before we knew how to fuck. But I realized a long time ago that it would be too hard to fight for your attention. So, you need not worry. I like having you for the time I have you. Whether that be for a week or a day or an hour or for five minutes up against the wall behind the Bottlebottom. I let you be you."

She glanced away as she spoke. She wasn't telling the whole truth.

But with everything floating around in Jathan's head he did not have time to add this one to the stew, not right now. And perhaps that was exactly what she meant. He was never ready to become that person for her *right now*. He felt quite certain that he would be, one day very soon. But it had been one day soon every day for years now, and still that day had not quite arrived. So he brushed those thoughts away. He would come back to them another time.

He shook a little laugh out.

"What's funny?" she asked.

"Obsession. I think we have our parents to blame for that."

"Jathan Algevin? Trying to blame someone else for his trouble? No." He didn't need to see her eyes roll to know it was sarcasm.

He closed his eyes and sighed. "Just that I remember they were so invested in this weird god, his rituals, his rites. Always purifying themselves, always bathing themselves with different soaps and powders, always in the same order, always in the same colored jars—violet and green and grey. Always washing with the same methodical motions, with the same brushes in the same order. Lighting censers of fragrant smoke. A whole ordeal each time. It was like a sacrament to them."

"Sounds like the kind of thing a god would make his worshippers do. They must have been quite devout to do it the right way every time. Ouleem calls himself devout to Abraxas, but he skips every third prayer and four out of five of the sacred observances on his holy days."

"What can I say? You are right about us. We are Algevins. We obsess."

"Which god? Do you know? My father is obsessed with all the gods, from everywhere, but in a scholarly way."

He shrugged. "I never asked. I don't know why."

"Maybe Lyra knows."

"She weeps when I bring up things like that, things they used to do together especially. They said it took the god Gabrias a whole day to make every waterfall in the worlds; I can make two out of Lyra's eyes in an instant just by mentioning our parents feeding each other bites of cake."

Nessa made a frown of rich sympathy. "Poor Lyra. Poor you."

"I could have pressed her about it. I just didn't care. Religion has never been something I was concerned about. I don't rely on gods for anything. I rely on myself to make my own way. Like a true Kolcha native."

"Hmmm, I guess I never realized you had no gods of your own. I suppose I don't think much about them either. Though my family raised me to pray to Analea."

"I think I heard she was quite the lover."

Nessa winked. "She can be."

He glanced up at the ceiling playfully. "How is she feeling tonight? Oh, if only I had an oracle or a diviner to scree me the mood of her priestesses."

"I guess you'll have to find out the way mere mortals do," she said.

"I like it better that way. I like making my own destiny. I suppose that is why I never found a god. Because I hate the idea of being controlled. By anyone. By any authority—parents, magistrates, overseers. A god just seemed like one more yoke."

"By the look of you I would have thought it was because you rebelled against the idea of all that bathing." She sniffed the air "Or any bathing at all."

He laughed. "I smell. I know."

Now it was she who shrugged, her hands clasped together in her lap as she did so. "It's all right. I like your smell. Elsewise I wouldn't be sitting in a seat downwind of you."

He smiled and raised a drink to her and swallowed it. She matched him with a double shot of velvet brandy. He settled back into his chair. "So, you think I should leave her all alone?"

She shook her head. "I am saying I think you should cut her some slack. That's all. You see her past lovers, and you think each one was lust pure and simple. But to her it was never just lust. It was freedom."

"I told you I never tried to control her."

"Not freedom from you. From this place."

"The Bottlebottom?"

"From this city. From Kolchin."

He leaned back from her. "What does that mean?"

"She was willing to put up with their awful personalities because they brought her the promise of traveling far from here."

"What?!"

"Aroush promised to take her up the coast to Ethios. Kevander led her to believe he was Samartanian royalty. She wasn't after his gold. She envisioned a journey across the Karelian Sea to Samartania. And Xork Xorka had her all tied up in knots with a fantasy of going to Arradan. She was willing to put up with a lot of personality deficiencies if it meant she was able to go far away. They weren't her lovers as much as they were escape routes."

"I don't understand," Jathan said.

"You never noticed that she wants to leave?"

"What are you talking about? This is our home. This is where our parents made a home for us. We can't leave it. How could we leave it? They did everything for us and then they were taken away. That house, the place they raised us, is all we have left of them. This city is our home."

"This city is *your* home, Jathan. Not hers. It hasn't been hers for a long time."

"What you are saying makes no sense."

"It makes no sense to you. But to her, it is not a home you are helping her stay in. It is a prison you are forcing her to stay in."

"Forcing her? What?"

"Oh, she would never tell you so. She would never say it aloud. Because she loves you."

"When we were separated after it happened, and sent to live with different sets of secondparents, it was her idea to have Aunt Dresa make the payments so we could keep the house. Jolly Uncle Aren left her a fortune after he died so it was a gift she was glad to give, as long as we stayed together. But it was Lyra who thought up the whole thing. It was her plan that stopped them from sending us to different families. She worked hard so that we could be reunited."

"She worked to save the house because you were both children. Children without a home were torn apart and given to secondparents. You were just a little boy. Her sweet baby brother. She couldn't stand to have you on your own. She couldn't stand to be without you. But you are not children anymore. And she doesn't want to live in the house where her parents died anymore. She doesn't want to eat her meals at the dining table in the very spot where the bodies of her parents were found. Tell me you understand this."

"I..." He thought of nothing to say. He had no witty retort. He had no question to ask. No anecdote to use to change the subject. He was stuck with that one thought. *Our house is a prison.*

Her face softened into a smile so sweet he stepped back from the abyss of tears. "She didn't want me to tell you. But I feel like I finally must. I want you to know she stays here out of love. Not for the romance of strange men. For the love she has for her baby brother. For you. I want you to remember that when you get angry at her, and I want you to remember to cut her some slack."

"I will try."

"You really are so good to her, Jathan. We all know what a good man you are. You just need to learn how to stop sometimes."

"I want to stop."

"I can help you stop. If you let me."

"I want to let you. I don't know if I can."

"I know. And I will never push you, Jathan. I hope you know that."

"I do."

"I just want you to see me when you look at me, and not one thousand other things."

"I want to see you."

His head was spinning. The summerwine wasn't helping. The brandy he snatched from Cristan wasn't helping either.

Nessa's hand on his trousers was helping though. And when she reached over to wrap her arms around him and tell him it would be all right it helped as well. Breathing in her hair and resting his forehead upon her soft shoulder helped even more.

And when he lifted his head up and found her lips there waiting for him it helped most of all. He lost count of how many centuries he sat there, her tongue wrapping around his, back bent awkwardly, her lips mashed against his own in one long unbroken crush.

He lost all concern for what the others might think and he simply devoured her, and let himself be devoured. He could not be certain if it was she who stood first or he, but their mouths never separated through it, even when his leg accidentally kicked his chair over backward. He could not have told how many eyes were on them as they staggered out the door and wandered around the corner to the alley beside it.

He heard music rumbling and twanging through the windows, and the ocean of a hundred different chattering voices washing through it all like a distant surf. The air outside was cool and made him realize how hot it must have been inside by the sweat on his neck and down his chest.

Her hands fumbled at the strings of his trousers while her mouth opened wide for his tongue, wetting his lips, swallowing his mouth. His hands wandered over her shoulders, down her back, lower and lower, grabbing her, squeezing her cheeks, pulling them apart, again, again, again. Every time he did, she released a moan into his mouth, a bit of the sound escaping like steam out the cracks at the corners of their lips.

She had one hand down his trousers before she even managed to get them untied, holding him, hardening him to stone. Her touch was familiar, her fingertips a half-remembered dream roaming between his legs until his trousers dropped to his ankles.

He pulled away from her mouth and lifted her dress, hand over hand, until it was up above her waist, kissing and biting her neck, tasting her salty skin, inhaling her scent, hopelessly lost in her.

One hand drove between her legs, frantic, urgent, searching, pressing over silken hair, sliding on skin, plunging into softness. She was wet as autumn rain spilling across his fingers. Her voice became one long inhale, each new part a higher pitch than the last, until he was not certain if she ever managed to let that breath go.

Her mouth collapsed against his once more as he took her right up to the edge of the little oblivion, hovered there until she begged him with her kisses, and then finally pushed her over it. She shuddered and shook, pressing herself against his palm, squeezing his fingers, her thighs humming with their own subtle earthquake, her head falling onto his shoulder, finally exhaling in an endless moan of relief. Heart racing, legs shaking, breaths churning the air, eyes leaking tears.

She took his chin in one hand and stared hard into his eyes before turning herself around and looking at him over her shoulder, biting her lip, wagging her hips.

Fuck.

He did. He dove into the autumn rain. Carefree as he danced and played. Sweat coated him, dripping down his chest. He couldn't tell if he was still breathing. All he knew was the smell of her, and the feel of her hips beneath his fingers, the wet crush of every thrust, the sharp smack of his hips against her, and the groans each one shook loose from her trembling mouth.

She looked back over her shoulder at him only once, biting her lip, eyes watering, mouth parting to say one word. "Yes."

He felt warmth spreading like hunger across his chest and down between his legs. His eyes glossed over. His breath misted. His fingers clawed at her hips. He was aware his legs were cramping but the part of him that cared was asleep.

She rocked savagely against him, the muscles in her shoulders taught, her palms locked on the wall, pushing back against him, meeting every sway of his hips. She cried out, her skin flushed, heat radiating off her in waves, the smell of her body taking hold of him, the softness of her gripping him so fiercely.

His body dissolved its partnership with his mind. Driving on without him, heedless of the ocean of pleasure he was losing himself in, cutting him loose amid the waves, letting him plow through the swells unguided, to shipwreck on her shores.

"Yes, Jathan," she gasped. "Yes. I want it. Give it to me."

He pulsed against her savagely, rhythmically, like the pounding of drums, driving him onward to oblivion.

"Oh fuck," she said. "Oh fuck."

He spiraled out of control. Overtaking her. Surging into her. Giving her everything. Losing himself inside her.

He released a pair of ridiculous grunts, every muscle straining, veins bulging, hips locked against her, deaf and blind, his body dissolving within her. His legs bowed like reeds, his knees weak. He tipped forward and nearly collapsed atop her, reaching out one hand and pinning it against the wall beside one of her own, holding it there for breath after breath. She moved her hand over until it was on top of his, holding it against the wall, feeling the pulse of his heart through his fingers.

"Yes," she sighed between breaths. "Yes."

He leaned over her for what seemed hours, catching his breath for years, finally sliding out of her after a century had elapsed.

Her dress dropped down over her when she straightened her back. She stood, face flushed, eyes half-asleep. She pulled her hair back behind her head and held it there with one hand, fanning herself with the other. "I do believe I like you quite a lot, Jathan Algevin."

"I do believe I like you, too, Nessifer Everad."

She leaned forward, balanced on her tiptoes to kiss him. Her lips were cold and sweet. He didn't stop until he realized he was kissing her smile. She slapped his cock playfully as she plopped back down on her heels.

"Pull your trousers up, you silly boy," she said laughing.

He reached down for his trousers. The Jecker monocle flopped out of his pocket as he lifted. He cursed and grabbed it, slipping it back to safety.

He managed to get his trousers halfway up his calves before they arrived.

"Look at what we have here," someone said.

He expected it to be Cristan, or maybe Ouleem. But it was not.

It was not one of his friends at all.

It was someone else.

It was a voice he recognized.

It was Ressic.

10

Gangers

JATHAN WOULD HAVE SHIT his pants if they weren't already around his ankles.

Ressic was waiting at the end of the alley. Just shy of ten long strides would have put them face to face. He had all three of his enforcers with him—Pranji, Torp, and Graekor. They were all dressed in their ganger colors—dockwork trousers and blue vests over ivory tunics, sleeves rolled up to the elbows. Ressic had his hair in a topknot, his golden beard catching the lamplight.

Jathan stood staring. Frozen. Unable to believe it. Unable to move. Unable to think. Trousers like shackles about his ankles. His arms and legs were on fire, his hands ice, his knees water, his heart a block of lead.

"Looks like we're just in time," Ressic said, eyeing Jathan and then Nessifer. They sauntered down the alley, hips out, leaning back, laughing grotesquely.

You piece of shit. Don't you dare look at her.

Jathan's heart raced. His mind was flying, searching for a way out of this. He yanked his trousers up and tried to tie them, caught his finger in the knot, stopped, tried again, tied them some kind of terrible, but it held them up at least, freed his legs for movement.

He exchanged a glance with Nessifer. Her eyes were wide, afraid, but her brow was defiant. She would dare them to come anywhere near her.

They made a half-circle about them, hemming them in against the same wall they had been fucking against.

"I hope you didn't think we were done with you, boy," Ressic said.

"I didn't think about you at all," Jathan said, puffing up his chin.

Ressic's gaze fixed on him. "Well, I think you are going to remember this time. For the rest of your life, every time you try to chew you are going to remember what it was like to have teeth, every time you try to walk you are going to remember what it was like to have legs, every time you think of a woman you will remember what it was like to lose one."

"At least I'll be able to remember," Jathan said. "If you try to remember a time before you were ugly, you'll be doomed for eternity."

Ressic's eyes blazed with rage. His knuckles turned white on his fists.

Yes, focus on me. You want me, so hit me. He hoped he could get all their fists onto him at once, such that they would ignore Nessifer and let her slide from their minds, slip away. The door to the Bottlebottom was so close, around the corner. He heard the people inside. There was time. She could get away. She had to get away.

Jathan could take a beating. He had survived enough of them from the time he was a child that he knew how to best cover himself to prevent the most severe damage. They couldn't hit him forever. Someone would hear. Nessifer would warn people inside. He could take it.

But no matter how angry Ressic became, his eyes always glanced over at her, mouth dangling open as he looked at her bare shoulders, her ruffled dress, her unkempt hair. "Isn't she lovely, Torp?"

Torp reached in a hand and snatched a lock of her hair, lifted it, gave it a little tug. "So lovely," he agreed. His hideous toad eyes crawled all over her.

Nessifer leaned her head away from him, but Pranji was already lifting her skirts. She swatted his hand away and he let go, but he just tried again, like it was a game of slap the cobra.

Jathan reached an arm across her trying to dissuade them, but it only brought Graekor's hand in to grab his elbow and throw it aside, his expressionless mask of a face terrifyingly calm.

Jathan's heart was in his stomach. His hands felt cold, numb. Every time he looked at one of them, judged where his hands would go, a different one would reach in, grabbing, pinching, slapping.

Then the grabbing became squeezing, the pinching became tearing, and the slapping became punching. Jathan threw himself in the way of as many as he could, taking open palms and fists.

"Stop!" he said. "Just stop."

"Stop, he says." Ressic laughed. "I don't think you understand how this is going to work."

"We aren't going to stop," Torp agreed. "Not til we've each had both of you."

Jathan stepped in front of Nessifer instead. *Through me first, you stupid shit.*

Pranji swung a fist at him, laughing. Missed. Swung again. Knuckles smacked Jathan's jaw. Head snapped back, ankles went weak. The hulking Hylamari's odor hit his as hard as the fist would have, leaning into every swing like he was trying to crush Jathan into the wall.

Jathan ducked his head to the side in time, but another came. He dodged again. But Pranji only laughed harder. Jathan took a hit to the shoulder, and then one to the gut. He swatted the fists away as best he could, but some kept getting through, hitting, brusing, tearing, cracking.

Every time Jathan deflected a blow with his hands, Graekor pulled at the ties of his trousers until they came loose, forcing him to drop a hand to keep them from falling and tangling his legs.

It wasn't working. They were intent on keeping them both against the wall. He couldn't take enough of their eyes off her. And he couldn't fight them all at once.

There was only one other choice. If Nessifer couldn't slip past them, perhaps he could. His feet danced better than they, and he could bend and twist between them well enough to get by them. From there he would have to try to outrun them, hide from them. Or outlast them.

But he couldn't do any of those things if even one of them remained behind with Nessifer. He needed to free up the path for her to get inside. They would give up once she got close enough to the door, where all it would take was a slap and a scream to the people inside the Bottlebottom. There were big men inside, fighters, drunk enough to fuck up a few gangers and smile about it. And it was not a good look for Vorlo Wauska to have his people seen in the fiestreets, even if it was only Brandytown. It would surely bring eyes to his operation he would rather not have. But if Ressic and his gangers were stupid enough to blow off their actual duties and come here for a lost payday, then they might be too stupid to realize the trouble they would be in.

He wouldn't leave Nessifer alone with any one of them. He wouldn't. He had to make them *all* chase him, or he would stay and fight until they flattened him.

He felt the weight of the monocle in his pocket.

He remembered the first night he found it on the body of a dead Glasseye. He remembered who had been there that night, fighting over his spoils—Wauska's gangers. Ressic may have been a fucking idiot, but he knew what a Jecker monocle looked like. And he knew how much it was worth.

There was only one thing he and his crew wanted more than the simple pleasure of beating him and Nessifer both senseless.

The prize denied to them that night.

It was the only way.

But if I show it to them, it's all over. The game would be up. His nights following Seber would be over. His window into the invisible world of insidious magick all around him would be taken away. Word would spread. Every ganger in the city would be after him, and every magistrate, and every Glasseye from the capital. Even if he publicly surrendered and turned it in and somehow avoided time in a dungeon, gangers would still be coming around Mistine's place looking for him from here to Chal's Day.

It would destroy the life he had meticulously crafted for himself and Lyra.

It would turn all his hard work into dust.

But he would not let one hair on Nessifer's head suffer for his mistake.

That made his decision.

I swore tonight I would make a choice. It seemed now that Ressic had forced his hand.

He looked at Nessifer over his shoulder, made sure her eyes were on his. "Trust me," he said.

She somehow managed to nod without moving anything but her eyes.

Jathan turned back to the gangers, eyes narrowed.

The next fist Pranji jabbed at him, he reached up and caught the wrist, wreathing it with both hands, squeezing, dragging him forward. He pulled Pranji off balance, drew him into a stumble, released one hand, twisted his torso and brought his elbow into Pranji's face. He missed the nose, but he took one of his cheeks with a loud snap. Blacked his eye, cracked the socket.

Pranji cupped his face, went to one knee.

None of them had been expecting that, and the surprise bought him enough time to swat Torp's fist away, spin himself through their grasping hands and dance across the alley until his back slammed into the opposite side. His head smacked on the bricks, but he was away.

They all turned toward him. Graekor even started after him. But Ressic and Torp were still reaching after Nessifer.

Jathan fished the monocle out of his pocket and held it up for them to see. He flipped the cover free and unfurled the rainbow of filters.

Ressic's eyes went wide. "Where...?"

"You see this?" Jathan asked, smiling. "You stupid gangers have been looking for this thing for weeks and I had it the whole time. You let me get away with it every time. And now you're going to let it walk right out of your hands again."

He skipped into a trot, then double-stepped into a run down the alley. When he reached the corner he looked back, one hand holding the corner of the wall.

"Get that thing!" Ressic shouted.

If even one of them wasn't chasing after him, he would go back and face everything. If not, then it was on.

It was on.

"Get him!" Ressic screamed, shrill, more screeching bird than man. "Take it! Get him! Get him! Get him!"

And they were all after him, Graekor out front followed by Torp and Pranji, with Ressic himself whipping them up in the rear.

Jathan tore down the Brandytown Road and took back alleys through the finestreets all the way to Winesink Row, using one of the mudwater holes to hide, hoping to throw them off his trail. It bought him a good twenty seconds as they milled around before they heard him vaulting the white wooden gate on the other side. He ran through one door of the Sturdy Fundament and out the other, leading them along, as the sleezy soothing yellow lamps of Winesink Row faded like the last groping fingers of a dirty sunset.

Every time he glanced back all four were still coming.

But he finally reached Tenement Lane.

The odds of lit lamps from here on were little better than a coin toss. That was good. The pitch would be useful here. Shadows to hide in, voids of opaque darkness to confuse their eyes.

This was the one place that he knew better than any other living person. Even the tenement gangers who lived their whole lives in there did not know every tunnel and every door the way Jathan did.

He ran down the south bowl ramp, cut left through a tenement block tunnel, crossed a tree-crowned atrium, burst out the other side to the next street, cut left, then cut right, then took a switchback until he was nearly running the opposite the way he had come. Everywhere he went he was hemmed in by hulking tenements on all sides, a maze of ravines with old grey stone walls and dark windows.

He watched the gangers fly by in the other direction, but they saw him. They turned. They followed. Tenement Lane was a magnificent place to lose a tail. But he was also under no illusions that he would be dead the instant they caught him.

Jathan ducked into a drainage tunnel, splashed his way through to the other side, ended up in the atrium of another tenement, its tree dry and dead, startling a large family milling about with cups of sour moonwater. He slithered through them and belched himself out into another street.

When his legs began to burn, he realized with stunning clarity that he had not bothered to think up anything remotely resembling a plan. He had assumed they would give up or wear down before long. But the incentive he had given them to follow was too rich a prize. He realized they might outlast him if he was unable to shake them. He needed a way to get rid of them.

He tried to remember the borders of the different ganger territories. If he drew them into another gangers' domain, he might be able to spark a brawl and speed himself away while Ressic and his enforcers were stuck in the thick of it. He wagered he was close enough to Savage Henri, Qleen Town, Togar Roshe's Evergang, and the sweetkillers of Quiet Quenby to make a fair chance of reaching one of them before his wind died or his ankles snapped.

Who had they been fighting that night? When he first found the monocle.

Greencoats. Qleen gangers. But fighting on Evergang territory. That narrowed it to those two. Gangers nursed their grudges like it was an art form.

He raced down a long straightaway with five massive tenement blocks on either side. He had until the next intersection to choose. To the left was Qleen Town, and to the right was the Evergang zone.

But a little thought nagged at him through the anxiety, creeping up and around the edges of his surging heartbeat, seeping through the cracks in his fear.

That no matter which gangers he bogged them down with, his life was over. Wauska would know he had the monocle. Or Soreb Qleen, if they were to take Ressic captive they might be able to beat it out of him, and Ressic was precisely the kind of coward who would volunteer that juicy tidbit to try to by himself a quick release, rather than sit around waiting for Vorlo to negotiate for his freedom.

Someone would inform to the magistrates. They would come round for him, either for justice or for their own corrupt greed. And with a Glasseye in the city looking into the death of his colleague, even if Jathan avoided everyone else, there would still be a knock on his door.

How many days did he have left? Three? Five? How much time before his whole world came crashing down?

Every step closer to the intersection was one step closer to the end of his life. Every heartbeat rattling in his chest was a countdown to the surrender of his freedom.

I'm not ready.

But the world did not care if he was ready.

Sometimes the world dropped your fate in your lap.

Like his parents.

Like the monocle.

Like Seber Geddakur.

Wait.

He finally reached the intersection.

But he did not turn. Not to the left. Not to the right.

He kept going straight.

You are just meat and bone. There is nothing more to you.

He raised the monocle to his eyes and gazed through it as he ran, his lips pulled back, spittle leaking out the corners of his mouth, breaths scraping his throat, burning it like acid.

The night was deep and dark, waiting for one of the moons to rise. Shadows to hide in. Voids to obscure him. Silence to wrap around himself like a blanket.

If he could time it right, he could use the darkness to keep himself whole, while the brash, noisy, careless men on his heels roared toward a fate of destruction.

He took a turn into a tunnel, through another atrium, and out into a switchback alleyway, through another tunnel, kicking a door open, racing up a flight of steps and across the stone slingball park.

The other-dimensional colors splashed across everything. Dozens of examples. More than all he had seen combined. He saw core colors of sapphire blue and pale pink, and sour yellow, and savage purple. They were all distracting him, pulling him away from his goal.

He had to get to the one who terrified him above all others. The one he was obsessed with. The one who had taken over his life.

If I can find him.

He wore the monocle over his eyes as if it was a part of him, another feature of his face. He stared through it and prayed to his mother and father to show him the way, to give him a sign.

And then he saw it.

A splash of silver afterglow on the railing beside a stairwell. He raced toward it, all four gangers hard on his tail. He ran down stone steps leading into a tunnel beneath a tenement wall, then back up the stairs on the other side into an atrium, to another tunnel, across a street.

There he saw more.

He remembered to switch to the blue filter. The afterglow core color was a lush green, like sunlight through emeralds.

He knew who it belonged to.

He saw still more smeared on the edge of a door within a cupola twenty paces away. He barreled through the door. He streaked his fingers across the stain, smudging it onto his fingertips.

He held both fingers up before the monocle. He focused every thought on them to deem which finger-smear of afterglow was blueshifting harder, which direction was taking him closer to the owner of the afterglow.

He blinked. He shook sweat form his eyes. He strained to see the difference as he ran, his vision shaking and blurring, eyes opening wide enough to swallow the world.

He saw it.

One finger a tiny bit more blue. So that was the direction he veered, every step making the fringe color a fuller and sharper blue. He did it again and again. At every turn, before every tunnel and arch. Before every door and walkway. He let the afterglow tell him whether to turn right or left, his memory of the winding maze informing him which turns to avoid, which were blocked, which turned back or dead ended. The layout of Tenement Lane was like a map in his mind.

It was the only thing keeping him alive.

He heard a thunderstorm of footsteps behind him as he went past, around, and through each tenement, along every passage, beneath every atrium tree. His eyes were stinging, but he was unable to close them. He dared not even blink. The afterglow on his fingers turned ever more blue.

He recognized where he was. Around the corner of the next tenement was a hidden atrium overgrown with vines and ferns, a massive oak tree rising above it. Seber Geddakur would always stop at a bench beneath its leaves to eat a slab of fried spiced lamb in a wedge of bread he bought from the midnight frier cart on the edge of Bowl District. He always ate alone on the days before he intended to visit his third mistress, waiting for her husband to be asleep at the bottom of his bottles. No one ever wanted stand or sit anywhere near him. Not even the kind of men who would be wandering the tenements at midnight. He terrified everyone.

Jathan knew there was a tree there. A large one. Overgrown. Thick roots. If he timed it right, he might be able to hide, survive. If he timed it wrong, well, Seber would make sure he had nothing else to worry about for all eternity.

The glow on his fingers was so blue. He had to be close. Jathan's heart froze. His blood turned to stone. His lungs ceased to function. His conscious mind turned and fled from him when it realized where his feet were taking him.

He turned the corner.

He saw the old coat. Seber was sitting down, facing the other way, hunched over something in his hands. He paused when he heard Jathan's footsteps.

There was a large overgrown tree in this atrium, just as he remembered, with branches touching all sides, leaves climbing the walls, roots crawling on the ground before plunging beneath pavement.

Jathan looked over his shoulder and watched the gangers all follow him around it, too. Ressic and Graekor and Torp and Pranji. All four. All here. The only men alive who knew he was the one who had the Jecker monocle. All accounted for.

Seber began to turn around.

That was the moment Jathan sucked in a deep breath and shouted at the top of his lungs. "Seber Geddakur, we've come to take you in!"

Seber completed his turn.

Jathan threw himself to the ground behind a bulbous root snaking along the ground. His body flopped and rolled. He managed to smash both knees and both elbows into the ground, sending shearing pain up and down his limbs. The end of a stick caught on his cheek and tore a gash from chin to eyebrow before he finally skidded to a halt.

He could not tell for certain if Seber had seen him. For a moment he feared the user would sidle up to the trunk of the tree, lean over the root, and blast him to pieces with magick.

But he did not. He addressed his words to the gangers. "Are you the shepherd? Are you one who brings me lambs?"

Ressic started aggressively toward Jathan, only three paces away, hovering over him, looking down at where he lay on the ground. "You little shitsack. I'm going to take a hammer to every bone in your face."

But Seber could not *see* Jathan, only the gangers. So he must have assumed Ressic was speaking to him. It was a violation of their deal.

Jathan barely saw the side of Seber's face over the curve of the root.

Seber's lips peeled back and he spoke. "Lambs. You are only lambs."

"What did you just call me, old man?" Ressic demanded.

Seber did not answer. He walked toward them.

Jathan tried to flatten himself, dissolving into the grass, becoming a part of the root. *Please don't see me. Please don't see me.*

"We are going to break you apart and shit on the pieces, old man," Ressic said.

"You are going to try," Seber said. "That is what is so adorable."

Ressic opened his mouth to mock him once more.

But before he was even able to put voice to words Seber raised his hand and pointed at him. The air whistled and something invisible struck Ressic in the face. His lower jaw exploded, spritzing the grass with blood, showering Jathan with broken bits of teeth. What remained of Ressic's mouth dangled askew from one side of his face, his tongue wriggling and writhing like a hooked worm. He tried to scream but it only sounded like he was gargling blood.

Graekor was so dumbfounded he did not even bother to move. Seber pointed, and Jathan heard wet smacks as invisible objects slapped the big Kolkothan's chest, burrowing beneath the skin, tearing muscle, splitting tendons, shattering bones. His left arm was blasted off his body. It fell to

the ground, still flexing and releasing on its own. By the time the burly
ganger decided to scream, he had already been struck three more times,
snapping ribs and blasting holes out his back. The only sound he made
was the soft squishy hiss as air bled out from deflating lungs. He dropped
to his knees, looked directly as Jathan, and then toppled face-first into the
grass, his expressionless mask mere inches from Jathan's eyes, staring into
them.

Jathan struggled not to vomit.

Torp at least managed to raise both hands above his shoulders in
stupefied surrender, and say, "please." But it did nothing. Seber blasted
his teeth down his throat, crushed his nose to powder and pushed it back
into his brain. He was likely already dead before Seber bored holes where
both bulbous eyes used to be. Torp tipped backwards, his skull cracking
like a stone pot on the ground.

Pranji turned to run and made it halfway back to the corner before
something shot into his spine just above his hips. His legs turned to ooze,
and he went down. He was finished by one more to the base of the skull,
spilling blood and brains out onto the stone.

Ressic was halfway to drowning on his own blood and tongue, his arms
jiggling like a marionette held by an epileptic puppeteer. His eyes looked
down at Jathan and saw him, stared into his eyes.

Seber walked up to him and calmly touched his forehead with one
finger. A hole popped through his skull, and he dropped.

Jathan clutched his head in his hands, face down in the grass. He held
his breath so long he thought he must have already asphyxiated. He was
sure his heartbeat was loud enough to give him away.

Seber hovered above him, looked back and forth across the atrium, then
turned and walked back to his bench. Jathan listened to him patiently eat
the rest of his fried lamb sandwich, bite by bite, while the bodies slowly
drained of blood behind him.

You are just meat and bone.

There is nothing more to you.

No bright light.

Everything just ends.

Jathan dared not move, dared not open his eyes. He took each breath over the course of minutes, terrified that even the faintest hiss of an inhale would bring Seber Geddakur over to mutilate him.

Seber quietly finished his meal, licking his fingers clean.

Jathan had been holding his breath for what felt like centuries. Every exhale took a millennia. He was trying so hard to imitate a dead body that he feared he might fool his own tissue into believing it, that he might think his own death into reality.

He felt a pair of hands brush over him and he screamed inside his own head. His heart exploded in fear. He was certain he had died, his blood becoming steam, his body becoming ash. He could not comprehend so much fear being inside him and not killing him. His mouth barely moved, the only sound escaping him a panicked hiss of breath.

The hands felt around inside his tunic, searching for something.

Jathan lifted his head an inch. Twisted his neck a degree. Turned his eyes as far as they would go.

He saw a small shape in the shadows above him. It was only a child. A little boy. Dressed in rags with an oversized maize-colored coat over them. He looked like a little bear digging for food.

Jathan recognized him. It was the little boy he had held behind the wall to keep him from being seen by Seber Geddakur. *You?* His mind reeled.

The boy noticed his eyes were open. "Where are you hit?" he whispered.

Jathan shook his head the slightest bit, trying to wave him off.

The boy kept checking him. He was searching for wounds.

He thinks Seber struck me. Jathan shook his head again, urgently, over and over. *No, get away. Hide. What are you doing?*

"You saved me," the boy said. "I save you."

"Get out of here," Jathan mouthed the words, barely putting any voice to them. The boy didn't understand he was only playing a corpse. He couldn't fathom someone coming to the sorcerer on purpose. He could not understand someone luring people to the spider's web. "Please go. Before he sees you." *I'm not hurt. I'm pretending. Run!*

But the boy refused to leave him.

Jathan shook one leg, kicking him harshly, making faces, trying to help him understand. "Just lay down. Just lay down."

The boy shook his head. "We don't leave ours."

I am not yours.

He tried to will the boy to run, hide, or simply lay down and stop moving.

But the boy continued trying to find where he needed to apply a bandage.

But the sound of Jathan's tunic moving must have reached Seber. His head shot up. He cocked it to one side, listening. Then one arm shot out, pointing behind him, past Jathan, aiming for the sounds the boy made without bothering to look.

Jathan lifted his leg and kicked out, his heel caught the boy's sternum, shoving him over.

But not fast enough.

An invisible projectile struck him in the belly before the boot hit. Blood roared out. The boy tried to speak but no sound came out. He tipped over onto Jathan, collapsing against him, arms out, as if laying down for a nap.

No! Jathan flailed in agony. *Please no.*

Seber did not bother coming over. He heard the same silence Jathan heard. And he saw the same bodies unmoving in the grass. He had no reason to check his accuracy. He knew he had hit. And his eyes saw those of the boy begin to roll back before he even fell. He did not come to check on his work.

Jathan felt his trousers and the bottom of his tunic slowly warm and soak. He saw so much red.

He tried to reach the boy back through time. *Don't make noise. Don't move. He'll hear you. Please. No, no, no.* But the boy was already hit. It was too late. Jathan kept wishing his warnings anyway.

He was so certain Seber was going to walk over and finish them both, as he had done to all the others.

But he didn't.

He rose, smoothed his coat, and strolled calmly out of the atrium, disappearing beyond the lamp light to a tunnel back out into Tenement Lane. Off to see his third mistress.

Jathan did not move until it seemed that hours had passed, but it was only seconds. He finally lifted himself off the ground. He looked at each of the bodies, so still that they were like mere objects that had always been there.

Magick doesn't change when it touches flesh. Only the flesh does.

He flipped the boy onto his back, hands rifling through his coat. There was an ocean of a blood puddle between them, the boy's face cold chalk, arms limp, jaw slackened. Jathan's probing fingers found the wound, slipping into the edge, blood flushing out onto his hand.

Oh no. Please no. Oh damn all the fucking gods at once.

He tore the boy free of his coat, lay him gently on his back. Pressed the coat against the wound. Felt cold skin. Saw vacant eyes. He did not feel a heartbeat. He shook the boy. He pressed on his chest in a steady heavy rhythm. He punched his sternum over and over again.

Please don't die.

Jathan slumped back onto his knees, arms limp and useless, hands in his lap, head tilted back, looking up at the sliver of sky above.

He heard the footsteps of a dozen people, echoes coming from every direction, filtering in from every arch, passage, or tunnel. He did not bother opening his eyes. If it was gangers, they would kill him, and he would deserve it. If it was Jansi and Mister Shine and all her people, they would kill him, and he would deserve it then, too.

He opened his eyes and saw her there, wearing her same clothes, leather sewn upon leather, keeping her tight coat in use three lifetimes longer than it should have been worth.

Jansi Wake.

He already knew the look that would be on her face, the sorrow buried beneath a thousand feet of stone, the grim resolve making her teeth grind, the raw anger of an oracle being proven true.

The boy would never have been here if it hadn't been for Jathan. He would have been somewhere else, safe. Not here. Not with the one man who sought out the danger of the ghost sorcerer.

She had been right. Simply by being here, Jathan had brought about pain. He caused this agony to exist. He was the maker of his own sorrow. He had fashioned it out of his desire, out of his selfishness, out of his obsession.

He made it for himself, but also for all these many other people.

He saw the bald head of Mister Shine, sharp eyes, soaring nose. He saw another man, wearing a coat of many pockets, over a tunic with layer upon layer of belts, straps, loops, and pouches. He was younger than the bald man, but older than Jathan, hair like shivers of black grass, a white scar running down his cheek. Others, men, women, and children of all ages, came together with them, gathering as one.

Then he finally heard what he had been dreading. The moaning wail of pure terror and agony that could only be the boy's mother. Her voice speared through him, like a dirge made of cold steel. Her cry was one long slice of a blade, splitting him open, emptying him onto the ground.

She shoved her way to the fore, falling to her knees like a mountain crashing down, mouth twisted in a tortured rictus, eyes bursting with tears. Her hands drifted down to him like feathers, feeling the boy's chest, head thrown back, screaming up at the stars. Arms scooped him up and pulled him into an embrace. His ghost-white face lay on her shoulder, arms limp. Asleep for the final time.

Jathan felt like he had been bled out, his veins full of nothing but ash, his stomach a stone, his eyes falling into his face and dropping into the very center of him.

The boy's little eyes were closed at least. It made him look like he was at peace. Jathan almost fooled himself into thinking that he was.

You are just meat and bone.

There is nothing more to you.

No bright light.

Everything just ends.

Jathan stared so long at him that his eyes felt like they had turned to glass, his legs grown into the ground like roots, locking him here in this one spot forever. Like the tree.

Some of the other people jostled him. Most did not feel intentional, but some certainly were. He did not react. Did not even move. He felt shoulders and elbows knock him this way and that. They were the very strikes that only hours ago would have seen him turn and bake the shape of his fist into each of their faces.

But he couldn't.

His anger was meaningless now.

It didn't matter anymore.

It had probably never mattered.

He had only had the luxury of pretending that it did all these years.

"His name was Ebel," Mister Shine said. Jathan recognized his smooth bald head, a fine gloss to the skin. He wore a tunic with short sleeves, showing off slender bony elbows wedged between thick muscle in biceps and forearms. His eyes were thin lines, his forehead half the height of his face.

"Ebel," Jathan repeated.

"Ebel Soar," the man said. "That is his mother, Mina."

"I...I'm sorry."

"You had better be," Mister Shine said. He had to be barely older than Jathan. He had the same slits for eyes as the old man, but his hair rose and arched like a tube wave on a Kolcha beach.

"He is, Ben," Jansi said. "He is."

He was. But hearing Jansi say it for him made it worse.

"My son is emotional," an old, wrinkled grey said. "He loved Ebel dearly. He was teaching the boy to use his power."

"Power?" Jathan asked. "You mean magick." *Abomination.* He could barely keep his mouth from sneering at them. He knew he was supposed to hate them both. But then he looked at the boy. The boy was no monster. He was so small. He couldn't hurt anyone.

Ben Shine nodded. "Little Ebel was learning how to help our people light the ovens to cook their food. The city-funded wood piles sometimes run low by the time they get to us. He was going to be a great help to us."

Ebel's mother burst into sobs again.

"Now he's gone," Ben said.

"Forgive me," the old, wrinkled grey said. "Introductions to strangers are rare for us. I am named Wikal Shine. This is my son, Ben. Mister Shine. You may remember that little girl there. Her name is Lani Shine, my granddaughter. She is the other child you saved that night."

Jathan turned to look over his shoulder. He recognized her, curious brown eyes, curly hair. She hovered over the mother, Mina, peering down at the boy's lifeless body.

"And for that we are all ever grateful," a third man said, stepping forward between the others. This man dressed in a long dark coat, collar turned up high, his jet-black hair rising and unfurling on his head. He had piercing blue eyes, a slender face, and a slender frame. "But surely Jansi warned you that things happen differently in our world. The rules are of a different sort here in Tenement Lane."

Jathan nodded. "She did."

"I am Lanhamer Rise," the man said. "I am a teacher and a warrior and an artist and a father. I like to use every bit of my skills to help my people, to lift them up to their potential, to help them rise and hold their heads high."

Jathan nodded. "Family is family, whether in blood or no. I get it."

"Do you?" a young man asked. His whole damn face was a sneer.

"This is Ravi Soar," Jansi said. "He is Ebel's brother."

That one hates me with a fury. "I do. I know how important family is. And I know what it's like to lose them."

"Do you know what it's like to be hunted?" Ravi asked. "Every day of your life? Do you know what it's like to raise children knowing there is a monster who walks the same places they will play every day?"

"No," Jathan said. He glanced at the boy again. He couldn't stop himself, no matter how much it hurt to see him each time.

"He has been following the children for a long time," Lanhamer said. "He knows we will fight the hardest to protect them. He knows it will lure us out to face him. That is what he wants."

"What?" Jathan asked. "What does he want?"

"Us," Ben Shine said. "The magi of Tenement Lane."

"So, he isn't after normals."

Ravi sneered. "Only if they get in his way. He would walk right past you, lushborn. If he didn't see that glass eye of yours."

Jathan nodded reflexively. "And he isn't after the gangers."

"Why would he be?" Ravi asked. "They pay most of the magistrates around here to look the other way. Their corruption is helping him. Your corruption, lushborn."

Jathan recoiled. He looked down at the boy, ice white. "My corruption."

Jansi frowned, closed her eyes to swallow tears back up. She took Jathan's hand. "This is what I meant. Do you understand now? Do you know how angry I am with you?"

Jathan recoiled. "I didn't mean for this to happen." He looked into her infinite eyes. "Are you? Like them?"

"Not me. I am a normal, named so by the ones who call everyone else abnormal. But we live side by side with ones who are. They are a part of our community. They are our family. They are our friends. We do not burn our friends."

He was about to spew an insult about them, but her last words shook the conviction right out of him. "You do not cast them out. No wonder I have seen so much afterglow here."

Lanhamer nodded. "The magistrates almost never come here. The gangers hold us in such a grip. Only the most honorable magistrates in all the world would set foot in this place. And Kolchin is not known for its honorable magistrates. They are as likely to be as lazy as they are to be in the pocket of the gangers themselves."

I think I witnessed the only handful of honorable magistrates in the city my first night in here. And they did not survive one minute in the face of Seber Geddakur. "But why does he hunt you? His own kind?"

Jansi shrugged. "Why do you normals spend your nights and days hurting each other? Because you can. Because you like to. Because there is no one to stop you."

Jathen felt the tightness in his knuckles still from when he had cracked a jaw and rattled teeth. His body still ached from the fists and boots of Ressic Wauska's gangers. "He likes killing your magi. He likes the challenge."

She nodded. "He is always smiling." She paused. "You may have noticed that he always seems to be where we are, where our street children walk."

"Yes. The children. They stumble upon him."

"That is not because we are fools who let our children run into dangerous places," Lanhamer said. "These children have no homes in the tenements. Their families can only sleep in the tunnels, in the walkways, beneath the bridges, in the alleyways. And many of them have more children that they can keep track of as it is."

"They live in this?"

Lanhamer nodded. "Some have no choice."

"They hide as best they can," Wikal said. "We help each other however we are able."

Jansi grimaced.

Lanhamer nodded. "They hide, but he always finds them. He finds them because he is hunting them. He moves from neighborhood to neighborhood. He is in a new place every night."

"Hundreds of families sleep in fear whenever the stars come out," Wikal said. "Always in an unfamiliar place just hoping that it will not be one of the ones he walks down that night."

"We do not stumble upon him," Lanhamer said. "He comes to us. He waits for us. That is why some of us keep watch." He nodded to Jansi.

Jansi looked up, mouth frozen somewhere between a smile and a frown, eyes frozen somewhere between glass and oceanwater. "We send warnings to the rest of our people when we can. Sometimes we are too late. But we always try."

"It sounds like hell," Jathan said. He was feeling his thoughts peeling back, exposing raw stinging emotion. He should not have felt any sympathy for users of magick. He should have been glad Seber Geddakur was cleaning them out of Kolchin. But he wasn't. He couldn't be. Because if he said it aloud it would be the most horrific thing he had ever said. His mind wanted to hide that thought way down deep where it wouldn't have to do battle with it, but it kept rising.

Jansi looked at her feet. "I was born Jansi Give. When I was grown to a woman, I chose another name. I chose the name of the thing I do. I run rooftops, following a monster through our streets. I watch where he goes, and if he comes too close to where the roofless families are sleeping, I come down and I wake them. I wake people up. To hopefully save them from being killed. That is my name. That is what it means. I wake people up. And that is all I will do for the rest of my life."

"Why can't you just leave?" Jathan asked. "Go. Run. Get out of here. All of you. Leave Tenement Lane and never come back."

Ben laughed.

Wikal shook his head.

Mina held her child close.

Jansi looked away.

"We can't leave," Lanhamer said. "Many of us have tried. Some still do. But the lushborn don't suffer us to walk their finestreets."

Ravi snorted. "They kick us. They spit on us. They throw rocks at our children. They call the magistrates on us. If we spend one night under the stars out on the finestreets they beat us or imprison us. They don't let us exist out there. We always end up back here or face down in the Float."

Jathan did not believe what he was hearing. "Beachside? West End? Tannery Town? There must be someplace."

Wikal shook his head. "If we go there, we find the gangers are there waiting for us too. And the magistrates. And the lowers and the deservingless who live all their generations in those places make common cause to get rid of us so that their tiny pie doesn't shrink any further."

"We are not permitted to exist outside this maze," Ben said.

Wikal nodded, but his mouth bent into a smile of pride. "But at least we know where we are here. We can meet fate on our own terms. It is all we have. Starve to death in your streets out there or hide and scrape by in our own."

Jathan felt anger bubbling up, he thought it might rupture his skin if he didn't keep it under control. "So many troubles and then this killer on top of it."

Jansi nodded. "Seber is the one thing standing between us and rising against the gangers. Our people are strong. And determined. We want to be free of them all. We have struggled and strived."

Wikal was still as stone. "We have tried to kill him, destroy him, throw him out. Every time has ended in disaster. Every plan has failed. Everyone who chose to rise against him, to face him down, to ambush him, has paid with their lives in the attempt."

"He is too powerful," Lanhamer said. "The best one hundred of our people with special talents combined could not match the power of one finger on his hand. His power and skill and experience combined in one man is a once in a generation event in a city like Kolchin."

"He is like a god," Jansi said. "How do you kill a god?"

Jathan didn't know. Maybe you couldn't. Maybe there was no way to stop a sorcerer when they became what he was. If all the magick users, magistrates, gangers and citizens of Tenement Lane couldn't stop this one man, how could anyone?

But Jathan wanted to. He wanted to stop him now. Nothing would make him forget that now.

"This is how we live," Ben said. "This is the life people like you made for us."

Jathan nodded. "I wish there was something I could do."

"There is nothing you can do," Jansi said. "That is the whole point."

He kept glancing back at the boy. His mother was rocking his little body back and forth in her lap, singing quietly to him. "I need to do something."

"You can do something," Jansi said. "You can leave. Go. Get out of here."

"I can't just leave," he protested.

"Look at this," Jansi nearly sliced him open with her whisper. "Look what your help has done. Look at him. This is what happens when you bumble in here and try to help."

"I didn't know."

He saw a tear fall from her eye. "Please just go, Jathan. Please."

It was the first time he could ever remember her saying his name in earnest. It stopped the words in his mouth. He looked at his feet. He looked back up at her. There was nothing else to say. He turned his back to her and walked away.

"See you around, lushboy," she said.

"No, you won't." He didn't turn around.

He flowed out of Tenement Lane like water down a hill. He was gone. He was finished there. That dark mysterious underworld was in the past now. He was leaving it behind.

She was right. He was never supposed to be in that world. He should never have gone into it. He should never have taken the Jecker monocle. He should have just left it all alone.

He had been so happy not knowing. He had been so happy when these places and these people and this magick and all of it didn't exist for him. He changed everything by deciding to look where he didn't belong.

It was all over.

It was time to go home.

He staggered back across the city. He did not remember navigating his way out of Tenement Lane, or across the Bowl, or up Winesink Row. He did not remember passing Brandytown or the Promenade. He did not remember slipping past the gate at Fencepost Pike. He did not remember any step along the way. He did not remember to look for afterglow. He trudged up the finestreets until he finally made it home.

He opened the front door and left it ajar. He threw the high cabinet door open. His fingers swam through the glass containers there, every shape and color, green and violet and many others between a forest of brown for the wine. He sought something as heavy as his thoughts. He scooted the bottles of wine and whatever else out of the way, carefully avoiding the whiskey that had been opened the day his parents had died.

He took the bottle of brandy that had been in the cabinet for a year. He sat in the dining room in darkness, drinking brandy while his feet rested on the same floorboards where they had found his parents' bodies. He passed out in the chair, fingers still cradling the neck of the bottle resting in his lap.

He woke once in the early hours, still black as pitch, to see Lyra awake, wrapping a blanket over his shoulders and tucking it around him. He felt her take the bottle from his fingers. He heard her cork it and place it back in the cabinet. She removed his boots, put a step stool beneath his feet, and wedged a pillow between the backrest and his neck. Then she left.

His eyes closed again and did not open them until dawn.

11

The Bottom Of The Bottle

JATHAN WAS ALREADY DRUNK before noon.

He hadn't bothered to go to work. He was sure Mistine was furious about now. In another hour or two she would begin to worry.

He took another swig of brandy.

The Bottlebottom looked so different at this time of day. Light streamed in through the skylights and windows that he was used to being pitch black when he was here at night. There were so few people, and yet everything seemed louder. The daylight was like a horn, amplifying every sound in his memory.

He sat in the same chair he had the night before, where he had kissed Nessifer, on one lonely side of an empty ten-seat table five quick strides in the door. He was staring at the wall. On the other side of it was the alley where they had both been attacked the night before.

He had an untouched glass of summerwine on the table, something to sip from if anyone he knew showed up. Until then, he would take the brandy, one gulp at a time.

He blinked and saw the little boy's face carved from empty ice.

He swallowed more brandy.

He watched little scullions mopping last night's vomit. The smell was foul enough, but it did not make him sick. Nothing so ordinary made him feel that way anymore.

He closed his eyes and saw the pain etched into his mother's face.

He took another swig of brandy.

He blinked and saw blood pouring out of a man's neck.

He needed another brandy already.

One by one his friends came in.

Nessifer was first. She came through the open doors like a hunter, looking for him, finding him, eyes going wide. She flew to him, dropping to her knees, one hand on his leg the other cupping the scrape on his face, brushing back his hair. Her eyes were wide and worried. The corners of her mouth curled down in those little arcs that said she only wanted to care about him and only wanted to know he was all right.

He glanced down at her, smiled out of reflex when he saw her face, then looked away before he fell apart.

"I looked for you at home," she said. "Ouleem said you didn't come to work today."

He nodded, fingers swirling the rim of the wine glass, another cup of brandy lurking behind it. "I came straight here."

"I looked for you last night," she said. "I waited here all night, until the last beat of the drums, the last pluck of the lute. I waited until they extinguished the candles and closed the doors. And then I waited outside."

He wanted to reach out to her, to throw his arms around her, and bury his head in her shoulder and let himself feel her warm heartbeat and breathe her hair.

But when he blinked, he saw dead eyes staring at him in the grass, rough bark scraping his cheek, blood leaking in a slow flood toward him, wetting his face.

He threw back more brandy. But it was already not enough.

He saw the boy's eyes eternally open, staring back into him forever. *Ebel. That was his name. It would be his name still if not for me. If not for Seber. If not for Ressic. If not for the day I found the damned monocle and every day since.*

He drank more. And more. And more.

She noticed. "Jathan..."

"I'm sorry I wasn't there," he said. "I'm sorry I didn't come back."

Her eyes were full of sadness, but he saw anger in the way her jaw clenched. "I was so worried about you I thought I was going to be sick. I thought I was going to have to lie down in the gutter. I couldn't feel my legs."

"I'm all right. I was all right last night. I lost them."

"I don't want you walking alone for a while," she said. "They knew who you were. They could come here again and..."

"They will never come her again," he assured her.

That stopped her. She paused, mouth closed for three long breaths. "What do you mean?"

"I mean we won't ever have to worry about them again." He wanted to tell her more, but he couldn't make himself say it.

"Did you do something? Are you in trouble? What did you do, Jathan?" She was half-fear and half-anger again.

"Don't ask me that. Just trust me. We are safe from them now." He blinked and saw the little boy in his mother's arms, eyes closed forever.

She didn't ask him about it again. She waited a long time. "What was that thing? That made them chase you? What was it?"

"Don't ask about that either," he said. "It is something you are far better off not knowing."

"What have you gotten yourself into, Jathan? What is going on? You have been different lately. Like you are somewhere else all the time."

"Nothing."

"What was that thing?"

"Stop asking me about it. Damn all the fucking gods at once, just shut the fuck up about it."

She laughed half a laugh, until she realized he was not being playful. He was not joking with her. Her face cooled to ice.

He blinked and saw a man's face crushed and crumpled, he felt teeth bouncing off his cheek while he pissed himself in the grass. "Stop concerning yourself with what I do."

She recoiled from him. "I thought...I..."

"You thought what?" he snapped.

Her mouth bent into a frown so full of hurt it crippled him. His arms and legs became lead, and everything inside him screamed at him to say he was sorry, and that it wasn't her fault, and that he was a twisted mess, and all he wanted to do was hold her in his arms, but he couldn't say it. He couldn't. He didn't know what was wrong with him. He should have told her that, too, but he couldn't. His mouth wouldn't move.

"I always thought you told me everything," she said. "I thought you liked to...I thought..."

"What do you want from me?"

"I just wanted to know you were all right."

He pointed at himself. "I'm here, aren't I? I'm alive. Now you are free to go on living your life. Your question is answered."

Her frown turned into a bitter scowl. "I waited alone all night because I was afraid you were hurt. I was afraid you were lying alone in some gutter, needing me, needing someone to find you. I was afraid you would call out and if I went home, I wouldn't be able to hear you. I was afraid if I went home, it meant I would never see you again. I was afraid if I gave up on you then the gods would let you die."

He laughed condescendingly. "Well, you worried for nothing. Your gods didn't kill me."

She rose to her feet, looking down at him, hands clasped at her waist. "Thank you for keeping them away from me." She said it formally, perfunctorily, like thanking a nightwatchman for shooing a mangy old dog.

He waved his hand dismissively. "You're welcome." He lifted his cup of wine and looked away out one of the windows.

He couldn't see her face, but he knew she was crying. He heard a tiny sob escape her lips, and he knew for that one he heard there were twenty more that she swallowed back down and hid. He knew if he turned to face her, he would see tears on her cheeks.

He waited until he heard her turn and walk back out the door.

She was gone.

No one in all of history had ever hated anything more than he hated himself in that moment.

He set the full wine cup back on the table untouched. He reached for the velvet brandy hidden behind it and took another swill to chase the blood of a dying child away.

It was either a few minutes or a few hours before Cristan and Ouleem showed up with Branderin in tow, his face was bruised to hell and back, one eye swollen, lip fat and purple like a ripe garden grub. He had at least three days' growth of beard on his face, which was startling to see on someone as kempt as Branderin.

They set him down in a chair across the table form Jathan. They both clapped him on the shoulder.

"There's the lad again," Cristan said. "I see you found your way out of Nessifer's mouth long enough to have a drink." He heaved with laughter in his old ivory shortcoat, jingling the dozen pendants around his neck.

"By the many gods, look at him," Ouleem said. "It's barely noontide and he's already at the bottom of his bottles." Ouleem watched him closely. "Are you all right, Jathan? You look like you've been to hell and back and paid the price." He rolled up his blue sleeves as if the question meant he would have to labor to get an answer.

"You could say that," Jathan said.

"Well shit and shit and shit some more," Cristan said. "Now I have two of you bastards to nurse back to health."

"You weren't at work today," Ouleem said. "Mistine is going to break you in half when she finds out you were sitting here with your head stuffed down a bottle."

Jathan shrugged. "I don't care. It doesn't matter right now. She'll get over it."

Ouleem rolled his eyes. "If you say so. At least you didn't have to hide from that creeping Glasseye. He came around again. Three times. He left quick enough though.

Looking for me. What in the seven hells does that filthy creature want from me?

He asked the question, but he knew the reason.

Jathan glanced at Branderin, but the man refused to make eye contact. He looked like his tunic was a day dirtier than Jathan's, and it was wearing thin. "What happened to you?" Jathan asked.

Branderin took a long time to answer. Too long for Cristan's liking, and by the time Branderin's mouth began to move, Cristan was already shouting across the table. "They dumped him at the edge of Bridgetown two days ago.   Rolled him down the Hillroad Crossing, the fucking bastards. Paden and Swani found him, and since their arms are unsuited to lifting anything heavier than a pair of twigs, they came and got me.

"What in all hells were you doing there?" Jathan asked, sipping a newly delivered cup of brandy. "Which gangers crossed you?"

"It wasn't gangers," Branderin said.

"No?" Jathan was confused. More so than just what his bottom bottling would account for.

"I was following your advice," Branderin said.

Jathan spit half his mouthful back into the cup. "My advice?"

"You told me to go see your friends, Vaen Osper and Felber Klisp. Go see them, you said. They might be able to help."

"Where did they send you?" Jathan asked. "Please don't tell me those smelly shits sent you looking into Bowl District or Tannery Town. That is ganger territory." He was angry. The brandy made him forget his pain by making him remember his rage.

Branderin seemed confused. He looked down at his hands on the table. "No. No, they didn't send me anywhere. They beat me."

Jathan set his cup down on the table. "They beat you?"

"They beat me."

"*They* beat you. The magistrates beat you."

"I went to them to ask about my sister, like you said. I said she had last been seen out on Winesink Row heading the wrong way home, heading toward Beachside. They told me to walk into the sea. It made me so angry, the way they dismissed me like that, the way they dismissed her. Like they didn't even care."

"This sounds all wrong," Jathan said.

"They told me to go, but I wouldn't leave. I stood up for myself. I demanded that they help me find my sister. I asked them if they even cared about the people in their district."

"What happened?"

"One of them struck me over the head. I fell. Then they beat me with fists and kicked me on the ground."

Jathan leered at him skeptically. "That can't be all. You must have done something else to provoke them. They wouldn't have just attacked you."

Branderin gave him a stricken look. "They told me to stop looking for my sister. They told me she probably ran away. They told me I shouldn't bother with a runaway whore. They spit on me."

He opening his mouth to speak but stopped. *That sounds like something a shit like Vaen Osper would do to someone who got between him and his money.* The way he had been acting of late seemed to align with Branderin's story. But it made no sense. None. Why would simply asking for help cause a beating?

What the fuck is happening to the world?

Jathan's head spun. He wasn't sure if it was the brandy or Branderin's story. He tried to close his eyes before his stomach returned its contents to him, but he saw a man with bloody eyes and no mouth.

His eyes flashed open, and he nearly vomited across the table. He saw Branderin staring at him.

"You think I'm lying," Branderin said. The bruises made his eyes look sunken in, twice as sorrowful as usual.

Cristan yawned and reached out a hand to playfully swat his shoulder. "No, he doesn't. None of us think you're lying. We just think you forgot a piece of what happened."

"I am not forgetting anything," Branderin insisted.

"Vaen and Felber come around all the time," Ouleem said. "I have seen them at Mistine's before. They do not seem like the kind of magistrates who would raise a finger to do anything. The don't get angry about anyone."

Except their money spigots apparently. But how did a missing girl in Beachside have anything to do with the sources of a magistrate's coin?

"Something set them off," Branderin grumbled.

"I'll talk to them," Jathan promised. *I have to give them Seber anyway. Don't I?*

He let the others argue back and forth over what kind of blasphemy would make a magistrate lose his cool, going around and around in circles.

But the more he thought about it, the more he wondered if he was still prepared to give his secret sorcerer up. The only ones who knew about the monocle were Lyra and Trabius. Ressic's crew had gone to graves without telling anyone. And when a man is gone to grave, he doesn't tend to say much after that. *The murder-dead tell no tales.* Even Nessifer didn't know what precisely he had shown last night.

Do I still have to give it up?

He thought of the gangers standing at the mouth of the alley. Looking for him. Waiting for him. It was an ambush. A pack of gangers from Tenement Lane wouldn't have known the Bottlebottom from a hole in the head.

How did they know I would be there?

Someone must have told them he would be there. It was the only way. Who else knew he was going there that night? Cristan of course. And that meant Sethleen and Ouleem knew. And probably Lyra. But that was it. Even Nessifer had not known he was going to be there until she arrived.

He couldn't think of anyone else he had told.

What the fuck is going on?

He felt a tingling in his spine, fine hairs standing straight. He practically felt fingers running up his neck. The day faded. The light turned grey. Scullions emerged to light the hundreds of candles, standing on ladders to reach every wick with flame.

Before he could blink, the Bottlebottom was full to the brim with a raucous ocean of sweating bodies, talking and colliding and swaying and dancing and moving. Wine flowed like waterfalls, and plates of spiced meats and potatoes floated like lifeboats lost at sea.

Sethleen arrived with two of her gossipy friends, gave Cristan a kiss and a cocksqueeze, and swayed into the next room to converse at exponential volumes.

The way they all pawed at each other made his mind snap back to the night before, the way the gangers pawed at Nessifer, the way they swiped at him.

He glanced out the front door and thought he saw a man in blue trousers and a blue vest. *A Wauska ganger? Again?* He blinked. The ganger vanished, either down the street or back into his imagination. *Was he real? Are they following me?* He was imagining it. Had to be.

"I need a sword," he said abruptly.

Everyone stopped and turned to face him. The table was silent for a long exhale. Cristan abruptly burst into laughter, an arm hanging off the back of the empty chairs on either side of him. He tilted his head so far back Jathan thought it would roll right off his neck.

Ouleem joined him, though nervously. Even Branderin gave a chuckle.

"What are you laughing about?!" Sethleen shrieked over her shoulder from the next room.

"Nothing!" Cristan called back. "Shut up!"

She made the Bravonian finger at him and went back to whatever three drunken conversations she was entangled in.

"You aren't serious, are you, Jathan?" Ouleem seemed genuinely frightened by his statement, even more than he had been at the idea of Branderin being beaten by magistrates.

"I am serious. I want one. I think I need one. I need it now."

"For what?" Cristan asked, laughter infusing his every word. "So, if someone accosts you, you can what? Model it at them? You don't know the first thing about handling a sword."

"And you do?"

"I have used one. I trained. It's a long time ago now. Doesn't matter. All that matters is without at least *some* training you are twice as likely to cut yourself with one as you are to wound an enemy."

"You are trying to talk me out of it."

"The city guard can spot a hidden sword. The new law says no swords on the streets. Trier's rules. Been Lord Protector less than half a year and already he has nearly done away with the epidemic of street dueling. His police up in Vithos, the Orange, they call them, they crack heads open over even *seeing* a sword in the capital. Now, Kolchin's city guards may not crack heads, but they definitely crack down so hard on it even the gangers judged it more profitable to switch to clubs and knives."

"Can you get me one or not?" Jathan pressed him.

Cristan turned to Ouleem. Ouleem shrugged. Cristan rolled his eyes. "Yes, I know a man. But it is not cheap. And the city guard have gotten quite good at spotting a hidden sword in the cloak. So you best know full well what you are getting into with one."

"I don't even know if I can afford one," Jathan admitted. "For now, at least." After he turned in Seber Geddakur to Vaen and Felber for triple the reward, he would have enough right away to at least get himself a five-fold broadsword with a spot of rust on it. It would not be a fancy longsword obviously. But it would be sharp and tough, and it would make blood come out wherever he stabbed it. That was all he needed. Until things settled down.

He thrummed his fingers on the table for what felt another hour.

And then...finally...Lyra arrived.

She was so busy making her greetings with the half a hundred friends she had not seen all week, that she had nearly finished her first glass of wine before she noticed Jathan was there.

Her eyes widened enough that he could tell even across the room. She flew to him. "I wasn't expecting you, brother."

"Does my being here affect your plans?" *With your magick-using lover?*

She looked up, rolled her eyes around, face wrinkling. "No. Why would it?"

"You are sure you don't need to go warn someone they might be better off not meeting you here?"

Her expression soured. "No, I don't. But now I want to know why you think there would be."

"I bet you do," he said. He looked down at his cup of brandy, realized he couldn't remember when he last sipped at it. He lifted it and gulped in anger.

"What is that supposed to mean?"

"Meaning your tiptoeing around the truth is growing a little stale."

She gave a horrified look.

Because she knows she has been caught.

"What have you been doing?" she demanded.

"What's the matter, sweetest sister of mine? Afraid I'll *see* the truth?" He slipped the monocle from his pocket and held it drunkenly to his eyes.

She swatted his hand aside so hard he felt the sting on the back of his hand. "Don't point that thing at me. I hate that you still have that. It's disgusting."

"It is suiting me better than the dead man who lost it," Jathan said. "I am going to find out. You might as well stop hiding it. I'm tired of your lies."

"Have you been this gigantic of a hole of an ass all day? Nessifer's half-brother says she has been upset all evening."

"Stop trying to bring her up to change the subject."

"I'm not. And fuck you, by the way. How dare you insinuate I would use my friends—our friends—as props to play some strange little rhetorical game with you."

"Afraid you'll lose the game?"

"You are being an ass. And I am not playing your game at all."

"If you say so."

She snarled at him. "What is wrong with you? You are not being you. You are being some shit person I don't even know. Enjoy your drinks alone."

"I will," he assured her. "I'm going to find out who it is, you know," he called out after her as she walked away.

"Good for you," she shouted over the twanging strings of the zinges. "Find out whatever you want. Maybe then you can go back to being kind again!" She crossed the dance square and vanished into another room.

He slapped the brandy cup off the table. He watched it bounce and chip and tumble across the floor, dodging some feet and smacking into others. He waved his hand until another cup came for him.

Shit. I shouldn't have said anything. Now she'll just double down on hiding it. But it was too late. The words were out. He could no more stop them than he could stop the sun from setting in the west.

He closed his eyes and felt the bite of men being torn apart in front of him. *Out, thoughts. Out. Get out of my head. Get out from behind my eyelids.*

How can I make them go away?

He leaned one arm on the table edge, forehead resting on it, his other hand a claw around his brandy cup. He sat there as the music swirled and the conversations swelled. The room grew hot. His thoughts grew hotter. All he thought of was Seber ruthlessly killing the gangers. Of the little boy cold and lifeless in his arms, the wetness of the blood soaking his tunic.

It made him think of the way he had found what happened to his parents, the blood. What remained of them had already been taken away. His only evidence of what had happened was seeing the spaces their bodies had occupied, outlined in their dried blood, so dark, nearly black in the candlelight, with beautiful and horrible sparkling silver clouds floating and hissing and steaming above them.

He always closed his eyes and imagined what they looked like, what their final moments had been like. But only for a moment. If he tried for longer his mind would switch to trying to imagine what their killers had looked like. Magi. Murderers. The thieves who crept up and stole the best part of life from him.

It made him think of the afterglow he had seen in their house, in Lyra's room, on her doorknob, on her undergarments, on her body where that scum had touched her.

I need to end this. He decided the next time he saw the afterglow in their house he would take samples and hunt the bastard down right then. He would gather some of it and follow it the way he had followed Seber's all the way to find him in Tenement Lane.

If he could do it with four murderous gangers on his tail, then he could do it when he was all alone with no problem.

He scowled so long and hard his cheeks began to ache from it. His eyes watered.

Lyra, why? Why are you doing this to us?

He felt only half alive. He felt like a ghost amid all these people. He felt no one understood what was happening to him. No one could know what it was like. No one could help him. No one could save him. He was on his own. Adrift.

He felt so utterly alone.

Cristan laughed and sweated in his ear. Ouleem patted him on the back like good friends do when they think they are helping by being there.

But Jathan *wasn't* there. He was nowhere.

He sobbed into his arm, touching the brandy to his lips, just enough to coat them in the flavor.

Sethleen was beside him at one point, kissing at his neck, working her hand between his legs, her tongue going in and out of his ear. She slipped into his trousers, and he felt her skin on his, her palm and fingers gliding and squeezing. She worked him to stone, and then coaxed every pitiful drop from him and he was too deeply depressed to bother stopping her.

He was so deep into despair that even coming felt like dying.

He blinked and Sethleen was gone. He lifted his head off the table. The room was spinning. Cristan's chair was empty, but he heard his voice nearby somewhere else. When he turned, he saw the lights strobing in his eyes. Weird faces and hot breaths. Spilled liquors and sticky boots. He slid down in his chair until his chin was bent into his chest and his ass was hanging most of the way off the seat. His head lolled to the right. He saw Lyra walking out into the night. Alone. Not saying goodbye. Not bothering.

Jathan thought about standing and then he suddenly was. He had no idea how he made it to his feet. He swung a fist at someone. His knuckles were bleeding. He felt something bounce off the rubber of his head. He saw a man fall down. He saw Cristan spreading his arms apart, holding someone back.

Jathan turned to look for Ouleem but ended up just vomiting over his shoulder onto the table. He wiped his mouth with his sleeve. He looked at a girl with the disgusted expression on her face. He looked through the servingwoman who sneered at him, washrag in hand.

He turned to tap Cristan on the shoulder, but Cristan was gone. There was a different man standing in his place. He looked under the table for his sword. He was supposed to have a sword, he thought. But there wasn't one. Because he didn't own one.

He was walking down the street. He swam through the light of a blue moon. His feet touched the ground, but he didn't feel it, like walking in the sky, his only company the stars and his own ruinous thoughts.

He was in Tenement Lane. His legs wobbled. He had a bottle in his hand. He was screaming. "Jansi!"

He swilled his brandy. Only it wasn't brandy. It was Cristan's whiskey bottle, still half full. He drank it again. And was surprised it wasn't brandy again.

"Jansi!"

He thought that he wasn't supposed to be screaming. But he was.

"Jansi Wake!" He didn't know how long he had been shouting her name.

She was by his side in the shadows. She put a hand over his mouth and dragged him into a dark corner, pressed him hard against the wall of a tenement. He felt her breath in his ear, and smelled her scent baked into leather. Her eyes were an infinite peaceful darkness where he could float across the universe.

"What are you doing here, you stupid finestreet boy?"

"I need to know."

"Know what?"

"What do you want from me?"

She shook her head. "What do you want from us? You are the one who keeps coming here. I told you to go away. I told you again and again."

"I can't. I don't know why. I don't know what's wrong with me."

"You need to go. You need to leave. You don't belong here."

"I don't belong anywhere anymore."

"That's not my fault."

"I know. It's mine. I don't know who I am. I just need to find a way out."

"The way out is not in here. There is no salvation in this place."

"You said you wake people up. Wake me up. Please."

"You are drunk and blind."

"I feel like I'm sleeping. I need to wake up."

"I can't wake you up from this."

"Tell me what I need to do. Tell me what you want from me."

"Nothing, Jathan. I don't take. I give. I don't want anything from you. Just you. Just you."

"I need you to tell me!" he shouted.

"Shhhh. Quiet. You'll bring ruin upon us both." She leaned hard against him, pinning his body against the wall with all of hers.

"I want it," he said. "I want ruin. If you want to give me something, give me ruin. Ruin me."

Her arms softened. Something in his voice or his words touched a part of her. Her arms coiled around him and held him, head nestled in his shoulder. Just for a moment. A single embrace. So simple. But in that moment the cliff he had been stepping off of was taken away, leaving him for one moment on solid ground.

She pulled back, arms still around him, body pressed hard against him, eyes looking up into his. Face so close he tasted her breath. "What are you doing, finestreet boy?"

"I don't know. I can't see."

"I can't help you see," she said. Her body snaked against his.

"Yes, you can. You—"

She cut him off with a kiss. Her face was cold, but her lips were warm as a summer day and wet as rain. Her mouth tasted like ale and sweetbark smoke. Her tongue writhed in his mouth. Her body moved against his, her belly rubbing him hard as stone.

The bottle fell from his grasp. It smacked down but didn't break, rolling against the wall. His hands wrapped about her waist, his fingers plunged down the backside of her trousers, cupping skin, squeezing, plying between her cheeks, pushing inside.

She bit his lip so hard he tasted blood. Her hips rubbed his trousers open, and he fell out of them against her belly. One of her hands took him by the back of his neck, holding him tight like a vice. The other slipped the buttons free on her leathers and shoved them down to her ankles until one foot stepped free of them. She raised her leg until her knee was high against her chest, her foot on the wall beside his shoulder. With her other hand she pulled him inside her.

His mind was swimming in whiskey. His body was adrift in pleasure. Hips pushing hard from the front and fingers pressing deep from behind, as she rocked sharply against him, smacking him into the wall with every collision.

She looked up into his eyes, her hand never letting go his neck. She kissed him again, tongue diving into his mouth, flicking the sour copper sting of her bite.

His oblivion finally swam up to the surface. He tried to pull away, but her grip was like iron, the thrust of her hips irresistible, the pleasure impossible. She kept going. She made him keep going.

She bucked and spasmed, one hand gripping him from behind, the other squeezing his throat. Her eyes rolled back, and she screamed into his mouth, the sound locked inside him by the seal of her lips. He groaned against her tongue and spilled until empty, pressing deep.

Her vice grip dissolved into gentle strokes of her fingers on the back of his neck. Her mouth pulled away and breathed hard into his ear as he slowly drifted down from the apex.

"You stupid blind boy," she whispered.

"I want to see."

She held him against the wall. "You're just a stupid boy. Stupid boys can't see."

"There has to be a reason."

"You need to go back to you finestreet life and your finestreet sister and your finestreet woman." She rocked against him once more, subsuming him in a flash of pleasure to accompany her command. "That is where you belong. With them."

"I don't know where I belong."

She rocked her hips into him again, her lips parting against his. "Your woman, I bet she is wondering where you are."

"She won't even talk to me." He devoured her mouth, desperate to taste her until he had memorized her.

Her tongue flicked against his teeth. "Does she know you came all the way down to the slum warrens to fuck a scumborn girl like me?"

"That's not the only reason. And that's not what you are."

"Then why did you come?"

"There has to be a reason for all of it," he said. "A reason I found this place."

"Life has many things, but it doesn't have reasons."

He leaned down and kissed her again. "I will get rid of him for you. The sorcerer. I know people. I can do it. I swear I can."

"If I know one thing it's never trust a boy who comes bearing promises."

"I mean it. I know magistrates who do this all the time. I will send them, and they will take him away."

She laughed, pulled away, dropped her leg. "Then I'll be waiting until never meets forever." She tucked him back into his trousers, hooked the toe of her boot into her leathers, and bent down to slide them back up, deliberately popping each of the buttons back into place. Not careless. Never careless. Even now.

"I'm serious," Jathan said.

"You're drunk. And an emotional disaster. You're so far at the bottom of a bottle you've fallen through the other side."

"This thought is clear."

"Why? You hate my people."

"I don't hate them."

"That is a stupid lie to tell me," she said. "I am a watcher. Remember? I see you when you don't know that I do. I saw it on your face when you looked at them. Lanhamer, Wikal, Ben, Ravi—you could barely swallow your loathing back down into your belly to be near them."

He grunted. He knew it was true. He was furious that she could read it so clearly.

"Even Ebel. The little boy. I saw you trying so hard to love him, but you just couldn't."

"Every time I see one of them it takes me back to the worst day of my life. How can I love someone that takes me to that place every time I look at them?"

"I don't know."

"Maybe I can't love them. But maybe I have enough hate for the one who is hunting them."

"My people don't need your help."

"Not for them. For you."

"I don't like promises."

"Call it something else then."

"A promise is a lie we tell ourselves," she said.

"Secrets and lies are the monsters we feed," he said Lyra's words.

"And the lies we tell ourselves are the hardest ones to kill."

"That sounds like something my sister would say."

"I should have slit your throat the first time I met you," she said.

Jathan smiled. "Yes, you should have." He leaned in close to her, pulled the collar of his tunic down, baring his throat at her. "You still have a chance. If you really don't want me to help you then go ahead."

She leaned up and kissed his neck, her mouth opening and closing against his skin, again and again, her lips gently tearing him apart, her tongue stirring against the pulse of his blood.

His eyes rolled back and closed as she devoured him, her mouth so soft, the pressure so hard. Eons passed. She finally pulled away, taking a gentle bite, letting her teeth rake against his throat all the way to his collar before they let go.

"You are persistent, finestreet boy. I'll give you that."

"That's a kind way of calling me stubborn."

"I don't believe what you say is true. I don't think it can be true. It doesn't seem possible."

"Everything is impossible until the first time it happens."

"But I'll tell you one thing, if it's true, if you got rid of him, then whether you hate us down to our bones or not, you'd be a hero for generations around here."

He shook his head and laughed. He picked up his bottle of whiskey. He took a heavy gulp. "I'm no one's hero. If I had a choice, I would choose to be literally anyone's hero but theirs."

"You say you want to help, but it sounds like you want to do the opposite."

"I learned a long time ago that there is a wide valley in between what I want and what I actually do."

She looked at him, bit her lip. "Fair. I believe that."

"Call me a villain if it suits you better. Just let me try."

"Believe me, stupid blind boy, I'd rather have the shit on my boots for a hero than you." She tied his trousers for him, kissing his bit lip one last time, tugging on it with her teeth as she pulled away.

"I need to do it. I need to stop it. I need to stop what is happening to me. I need to stop him. If he's gone then I don't have follow him through the shadows anymore. I can escape the pull of this pit that I am slowly falling into. I can be free."

"You can be free simply by walking away."

"You know I can't."

"You have to."

"Tell me you don't want my help. Tell me you don't want me here."

She didn't answer for a long time. "This isn't your place. You know you can't stay here forever."

"You didn't answer my question."

"I want you here," she said. "But you can't be here. I don't get to keep you here. This world isn't for you, and you know it."

"Has none of this meant anything?"

"Don't get me wrong, Jathan Algevin. You've done a thing or two that I'm grateful for. But you don't belong here. You are an outsider. It doesn't matter how much I want you to come back here to my world. I can't let you. For both our sakes."

Outsider. It hurt to hear that word, the word he had used all his life to point to the people he hated. "I can't be a savior for you. I can't save you from gangers and magistrates who have built this empire of oppression around you. Only you can do that. I get it. But if the *one thing* I can do is remove the single obstacle that is standing between you and your chance to save yourselves and run your world the way you want, I'll do it."

"You can't save us."

"I know," he said. "I can't fight your battles for you. I can't win your wars for you. But right now, you are all locked in a prison. A place where you don't even have a chance to fight for yourselves. I can't fight your fight. I know that. But let me at least unlock the door to this cage. So that you can fight them yourselves. Then I'll leave, and never come back."

She leaned in as if to kiss him again. His lips parted for it. But she pulled away, hovering an inch from his mouth. "If I ever see you here again, I'll be just as likely to kill you as to taste your lips, stupid boy."

With that she disappeared into the shadows. He could not hear her go. Her steps were silent, bred of a lifetime of hiding from an evil god.

Jathan took another drink of whiskey. Then another. It burned his throat savage like. But the burn was good, so good. He decided he would bring his lead on Seber Geddakur to Vaen and the other magistrates in the morning. He would do that one thing.

He drank himself across the Bowl, and when the whiskey ran out, he staggered down Winesink Row and found a bottle of wine a quarter full on the street outside the Rusty Salvage. There was blood on the glass. Jathan picked it up anyway and drank from it all the way home.

By the time he made it to the finestreets he was stumbling, his vision blurred and swaying back and forth. He hadn't been this drunk in months, maybe years. He could not look up or the sky would spin him to vomiting. So he kept his eyes down as best he could, stumbled and tripped and crawled and pulled himself up and stumbled some more.

He ended up on the Promenade. He walked past the home of Trabius, dark and quiet. He walked past the spot where the gangers had beat him. He walked past the spot where he had first seen Ressic. Where he had spilled that foul oil all over him. Where this nightmare began.

All the while Lyra danced away. He reached after her, but she leapt so high, flying over obstacles he could never hope to even climb. Rising on clouds. Climbing the sky itself. Hanging by the stars.

It had always been that way. She had always gone faster, and jumped higher, and sailed farther on every spring of her feet.

He was alone.

The Promenade was quiet.

The lamps glowed. But everyone was gone. Asleep. Or at the bottom of a bottle on Winesink Row. It was like walking alone at the end of time.

When everyone else had disappeared, and he was left by himself to walk the earth like an apparition for eternity.

He staggered into the Upper End. He recognized a lone patrolman at the gate to the vacant government square and waved. The man waved back. No words were exchanged.

Jathan stumbled to his front door. Key out. Turned the lock. Pushed through the door by leaning his whole body into it like a weak-kneed lover.

He swung it shut with a snap.

He turned about and lifted the Jecker monocle to his eyes out of habit. He gazed through it, a pint of drool streaming in a waterfall out the corner of his mouth.

He saw a raging storm of afterglow. He saw thunderclouds of sparkling silver rushing and colliding and mixing and combining. It was so bright. Too bright. It was fresh, thick, clear, real.

He turned and saw it smeared on the table. He saw it on a plate and the table, and upon the empty spoon like an oar halfway off the edge. He saw fingerprints in glowing color. He saw it on the cabinets, and on the chairs, and on Lyra's favorite blanket draped over the couch.

He turned with the monocle to his eyes and looked down the hallway.

He saw someone standing there in the grey gloom of the crystal lens.

Their hands were covered in afterglow, like fists freshly dipped into buckets of glittering molasses. It radiated and exuded and smoked silver color. Both fists glowed brighter than the moon, sparkling fumes slithering up the arms like liquid starlight.

His heart stopped beating. His mouth fell open. His knees wobbled.

He flipped the blue filter in place.

Lush purple glowed its core color.

They were here.

This was the person Lyra had brought into their home. This was the one, in his home, standing as still as a statue.

But even through the hazy blue world of the lens, he knew something was wrong. The body was slender, short, trim, curved, lithe and small with hair long and braided.

The magus was a woman. Wearing nothing more than her undergarments. Long legs uncovered, arms, chest and belly exposed.

He let the monocle fall from his eyes to reveal the person he had been seeking for so long, the one who had invaded his parents' home and poisoned it with their infernal magick.

He looked with his own eyes.

His real eyes.

The ones that told him the truth.

He was staring at Lyra.

She was staring back at him.

It was her.

She was the one.

The magick streaming off her hands was *hers*.

The magick he had been seeing every day since the day he found the monocle belonged to Lyra.

Lyra was one of them.

Jathan's blood dried to a crisp. His bones turned to powder, his organs turned to stone. His mind died, lived, died again. He was shattered, he was gone, he was splinters and dust. Jathan Algevin fell into a pit in the earth and was buried in tar and pumice for centuries.

He stared into his sister's eyes.

She stared back into his.

I am in hell.

He wanted to rip her eyes out. *How could you do this to me? How could you be this way? Why, Lyra? Why?* His teeth were grinding. His fists were shaking. Every muscle tensed and released, over and over, shuddering him with every spasm of rage.

He was crying. He felt tears soaking his cheeks. He heard them drip onto his shirt. He saw his hands take hold of one of the dining chairs and hurl it at a wall. It smashed plates and cracked the masonry. One of the legs snapped loose. He saw his feet kick another chair over. Its backrest hit the floor like a backhanded-smack.

The sounds jolted him, enraged him even more. He flipped the table over on its side, launching cups and a bottle to the floor, exploding in bright arcs of glass and stone. He kicked the rug beneath until it rolled halfway onto itself.

He punched two walls. He kicked three others, until he stubbed his toe, hard enough for the pain to slice through the whiskey and wine. He cursed. He drooled on himself and on the floor. He smashed his head against the front door, then yanked it open so hard the knob punched a hole in the wall behind it.

All through it, she just stood there, watching him, staring at him, trembling. No matter how many things he broke, no matter how loud the noise or how wild the movements, she never moved. She was still.

Jathan tore the high cabinet open, punched a hand inside, shoved his way blind through the bottles of grey and brown, violet and green, blue and gold, until his fingers locked about the neck of the one he wanted, the bottle of ancient whiskey, last sipped at by his parents alone and never touched again, half-finished ten years before, as old as his pain, as sour as his sorrow.

He pulled it out and thumbed the cork onto the floor. He stared Lyra in the eyes as he took the first gulp.

He blinked.

And then he was careening down the street. He looked down at his feet. They carried him down the finestreets. Past Brandytown. Through the Bowl District and Winesink Row. Around Tenement Lane. Past the fish friers, the oileries, and the salt merchants. Around the spice exchange and up to Hillroad Crossing. Down the low end of Bridgetown and over the Whalebone Bridge. Through the sandstreets of the Lower West End.

Until he came to Beachside.

He stepped over and around and through every dune sleeper and beach dweller and wave rat he passed. He didn't see them. They were too afraid of him to get in his way.

He did not stop until he felt the sand crunching beneath his boots on the steps of the magistracy.

He tumbled into the door, knocking on it by slamming his head into it until he vomited.

Vaen Osper yanked the door open, half-dressed. "You? What the fuck are you doing here now?"

"The lead," Jathan hissed. He drooled and spit ten times. Twenty. "I know it now. I know it of a certainty."

Vaen's scowl gradually turned into a smile. "Tell us your big secret."

Felber peeked over his shoulder. "We'll see if it's worth it."

"I want triple," Jathan said.

Vaen kept smiling. "If it's as big a lead as you say, you can have your fee times ten."

Jathan bit his lip, grinding his teeth, knuckles white, palms scraping on stone, feet blistered, legs shaking, bladder emptying itself into his trousers.

"Lyra," Jathan said. "It's Lyra."

12

Outsider

JATHAN WAS UP AND halfway to work before he remembered what he had done the night before.

Even now it felt unreal, like a half-remembered dream. But it was true. Dreams faded. Dreams were midnight pictures that turned clear as glass as soon as the light of morning shined upon them.

This picture didn't fade.

Lyra standing alone and half-dressed in the hallway of their home, her fists glowing like they were raging fires made up of silver stars, shimmering like a mirage, radiating like cold flames.

That image was burned into his mind, etched in stone, unforgettable.

How could she lie to me all this time? Our whole lives. She had pretended to be a normal. And he believed it, never questioned it. What reason did he have to think otherwise?

She was a monster all along. *The same cold slimy flesh as the things that killed our parents. My parents.* For she had nothing to do with them any longer. Not now that he knew. Every breath she took was a betrayal of their entire lives. Every day she slept under the same roof as he did made him a fool. How many years had she lied to him? How could he ever believe her again?

Every moment of his life from that day until now was a fraud.

Food felt superfluous. The coffee drink tasted like smoke. His eyes were paper-thin slits against the sunlight. The bright of day magnified the throbbing of his head. Every step cramped his legs.

He was nearly to Mistine's, coffee drink in hand, when he remembered the rest. When he remembered what happened after. When he remembered where he went that night.

I reported her. I informed on her. I turned her in.

The memory flooded back to him. He had felt so certain last night. It had been automatic. A reflex. Magick users were sorcerous scum. Magi were abominations. That is what you did when you found one. You turned them in. Especially when you caught them in your home.

But now that daylight was playing across the Promenade, and children were chasing each other and lovers were splashing in the water and the world was alive with the frenetic buzz of people, he was decidedly uncertain.

He turned in his own sister.

I turned in Lyra.

He had to.

I had to.

There was no other option.

There were many options.

It was the only way.

There were other ways.

She would have done the same to me.

You are a liar.

He stumbled through sunlight, his boots crunching on the grass, kicking up sheets of morning dew. One hand shielded his eyes from the sun.

It was the eve of the twentieth day celebration marking a half year until Chal's Day, and the Promenade was full to overflowing with people. Every frier, and sink, and baker, and cafe was packed. Chairs filled on the patios, people spilling out into the street and into the grass, sitting or standing. They were everywhere.

I need to sit down.

He wandered in the sweetfrier and wandered right back out the other side. Too many people. He couldn't breathe.

He tried the door of the icery, but he took one look at the line for the counter and fled back the way he came. He thought he saw a pair of

Wauska gangers in blue vests hovering near the cart of a meat frier, but he rubbed at his swollen eyes and looked again, and no one was there.

Jumping at your shadow, fool. The gangers are in your head. They have to be.

He had better luck on the far side of the lake. The Lazy Steward had seven of their twenty high tables free for the taking on their patio, and the shades were like a merciful cloud keeping the sun away from the grinding ache in his head.

He slid into the high chair, its rounded backrest hugging him. His elbows went at once to the tabletop, and his head at once went into his hands. A young girl sauntered by asking him for his drink of choice as she flourished past.

"Wine," he said.

"Which kind?" she asked.

"Doesn't matter."

He waited with his head in his hands, cradling pain both physical and mental. His heart was in anguish, as clenched and nauseated as his body.

I shouldn't have done that.

Why did I do it?

How could I throw away all the years of our lives?

Over one thing.

Just one.

A horrible thing.

A hateful thing.

But still just one thing.

Out of the millions of things she had ever been and ever done.

Was seeing her with those roiling silver fumes on her hands one time really worth the ten thousand of her smiles she had given him? Was it worth the hundreds of times she had reached out a hand to him when he fell? Was it worth the way she fought every day to get him back when the Protectorate separated them?

Without even giving her a chance to speak.

I let Ressic's gangers stomp me black and blue before I'd give them her name. And now I gave it away for nothing.

Not even for the silver; just for spite.

He imagined his mother and father sitting across the table, looking at him. He imagined them asking him to explain. Not only could he not think of an answer, he could not even bring himself to raise his chin, to lift his head out of his hands to even look the apparitions in the eyes.

Your anger has always ruled you, he heard them say.

You know how you get, he heard Lyra's voice in his head. She had said it to him hundreds of times. He heard those same words in the voices of every friend and acquaintance.

I know how I get. And then I pretend not to so I can convince myself it's okay.

He never looked up, not even when the cup of wine smacked down with sharp click.

He felt the hand on his shoulder before he heard the voice. The hand was strange, but it was so calm, so careful, cupping his shoulder like an embrace. Jathan didn't even jump at the touch.

"Don't run," a man whispered in his ear.

Jathan lifted his head out of his hands in laborious increments. He tilted his head to one side to look at the man the voice belonged to.

He saw a face slender and sharp, barely older than he, aqueous blue-green eyes, a sheen of whiskers, prematurely grey, cheeks sunken like he was partway to deflating, and a jawline the likes of which envious statues would fight over merely to possess one of its quality.

He wore a long coat, expensive but ancient. It had perhaps been black once, but was now more grey and brown, faded unevenly by the sun. Upon his left breast he wore the badge of a Render Tracer. Amagon's finest.

The Glasseye.

He knew at once that it had been the same one who had been coming to the Promenade for weeks, looking for Jathan, sitting alone at this very establishment.

Jathan's heart sank. His life was upside down. Nothing made sense anymore. Nothing in the world was willing to let him slide. He laughed to himself at the parade of madness that was rewriting the chapters of his life.

"Do you know who I am?" the Glasseye asked.

Jathan looked him up and down, resting one ear in his palm. "A Glasseye."

"That's right."

"From the capital."

"Right again."

Jathan held up his hands, wrists pressed together. "Aren't you going to arrest me?"

"Arrest you, eh?"

"How did you know I have it?"

"I have been looking for you for some time."

"I didn't think you lot would try so hard to get it back," Jathan said.

"Get what back?"

"I meant to turn it in, you know. There was just never a time."

"This...whatever it is you are talking about...stop it."

"Stop it?"

"Are you going to repeat everything I say to you?"

Jathan lowered his hands. "You aren't going to arrest me?" *He doesn't know? How can he not know?*

"Words often said by a man who knows he has done wrong."

"He was already dead, all right? It wasn't me."

He pulled back and regarded Jathan with wry smile. It looked hideous on him. The Glasseye had a face that was made for scowling. A smile on those lips looked like an insult. "If I sit here long enough, are you going to admit to every crime in the city?"

"You...aren't here about the body?" *Why has he been looking for me if not because of that?*

"While this event you describe sounds fascinating, I am not interested."

"Not interested?"

"Is everyone in Kolchin as slow as you are, Algevin?"

"How do you know my name?"

"I told you..."

"No, how do you know my name?"

"Everyone on the Promenade knows who you are. Jathan Algevin the double-orphaned."

The other children used to call him that when he was a boy. *Apparently some around here still do. Enough to tell a damned Glasseye about it.* "What do they call you?"

"Sarker," the Glasseye said. "Toran Sarker."

"Means nothing to me."

"It means little enough to me as well," Sarker said.

"You've been watching me. Following me. Asking about me. Why?"

He wrinkled his lip in some sick rendition of a smile. "I'm surprised you noticed, being that you have quite the habit of vanishing into thin air whenever I come around."

"Are you surprised, Glasseye? Really? That no one would want you here? We don't like your kind here. We don't trust you. High-and-mighties from the capital aren't welcome, what with your condescending attitudes, lording it over us, the Lord Protector's dogs shitting on our rugs."

"Trier has only been the Lord Protector for a few months and already you hate him."

Jathan shrugged. "We hate all of them. We hate all of you. Nosing around in our business. Local business. Kolchin business. We are Kolcha people. If you aren't Kolcha, then you aren't worth the shit on your boots."

"Your civic pride is astonishing. Good for you."

"I don't need your praise."

"No, of course not. You have Kolchin. The untamed city. The little metropolis where three quarters of the neighborhoods are run by gangers and street warlords. The quaint little seaside city without a functioning seaport. The place with the most corrupt magistrates in all of Amagon. The place where there were so many street duels, we had to ban swords to keep you imbeciles from killing each other."

"Fuck you. You think you capital people can just wander down from Vithos and tell us what to do?"

Toran Sarker shrugged. "As fun as it would be to carry on this argument to its pathetic and predictable conclusion, I should point out that I don't give a fuck what you think of me, or capital Vithos, or anything at all really. I don't care what anyone from your beloved city of Kolchin thinks about me. I'm not here to recruit friends."

"Why *are* you here?"

"I'm looking for someone."

Looking. For someone else. *He doesn't care about me. Why is he here then?* Jathan felt his heart leaping. His ears were ringing, and acid rose in his throat. *Glasseyes hunt magick users. Glasseyes trace magick. They don't hunt people like me. They hunt people like...my sister.* "You want *her*, don't you?"

He smiled wider. It looked like a cruel joke on his face. "Lyra Algevin. Your sister. That must be who you are referring to."

Jathan hated the way her name sounded on his voice. His hands balled into fists. "You're too late. I already turned her in."

Sarker widened his eyes in surprise. It seemed...genuine. "I had heard you hated them. But I had not realized how deep the current ran."

Jathan shook his head. His arms tightened, bent elbows, shaking. His eyes filled with tears. *What have I done?* His knuckles rattled the table. He paused, confused. "You don't seem upset by this. You don't seem angry that I handed your quarry to someone else."

He laughed and it was an abysmal grotesquery. He leaned in close, his nose inches away. "I don't care about her."

"How can that be? You are a Glasseye. How can you not care?"

"Your sister is a user of magick. I saw her afterglow all over this place... you call it the Promenade. I had to study her colors and patterns closely... to rule them out. So that they would not confuse my trace."

"What...? You...don't want my sister?"

"She is quite lovely," Sarker admitted. "But she is not my quarry."

"If you don't want me to give her up, and you don't chase people like me, then why have you been stalking me for weeks?"

Sarker turned and looked out across the Promenade. "When I first set foot in this city I heard certain names—Salavar Kimshan, Leno Togaris, Maya Chelsis, Togar Roshe and Vorlo Wauska, the Waverider, and Conor Halfsword. Names of people who are well known, for one reason or another." He paused, looking back at Jathan. "And I heard about Jathan and Lyra Algevin. Only children of Dain Algevin and Vela Tracontis."

"My parents."

"Those names stood out to me. They are famous in Amagon, after a fashion. You are likely to ask why, but based on what I have learned of you so far, nothing I say would make much sense to you. But hearing those names, I had a hunch."

"Why do you know my parents' names?"

"You mean, how do I know who they were?"

Jathan flinched. "They are the two greatest people who have ever lived on this earth."

"Such sentiment is shared by many in these parts, you should be pleased to know. They frequented this place back in their day, I have heard."

"They used to take me and my sister to the Promenade every day. We ate iced calpas fruit and splashed in the lake." Thinking of it made his heart hurt, like a cord inside it twisting, squeezing it shut.

"Everyone I spoke to said that both you and your sister frequented the Promenade as well. And so I came here. I have known your sister was a magick user from the first day. Her afterglow signatures were small, faint, clever, well-hidden. But I have been known to turn over rocks that others of my profession might not think to. They were not obvious, but they were everywhere. She uses little, but as often as you or I might stop for a drink."

Try as he might, Jathan couldn't make sense of it. "But you aren't trying to catch her."

"Certainly not. You have not heard my name before. There is a reason for that. I am not usually here in Kolchin. I am the one they send when things become serious. I am the one they send when the usual circumstances just won't get the job done. I am the one they call upon when every other resource has failed."

"I get it. You are their big man. You are King Glasseye."

"There is a very good reason for that. It is because I do not fail. One of the best ways not to fail is to avoid wasting thoughts on issues unrelated to your goal. A practical man such as yourself must surely agree."

Jathan nodded automatically.

Sarker looked away across the lake as he spoke, studying the people, dissecting their motions. "Your sister could use her magick right in front of me and I wouldn't raise a finger to stop her. I wouldn't take a single step to chase her. If she stole a sack of gold from the next table, I would not care. Do you understand why?"

"No," Jathan seethed. He didn't understand anything. It infuriated him.

"Because those crimes do not matter to me at all. She could rob the vault of the Moneychanger in front of a hundred witnesses and I would not be remotely interested. Because that kind of crime is not bad enough for me to even raise an eyebrow. Extreme larceny is a yawn to me. Theft, assault, fraud—none of them are even worth me opening my eyes and getting out of bed in the morning. Because they are not heinous enough. Because they are not horrific enough."

He flipped the clasps and opened his leather satchel, withdrawing a half dozen glass vials, each one a different color glass, setting them on the table one by one, green, then grey, then violet, then white, then clear.

Jathan stared into the contents—a thick pasty soap like liquid opals, then a dry coarse powder like black sand but it glittered like a night sky full of stars, and then a fine powder like diamond dust, one fine like chalk powder, one like rolls of honeyed treebark.

Jathan felt like he was seeing parts of his life out of order. Was his mind failing? He thought what he was seeing was cut out of a different place and time and put here. "What are those?"

The Glasseye retrieved a little notebook the vials had been sitting on at the bottom of the satchel. He opened it and pressed a tiny hummingbird quill to it, never once looking back at Jathan. "They have but one use. These are the things I use to clean my tools, to cleanse everything of magick residue, the afterglow of sorcerers. Ranum crystal powder, obsidian sand, granulum salt soap, Borean talcum, sedgewood bark. They are quite effective at wiping away the stains of magick, to prevent cross-contamination of my results. I am quite thorough. A Glasseye has to be. Our lives frequently depend on it."

Jathan felt his blood turn to ice. "What are you doing here? What are you doing in this city?"

Sarker tapped the notebook with the sharp tip of the quill. "Tenement Lane is said to be many things, but there is one thing everyone agrees...it is a labyrinth."

"Labyrinth," Jathan repeated. He felt his thoughts all dissolving into a trance, his mind transfixed on the substances in the little vials, by the way they gently glittered. "What do you care about Tenement Lane?"

"They say it cannot be navigated. Not even by locals, at least not perfectly."

Jathan nodded along with his words, staring at the vials. "Not even by most of the people who live there."

Sarker stared at the side of his face, tapping the notebook. "Especially not by Glasseyes."

Jathan's eyes widened. He looked down at the table. He looked at both hands, turning them over and over. He thought of the night he found the Jecker monocle. *Izimer Kohp.* The dead Glasseye. Lost and ambushed in Tenement Lane. "Wait, you mean..."

"They dispatched one of the best Glasseyes in Amagon. Izimer Kohp, he was named. Over a hundred captures to his name. Over a hundred brutal murderers sent to burn in the fires for the horrific things they had done. He never flinched in the face of the worst of them. Yet even he did not survive Tenement Lane."

"That is what the Glasseye was doing there," Jathan said to himself. "He got himself lost in Tenement Lane."

"So lost that by the time he finally found his bearings, he had not noticed he was being stalked by agents of the criminal underworld there."

"Ambushed by gangers." Jathan knew the rest. "Tenement Lane treats no man kindly."

"But everyone I talked to said there was one man they knew who could walk every winding route of Tenement Lane the way other men walk a straight line across an open field." Sarker tapped the quill down the page, landing each time before the name of someone from either the Promenade or Brandytown or Winesink Row who knew Jathan by name.

Jathan saw Mistine's name. And Harod the bookseller. Mazza the icer. Wenomyr the spicer. Gadrud the slingball ace. Half the tillers, cuppers, rhythmancers, nightbirds, sourhousers, midnight friers, and dancehall cocksqueezes were on the page.

"Oh gods." Jathan wheezed and groaned.

"And then imagine my surprise when I found a patch of afterglow on the door and window of Mistine's, where you are employed. Sensitized fluorescence, we call it. Afterglow that has been spread to physical surfaces, clothes, hair, skin. And then I saw more of it there on your hands."

Jathan realized what the Glasseye wanted. He sat very still, hoping if he just held his breath long enough the Glasseye would walk away, and this nightmare would end.

"Imagine my surprise when that afterglow signature, the core color, magnitude, and individual key pattern all matched the evidence in a composite folio I had brought with me across the country. A folio containing the evidence gathered from countless scenes of murder, torture, rape, mutilation. All matching one man."

"Seber Geddakur," Jathan said.

Sarker nodded. "The Ghost of Tenement Lane, they call him. No one knows where he lives. No one had been able to follow his movements without becoming hopelessly lost themselves. And no one who has found him has lived to tell the tale. Except for you, Jathan. I know you have been following him. You had his afterglow on your fingers. You stained the door at Mistine's with it. You have been where he has been."

"You want him. You want to capture him."

"Precisely. I have an entire team here in the city. They are primed and ready at a moment's notice. I have with me men who are able to block his magick, who I have personally taught the patterns of the pieces of the magick that he renders into reality. They sit out here on the Promenade every day with me. They are never more than twenty paces from me. We have been pursuing him for quite some time. We have everything we need to catch him, except his location. That is where you come in."

"You want me to lead you to him."

"Yes. Following his afterglow has led many a Glasseye before me into dead end after dead end. They could tell exactly how far away they were from him, but they could not get to him. The maze stopped them. But it doesn't stop you."

Jathan saw the blood spraying again. He saw the bodies of dying men, disfigured, broken, wide open eyes, right beside him. He saw the body of the little boy, the boy who only wanted to help him. "You want me...to go back in there."

"Yes."

"I can't."

"You can."

"I can't."

"You must."

"You don't understand."

"I understand more than any living man, Jathan. Whatever you know, whatever you have seen him do, I have seen what remained when he did it to innocent children. I have seen what was left when he did it to women who told him no, to weeping fathers, to hopeless infants. You think he is a dangerous murderer. And he is. But I would resurrect any ten murderers I have sent to burn if I had him in their place. Do you understand now?"

Jathan nodded, but his insides were liquified. "I...I don't know if I can. I...what if someone sees me working with you? They hate your kind here. I...I'll lose my job. I'll never work again. My friends will shun me. And..." *And I am afraid of what he might do to me.*

Sarker must have been able to see the terrible emotional state he was in. His voice softened unexpectedly. "Jathan, here is what will happen. Every day I am going to sit at my table here, at the Lazy Steward. Every day my team will be within my sight as I sit here. If you decide you are able to help us, all you need to do is walk past this patio and nod to me. You do not need to speak. You do not need to wave. You do not need to do anything that would give the people here the impression that you were helping us in any way. We will follow you from a distance. You will not know we are there. No one will. If we are able to keep up with you, you merely have to walk us through the maze to him and we will do the rest. Then you may walk away from all of this. No one will ever bother you again. You and your sister may go on living as you always have, and many blessings upon you both."

"No one has that kind of power."

"Jathan, if you give me one little head nod, and then walk me down the right street, I will make all your troubles disappear."

Jathan nodded along with the words, but he promised the Glasseye nothing. He only sat there until Toran Sarker finally walked away to his usual table and sat down.

It is a trick. It has to be. No outsider from the capital would ever help me. But he seemed very serious. *Lies. He is manipulating me. He will get what he wants and then drop me in a prison, or worse.*

He didn't know what to do. If he was going to death or a dungeon regardless, he would rather go to it without giving aid to some outsider scum. Maybe if he told Vaen Osper about it, he might be able to help. The indecision was ripping him in two.

Are you telling me the truth, Glasseye? Or am I dead no matter my choice?

Jathan glanced over at him, but the Glasseye did not even look up. It was as if he had never even spoken to him at all.

13

To Land Your Ship

On The Shores Of Regret

JATHAN WONDERED IF EVERYONE shared the same stagger when everything in their life had been upended. He wondered if the steps he took now were the same kind of steps taken by all those who had been so sure they had escaped trouble, only to have it fall into their lap tenfold.

He stumbled away from the Lazy Steward. His feet carried him past the lake and to the row of old shops along the north end. They carried him up the street and around the corner, until he was standing at Trabius' door.

What am I doing here?

He raised his hand to knock, but the door opened before his knuckles rapped the wood. Trabius was there, that relaxed yet astonished looking smile of his already on full display.

"Jathan," he said. "Please come in. Can I get you anything?"

"No."

"What brings you here this fine day?"

"I...don't know." But as the door closed behind him, he realized that it was obvious why his legs brought him here. This is where he learned how to use the monocle. This was where he needed to be to unlearn it now.

"I hope you have been avoiding those gangers," Trabius said. "They are quite vindictive."

Jathan shuddered. "They...won't be bothering me anymore."

"That is good indeed! Yet I sense unease in you."

"I'm in trouble, Trabius."

Trabius frowned. "I feared that crystal lens might lead you down a path it was difficult to come back from."

"I...saw something. In the lens. The monocle. I saw something."

"The world looks different when you can see it, when you know what invisible things you are missing out on."

Missing out on. Gods, how he wished he had missed out on seeing Lyra. *Why couldn't she just be normal? Why did she have to be one of them?* "It's more than that. I saw something that has changed my whole life. There is no way to put things back the way they were."

"Would you want to put things back the way they were? Now that you know what you know?"

Jathan shook his head. "I don't know. I don't think I could."

"Decisions are not best made during times of turmoil." Trabius set a hand on his shoulder. "We do not always have a choice to wait before we must act, but in those times that we do, it is important that we do. To do otherwise is the surest way to land your ship on the shores of regret."

Jathan shook his head, tears returning to life in his eyes. *It may already be too late for me.* "What would you do if you found out someone you love had done something terrible?"

Trabius puffed out his lips into a pouty bunch and squinted his eyes as he always did when concentrating hard. "It depends on what it was."

Jathan squirmed his shoulder out from under Trabius' hand and threw himself into a chair. It creaked and nearly tipped over backwards, but he managed to keep upright, one hand cupping his head. He was immediately surrounded by a legion of curious cats dressed as dogs. "I cannot say what it is. But it is a thing that I loathe, Trabius. It is something that I don't know if I can ever forgive."

"Hmmm," Trabius tapped his chin with one wiry finger. "Have you heard the whole story?"

"What do you mean?" He shot and angry glance, then settled back to staring at nothing in the corner of the room.

"What I mean is, this new thing you have come to learn about, do you know it's full story? Do you understand its context? When we are in distress our minds will focus our thoughts in a way to direct us to action immediately. This is why we know to run and climb when a direwolf chases us. Or how we know to look for a hiding place when a cave bear comes sniffing about. No one has to teach us these things. Our minds know them without us having to think about them. This is fine and well with wolves and bears, for there is little context to them chasing you; they want to eat you, you want to avoid being eaten."

"What is your point?"

"We people are more complicated than that. With our incredible creations—buildings, tools, clothes, words—come any or all of a thousand different iterations of motivation to any one action. We are so complex, so full of nuance, it can take time to deduce what the best course of action is."

"I have already acted rashly. But you don't understand, it was something irredeemable."

"I don't think *you* understand. That is my point. You must understand this new knowledge that has presented itself. You must confront it. By sitting here, pretending that you already know everything you need to know to make your decision, you are lying to yourself. You are lying to me. You don't want to know anything more because you think it will hurt. You think it will cause you pain and tears. If you truly wish to avoid that pain, then by all means do, but do not for a moment pretend that you are doing it for any other reason than cowardice."

Jathan flew to his feet. His shoulders reared back, fists clenched, knuckles white.

Trabius closed his eyes and held up one flat palm. He shook his head. "Are you really going to beat me? In my own home? Mere steps from where those men beat you?"

Jathan wasn't. He didn't know why he had jumped up. He relaxed his arms. His fingers uncoiled one by one. He felt utterly foolish. "I am not a coward."

Trabius opened his eyes once more, clasping both hands behind his back. "I do not believe you are either, Jathan. I believe that something happened to you that has you all turned around. You don't know down from up. Your mind is all twisted up in surprise. It is trying to hide from you what you must do."

Jathan fell to his knees. "What must I do?" He fished the monocle out of his pocket and held it up with both hands, like offering a sacrifice to the oracle of an infinite god. He looked up at Trabius, eyes swollen.

Trabius knelt before him, met his eyes with his own. "Ever since you found this device, you have been looking at the world around you through many filters, looking from a different angle each time, but always shading what you see and hear. You have been seeing many things, new things, strange things. You are fascinated."

Jathan nodded, shaking a tear loose.

Trabius reached out one hand, cupped Jathan's fingers and slowly curled them closed over the monocle. "Sometimes it is best to look at your world with no filter."

Jathan looked down at his hands, then back at Trabius. "My mind is in knots." He stared through all the drooping plants, jars of glow slugs, strings of beads, smoking censers, and sacks of crystals. He saw a high shelf with a row of slender cylindrical bottles, opaque glass, grey and green and violet.

Lyra.

He felt despair grinding him apart.

Trabius was calm, a rock to hold back his storm. "You know what you have to do. Think hard. Know your mind. Concentrate. Let all these feelings that are driving you mad wash away for one moment. Cleanse your mind of rogue thoughts. Become clear like glass. See your mind. Do you know enough about what you saw?"

"I don't know."

"Do you know enough about what you saw that you could write a truthful accounting of it in a Kolcha almanac? Can you explain it entirely? Completely? With certainty of every when and where and why and how and who?"

"No."

"No?"

"I don't know enough."

"What do you need to do?"

Jathan closed his eyes. "I need to go back. I need to go back there. I need to find out. I need to go back to where it happened."

Trabius helped him to his feet. He smiled. "Then go do that. There is still time."

"Thank you, Trabius. Thank you."

"You are quite welcome, young Jathan Algevin. Now go. Speed your feet."

Jathan fell back into the light of day. He worked his way across the Promenade. He took more than a hundred steps before he realized he was checking over his shoulder for Ressic and his gangers.

They are dead. Stop it, you idiot. He slapped his fingers against his forehead until he felt he had sufficiently punished himself.

He looked up as he was passing the lake and saw someone pacing back and forth outside of Mistine's.

Nessa.

For a moment his feet wanted to run. But he froze long enough for one of her glances to notice him. He had no choice. He walked directly to her. He did not stop until he stood directly in front of her, his head tilted slightly down.

Her face was sharp, glowing in the sunlight, her expression fierce. "Jathan, you owe me an explanation of whatever it was you think you—"

He took her chin in both hands, fingers barely touching her, holding her there with a subtle magnetism alone. He leaned down. His lips rushed to meet hers and everything stopped. Her hands fell on his elbows. They snaked up over his shoulders and clasped behind his neck.

After the gods new how long he pulled back. "I'm sorry," he said.

She smiled. "You had better be."

"I didn't mean it. Any of it. My head wasn't on right. I—"

"Shhhh. I know. It's all right."

"It isn't. I am...not a good man. There are so many horrible things I have done. Things I have seen. And then after all of it I yelled at you of all people. The one bright light shining in my life." He sighed. "I shouldn't have treated you the way I did. You deserve better."

"I do. And it's all right. Both at once."

"I don't deserve you, Nessa."

She gave him a look, with a hint of a smile hidden within it. "Yes, you do. You just have to admit it to yourself."

He nodded to her. He glanced away, past Mistine's, through the corner outlet of the Promenade which led to the Upper End, to his home.

"What is it, Jathan?"

He looked into her eyes. "I have to go. There is something I have to do. Something important. To end all of this and set me right again. You may not see me for a day or two. I wish it could be another way, but this has to happen now. Right now. There can be no delay. Do you understand?"

She nodded. "I can see in your eyes that you mean it."

"Just a day and a night. Then everything will be back to normal again."

"If I can have every day thereafter, then I suppose two days is not so long. Though I will miss you dearly." She made a sly smile. "But I will not be obvious about it. Decorum, after all."

He chuckled. "I expect nothing less. I will do my best to not look like I miss you as well."

She kissed him again, a brief flash, over far too quickly. She pulled back, holding his arms with both her hands for one last look. Then she stepped back and turned. She looked over her shoulder at him. "I expect you to come back to me, Jathan. Promise me you will."

"I promise," he said.

And then she was gone into the crowd flowing about the great circle of the Promenade.

Jathan turned the opposite way.

Time to go home.

Time to talk to my sister.

By the time he crossed into the Upper End his feet were throbbing, reminding him of every one of the ten thousand steps he took the night before to get to Beachside.

Now he was coming back.

He saw his house. The house his parents had fought so hard to have. The house where they had raised him and loved him and cherished him until his tenth summer when they were taken away from him. When he came home and found soldiers and city guards and magistrates there.

He had run past them all, darting between their legs to go inside. They had already taken the bodies. They never even let him see them. He remembered finding the places where they had been lying on the floor, beneath the dining table, their lives reduced to human shapes of clean floor outlined in blood, the air above them suffused with clouds of steaming glittering silver smoke.

That was the day he knew his parents had been murdered by magi.

He turned the knob and opened the door, letting light wash over the dining room, the place where he had seen all that was left of them both that day. He closed the door behind him and walked across the room.

His sister had put everything back the way it had been. Rug, table, chairs, all upright. The shards of glass and stonewear plates had been swept up and removed. She even reset the chair leg he had broken, rope securing it in place with an impressive tangle of knots.

That was what his sister always was. Always able to run faster, and jump higher, and do everything just a little bit better than him. It is what pushed him to be as strong and as fast as he was, forced him to learn the path of every street and back alley and shortcut in the city so that he could beat her when they raced home. Her speed counted for nothing when he knew the secret path that she did not.

She made him who he was. She fought for him, to keep the two of them together, and she looked out for him all their lives, until he was fit to take care of himself, and even a little more after that.

And all that time, beneath every smile, buried within every conversation, behind every good thing she had ever done for him...was this.

This lie.

This horror.

This abomination.

He had to know why.

He turned the corner and looked down the hallway, past the side doors to her bedroom, and his bedroom, to the door at the far end of the hall, the door to their parents' room. It stood ajar, a lamp on within.

Standing in the doorway, perfectly silhouetted by the lamplight, was Lyra.

14

This Is Who I Am

JATHAN WASN'T SURE HE could keep himself from strangling her, so he went no closer. "Our secrets and lies are the monsters we feed. You told me that."

"Jathan," Lyra said, hands cradling her elbows.

"The older they are the bigger the piece of yourself you must feed them. That is what you said."

She nodded. "Now you know how I learned that."

"Our whole lives. How is there any of you left?"

"I had to do it. To survive. I had no choice."

"Tell me," he growled.

"Tell you what?"

"Tell me what you are."

A long silence lurched by.

"What I am?" Lyra said through gritted teeth. "You damn me before I even say a word."

"What would you have me call you?"

"I am a person, Jathan. Like you."

"You are not like me. You are something else."

"Because I can do something that you can't. That is all it is, sweet brother."

"It is grotesque. It is a sin."

"It is beautiful. It is wondrous."

"It is sacrilege."

"See? You do not want to talk. I am garbage to you. I am a pile of refuse to your eyes."

"You have a sickness. An awful affliction."

"It is a gift, Jathan. It is incredible."

"Don't say that! You can't say that to me."

"My own brother despises me because I can jump higher than he. Because I can float on the wind. Because I can climb impossible heights."

He widened his eyes. "Your skill? Your speed? All our lives you were better than me. That was from your magick? I don't understand."

"Do you even want to understand?" She gave him a dubious look. "A man does not often ask his garbage to explain itself."

"How long have you been doing this?"

"I have not been doing anything. This is me. This is who I am. I have always had this power. I have always been this way. If you had never found that monocle you likely would never have known."

"You lied to me. All our lives, you lied to me."

Lyra glanced down at the broken chair and the dented edge of the table. "I wonder why. Why would I want to live my whole life without my brother calling me garbage and throwing chairs at me?" Tears squeezed their way out of her eyes. Her cheeks turned pink.

"I was angry."

"Exactly. You know how you get. Everyone has seen it. When your blood is up you only know how to break things. Branderin calls you Jathan Rage behind your back."

"What are you talking about?"

"Your anger. Your obsessions."

"My obsessions? I'm not the one leaping from bed to bed, abandoning my family and my friends for the cheap embraces of rotten conmen."

She leaned back, wounded. He saw the hurt in her eyes. "Yes, Jathan. *Your* obsessions. Swordstealing. Ship-hopping. Drinking. Fighting. Chasing down the girl who gave you a flower when you were seven summers old and scaring her and her children half to death ten years later. Spending a year tracking down that boy who beat you when you were small ten years ago so you could finally have revenge *last year*."

"I was not aware you were keeping track."

She rolled her eyes. "You have been filling the ears of every single one of our friends with lies and assumptions. Telling them I have taken some new lover and how concerned you are about me. I have had them coming up to me for weeks treating me with pity because of your gossip."

"I was looking out for you like I always have," he said, his voice breaking. "You can't pretend there was no history of you doing that. You can't pretend there was no history of you begging me to sort out your life again."

"I stayed off the Promenade for one day, Jathan. *One day!* And that was all it took for you to pass judgment on me. One day for you to start rumors about me. I change one little thing and you just assumed the worst about me."

"Smug coming from you. With your history."

"Fuck you, Jathan. Do you want to know why I haven't been going to the Promenade these past few weeks? Because of the fucking Glasseye. I know you are so damn thick-headed that you can't see the back of your own hand sometimes, but by all the gods at once, did you never once stop to put two and two together?"

"You never told me anything."

"Because you stopped fucking coming home at night. You stumbled in after I was asleep and woke after I was gone. You never asked me about it. You never even tried. Because you already knew the answer. Your answer. The one you made up in your head and decided was right without any evidence at all. Because that is what you do, brother. And once you do that, you stop trying to find out the truth, you stop thinking to come to me and ask me where I've been, because you think you already know the answer."

"You...You are always...I never..."

"*You* are the one with the mysterious new lover, Jathan. The damned Jecker monocle. You are in love with it. More obsessed than I ever was with one of those men I tried to find a way out with. You found it and you just wouldn't let it go. You always ask where I have been? I was at home. I was here, alone. You would have known exactly where I was every single night, if you had ever bothered to come home and see."

"Lyra, I..."

"But you didn't. You couldn't. Because you were out there. Walking dark streets at night, holding that awful thing to your eyes, staring into the gods know what horrors."

"I can explain..."

"You didn't see me because you *stopped looking!*"

He opened his mouth to speak but nothing came out. Because there was no possible retort. She was right. He was so convinced she was out with someone, that he simply assumed that was where she was. But it was not true. He let himself believe it so he could justify sneaking through the darkness following the infinitely mesmerizing danger. "I don't know why I can't stop using it."

"Because you always want to be in control. Of everything. Of this house. Of our lives. You plan everything."

"You say this like it is a bad thing that I wanted us to be safe and comfortable."

"It isn't bad. It's good. It's one of the amazing things about you, Jathan. But you fight so hard to bring the world under control that you lose control of yourself."

"I...I know. I just wanted to see where they had been. So I would know that we were safe. So I would know which steps not to take."

"You went too far," Lyra folded her arms. "You became so obsessed with finding the danger and knowing the danger, that you forgot why you were trying to see it in the first place."

"You're right. I wanted to use it. At first. I thought I could find them, turn them in. Help our local magistrates, keep those damned Glasseyes from the capital out of our business. If we already caught all the magi in Kolchin, there would never be a need for them to send filthy Glasseyes to walk our streets anymore."

"And now that you have seen it, you cannot unsee it."

"I...found them. More than one. Especially one. And he terrified me so much that I became obsessed. I followed him. I wanted to see where he went, what he did, who he was. I wanted to *know* him. I wanted to know *them.* I wanted to know who had done such terrible things to my parents."

"To *our* parents."

He pretended not to hear her.

"I love you," she said. "I love you because we are blood. I love you because you are funny and talented and headstrong and brave and fierce. I love you because you take care of things for us. I love you because you are kind. Even if you are not able to be kind to me anymore." She began to cry again.

He reflexively reached out to her, a comforting hand. One of his feet took a step. He had to force his limbs to recall themselves, so they would remain congruous with the loathing he commanded himself to feel. "I loved all those things about you, too," he said. "But I loved one thing about you above all the others. Do you know what that one thing is? Your honesty." He liked that his words made her cry harder. It felt good to know she was in as much pain as she had put him in. It felt just. It felt *fair.* "Now that is something of yours I can never cherish again."

She wept a long time in silence, the only sound his gruff exhales and her wounded sobs. "Love means knowing how to hurt each other," she said. "And you have hurt me more than I thought anyone could ever do, and you did it with nothing but words."

"Funny," he said. "I feel the same about what you didn't say. Because I had to find out about it now. Because I had to find out about it this way."

She wiped her eyes. She stood up straight, chin up, eyes narrow, defiant. "You are stubborn, Jathan. More stubborn than anyone I've ever met. Every idea you get in your head, you are so certain you know all there is to know about it. When your mind is set on one thought, no one can argue you out of it. You get so stone-headed I couldn't crack your skull open with a hammer. When you think you know something no army can change your mind, no mountain can stand in your way."

"What ideas?"

"Not trusting people from other places for the gods know why, blaming the lower classes for what happens to them because you once heard someone give a speech saying you should, being so sure you can't trust authorities from the capital because of what your secondbrothers told you *ten years ago*, being so sure you *can* trust the local magistrates because of no reason I can surmise, thinking that because you live in a nice place that it means you can ignore all that goes on everywhere else, thinking you truly love this city because it makes you feel like you belong when really you only love one small part of it and spend all your time loathing everything else about it." She paused. "You convince yourself of things. You always have. You have been doing it all your life." She sent a pair of tears down her cheeks when she said the last words.

"What?"

"You have been doing it since the day our parents died."

"You have some nerve to call them *our* parents. The thing you have become. You insult the very memory of them."

"Fuck you, Jathan. Fuck you. We are family. We share the same blood. And now you think you can be cruel to me because you found out something about me. You discovered a secret that I have been holding, not just from you, but from everyone we have ever known our whole lives. Everyone. Do you know what that's like? At all? Do you? To have to hide who you are from everyone? To have to keep one of the most special things about you a secret from your closest friends? From your own brother? To have to always laugh at the jokes everyone else makes at their expense so you don't give yourself away? To have to always hide it? To have to always be vigilant? Because if you slip up just once they will drag you off the street and set you on fire?"

"I didn't think—"

"Exactly. You didn't think. Because you decided you hate people who can use magick. You decided you hate people who can touch the source. So now you see me and you don't think. Because you don't want to think. Because thinking is hard. Anger is easy. You would rather hate me and never see me again than have to face the truth."

"I decided?" He growled the question, shoving the words down the hallway at her. "I didn't decide. They decided. They decided it for me the day one of them killed our parents in this very house!" He pointed at the dining table. "Right there. That is the place where they decided for me."

"And so all are guilty. Even me."

"Even you."

She swallowed a sob, her eyes red and quivering. "That is not the moment."

"What the fuck are you talking about?"

"You don't remember. Maybe you forgot. Maybe you just would rather not face it. But you did not hate them all that day. You were in pain. You were angry. But you didn't have these thoughts until I brought you back from the secondparents they sent you to live with. It wasn't until you came back that I heard those words come from your mouth."

"What are you saying?"

"You weren't born hating people like me. Someone taught you to."

He had a mouth full of words, but they all leaked back down his throat. "I...I remember. The old man and his sons they lodged me with, they told me it was only a matter of time with people like that walking about free. They said it wasn't my fault. They told me the truth. They told me how the capital chases all its sorcerers away with their Glasseyes, and how the sorcerers all come here, where the people in charge of our nation don't care what happens to us. It is not some great revelation that I learned this. They opened my eyes to what was happening."

"They told you the *truth*." She laughed through her tears, throwing her arms up in resignation. "Funny how you just decided it was truth. You just believed everything they said. You never questioned it."

"Because it made sense!"

"Because you wanted to believe it. Because you had infernal forces to blame. So you could hide the pain by always being angry."

"This is not about me," Jathan hissed. "This is about you. You are the liar. You are the one who needs to explain things to *me*!"

"Why do you think I was trying so hard to get you back from them? Why do you think I fought so hard for us to be together so soon? Because I was afraid of what ideas they would put in your head. Because I knew how you would get. I knew. I tried to tell you that night, but they separated us so fast and sent us our separate ways. They didn't even let us say goodbye. It was my one chance to tell you the truth and it slipped away. By the time I got you back your head was full of hateful thoughts like that, and you would rage every day about how much you hated everyone who had ever been born with magick in their blood."

He took a step back. Her words slapped him. They stabbed him. They cut him open and bled him onto the floor. They bored through his skull and pushed deep into his brain. "I don't know what to say."

She smirked. "That's a switch. You are always so sure of everything."

"Because I'm always right. I was right about what happened to our parents, and I'm right about you now."

"You are such an asshole."

"Like you don't deserve it? This is where our parents died!"

"Yes, I know. You think I have forgotten that? I remember it every second of every day. And even if I didn't you are always there to remind me."

"Because I loved them!"

"I loved them, too!"

Jatham ground his teeth together. "I don't know if I can believe anything you say anymore."

"Have you not been paying attention to what I have been saying? About that night? About what really happened? You don't know anything. You only know what you *decided* happened that night."

"I have been paying attention. I know what happened that night."

"You aren't listening to me. And you're wrong!"

He laughed. "Wrong about what?"

"Wrong about what happened to our parents."

His blood went suddenly cold. His eyes narrowed and he glowered down his nose at her. "You had better watch what words you say."

"Fuck you."

"Say it! Say what you want to tell me!"

She closed her eyes. "I hate you so much right now. You don't even know."

"Tell me, sister. Tell me how I'm wrong. How am I wrong? Tell me!"

"Fuck you!"

"Say it!"

She screamed. "Because magi didn't kill our parents! Our parents *were* magi!"

Jathan saw the room spinning. He fell hard into the chair with the broken leg, too hard for Lyra's quick rope-work to sustain. The leg snapped loose again. The chair tipped over backward. He fell. He cracked the back of his head on the floor. He was already on the ground, but he was still falling. Everything faded, dulled, disappeared into nothingness.

15

The Truth You Don't Want To See

JATHAN WOKE UP ON the floor. His head was already drawing constellations of pain before he even opened his eyes. Both hands went to his face. There was a cold damp cloth beneath his head. His boots were off, sitting against the wall. He remembered being in a chair. But now he was on the ground. The chair was upright once more, in its proper place under the table. He pressed aggressively against his forehead, trying to fight the pain, to crush it. But it persisted.

It was dark outside. That meant he had been down for hours. His stomach grumbled and roared to remind him that his math was very accurate. His lips were dry and cracked, but when he set his hands down, he found a full cup of water there waiting for him. He slurped from it greedily, choking it down in extravagant gulps, rivers running down either side of his mouth. He emptied it and let it roll across the floor all the way to the hearth.

He lifted his head and looked across the room.

Lyra stood at the entrance of the hallway, leaning up against one wall, arms folded. Her eyes were hidden within dark rings soaked in raw tears. She was bouncing her back against the wall, rocking forward and back, forward and back, looking at him.

It took the strength of untold heroes merely to hoist himself onto his elbows, head teetering, returning her stare.

"I could have killed you," his sister said.

"I know," he said.

"I didn't because I wasn't done yelling at you yet."

"I appreciate your honesty."

"Do you remember what words you said to me?"

"Yes. Every word. My memory is intact." *Enough to know I am awful.*

"And do you remember what words I said to you? Before you fell?"

He narrowed his eyes. "Every word."

"Do you have a response?"

"To what? To you telling me some story about our parents?"

"It is the truth."

"It isn't true. It can't be true."

"Why not?"

He closed his eyes and shook his head. "Because it makes no sense."

"What? That there was something about our parents you didn't know? That they could keep a secret from a little boy? You didn't know about my magick for twenty years of your life. Suddenly you are the expert on knowing things?"

"How did you know?"

"They told me."

"But not me."

"You were too young. They wanted to wait. Until you were old enough to understand."

He scoffed. "I was there. I know what I saw. I was in this room. Right here. On this very floor. This is where they both died. The blood showed where their bodies fell. Do you understand that?"

"I do. So very well."

"Well, I saw the afterglow floating all around, hanging in the air where they died, silver and glittering like starlight. I know what it meant." He sat all the way up, leaning his head over his knees. "It meant magick was used. Recent magick, and strong. So strong that it was visible to the naked eye for over an hour, they told me. That meant that a sorcerer had stood inside this very room. That they did something incredibly powerful."

"Our father *was* incredibly powerful, Jathan."

"Stop saying that."

"The afterglow you saw that day was not from some killer. It belonged to our father."

"You are lying."

"He was using his magick to protect our mother. He was trying to save her. She could not use her own magick because they had dosed her with a sedative that made her confused."

"If the magick all belonged to him, then what magi were he fighting?"

"Jathan, I...It wasn't magi he was fighting."

"Who?"

"Jathan..."

"Who?!"

"The magistrates."

Jathan threw up a little, leaned over to let it trickle out his mouth onto the carpet. Even if it was untrue—and it had to have been untrue—the mere idea of it made him sick. "Why would they come for our parents? Our parents were kind, wonderful people. They never did anything wrong. They never stole, they never defrauded, they never hurt anyone."

"Someone turned our mother in," Lyra said. "Someone informed on her to the local magistrates. Someone they trusted betrayed them. They told the magistrates how to take them completely unawares. They didn't even have to call for a Glasseye from the capital. They used their own tinwood leaf resin to sedate her. They took her completely by surprise."

"You are making me sick with your story," he warned.

"Good. Because it makes me feel the same way. I am only showing you the truth, after all this time. When our mother fell, our father fought to hell and back to protect her. They told me he killed so many magistrates, that he fought with all he had, but that it was not enough."

"I saw no bodies. No blood but theirs. No other signs."

"The magistrates removed them, pretended like they were never there. They dumped their own men into the Float to save themselves from the embarrassment."

"That sounds crazy. The magistrates of Kolchin..."

"Are more corrupt than anywhere else in Amagon. Everyone knows that. Even you know that. *Especially you* know that."

No. It can't be. The magistrates back then wouldn't have...

He kept trying not to believe it. But a thought kept trying it break a hole in his belief. He had turned them in before. So many. What she was describing was the very same thing he had been making a handful of double-silvers every week doing.

Have I been doing the same thing? Have I done this to other families? Am I the horror that befalls other people? Am I the nightmare demon who makes children weep?

Jathan tried to stare her into taking it all back. "If you knew this all along, why didn't you ever tell me?"

"For the same reason I didn't tell you about me. The bureaucrats of Kolchin separated us that day, as the law told them to, each to different secondparents. The slow grinding wheels of our city government kept us apart for months and months while I fought to get you back. By the time I did, you had all those ideas in your head. There was no talking you out of them. You were so certain that the story you put in your own head was true, there was no way to dissuade you."

"But Lyra, come one. Ten *years*, Lyra."

"I tried to bring it up. Every time I did, you punched a hole in the wall and stormed out to go swim at the bottom of a bottle somewhere. Even suggesting the slightest deviation from your own preconceived truth set you into a rage. You believed they were killed by sorcerers, and that all sorcerers deserved to die. You know how you get. You were hurting. I was hurting. I just finally got you back. I didn't want what was to be the rest of our lives to be ruined by you hating me. I didn't want you to leave me. I wanted us to be together, family, to protect each other and watch each other's backs. It wasn't worth the price to try to change your mind."

He rolled up onto his hands and knees, leaned back on bent legs, back straight, looking at her once more. He felt suddenly horrible. He despised himself. For whatever else she was, Lyra was his sister. He had betrayed her every bit as much as someone could.

What exactly did he want them to do with her? They only did one thing. And it was horrifically painful, and final. Did he really want that for her?

He was disgusted with himself. He leaned forward and threw up again, this time merely by thinking about himself, how disgusting he was.

I don't deserve her. And she deserves leagues and leagues more than me.

"Make me believe," he said. "I want to believe it. Please make me believe it. I can't do this if I don't believe."

"You always called it our parents' religion," she said.

His eyes snapped up at her. *Religion.* "What does that mean?"

"The strange rituals?" she reminded him. "The special soaps? The washing?" She pointed at the crystal eye in his pocket. The Jecker monocle. "What was it you thought they were washing away? Sin? Cleansing their souls metaphorically? Some symbolic gesture?" She held up her hands, the same ones he had seen the cool lambent liquid smoke of afterglow shedding from. She clenched her fists. "This was their sin. Magick was their sin. Every time they used it, they had to cleanse themselves of their afterglow, the evidence of their crime of existing."

"No. No, no, no. I remember...I saw...They were always..."

"Always what, Jathan?"

"They..." His own tongue rebelled against his excuses. He nearly choked on it. "The bottles."

Lyra nodded.

He stood. He walked to the high cabinet. He opened the door. He reached inside and touched the bottles he had spent half his life shoving out of the way to reach his alcohol. He took one of each of them down and set them on the table. One was violet. One was grey. One was green. The bottles he had always seen his parents use, still here in their house. Glass that had felt their touch.

He pulled the corks free. He spilled some of each onto the table. The first was a soft white powder with a prismatic shimmer shine. The second was like a coarse black sugar sparkle. The third was a thick glistening opalescent salt cream.

He realized it all at once, with stunning clarity, his mind like glass for the first time in his life. The same colors as the vials carried by the Glasseye. Within them were the same substances. *To cleanse everything of magick residue.* The Glasseye had named each of them, the same names

Trabius once mentioned his parents came to him for. These were the very bottles that Trabius imported for them. *They have but one use,* the Glasseye had said. The same salts and powders he had seen scooped in the pockets of the little magi children when he talked with Jansi. *They are what we need,* she had said.

There never was a strange religion, a superstition his parents subscribed to. He had thought it so many times as a child that he had come to accept it as fact. And carried it with him all this time. Like everything else in his life, he hid what was real behind veils of assumption, pure inventions of his mind. He imagined the world around him to fit his notions, and then he populated it with himself, living in a made-up world, willingly deceived.

His parents had bathed and cleaned themselves with the stuff of these bottles for as far back as he could remember. There was no other possible reason for them to go out of their way to order such expensive rarities.

They have but one use.

"I...should have asked about these," he said. "I don't know why I never did."

"I do," she said. "For the same reason you never looked at the truth of so many things in your life. Because the world you make up inside your head is safer that the one that actually exists. It follows your rules. It behaves the way you wish. Everything in it is perfect. Even the hard parts are the way you think they should be. You walled yourself away in there. And how can I blame you for that? Our lives had just been destroyed. You needed something to feel in control of. I didn't want to break you out of it because you were so very young, and I was afraid you would fall apart and never recover. But you kept adding beliefs to your world, and they grew stronger and stronger. And then when you were older it was too late, you had lived in that place too long."

"I'm sorry, Lyra. I'm sorry I didn't know. I'm sorry I didn't see. I'm sorry I'm such a fool." He looked up at her. "What is the truth?"

She looked down at her feet. "I have the sealed magistrate records of that night. Not the one they made public, for the criers to roam the districts shouting about with the news of the week. The real ones. The unflattering ones. The ones that show how even with all their surprise and advantage, our parents very nearly prevailed against them. I needed to know that much. I needed to know that our parents fought for each other to their dying breaths."

The room sucked all the wind out of Jathan's lungs. He gulped at the air but only brought in a sip. He coughed and croaked an exhale. His whole body shook. His eyes watered.

She turned and disappeared down the hallway. He heard her rustling about in their parents' bedroom. She turned the locks on the old chest. He heard the hinges whine. He heard the lid thump back down when she closed it.

And then she returned, holding a leatherbound folio in one hand. She handed it to him. "Read it. Believe me."

It was thin, but there was so much written in it. It was so complete. He tried to find evidence that it was a forgery. But he had seen magistrate documents when meeting with Vaen before. They looked identical. Down to the little abbreviations they used. Everything about it screamed that it was legitimate.

And oh, how he tried to believe it wasn't true when he read the first words. His eyes bounced around every page. There were many things he did not understand at all. But he understood the narrative of that night.

He read about how his mother, Vela Tracontis, fought them with her bare hands even after they had drugged her, fought them until she passed out on the floor. He read how his father, Dain Algevin, fought them off while kneeling over her body.

He was already crying by the time he read how his father killed dozens. How he broke free of their restraints not once, but twice. How it was a lucky shot with needle drenched in pure sedative resin that took him down, and even then, he fought them all the way to unconsciousness.

His eyes were swollen halfway shut with tears when he read how when they were both down, holding each other's hands in sleep, they were each killed with a knife through the temple, and another into the heart. How they were left to bleed out on the floor in each other's arms.

This floor.

Right here.

Where Jathan had found the shapes of them, outlined in blood, the spaces they had last been alive. Right here. The moment they took their final breaths together was on this floor in this room.

Jathan let the pages fall away. His head leaned onto his knees. He pushed the pages away from himself, afraid he might wrinkle them, or wet them with his tears. He did not want anything to tarnish the written word of their final moments alive. He wanted to hold onto those words forever. How they loved until the end of everything.

This sterile report had just become a sacred document in his hands. These few flimsy pages were his holy book. He now not only loved his parents, but was also in utter awe of them.

"Why didn't you show me this before?" he asked. He wiped tears from his eyes with the backs of his hands.

"Oh Jathan, I tried. I tried so many times. But every time it sparked an argument. The one time I got the pages into your hand, you tried to set them on fire before you even looked at them. I had to fight to get them away from you. You are not easy to dissuade from anything. And so much time had already passed by then. It took me years to find out that report even existed, and years more before I saved enough to bribe someone to bring it to me. By then your ideas were set in stone."

Magistrates killed my parents.

And all this time he had been praising them. All this time he had been fighting to throw the agents from the capital out of this city so the local magistrates could do the real justice.

I have been wrong my whole life.

He had been fighting on the wrong side all along.

I thought I was exalting my parents. But I wasn't. Every time I turned in a magus I was shitting on their memories. Lyra didn't betray us. I did.

He heaved his aching, shivering body up, bracing himself with both hands on the edge of the dining table. Lyra was at his side. She eased him down into the chair with all the legs intact. She brought him another cup of water which he downed in an instant. She carefully put the pages back into the folio and clasped it shut. She took it back to their parent's room and replaced it where she had found it. Then she came back and sat down across from him at the table.

"Who? Which magistrates? Was it anyone I would know?"

She shook her head. "They are all retired now. Or dead. Many of them were indebted to gangers and wound up face down in the Float. One moved away to the capital—Aldarion, I think his name was. He was the youngest, just a boy back then, no more than your age now. It doesn't matter. They were just the hammer. It was the one who turned them in that caused everything."

"Who was the informant? Who betrayed them?"

"It doesn't say. Not even in the secret file. Whoever among the magistrates who knew did not survive the night. But it says that the informant was a close confidant to our parents."

"It may have been any of their friends."

"I have asked everyone they knew. Nothing. Not ever a name."

He shook his head. "It doesn't matter anymore, I suppose."

"I wanted to tell you, Jathan. All these years, but I just couldn't. Not when you were so sure."

"It's not your fault," he said. "You're right. The way I was—the way I still am—made it impossible for you to tell me. I see that now. I was wrong. I wronged you."

"It's all behind us now. You understand now. You see. We can go back to the way it was. More or less."

"Not exactly quite yet."

"What do you mean?"

"I mean there is something I have to do first." *I have to call off Vaen Osper and the damned magistrates.* He was too disgusted and embarrassed to admit what he had done, how he had betrayed his own sister, turned on his own blood. It did not matter that it was in a moment of drunken confused pain when it happened. It did not matter that he thought he was paying her in kind for what he perceived to be an even worse betrayal. None of that mattered.

It is the worst thing I have ever done.

"What thing?" she asked.

"Just a little thing and this will be behind us. I...am going to turn in the monocle."

Her eyes lit up. "Truly? Jathan, that is wonderful. You have no idea how happy it makes me to hear you say that."

He smiled at her. "I have a deal with the Glasseye."

She squinted. "With the Glasseye?"

"I do a deed for him, and he does a favor in return. And then he leaves Kolchin forever. I get two birds with one stone. It's late tonight. In the morning I'll stop at Beachside, make arrangements, and do the favor tomorrow night."

"Why do you need to stop by Beachside? The Glasseye is on the Promenade practically every day. At the Lazy Steward."

"I...It's all about setting things up right. Don't worry about it. I'll take care of it."

"I believe you, brother," she said.

The words made him feel smaller and more undeserving of her love and kindness than he had ever known. *I will make this right. It will be easy enough. I will just wave a different shiny object in front of Vaen and Felber. They will go wherever I move the carrot.*

"I wanted to ask you something," Jathan said.

"Anything."

"What is it like?"

"To render magick? In a word—incredible. It feels the way it must feel to have any skill that very few people have. To know that you are capable of amazing feats that are so rare."

"How does it work? I have seen it done from the outside, but...how do you know what to do?"

"Well, I didn't know how to do a lot at first. But our mother and father taught me how to feel it out. There is a source, a place where the possibility of all these things is lying dormant. And when I think about it, the source just opens for me."

"Trabius said you made a pattern, a key."

She shrugged. "It doesn't feel like anything. It's not like I tap out a code to enter it, I just think it and I can touch it. Though I suppose key is a good metaphor. Only people like me can open a path to the source."

"How do you think the right thoughts? How did you learn to do it?"

"It is like reading and writing. Like learning how words are spelled, and how they go together in a certain order to make sentences, to convey thoughts. It is like the way you know your letters. If you wanted to write a message to Cristan, you would think of what information you want him to know, and then you just write the words to say that message. It is as simple as that."

"It doesn't sound mysterious at all," Jathan said. "It sounds so... mundane. Like writing in your mind, but instead of paper, you are writing onto the world around us."

"Now, sometimes you may want to add nuance, or add flair to the message so that there is additional meaning, and you might labor over which words to write, but you know the words. You know how they are spelled. You just do. Once you learn them, they are yours. When you think of those letters, they come into your mind automatically. It is the same with the pieces of magick. Once I am strong enough to grasp them, I can just think of them, and they will be there. And I bind those pieces into a single thing, the way you put words together to make sentences. And once I render magick, I can edit what I have made. I can change out one piece for another. If I want to make the table lighter but the piece I choose from the source is not enough of a change to lighten it to lift, I can swap in another piece that will change the weight further still. It is as simple as a thought."

"But you said you don't know everything. You haven't figured out everything."

"Of course, you have to learn how to spell strange new words in order to use them. So must I do with magick. I don't know what new things are out there waiting for me until I discover them."

"Can you do anything? Anything at all that strikes your fancy? Could you set this table on fire?"

"It doesn't work like that. There are pieces there, in the source, just waiting there. They are like little pieces of the code of how the world works. Each piece can change one little thing in the real world. If I put enough of the pieces together and then bring it over to this side, it can change something in reality in a very serious way."

"How do you know which pieces you can use?"

"I can use any of them, I suppose. But I have to be strong enough and concentrate hard enough to make them want to come to me. It is one thing to just feel them in the source, it is another to take them and manipulate them. The ones I am not strong enough for just slide out of my grasp before I can build anything with them."

"What changes do these pieces make?" He kept thinking of the *changes* Seber Geddakur had made to reality and it terrified him.

"For me? I can change the weight of this table," she said. "I can change the speed a crabatz ball flies through the air. Or the direction. I can make physical things, with shapes and dimensions and strength."

He recoiled. "You make objects? Things you can move through the air?" He could not imagine Lyra sending out projectiles, killing people the way Seber had. But...well, couldn't she?

"I can," she said. "I only make flat things. That is what I focus best on. I make shelves in the air, steps to stand on, or little walls, invisible ones. No one can see. I can make weak ones and strong ones. But mother could make ones a hundred times stronger than me. I hope to be as strong as her someday."

"What do you use it for?"

"Me? I use it to jump."

"Jump? Just to jump? That's it?"

"And to climb. Or to speed myself along. I love to feel like I can fly free like a bird, just for a little while. This might sound silly, but I imagine father's hand, the way he used to push us up when we needed help to climb or push us with a hand on the back the set us into a run. I imagine that and a flat surface appears where I imagine his hand would be—under one foot, on my back to push me up or move me along faster, on my chest to slow me down so I don't stumble, or beneath me so I don't fall."

He studied her for a long time, his face a smirk.

"What?" she asked.

"So you cheat. Every single one of our competitions when we were younger, the ones you *always* won, it was all because you cheated?"

Lyra shrugged, her face dancing into the goofiest grin. "Sorry?"

"You asshole," Jathan accused. "You raw, wrinkly hole of a butt."

"I made you work harder, didn't I? You are so quick and strong now because I pushed to you be. You know every place in this city because I pushed you."

"You are trying to trick me into thinking you aren't a lying little shitstain." Jathan leaned back and folded his arms, mouth in grimace.

She held up her hands apologetically. "Does it matter that I am very sorry?"

"No."

She dropped her head onto her arms on the table in mock tears.

He laughed. He didn't want to, but he laughed. He looked down at the table.

She lifted her head once more and they sat in silence, just being together.

Jathan finally looked up at her, his lips turned down into a frown.

"What is it, Jathan?" she asked.

His eyes met hers. "Nessa said you wanted to leave this place."

"Oh, so it's Nessa now, is it?"

He cracked an exhausted smile. "Is it really true?"

"It is."

"But why, Lyra?"

"Because where we now sit our feet are touching where they lay when they died, Jathan."

"It's their home. Every day we stay here it makes what they did for us that much greater."

She shook her head. "It is a way to hold on to sorrow well past when it is ripe. It has been ten years, Jathan. Our sorrow is no longer ripe. It is rotten."

"It is a way to honor them," he protested.

"It is for you, sweet brother. It never was for me."

"You are the one who fought to keep the house."

"It was the only way to get you back from the secondparents they gave you to. It was for when you were a boy, so that the law would let us come back together. Do you remember what I said to you that day? The day I got you back from them?"

"That we were together again now, now and from now on."

"Now and from now on," she repeated. "I meant us, that we would be together, our minds and our lives. That from then on it would be us against the world, that we would look out for each other from then on. It never meant this house. Because we are who we are wherever we happen to be."

"So, you never loved this house?"

"I did, Jathan. Once. But no longer. I...can't any longer. I want to leave. I stayed because if I didn't then they wouldn't let us be together. I don't want to be here anymore. I hate it here. This house, this place, this isn't our parents' life of joy to me. To me, this is their tomb. And every day of my life you make me live in it."

"Gods high and low, Lyra, I had no idea. I am so sorry. I am *so* sorry."

She reached a hand across the table and held his. "I know." She smiled.

"I don't deserve you," he said.

"Yes, you do. You are my baby brother. You deserve the whole world."

"We will talk," he said. "About this. About the house. About what to do next. As soon as I am done with what I have to do tomorrow, we will make a plan. You and me. Now and from now on, I swear. What say you?"

"And Nessa?" she asked slyly.

"And Nessa."

"That sounds amazing. I can't wait."

"After tomorrow," Jathan said. "After tomorrow. I promise."

16

Feeding Monsters

"WHAT DO YOU MEAN they're gone?" Jathan asked.

He pounded his fist on the old process desk of the Beachside Magistracy station. The scarred wood scraped his knuckles, pitted and grooved from a hundred years of biting teeth and scratching fingernails of the malagayne smokeheads, horocaine fiends, and the deservingless class who had been dragged through here on the way to beatings, breakings, slicings, and poisonings until they were either released back onto the streets, into a noose, or face down in the river.

They didn't call it The Float for nothing.

"Gone is gone." Sau Ruda shrugged. "Not here. You want me to change the definition for you?"

He glanced out their front window at the long shadows of a very bright dawn. "I can't believe the lot of them would sleep in like this. How can they not be here yet?"

Sau looked at him oddly. "You have a message? I can deliver a message if you have places to be."

"I need to do it in person. I have to call them off. I was wrong. I was fooled. A clever joke is all. I have the real name now, a different name. I reported the wrong one. I need to clear it up."

"You mean that girl you turned in?"

My sister. "The girl? You don't know her name?"

Sau shook his head, nearly laughed. "They never take down the names. Not with these folk."

"What do you mean they don't take down the names? I come here, I give them names, I give them locations. They must write down the names. Why wouldn't they write down the names?"

"They don't need to. Only name they need is yours."

Jathan froze. His hand slid to a stop on the countertop. His eyes were sharp enough to cut Sau Ruda open and spill his bellyguts all across the floor. "What do you mean they need *my* name?"

Sau Ruda chuckled as though it was obvious. "The overseers and the marshal have been riding every station hard to count results."

"You mean count heads," Jathan said. "Count the people you burn alive in the fires."

"They aren't people. They are magi. At least that is what it says on the death orders."

"Explain to me very carefully what you are talking about, Sau."

"You know if they can't find a person matching the name and description you provide, they just...provide their own."

Jathan's eyes stretched until as wide as the twin moons. "They write their own names? I don't understand."

Sau shrugged, barely looking up from some document he was skimming. "They have to make their quotas. They very rarely find any actual user of magick out there. Hell, even if they ever did, they don't have the resources to capture one. Not without going through channels, not without calling for a Glasseye and their team. Those freakish sorcerers are dangerous. Even the little children. Only way Vaen and Felber can catch one is if they strike when they are totally unawares. Like if they are sleeping or looking the other way. They have to ration their tinwood resin sedative. The cost is astronomical. So they do it mostly with knives, clubs, batons, or the swords if they are feeling showy."

"You mean they just grab whatever girl off the streets that they happen to see? Then they write down her name in the place of the name I actually gave?"

"More often than not. Far more often."

Jathan thought he was sinking into the floor. He felt his morningwine rising high in his throat. They just...took innocent women. Took them and drugged them and then burned them alive. And all the while they knew they were the wrong ones. How many had they done this to?

There was a different room for them to bring in the captured magick users. Jathan had never seen it, but they had told him it was there. He dared not think about what they did to those they brought in.

"Why do they need the names I bring to them then? Why have they been harassing me for names and leads? If they are just doing whatever they wish out here, then why?"

"Why? Because they couldn't do it without you. They can fill in their writs of capture and their many warrants with whatever description and location that matches the person they decide to bring in. That part doesn't matter."

"Doesn't matter?"

"The Superiors don't bother verifying *who* the captured are. If they happen to come poking their heads in our operations, all they will care about is that a man of good standing signed his name to it. Even if they bothered to come ask you about it, it would only be to make sure you were the one signing your name. And you would say yes and be telling the truth because you did give them the name. You would have no way of knowing that you were attesting to something they made up. The captured are never second guessed. The only name that ever matters is yours."

"Why are you telling me all this?"

Sau shrugged. "It's how they've always done it. No one will ever see a punishment for it. Not the way they will if they don't see their quota."

Jathan felt weak. His head throbbed. He thought his skull was cracking apart. *I give them license to murder. I give them cover to beat girls, starve them, burn them. By every god of every rock and stone, what have I done?*

They were never interested in clearing magick from the streets. All they wanted was a steady stream of guilty people that they could capture easily without help from the capital. All to make themselves look good to the Superiors. He knew at that moment that even if he had given them Seber Geddakur's name they never would have done anything about it. They would never have gone near him. They would have killed some other man in his place and called it a day.

They were monsters.

Vaen, Felber, the whole lot of them.

I feed monsters.

And I turned them on my own blood.

"Give me my report back, would you? The one I made the other night. I need to amend it. I have to change the name and location of the magick user."

At least I can change it to a man. Then they would have to go find some stranger and Lyra would be fine. At least I can do that. Like I promised. I can change the name and give them what they want.

There had to have been a pretty pocket jingle in it for them to bring in someone and claim it was the Ghost of Tenement Lane. They would be the talk of the town. They would reap one hell of a payday.

Jathan was reeling from what Sau had told him, but he could do this one last thing before he severed ties with them forever. He could keep from hating himself just a little while as long as he did that.

He noticed Sau hadn't handed him anything.

"Give me the report, Sau."

Sau seemed confused. "Hmmm. Too late for that now, I suppose."

"Too late? What do you mean?"

"They aren't late coming in," Sau said. "They already left. They are already on their way to get her."

Jathan's blood surged so hard into his legs that he collapsed. He landed hard on his backside. His eyes danced around the room. The pegs on the far wall where they hung up their swordbelts overnight were all empty.

Why had I not noticed that?

Think, Jathan. Think.

Sau leaned out over the counter, peering down at him. "The matter you, boy?"

The matter me? Fuck you, Sau. "I...I am unwell." He was. He had thought everything he had known all his life had already been upended. But the universe was not finished with him. It still had today to twist the knife a little more.

He made it to his feet, but his heels felt like water, and he stumbled backward until his head cracked against the glass of the door.

"Heya, boy!" Sau called out, annoyed. "That is real transparent glass. The kind that costs. Not that shit opaque trash you lowers use."

Jathan used to swing a fist or two for an insult like that. Sau Ruda was lower than Jathan's boot heel. But on this day the words sailed right past him. He fell out into sunlight, fell to his knees, palms caked in rough sand, feeling it crush, squish, and scrape between his palms and the stone street.

They are already gone.

All five of them. Vaen Osper, Felber Klisp, and their three dung-brained brutes—Tylar, Sejassie, and Belo. Men known for their self-absorbed strength and their stupid cruelty.

Jathan had once liked that about them. He liked that the men who would be collecting the awful magi he handed over would give them trouble and pain. Before he knew what he did now. Back when he was still blind.

Now he hated himself for every name he had ever given them and hated himself more still for every coin he had every taken, to buy extra wine with the lives of all the poor girls who wandered the wrong street.

He was disgusted, furious. He was bitter and afraid.

He had to get home.

As fast as his feet could carry him.

He took the shortcut through the magnificent stench of Tannery Town, running down the inland slope of the Bowl District, and cutting through the culvert beside the old mill. He tore along the fenced-off embankment beneath the old Arradian aqueduct and followed it to the Upper End, leaping through the hole in the fencing, ripping his trousers and fraying his tunic on the sharp claws of iron ringing its mouth.

Sweat was running rivers down his face and back. His palms were so slick he barely gripped the doorknob.

He flew inside. Lyra was washing dishes at the basin in the kitchen, and he startled her into dropping one on the floor.

"Jathan!" she shouted. "Slow down. Look at this mess."

"Lyra," his voice screeched at her. "We have to hurry."

"Hurry for what?"

"I need to get you someplace else until they give up for the day."

"They?"

"Once they give up for the day I can go back and point them somewhere else."

"Point *who* somewhere else?"

"I thought for certain there was no way they would be awake before the dawn. I thought we were home free."

"Jathan, tell me what is going on."

"Lyra, I am so sorry."

Her anger faded when she recognized the fear in his eyes. She knew his expressions well enough to know what it meant.

He heard a heavy thump on the front door, like someone hitting it with a log.

Lyra backed up against the basin. "Jathan, what did you do?"

"I made a mistake," he said. "I made a terrible mistake."

17

Magistrates

ON THE THIRD HIT they broke through the door.

They poured in, swords drawn.

Vaen Osper sent the others in first. Jathan knew he would. Vaen was the kind of man who would risk as little as possible to take all the credit.

Tylar and Sejassie burst inside, one cutting left, the other right around the dining table, thirsty to get their hands on Lyra. But they stopped when they saw Jathan standing there.

Belo was behind them, short slender weapons in either hand, knives or needles, the ends black with shiny liquid.

Tinwood resin.

They are going to take her down with those.

They were going to stab Lyra with one and then let the resin confuse her until she couldn't concentrate on magick, and then they would simply drag her away.

But Jathan being here complicated things.

"What are you doing, Jathan?" Vaen asked in an insidious sing-song.

"This is my house, Vaen. Get out."

"Afraid I can't do that," Vaen said. "We were invited. You invited us."

"It was a prank," Jathan said. "A joke."

"What joke?" Lyra asked, her voice nearly a whisper.

"You were shaking and crying," Felber said over Vaen's shoulder. "You didn't seem in a joking mood."

"What are they talking about, Jathan?" Lyra's voice was as faint as a strand of wind.

"She is not leaving here with you," Jathan said.

Lyra stopped asking what was going on. She knew. He felt the betrayal staring holes in his back. She became so quiet he could not even be sure she was still there, except for the eyes of the magistrates. They all looked at her, even when talking to him.

"Get out," Jathan warned. "Go. Find another. That's what you've been doing all along, isn't it, you piece of shit?"

Vaen's eyes widened. "Like you ever cared, you little shit."

"Don't you ever want me to give you another name?" Jathan asked.

"We found another informant, Jathan. To replace you. We don't need you anymore."

"What?"

"You were becoming more trouble than you were worth," Vaen said. "Setting up a bidding war for your leads with other magistrates."

"That never happened," Jathan protested.

Vaen talked right over him. "And you sending that whelp over to threaten us over that girl, well, that was the last straw."

"What are you talking about?" Jathan asked. "I never harassed you. You always came to me."

"You sent that shit to us, asking uncomfortable questions about his sister. I don't know how you found out about it. She wasn't even one of the ones on your list. We just took her and marked her by your name."

Jathan felt a pit open in his stomach. "You killed Branderin's sister."

"You should have let it go," Felber said.

"You should have given us the names," Tylar said.

"You should have left it all alone," Vaen said. "I don't know how you found out, but that makes you a loose end."

Jathan's eye twitched. He suddenly remembered the last time he had seen Vaen Osper on the Promenade. "You. I told *you* I was going to be at the Bottlebottom that night. *You* sent Ressic's gangers there. You gave me up to them. You tried to get me killed."

Vaen shrugged. "It seemed more natural that way. A pity they failed, lazy shits. You won't be so lucky this time."

"Jathan," Lyra whispered behind him.

"I take back everything I said," Jathan pleaded. "Let's all just walk away."

"Doesn't matter," Vaen said. "We already told the Superiors we'd be bringing in a little bird to burn."

"It's too late," Felber said. "We're here now. And we're not leaving without her."

Jathan narrowed his eyes at them. "Then you're not leaving."

Vaen's smile vanished. His hand went to the hilt of his sword and slid the blade partway free.

Jathan bent his back, lurched into the table, and snatched up a half full bottle of wine. His hips slammed into the table edge, bruising and biting, but he had the bottle. He let it fly at Vaen Osper.

The bottle struck him in the lips and nose with a sharp crack. His sword slipped back down into its scabbard, and one leg lifted up to waist-height, before he tipped over backward and crashed down on the floor.

"Lyra," Jathan said. "Lyra!"

Her eyes darted to him.

"Run!" Jathan shouted.

"Get her!" Felber screamed.

Tylar and Sejassie leapt at the command, legs churning, swords swaying, each taking a different route around the dining table.

Lyra was backed so close up against the wash basin she was practically sitting in it.

Jathan eyed both men and chose to move toward Sejassie. But as he went, he kicked one of the chairs out from under the table. It skidded across the floor in Tylar's path. He tried to stomp it back out of the way, but it was the one with the broken leg and it collapsed under his foot, making him stumble, fall to one knee, and accidentally dig the tip of his sword into his own thigh.

While Tylar was shrieking, Jathan moved on Sejassie. "Come on, Sejassie. Swing your sword at me."

He did. A wide horizontal arc. Swung as hard as an axeman chopping at a tree, and only missed by a hundred miles. Jathan danced back, let it go by, and then lunged. He caught Sejassie's sword arm. Tried to lock both hands about the wrist but lost his grip. One hand slipped off and the other slid up to the elbow before Jathan convinced his fingers to close again. Sejassie tried to stab at his ribs, but Jathan was able to hold the elbow out so that the blade was only slapping harmlessly at his backside.

Jathan heard Lyra scream, and without looking, drove a fist into Sejassie's eye. He felt the same crunch as he had the very first time one of the other children in the orphan pits had made fun of his mother.

Sejassie shrieked and covered the eye with his free hand. Jathan locked his grip about the wrist and twisted, hoping to snap his sword arm. He was not so lucky. Sejassie was so preoccupied with his eye that he offered no resistance at all. His body twisted and rolled right along with the arm, and he flipped over into the table, his sword careening toward Vaen.

Vaen swatted it aside with one gauntlet, blood trickling from his lip and nose. The sadistic fuck never stopped smiling though.

Oh, how Jathan wanted to make him eat that smile.

But it would have to wait. Jathan turned toward Lyra, her scream still echoing in his head. He saw Tylar across the dining table, on his feet again and lunging.

Jathan leapt at him and slid on his boot heels, losing his balance, dropping into a squat to keep from toppling over.

Shit!

He locked both hands under the near edge of the table and heaved it up and over. It slammed down on Tylar's shoulder, then dropped edge-first onto one set of his toes. Tylar squawked and whinnied, dropped his sword again, fell into the wall, his head punching a divot into the masonry.

Vaen smirked and stepped forward, but he walked into an invisible wall. His sword tapped it first, then one knee, and then his face. He snapped his head back. A river of blood charted a course down his lips and over his chin. And then he was shoved backward so quickly he stumbled and fell over into Felber. They both went down.

Jathan turned to look back at Lyra. He saw wisps of silvery smoke rushing off her hands, fading quickly to his human eyes.

Sejassie was up again. Jathan kicked him in the face.

Tylar was up again too. He reached out to stab Lyra.

Lyra shrieked and Tylar flew sideways through the air. His body smashed out through a window, and he was just gone, sword and all, like an invisible broom had shoved him through the glass. Jathan's jaw hit the floor. Even Lyra seemed surprised by what she had done.

Jathan looked up and saw Sejassie rising and Belo rearing back to throw one of the black needles at Lyra. Jathan snatched another chair and swung it into Sejassie, crushing him into the wall.

Belo hurned the needle.

Jathan leapt into its path, waving the chair, batting the needle down. He heard a crack of wood, and then a ping as the long needle slammed to the floor.

Jathan brought the chair back around, aiming for Belo, missed, hit the wall instead. Before he recovered, Vaen grabbed a leg of the chair and wrestled it down, leveling his sword above it. Jathan sensed the stab coming. He let go the chair and brought one knee high into his chest and kicked out with it, crushing the chair against Vaen and sending him sprawling.

He raced to the shattered window, looking for escape, but Tylar was there, already coming to, reaching for his sword. Sejassie was standing, cradling his face, spitting blood. Felber was climbing to his feet. Belo was scrambling along the ground trying to get his hand on one of the needles.

He saw Vaen smiling, blood coating the bottom of his face like a crimson beard. He had his sword again, blocking the door.

Back where we started. Only this time Jathan was already exhausted. He felt the walls closing in.

Surrounded.

Jathan heard Lyra grunt behind him. He turned around, ready to lunge to keep them off her.

But she was still out of their reach

Her eyes were closed.

Lyra, what are you...?

She began to gently sway, back and forth, like she was doing a dance. Her hips rocking gently from side to side. Her arms writhing, twisting, bending. Then suddenly her movements would stiffen, sharpen, freeze, palms out. She swept both hands to the right, like slamming a door.

Jathan felt a gust of air blast through his hair and turn his tunic into a sail. Tylar was knocked back out the window all over again. She danced the other way and did it again, sweeping Sejassie off his feet next.

Jathan saw Vaen coming on. But Lyra's arms moved and Vaen's sword leapt from his hand, spinning in the air. She moved again and the needle Belo threw was swatted away. She moved again, and Vaen was knocked onto his backside. She moved once more, and Belo went sprawling down the hallway and out the front door.

Jathan understood. These were her flat squares, planes, simple surfaces, each positioned, directed, and sent out with incredible force. Incredible violence, shoving, throwing, smashing through them.

This was how she rendered her invisible magick. This was the way she concentrated. This was the way she focused all of her attention on just one thing despite the chaos around her. The very same way she danced at the Bottlebottom, eyes closed, mind turned off to the moving bodies, the roar of conversations, the shouts, the crashes and thumps of a hundred intoxicated fools.

And now she moved the same way here, ignoring the sharp blades, the tainted needles, the angry grunts, the furious faces. She was only dancing. But her mind was throwing men around like dolls.

When they were all down again, she opened her eyes. Her legs wavered. Her face had gone pale, her brow narrowed in pain. "Jathan, I'm so tired."

Magick exhausts those who use it.

She was crying. "What are we going to do?"

He turned. He held her face between both hands and looked deep into her eyes. "We are going to make it. I am going to get us out of this, Lyra. I swear I am."

She nodded. "Okay."

Jathan pointed out the smashed window. "Go."

She climbed through first. Jathan was close behind. He kicked Tylar in the teeth along the way.

They scrambled over her little garden, and down their private walkspace, bounded by the exterior wall of the house on one side and the high side of a courthouse on the other.

"Which way?" she asked.

He pulled her along to the left, racing down the side of the immense building, before cutting through an alley, and out one street over.

From there he brought her to the Promenade. It was the nearest place with crowds of a size one could get lost in. As soon as he set eyes on it, he realized it was a mistake.

He heard the shout and turned to see all five of them one block back, racing to catch up to them.

Of course, they would think we would come here. We are always here. Shit.

He tore into the crowd, dragging Lyra along. He turned to look over his shoulder. Just to see how close they were. Just to know.

That was a mistake. He saw a flash of ganger colors in the crowd, blue vest over ivory tunic. The sight of one of Vorlo Wauska's gangers startled him. He caught the toe of one boot on the wheel of a meatseller's cart. He found himself horizontal in the air. Then he found himself flat on his stomach. The impact was not kind. The wind gusted out of him, pain screaming up along with it, as if a clawed hand had reached down his throat to yank the air out.

He cracked both knees on the pleasant Promenade walkway, and his forehead thumped down soon after. His body bucked and heaved and squirmed, unsure which pain to prioritize, eyes closed to the sun. He sucked at air, fighting for even a drop of wind to come back to him.

He felt himself thrumming his hands on his thigh and didn't know why. It took seconds of this before his eyes would even open. When they did, he saw the magistrates racing past him—Vaen, Sejassie, Tylar.

He scooted himself back, trying to wedge himself beneath the cart. Belo and Felber finally ran past.

Jathan sighed.

Then he remembered he was not out here alone. He rolled onto hands and knees, scanning the crowds for Lyra.

The five magistrates spread out around Mistine's, some on the paved walkway side, and some on the grassy lakeside. Tylar peered in the window of the storeroom and moved on.

Jathan scraped his way out from under the cart. Heaved himself upright. Tipped over backward. Slammed both elbows on the cart and earned a disgruntled caw from the furiously mustached meatseller.

Jathan leaned forward, falling, hoping his legs would get moving in time to turn his immanent collapse into mere walking. One foot touched down, then another. He was moving.

Then he saw all the magistrates turn as one. Felber pointed, but it appeared more out of reflex.

Jathan followed their eyes and saw Lyra crouched behind a little round white table, fingers and eyes only visible above the tabletop, a host of confused occupants of the chairs around it squawking at her.

Damn it, Lyra, they see you.

Tylar ran along the walkway, and the others moved along the grassy park, spaced evenly between Mistine's and the lake.

Shit.

Jathan launched himself into a run.

I won't let them get you.

I will turn the world inside out to save you.

He caught up to Felber first and tackled him. They rolled in the grass, Jathan fighting with both hands to wrap around the hilt of the sword, Felber trying with all his might to pry Jathan's fingers off.

Jathan head-butted him but hurt himself nearly as much as he hurt Felber. He twisted his body around, yanking on Felber's arms, swung his elbow at the neck. Felber was savvy enough to keep his chin down, but Jathan landed crushing hits on his teeth and nose. Felber spat blood and grunted. But on his inhale sucked a long viscous strand of blood back into his mouth and down into his lungs, setting himself to choking and gasping.

Jathan managed to pry three fingers loose, enough to jolt the hilt free, swinging down, dropping to the grass. Felber reached after it. Jathan ignored it and used Felber's sudden distraction to wrap both arms about his neck and flip him over into a table, snapping it and scattering the chairs.

People leapt up, some still holding cups or plates of food, some holding nothing at all. Most backed away, shock in their eyes.

He looked up and saw Lyra on the run. She spun away from Sejassie's arms, but wound up spinning herself right into Tylar, coming at her from the other side. He reached; she raised hands. He lunged; she closed her eyes. He struck a flat wall, invisible, not even reflective of the ample sunlight. Her wall was unforgiving to Tylar's intractable nose. The bones snapped and cracked, and a gush of blood erupted on the wall, for a brief moment showing the orientation of the flat surface. But the wall had no friction imparted into it. The blood ran off it, splashing onto her feet, leaving the shield clear.

Tylar sat down hard, cradling his nose and groaning.

But Sejassie was already behind her. He wrapped his arms about her waist. She pushed down on his hands with both of her own and squirmed until he released her. She flopped to the grass.

Vaen was already standing over her, sword in hand. She raised a shield wall in front of him, stopping him cold, but he did not seem to fear it, he tapped around it with his sword, discovered it was barely taller than waist-height, leaned over it and stabbed her in the arm.

Lyra screamed.

Jathan went deaf to the whole rest of the world. He only heard his heartbeat filling his ears, swelling, threatening to break open his skull.

Lyra waved her hand and the wall moved away from her at speed, taking Vaen's legs out from under him and flipping him over forward, putting him on his back in the grass.

She swatted sharply with both hands and another invisible wall swept Sejassie aside, shaking him to his knees.

Screams erupted from the crowd. People ran, exploding in all directions like a startled swarm of bees. Some fled down by the lakeshore, but most flew as fast as they could off the grass and across the wide Promenade walkway, seeking shelter within and around the ring of shops on the near side. Jathan wasn't sure if they were more afraid of the magistrate's angry swords or of the little girl who walked on air.

Lyra, spurred on by the chaos, leapt up and ran. Vaen was up and after her. She darted between tables and leapt around merchant carts. She was leaving them behind until she ran headlong into a tall merchant stall parked in the grass, built up out of the back of a wagon, nine feet high at least. She took stilted, joltingly uncertain steps, as if she could not make up her mind whether to drop to hands and knees and go under or take her chances trying to go around.

The few moments of indecision were all it took for Vaen and Tylar to catch up, hemming her in on either side. She blew a strand of her hair out of her face and ran toward the wagon. She jumped. And then her foot pushed off a step that wasn't there. Then another. And another. She kicked off each one onto the next, until she was high in the air, scrambling over the top of the wagon and taking more invisible steps down the other side.

Jathan heard a hundred gasps. The crowds on the walkway and the tables teeming with people, none of them knew what exactly they were seeing. But they knew what was causing it.

Magick.

Everyone knew. Everyone with a pair of eyes on the Promenade saw Lyra walking on air. They saw her send men sprawling with a wave of her hand. Jathan saw their confusion, their fear, their disgust.

Coming here was a mistake. We have to get out of here.

Jathan glanced left, saw Belo standing down by the lakeshore, holding a resin needle, taking aim. He raised his arm, holding it behind his head.

Fuck you.

Jathan was already running toward him. He leapt, he flew, he wrapped up Belo with both arms and dragged him backward into the water. He splashed down and water stabbed like knives up his nose. Belo squirmed beneath him. Jathan tried to hold him, but a knee rose and jabbed his stomach, reminding his body how much it still hurt from his last fall. He kicked himself off and splashed backwards, dragging him back through the reeds onto the grass, unable to drown Belo. But at least the damn needle was lost in the lake somewhere. No way he'd find it again.

Jathan smiled. Lyra was going to get away, and he could slink off back the way they had come, and circle around to find her again once he was certain he lost them.

He smiled.

But then Lyra faltered.

His mouth dissolved into a gaping hole. Terror overflowed him, bled into his belly, rising in his throat, drowning him within his own body.

She went for a step that she seemed to think would be there waiting for her foot. But it wasn't. Her foot dropped. Her body tipped forward, plunging to the ground. She landed on the grass at least. But she was stunned, barely moving.

Belo was sloshing out of the water. Felber was kicking chairs aside and swatting anyone who wandered into his path with the flat of his sword. Vaen was picking himself up. Tylar and Sejassie were slower than he, but even they were going for their swords.

No. No. No.

Lyra was barely crawling, her belly shivering across the grass.

Jathan had chewed on his fair share of pain before, and he had fought poor odds before and won. But not against magistrates. Not against swords. Not when he didn't have the option to simply run away if he felt he was beginning to lose.

He began walking toward them anyway.

Lyra, I'm going to get you out of this. I swear I will.

18

Lambs

JATHAN STALKED BEHIND THEM.

The magistrates had gone blind to him once more. Seeing Lyra down, seeing her weak, emboldened them. They knew if they kept her hurting, keep her tired, her magick would fail. They would have her. Then they'd take their time with Jathan.

They were all between him and Lyra. Between him and the sister he had loved all his life only to fail her now.

Jathan had never tried to kill anyone with his own hands before. Not in any of the brawls and spars, not any of the orphans, and urchins, and bullies, and thieves. He had taken his licks and given plenty more and he had survived. But so had all of them. Even the Qleen greencoat had been an accident. He had thought he would live his entire life without having to murder anyone with his own hands. If anyone had asked him yesterday if he thought he would ever have to kill a magistrate he would have laughed them away.

Not today.

He moved on them, even as they were moving on Lyra. His knees were burning coals beneath his skin. Bright white pain streaked up and down his legs at every step. His throat was torn. Every breath had to scrape its way out of his lungs.

But he kept putting one foot in front of the other, faster, faster. He caught up to Belo first, slowed as he was by his slog through the water. Jathan reached down and picked up an abandoned wicker chair. He reared and swung his arm like a windmill, hurling it in a high arc. It crashed down on the back of Belo's neck and flattened him into the shore with a splash.

Four still on their feet.

Jathan was keenly aware of his empty hands. And even more aware of the swords in each of theirs. He looked every which way for something to use as a weapon.

Something. Anything.

Upon one of the tables, he saw a heavy leatherbound book with sharp metal edges and a heavy lock joining front cover to back. It was splayed open upon one of the white tables, left at whatever page its owner had been reading before they ran off when this madness began.

That is my weapon.

Jathan took one cover in each hand and slammed it closed, iron lock clicking shut. It's pages all together were as thick as his fist, and it was wide enough from end to end to hold comfortably with both hands.

The tome was enormous. Different from an ordinary book the way gods were said to be different from ordinary people. Its weight was daunting.

Felber was only two strides ahead, beside the frier cart, sword in his hand, blade sharp, well cared for, not even a hint of rust. Felber was a careful man, lazy, but careful.

But as careful as he was, he sure as shit didn't have eyes in the back of his head.

"Felber!" Jathan called out.

Felber turned to look over his shoulder.

Jathan brought the book down over his head. There was a snap and a crunch, and down Felber went, his nose collapsed, his eye turned red, shedding blood from his forehead where the sharp metal corner cut him.

Fuck you, Felber.

The others heard him. They all turned to face him. He knew no matter how badly they wanted Lyra, they would now have to deal with him first. He threw the book end over end into Vaen's knee, just in case he was wavering. The book spun like a windmill, its momentum smacking Vaen's entire leg out from under him. He fell, barely able to avoid stabbing himself with his own sword.

Now I have your attention.

As to what he would do with it now that it was his was another question entirely.

Tylar and Sejassie moved toward him, passing the abandoned cart of a lamb frier, fire still burning in its basin, a lake of oils bubbling, chunks of meat on sharpened sticks sitting on a platter, covered in the handful of coppers that had been intended to buy them, dropped when the buyer fled along with everyone else who scattered after the fighting began.

The two magistrates swept in from either side, swords biting the air, swiping at him in long cuts. Jathan backed away the first few times, but that move wouldn't last forever. Lyra was behind them. Running away wouldn't help her. He had no choice but to go through them.

Vaen was still there, still coming up behind the other two, but slowly, leisurely. No, lazily. Vaen was only good at one thing—letting other people do his dirty work for him.

One way or another, Vaen. I'm going to see you dead today.

He danced away from Tylar and Sejassie, and sidestepped around the frier cart just in time, the swords biting wood and metal instead of his skin. The two split up, rounding the cart and coming at him from either side.

Shit.

He had no weapon. He had nothing at all, save for the monocle. It was bronze. It would take a hit from sharp steel, but it was barely the size of his palm, with no way to keep a solid grip on it. It would deflect a sword right into shearing off his fingers.

Something else.

The book was on the ground behind Vaen. No tables or chairs nearby. Only the cart.

The cart. The damn cart.

Sejassie swung hard, overhand, missed. But he recovered and readied to return with an upswing.

Jathan felt about the cart with his hands, fingers fumbling, finding metal clasps, flipping them open. A cabinet door in the side of the cart creaked ajar. It rose barely above his knees, swinging free on squeaky hinges. Jathan threw it open.

Sejassie's sword caught in the wood, burying itself between two slats.

Jathan spun, ducking under a high horizontal cut from Tylar behind him. He stuffed both hands inside the newly open cabinet. The sides felt hot from the fire in the metal basin on the far side. He heard the oil bubbling, waiting for lamb that would never arrive to be fried.

Tylar tried to stab down at him. But Jathan managed to pluck a stiff unripe calpas fruit from the cabinet. He held it up in both hands and Tylar's blade speared through it. Unripe calpas was as stiff as ironwood bark, and the rind stopped the blade before it carried on through into Jathan's belly.

Jathan held fast and twisted the fruit with both hands. The sudden torque flipped the blade and yanked the hilt out of Tylar's hand.

Jathan's eyes went wide. He did not think it was going to work. He rose to his knees. Tylar reached after his blade, Jathan lifting it away, Sejassie still behind him, still trying to yank his sword out of the cabinet door.

Jathan raised the fruit with the sword sticking out of it until it was high above his head. He turned around and brought it down hard on Sejassie's skull, just as the magistrate succeeded in yanking his own sword free of the cabinet door, freeing it only for it to go flipping through the air, splashing down in the lake, his ass splashing down in the wet grass, head cracked and bleeding beneath the heavy impact of the calpas.

Jathan turned back to Tylar. "Here." He hurled the calpas, sword and all, into Tylar's face. That face was not well served by the calpas. It took him by the nose and mouth, splitting each, spraying blood, snapping his head back.

Jathan felt an abrupt searing pain along his ribs under his arm. He looked down and saw Vaen's blade there, sliding under his arm, tearing skin. He tipped over away from it before its owner had a chance to draw a second cut, deeper into his flesh, when drawing the sword back.

He succeeded in dropping away before it did more damage, but his reward was falling on his side, slamming one arm into the ground, going numb, leaving him surrounded, kicking and scrambling.

Jathan felt under his arm. His tunic was torn through. His fingers touched split flesh along his ribs, it was peeled back more than a knuckle-width in the center.

This is not good.

Vaen Osper leaned over the top of the cart, sword extended, reaching, stabbing down at him. He rolled away but thumped against Tylar's boots. He wrapped his arm around Tylar's ankle and twisted. Jathan felt the split flesh tearing further under his arm and he screamed, but he kept twisting until Tylar was flat on his back again.

Jathan threw himself to his feet. Saw Sejassie trying to stand, one hand on his knee. Jathan offered to help by kicking him hard in the face, sending him sprawling all over again.

Vaen reached over the top of the cart again, waving his blade in a wide arc, clipping Jathan's elbow. Jathan stepped just outside the arc of a backswing, let it go by, leaned in, reached, took hold of a sharp skewer of cubed meats, and brought the pointy end down hard on the back of Vaen's hand, spearing it through. Vaen screamed, dropped his sword, stared bloody hatred back at him.

Tylar was up again already. Sejassie was rising. Vaen was trying to pull his hand free of its skewer.

Jathan had been holding his own, but he admitted it would not last. He was exhausted, in raw agony everywhere he could imagine, his body opened up, soaking one side of his tunic in blood. Getting weaker by the moment. He was one misstep from being carved open. He had failed to wound any of them well enough to take them out of the fight. And he had not even managed to slow them enough to get a head start in flight.

Jathan felt defeat rolling over onto him, crushing him.

But then he saw Lyra.

Where in the...?

She stood calmly behind Vaen, her hands at her side. Suddenly a flat horizontal surface appeared on the ground beneath one half of the cart. Jathan did not see it, but he saw the grass flattening beneath it.

Vaen saw Jathan's eyes and turned. He saw Lyra, too.

"Lyra!" Jathan screamed. "You have to run. Go! Just go!"

She stood perfectly still. She did not flinch when he screamed at her. She did not move when Vaen reached after her.

What the fuck is she doing?

Then the flat squared plane *moved*.

Her rendered square lifted straight up in the air. Catching one pair of the cart's wheel. The entire cart tilted up and flipped over, slamming down and smashing apart. Logs from the fire basin tumbled free and boiling oil from the frier pots sprayed into the air, splashing down and peppering Vaen and the others.

Jathan heard screams and shouts. He did not bother to look at what happened to any of them. He ran to Lyra, wrapped his arms around her and pulled her away from them, backing up against the lake shore.

But Belo and Felber were coming. Blocking any escape back the way he had come.

They were still surrounded.

Jathan and Lyra backed up against the shore of the little lake, the very injured, very enraged magistrates coming now from both sides.

He looked over his shoulder at the calm water.

"What are you thinking?" Lyra asked.

"I hope you're ready for a swim," he said.

He turned and clomped his feet down hard, churning the water, dragging Lyra along behind him. The water would make for slow going. But if any followed it would slow them, too. And the lake's ovoid shape meant it was far narrower in width than it was in length. If they chose to try to run around and head him off, they would have quite the sprint ahead of themselves on those stabbed knees and bruised ankles.

By the time the water was up to thigh level, the mud beneath him sucked like a pair of mouths at his boots, sinking him into its morass.

"I lost my sandals," Lyra said over his shoulder.

"Hold on." He tried to kick with one foot and push off with the other. That seemed to help, but Lyra couldn't escape the mud on her own. He had to pull her up onto the water, face turned up, floating. She was able to wave her arms through the water and paddle with her feet, helping far more than Jathan thought it would.

The deepest point brought the water up as high as his chest. He waded through it, pulling Lyra like a little barge on the water behind him. It seemed to take years to reach the other shore. He crawled up and collapsed on his back, every muscle revolting against him.

Get up.

His arms and legs wanted to drift back out into the lake to float away.

Get up!

He ripped Lyra free from the water. Her dress was flattened to her, sticking and squeezing around her at every step, tightening like a rope around her thighs, clogging up her steps.

Jathan looked right and left. There were more people here, milling about, curious, some watching with rapt attention and others eating their midday lunch, staring wide-eyed at him over mouthfuls of meat and potatoes.

Jathan's eyes locked on the vaulted shade canvas of the patio outside the Lazy Steward, rising like the great sails of a mighty ship, blanketing the tables with pleasant shade. He saw the high tables. He saw people at them. He couldn't tell if the Glasseye was there.

Did you mean it, Glasseye?

Jathan decided it was time for some hedging of his bets. "This way." He got Lyra moving, and she stumbled along. She was so weak, exhausted, uncoordinated, distractible. Jathan had a lifetime of experience wrangling his sister down this street or that street when she was too drunk to know where she was.

But he had never had to make her run before. And no one had ever been chasing them before either. This was new. He wasn't sure how good he would be at doing this.

He stormed through the crowds, pulling Lyra along, both of them shedding drops of water as if they were two little rainstorms scudding across the Promenade. His tunic might as well have been made of lead, the torn skin over his ribs burned, and his knee felt like something was about to snap loose in it.

But Lyra was keeping up, saving him some strength. For the moment at least. The people parted for them. No one tried to help the magistrates by slowing him up. That was good.

Odd, that.

He heard more splashing behind him. Sejassie and Belo were nearly at the shore. Ahead and far to the right Vaen and Tylar were racing to round the lake, Felber tromping along weakly behind them. Jathan judged the distance and the speed. If he kept this pace he would fly away through the Promenade's northeast outlet and be gone into the streets fifty steps before they reached it.

That was not much of a head start. But it was something.

Jathan was so busy trying to gauge how much wiggle room he had for this escape that he almost passed the Lazy Steward without looking for the Glasseye.

Is he even there?

He was. The Glasseye was seated at the same high table as he had been every single time Jathan had seen him there. He was gently flipping through his little leather notebook, lifting and sipping from a tall cup without even looking up at it.

Will he even see me?

He did. The Glasseye looked up at the precise moment Jathan glanced over at him. Jathan stared hard at him for three or four heartbeats, feet slapping wet footptints into the pavement as he went by.

Should I do it? Should I do it?

He did. Jathan locked eyes with the Glasseye—Toran Sarker, outsider, untrustworthy creature slinking into his home from the damned capital. Jathan held his gaze and then gave a nod of the head away and to the right, toward the direction he was running.

The Glasseye never moved. His eyes settled back on his little notebook, and he raised his hand and wiggled a little finger.

Ordering another drink. Damn it. I should have known he didn't give one shit about us. I should have known nothing would happen. I knew he was a liar.

They were on their own.

Jathan did not feel his heart any longer. He had no way to tell if it was beating. His lungs disappeared. His breathing became glass gasps of cutting shards, every inhale and exhale. The weight of the water bogging down his tunic was stretching it at the neck, tearing it at the sleeves. His boots were coming untied and were as heavy as lead blocks besides.

He kept running.

He kept guiding Lyra, holding her by the hand. Never once letting go.

Sloppy wet steps down the Promenade, splitting the crowds like a log of wood when the axe bites into it.

Run, run, run. We have to run.

From the outlet he knew a shortcut to Tenement Lane. He could lose a pack of incompetent magistrates in there.

I must lose them.

His mind revolted against the alternative.

Jathan's legs cried out at him, his feet cramping. Lyra's pace varied from running along with him, to stumbling, to being carried, toes scraping the ground.

He looked over his shoulder. He saw the magistrates all coming after him, kicking their way through tables and chairs. A man as lazy and cruel as Vaen Osper would not stop until both of them were dead.

There was nowhere else to go. This was the only play.

He looked everywhere for some sign of Toran Sarker and his phantom team, but there was nothing. No sound, no faint sight in the distance of men moving. Nothing.

He lied to me. It was all bullshit.

Jathan took corners and back alleys, sometimes throwing Vaen and the others off his trail for a moment or two. But with five men on him, unencumbered, determined, he was always seen before he rounded the next corner.

The buildings gradually turned form the gabled roofs and soaring facades of the finestreets, to the sagging roofs and doubled pediments of the Bowl. He dragged Lyra along by the hand, guiding her under the cloudy sky into the first fateful turn into Tenement Lane.

Through a tunnel, into the first atrium, past the shadow of its enormous overgrown tree. The wide mouth across the way opened to a street surrounded by the high grey stone walls of the massive tenement blocks, four stories high.

He rounded a corner into a shallow alley that dead-ended against a stone wall. If he worked fast enough, he could get Lyra over the top before the magistrates saw.

"Lyra," he barked.

"What?" she panted.

"Over the wall," he said, spitting each word between breaths.

"Are you sure?" Her voice had a raw, cracked urgency to it.

"Step on my hands. Pull yourself up. I'll be right behind you."

"Okay," she said.

Jathan pressed Lyra up. Her fingers locked on the top of the wall and she pulled herself up out of his reach. He let her go, his fingers wanting to keep holding her up. But they pulled apart.

He looked over his shoulder and saw they were still clear. She swung her legs up, and then she was over and down the other side.

He glanced at her once, seeing her rolling over the top, safely out of sight.

This is the last time I'll ever see you. Goodbye, sister.

Jathan sighed in relief. They wouldn't think to look over the wall.

Because they will be too busy chasing me.

He tore out of the alley and flew down the street. The magistrates were almost right on top of him.

Sorry I lied, Lyra. I had to get you to go over the wall. This is the last time I'll ever lie to you, I promise.

He knew it was all his fault. All of it. From the moment he first picked up the glass eye, every step he took, it was always going to end like this. He had one chance to make things right. His only chance.

To do one last thing for Lyra.

To save her one last time.

To save her from one more worthless shit, hellbent on ruining her life.

To save her from himself.

The magistrates were on him like horsefish on a wiggly lure. All five were on his heels. None of them saw Lyra go over the wall. Only him.

Just the way he wanted.

No matter how many turns he took, they were always there. Always behind him. Always coming. He would never outrun them.

He hadn't planned to.

Jathan brought out the Jecker monocle and peered through it.

Please. Please be here. He had to be. He always was. And he was always using his magick.

He ran through the steep artificial ravines, taking turns, stairs, ramps, tunnels, deeper and deeper into the maze of Tenement Lane, the five men always right behind.

He spotted numerous signs of afterglow. At least four belonging to other people. Those were useless. He ignored them. He needed to follow the trail of one man and one man only.

At last, he saw it. A sign. Shining to him in polychromatic effulgence. A glittering wave of vibrating color. He switched to the blue filter. Green. Oh, so green. Here he was.

He tried to slow down enough to touch it, to take some of it on his fingers, but he could not slow enough. The magistrates on his tail may have been hobbled by their wounds, but they were not undone. They were coming.

Luckily, he saw another sign ahead atop some stairs. And then another at the lip of a tunnel. And then another across a street on the top slat of a gate.

As each new sign presented itself to him, he slowly realized he had been this way before. This was no random spot. Up ahead was the place where he first saw Seber Geddakur, the space between two high buildings where Jathan had first watched him kill.

The tree there did not provide enough cover to keep him out of sight, and broad daylight left no shadows to hide him. If he rounded that corner, he was deciding his fate.

If I go through with this, it's all over. No way to hide.

But at least I'll take them all with me, so they will never bother Lyra again, or anyone else.

He thought of Lyra, his sweet sister, finally free to leave home like she always wanted.

He thought of Nessa, weeping on Lyra's shoulder when she went to tell her that he couldn't keep his promise, that he wasn't coming, that he wouldn't have the chance to become that man she always knew he could be.

He thought of Jansi Wake leaping down from the rooftops to find his body here on the ground, looking into his dead eyes, telling him how stupid he was, and shedding a tear for him, one more victim of the murderous god, one more man who failed to do what he promised he would.

This was where his obsession began. And this is where it would end.

A glance over his shoulder told him that they were gaining on him. This was going to be it. He raced across the street. He ducked behind the hedge and turned the corner and found himself between the two hulking tenements. To the left was an ancient, gnarled tree, its leaves dry, its branches like claws.

There in the middle Jathan saw him.

Seber Geddakur. At the far end, past the tree. Leaning against a stone bench, waiting for one of his mistresses.

Jathan felt his stomach rise until he thought it would float out his mouth and pull him into the sky like a balloon. He saw Seber's head begin to turn, as the sound of so many running boots reached him.

He heard the steps of the magistrates, sharp cracks and echoes informing him that they too had rounded the corner behind him. He looked back at them as he ran, as his feet carried him closer and closer to the sorcerer.

Time slowed to a halt.

Seber turned his head, the side of his face slowly coming into view, his eyes cresting his shoulder. Once he was sure the murderer saw all who had entered his domain, Jathan drew in a breath and opened his mouth to shout the words.

"Seber Geddakur! We've come to take you in!"

The murderer smiled.

Lambs to the slaughter.

19

A Whisper Through Tears

JATHAN KNEW WHAT WAS coming, and this time he had nowhere to hide.

He watched Seber Geddakur turn. He watched that same coat slowly come around. Jathan realized he was reliving the very first time he had seen Seber, when he had watched him kill magistrates in the middle of the night.

Only that time he had been hiding high above, in the dark of night, behind the wall of the walkway three stories up. He had been looking down at the men who would die, observing them from the outside.

This time he was one of them. This time he was facing those eyes. He was facing that terrifying magick. He was the one who was going to die.

He looked up at the balcony where he had been that night. He wasn't sure why. For some reason he thought he would see someone there, watching him in turn, but there was no one.

Jathan slowed to a jog, and then a trot, and then a walk, and then he stopped. He heard the steps of the magistrates behind him. He heard Felber Klisp wheezing. He heard Belo and Tylar and Sejassie, breaths heavy. He heard Vaen Osper stop behind him. Blades were freed from scabbards, the fancy bright colored rigs Jathan had always been so envious of. Only a few quick strides until they would run him through.

Seber's eyes fell across them all. He only spoke one crucial word. "Lambs." His lips curled into a snarl. His eyes were dark and unforgiving. Looking at him was like falling into a deep well, the dark kind, the leg-breaking kind, the kind you never climbed out of, and no one ever found you until you were made into nothing but old bones in black water.

He raised his hands.

Jathan fixed his feet in one spot, and then he let himself tip forward. He heard the strange whistling sound of the invisible projectiles flying from Seber's hands, whizzing past his ears.

He had never heard anything like it before. It was the sound a god made when they flew to earth. It was the sound of terror. It was the sound of awe.

Jathan felt the bite of the invisible projectiles. One of them punched into the flesh above his hip, another tore through the meat of his shoulder, and another bored through the muscle of his calf. The pain erupted like a blossom of flame inside his body. It was simply everywhere at once.

He crashed to the ground face-first. His arms barely cushioned his fall. He felt blood on his trousers, spreading beneath him, pooling around him. He had dirt in his mouth. He lay there, still and quiet, listening to the strange ethereal hum of the storm of swift objects Seber created with his magick.

And when that sound was gone, it was replaced by the screams and cries of the magistrates.

Jathan closed his eyes. He felt blood spraying onto his back. He heard the heavy smack as they each fell, one by one. One of their bodies tumbled and rolled until one of its arms flopped across his leg. A pair of swords clattering down.

Then the world descended into a hell of silence. Jathan thought his own breath hissing was like a streak of thunder in comparison.

Seber noticed him. Must have seen his body rise and fall with each painful, shuddering breath. He tapped Jathan's face with his boot until Jathan rolled over onto his back.

Seber made an odd expression at him, as if there was a hint of recognition. But his hand raised all the same, pointing one finger at him.

Jathan smiled.

The only reason Seber was standing over him was because Vaen Osper was dead. Felber Klisp was dead. Tylar, Sejassie, and Belo were all dead.

That meant Lyra was safe. It meant she would live. It meant she would go on. She was finally free.

And so was Jathan.

You are just meat and bone. There is nothing more to you.

Knowing that was freedom.

He looked up as Seber, unafraid. "Do it, you coward."

Seber sneered. He made the same face he made whenever he created magick to kill.

Jathan closed his eyes, ready to receive it.

But nothing happened.

Jathan opened his eyes.

Seber's face changed, eyes peeled open into twin moons. His head turned. Before he could react, something hit him, something invisible, something heavy, something that shoved him off his feet. He was dragged across the ground until his coat was torn and his body rested up against the far wall.

What the...?

Jathan rolled onto his side, lifted his head, saw motion in the corner of his eye.

She had followed him. She had rendered magick. She had attacked Seber.

Lyra, no!

But it was too late. Seber saw her. He floated to his feet.

He rendered attacks at Jathan, but Lyra waved her hands again. This time a flat wall smacked into Jathan, shoving and rolling him out of the way, leaving a bloody streak on the pavement behind him.

He heard loud pops, as the projectiles peppered the ground, and a strange whistling twang as they struck Lyra's invisible wall.

Lyra's wall finally vanished. Jathan tumbled to a stop. He tried to climb onto hands and knees, but there was so much blood pouring out of him.

Lyra sent another square shape sliding toward Seber, but he must have rendered something of his own. Her moving wall did nothing.

He then rendered more projectiles and sent them flying toward her.

Lyra made yet another square wall, stationary, for protection, but Jathan heard the sharp slap as it was hit. Seber cracked it, punched through it, destroyed it.

Lyra screamed.

One of the objects clipped her hip and spun her. Her little wall went away. She fell onto her hands. Rolled onto her side. Tried to stand. Failed. Her hand fastened to her hip, holding onto the blood and the pain.

Seber walked over to her.

Jathan was on his feet.

No! You leave her alone!

His side was splitting, like burning coals inside his flesh. He took a step, winced. Took another. The pain drove him to one knee.

Lyra looked at him.

He met her gaze, inched forward, trying to do something, anything.

Lyra was shaking, her dress frayed and torn. She had dirt in her hair. She had tears running down her cheeks. She had blood on her lips.

Seber looked down his long arm and one raised finger at her. Ready to punch a hole through her.

But he stopped. Changed his mind.

For a moment Jathan thought he might spare her.

But that was not what Seber intended at all.

Seber let his little projectile render vanish before it had a chance to exist. He made a new one in its place, a giant sphere, pregnant with incredible mass, something so impossibly powerful and violent that space bent and warped in anticipation of it existing.

He wasn't merely going to punch a little hole through her heart. He was going to crush her into paste, and mash her into the ground.

Jathan kept pulling himself toward her, pain scraping all through his body. He wept. He screamed. He vomited into his hands. But he kept going. He kept moving. He kept crawling. He kept reaching.

But he was too far. He couldn't save her. By the time he reached her there would be nothing left. He saw her face bent in fear, tears streaming from her eyes.

Why did you do it, Lyra? Why?

You were safe. You were free.

Why?

Why did you come back for me?

Seber raised the hand and pointed his finger at her, the way he had seen him kill so many.

Jathan reached out to her, his fingertips inches away from hers, but forever apart.

Lyra looked at him. "Jathan." A whisper through tears.

Jathan looked back. "Lyra." A murmur between groans.

Nothing they did could stop what was going to happen next.

It was inevitable.

Except something odd happened.

Nothing happened.

Seber glanced down at his own hand. He pointed at her again.

Nothing.

Something happened then that Jathan had never seen before. Seber's eyes widened, eyebrows raised infinitely, lips pulled apart, severing his grim sneer and making it into a gaping hollow well of surprise.

Seber Geddakur was afraid.

Jathan turned his head. The echo of footsteps rippled in his ears. He looked out at the street that had brought him to this place. He saw people passing the hedge and walking into the space between buildings, coming toward them.

He recognized the one out in front.

The Glasseye.

"Tsk tsk," Toran Sarker said, strolling calmly up to the most dangerous man ever to walk the streets of this city. He wore the same old coat, and he carried a cane even though he could walk just fine. He kept adjusting his grip on it, twirling it this way and that. There was a heavy runic moon at one end, making it look like a slender club.

He was accompanied by a team of swordsmen all in black capes, four spearmen from the city guard, and a host of other unarmed men, some carrying bags of enormous books and jumbles of unseeable, unknowable equipment, and some carrying nothing at all, walking calmly, eyes barely open, lips pressed together as if focusing all their attention on something Jathan did not see.

His eyes darted back and forth between them and the brutal killer hovering above his sister.

He hasn't killed them yet.

He hasn't killed her either.

He's not doing anything.

Because he couldn't do anything. Because Sarker had not been lying. He did have an entire team with him. A team of people with the power to block magick somehow.

Jathan didn't understand. He didn't need to. If it was working, the result was all he cared about.

Sarker stepped up to Seber Geddakur and stared fearlessly into his eyes. The Glasseye had the look of a predator one moment away from starvation finally staring down the delicious meal he had been waiting for.

The sorcerer did not move.

"You're very clever," Sarker said. "Hiding from us in here. The beast at the center of the labyrinth. You knew our tools would tell us exactly where you were, so you came here, to this place, where every other turn is a dead end, or a dogleg, or a tunnel to nowhere. We could know your precise location and still not be perfectly certain how to get to you. I like that. The challenge. It will make your burning skin smell all the sweeter when they put you in the fires."

Seber snarled. He released a hiss of a breath, spitting the air between clenched teeth. His eyes bounced from Sarker to Jathan to Lyra and back again.

He must have been using that time to make a decision, because as soon as his eyes had completed their circuit, he turned and ran, feet twisting around, coat fluting up like the tail of a hideous bird. The motion was so fast it was hard to believe he didn't break his own ankles.

But he only made it two steps before Sarker caught up to him. He reached out with his cane, cracking Seber on his skull, just above his right ear. He dropped to his knees in absolute silence. His head turned to the left and he drooled before collapsing.

Sarker was mildly amused. "Trying to evade my Stoppers, Seber? This handful of men can concentrate so hard they can stop you from being able to touch your magick. Specifically, you. They block your magick in the source and keep it from reaching your fingertips, the way a cork blocks the wine from reaching your mouth. I have coached them on everything they need to know to make your infinite powers..." He snapped his fingers in Seber's face. "...disappear."

The sorcerer looked so weak. He was no longer this towering object of fear. Without his powers, he was not frightening at all. He looked so harmless.

He looked so...ordinary.

Sarker was smiling as if he was merely a guest at a dinner party. "That is the funny thing about undoing magick, Seber. It is so...anticlimactic. All it takes it a handful of Stoppers to block your magick, as long as a trained Glasseye who has studied you for months is guiding them on what to do."

Seber growled through gritted teeth.

"Poor little Seber," Sarker said. "You think you deserve to go out in a blaze of glory, firing off your violent magick this way and that, valiantly blocking attacks with your shields, taking a hundred men with you when you go. Only it isn't like that. You simply *stop* being able to use your magick. It makes it all the more satisfying for me to know that you will go into the void with a whimper, that the only blaze you will see is when they set your face on fire."

Two of the men Sarker had brought with him muscled Seber up and held him upright on his knees. His eyes were already swimming around, glancing at Jathan and everything else but not seeing them.

Sarker produced a little metal flask. He unscrewed it and flipped the stopper up. He poured the contents down Seber's throat. "There, there, Seber. Tinwood leaf tea is good for the soul. If you're lucky I'll give you a double dose on the way to the fires. It may last long enough that you will not even realize you are burning alive. Who knows? Perhaps the gods will smile on you and decide your demise alone is enough."

Seber never answered, mind sinking into a quicksand of sedatives and blunt force trauma. The two men lifted him and dragged him away and set him down under the mighty tree.

Then Sarker's people set to moving about, setting up devices and lighting firesticks and flares and copying down everything they saw into notebooks. One of them had a Jecker monocle. The mere sight of it made Jathan panic out of reflex. His hand slapped to his pocket, only to find the one he had stolen still safely there.

Jathan and Lyra scooted toward each other, half embracing, and half holding each other upright. "Thank every god, Lyra." He felt all about, checking her clothes for signs of blood, brushing her hair aside to check for wounds.

"You don't believe in any gods," she whispered.

"Are you all right? Are you hurt?"

"Yes, I am hurt. I don't think there is a single part of me that is not in pain at the moment, but I will be fine. My shield slowed his cheap tricks down before they hit me. They bruised, and I may have a broken bone. But I will live. I am not so sure about you though."

She tore away the lower fringe of her dress into strips and tying them tightly about his shoulder and leg. Tight enough to make him grunt. She made him press his hand hard against the wound on his hip. And she made a face at him when she saw the wound over his ribs.

"This is all my fault. You are my sister and I failed you. Lyra, please believe me. I am so sorry."

She shrugged. "You didn't know. I should have told you sooner. I should have found a way. But I was afraid. Yes, you get angry. No, you don't like to hear new ideas sometimes. I know that. And I know I told myself that every single day as an excuse for why I shouldn't keep trying to tell you. Why I should go ahead and skip doing the hard thing."

"I wish I could take it all back," he said.

She shrugged. "If you don't have a head full of thoughts like that then you haven't spent a single day on this earth."

"I shouldn't have told them."

"You're right. You shouldn't have told them. I shouldn't have made you find out about me that way. I should have trusted you. You should have trusted me."

"We fucked up," he said.

"You fucked up a little bit worse than me."

He chuckled and it hurt. "That's fair."

"I'm willing to say we're even. What do you say?"

"I say *even* sounds better than I deserve. I'll take it."

She smiled and wrapped her arms around him. It hurt. A lot. But he didn't dare stop her.

It felt so good to finally be rid of the itch of suspicion, the slow scalding of betrayal. It felt like they could just *be* again. Brother and sister. Like the old days. All his hopes and plans seemed like faint little shadows next to the voluminous light of that joy.

Assuming he didn't bleed to death before they fetched a physician.

She helped him to his feet, letting him lean on her as he hobbled. He looked around. There were two dozen men meandering around them. And none of them, including Sarker, seemed to care even one little bit about the two of them.

Is this real? Are we really free to go?

He was afraid to start walking. As if moving might remind them all that he and his sister were supposed to be going to face their execution.

Just then, as if in answer to his thoughts, he heard the syncopated rhythm of boots clattering on the street outside. He saw men pour in behind Sarker's people.

Jathan deduced at once that they were all magistrates and city guards. At least a dozen of each. Must have been actual Tenement Lane magistrates, or the Nearside Street staging office at least.

They heard about what happened at the Promenade. There were hundreds of witnesses. The know what Lyra is. They know she attacked magistrates. They know I attacked them too. They know everything.

And now they knew that the five magistrates were all dead. And Jathan and Lyra, who had been plainly seen attacking them with magick, were standing over their bodies.

20

Abomination

THERE WERE WORSE MOMENTS than this one to die.

"Arrest them!" the senior magistrate commanded. "Arrest both of them. The criminal use of the infernal magick. Evasion of lawful magistrates. Murder of lawful magistrates. Witnessed by dozens." He turned to Jathan and appraised him, scowling as if he was a pile of odious garbage. "Harboring an abomination."

Jathan knew there were far too many for them to evade. But he could lunge at them, tie up enough of them that Lyra might have a chance to run. Lose them in the maze. Escape.

And besides, he'd rather to go to his death having left the impression of his knuckles on that asshole's cheek for what he called his sister. He would earn the wrong end of a sword for it. He knew that much. Even the honorable magistrates considered resisting a killing offense.

He nodded to Lyra, then turned on the magistrates.

Fuck you all. I'm ready.

He took the first step of the final act he would ever perform in his life.

He thought of how happy Lyra was to finally be who she was in front of him, and how sad Nessa would be when he didn't come back to her the way he had promised he would.

He was ready to die.

Only he didn't have to.

Sarker, the Glasseye, stepped between him and the magistrate. "This man is not under arrest."

"What?" the magistrate asked. He made a face that clearly showed he had never heard anyone say that before.

"Trouble hearing?" Sarker asked the magistrate. "I was explaining to you that neither of them is under arrest. It is quite an uncomplicated statement. I apologize. I had not thought such a simple concept would cause you such confusion. Shall I reword it a different way? As if I were explaining it to a child perhaps?"

"Who the fuck are you?" an assistant magistrate demanded.

"Shut up," Sarker said.

That left the man wide-eyed. As a magistrate, he had of a certainty never heard anyone ever speak to him that way.

"These are criminals," the senior magistrate said. "They need to be taken into custody."

"No," Sarker said. "No, I don't think so."

"You don't think so?"

"No, I don't think so. But if you are in need of something important to do, you may go fetch me a warm Samartanian coffee drink. The Lazy Steward has a fair price."

The magistrate fumed, face turning sunset orange. "You have no authority over us."

Sarker pointed one slender finger off in a seemingly random direction. "Out there is a place called *away*. Go there."

"Who are you?" the magistrate demanded, his fists shaking.

Sarker yawned. He motioned to the men with him in the black capes. They drew swords on the magistrates, hemming them into a circle against one wall.

"What do you think you are doing?" the magistrate asked. "You will swing on a rope for this."

"Wrong again," Sarker said. "And to answer your question, these men are going to ensure you do as I say."

"We do not take orders from you," the magistrate said. His men reached for their weapons.

Sarker drew a small leather book from his coat pocket, opened it and flipped through it. "You are Senior Magistrate Ardos Bex, yes?" He did not wait for an answer before plowing on. "Born in Palatora but tell everyone you were born here in Kolchin. Father farmer, mother butter churner, fond of knitting pretty blankets. Brother Adem left for Westgate to join a mercenary company to fight in what has been labeled the Seventh Olbaranian War of Succession, never returned. You were a dock worker, river barge mate, dock watchman, and street captain before joining the local magistracy. You like to draw colorful birds and you aspire to be city governor one day. Am I close?"

The magistrate froze mid-step. "I..."

Sarker looked up at him. "You were about to say, *yes sir, you are quite correct, and furthermore I am going to get out of your way and let these people go.*"

"I was not going to say that."

"You are a magistrate, yes? The city of Kolchin is administered by a senior council, yes? They select a marshal to oversee the magistrates of every district, yes? And the current marshal of *this* district is named Everad, yes?"

The magistrate's brain seemed to melt and ooze out his ears. "What?"

"Please go ahead and fetch him," Sarker said.

"What?"

"Fetch Marshal Everad, your superior. We shall wait."

"No one fetches him."

Sarker yawned. "Tell him Toran Sarker is calling. We shall wait."

The senior magistrate growled but he relented. He sent a runner.

And they all waited.

Jathan did not know what to do. He kept glancing at Lyra, trying to give her a little head shake when no one was looking, to encourage her to gradually back away toward one of the exits in case things went sour, but she was never quite looking at the right moment.

Eventually an older man arrived, lanky but strong, wrapped in a dark ocean colored cloak. He appeared deeply annoyed. When he saw the Glasseye his eyes widened noticeably. "Sarker?"

"Everad, your dutiful men here seem to think you require them to arrest these two individuals. I have indicated to the contrary. I do hope I am not wrong. You aren't really going to have these two people arrested, are you?" Sarker gestured at Jathan and Lyra.

Marshal Everad glanced and them both, looked them up and down. He rolled his eyes. "No. No arrests. Call it off."

"Thank you," Sarker said. "That will be all."

Jathan did not believe what he just witnessed. *He just dismissed the city marshal as if he were some errand boy. Who the fuck is this?*

Marshal Everad turned and left without another word, leaving the stunned magistrates milling about like a wedge of stupefied ibises.

Sarker addressed the herd of cowed magistrates. "Feel free to do something or other with these various assorted dead bodies lying about. I have no interest in them. Do check the pockets. You never know when you might find something good." He winked at Jathan.

Jathan was too stunned to move.

"See you gone," the Glasseye said. He lifted one hand and shooed them like inconvenient children.

Jathan felt Lyra's hands clasp about his elbow. She dragged him away down the street.

The sound of men moving about faded away to nothing.

Lyra wrapped her arms around him. The sudden embrace startled him. His hands were slow to close in around her back, but when they did, he held onto her as if he was clinging desperately a ship's mast in a sea storm, to keep from being battered overboard by wind and wave.

He let his head drift down to her shoulder and closed his eyes. He slept for a thousand years. He opened his eyes. She was crying. So was he. Her sobs patted his ears, and her tears dripped onto the back of his neck.

"I'm sorry," he said. He didn't know what else to say.

"No need to be sorry," she said. She kissed him on the back of the head. "It's over now."

"I know. It's the end of everything."

"And the beginning." She looked him hard in the eyes. She made a face as if she suddenly remembered some clever jest. Her eyes widened. "We need to get you to a physician."

He laughed. "I almost forgot."

A block away. Over a bridge. Through a tunnel. Into an atrium and out the other side. Into a wide intersection where five streets of Tenement Lane came together at once. It was the brightest, most open space in the whole warren, with a wide view of the blue sky, and views down each of those streets.

That was where they chose to spring their ambush.

Men in blue vests poured out of every alley and side street. Most had trousers of a color to match. *Ganger colors.* They came from the tunnels, and through the broken doors of closed down midnight cafes, unused in the daylight hours.

Blue on blue. That meant these belonged to old Vorlo Wauska.

Just like Ressic.

They were suddenly everywhere, blocking off every street, in front, behind, closing in on all sides. And a large group of them was coming up one of the five streets. Many of them had some part of the heads shaved down to stubble. Jathan saw not a single hand without a knife or a truncheon.

At the head of them was a man with as many scars on his face as he had wrinkles. His hair grew up and out into an ancient, weathered monument, white as clouds, bristly and coarse as a wire brush. His beard coiled about his chin making face look as thin as a goat's. One eye had become a milky white sea. The other was a sharp as a hawk's.

Vorlo Wauska himself.

He was either the most notorious of the infamous, or the most infamous of the notorious. A bloodthirsty man, and callous. Put down women and children, it was said. A man who held grudges, whose memory was as long as the world was wide. If he came here himself, it meant this was not a courtesy.

"Jathan Algevin," the old man said, stepping out in front of the others until he was in the middle of the intersection, a mere ten paces away from where Jathan and Lyra stood.

They know my name.

"Not good," Jathan agreed. *Old Vorlo himself has my name on his tongue. He only learns the names of dead men.*

"I know you know who I am," Wauska said. "People who have never met me know my name. Care to know why?"

Lyra never stopped dragging him along.

Jathan could barely get a word out. So he picked some choice ones. "Fuck you."

"Because I have a reputation," Wauska went on. "There are certain expectations that come with my name. One of those expectations is that when you raise a hand to my enforcers you must pay the price. And I don't mean in gold coins."

"Not us," Jathan said. "Didn't do it."

"Funny you should say that. My informants saw you in here with my son. You were the last person to see him alive."

Ressic. Damn all the fucking gods at once. He knows about Ressic. "I heard... he took a...wrong turn at night."

Wauska ignored him. "When they found him, they said he was opened up like an animal carcass."

Jathan pleaded with his mouth to voice the words. "We...have... nothing...to do...with that."

"My son died like an animal. And you were with him, I am told. Tell me, Jathan Algevin. What happened to my son?"

"If he walked...into...Tenement Lane, that's his problem." He dripped blood onto the pavement from his many wounds. He felt his strength waning. He was leaning more and more onto Lyra to keep himself upright.

"You are lying to me," Wauska said. "With every word. You ought to know what happens to the ones who do that."

"Maybe I just don't give a fuck," Jathan said. His legs were close to putty. His hands felt so cold. He shivered. "Maybe your son just deserved it. Maybe he was just a little piece of shit that the world finally scraped of its boot."

Vorlo Wauska's face soured so hard he might as well have bit into a lemon. "We're going to cut you open all the way down," he said. "We're going to place bets on how many of your organs we can pull out and smash in front of your eyes before you die."

Lyra was so focused on dragging him to a physician she ignored every word. Jathan was proud of her for not giving them the satisfaction.

"I am bored to hell and back with all your talk," Jathan said. "Just get on with it."

Wauska smirked. He waved his men forward resignedly.

Like a flock of birds, they pressed in as one, weapons at the ready, a blue on blue ocean surging ashore in a storm.

Jathan felt Lyra's grip tighten about him. He wished she would just leave him and float herself away like a bird, but she wouldn't. His big sister was going to protect him to the very end.

Just then a loud boom slapped his ears. The shockwave sucked the breath out of him, and he gasped. The vibration fluttered the liquid in his eyes.

The gangers all stopped. Some backed away, others looked all around, every direction, even up.

Jathan knew what it had to be. Magick. Invisible. If he had the strength to fish the monocle out of his pocket, he surely would have seen the afterglow of whatever had been rendered into reality to create that concussive blast.

Jathan saw heads poke up from the rooftops. Dozens, hundreds. They were suddenly everywhere, blocking off every street, in front, behind, closing in on all sides. They came from the tunnels, and through the broken doors of closed down midnight cafes. They came from everywhere Wauska's people had, only these people were surrounding the gangers.

Jathan turned his head all around. Every rooftop was full. Every street was blocked off. He saw people wearing clothes covered in patches, sewed and repaired so often it was difficult to tell which was the original fabric. He saw rough leather and old coats, shoes that didn't match.

Lyra never looked up at any of them. She would not be distracted from pulling him to safety.

"You are not welcome!" someone called down from atop one of the roofs.

Everyone turned to look. Even Jathan. He saw Jansi Wake there, with Wikal Shine standing on one side of her, and Lanhamer Rise the other. Behind them were a dozen more.

"Who said that?" Vorlo Wauska asked. "Who decided their own death today?"

"My name is Lanhamer Rise, and you will not hurt us any longer."

"Dead man," Wauska said. "Dead, dead, dead. Get him. Get that man. Bring him to me dead."

A handful of Wauska's gangers made to cross the intersection to the find an entrance to the building.

Wikal stepped up to the edge next, hands folded patiently behind his back, a calm patience in his smile. "Get out! You don't belong here anymore! You will never harm the people who live here ever again!"

Wauska was so furious he was exhaling steam. "I'm Vorlo Wauska. Wauska! Do you hear? No one tells a man with that name what to do." He snapped his fingers and more men moved on the door, trying to force it open to find the stairs within that would let them up to take Lanhamer.

But the door opened on its own.

Jathan saw a single man there, wild hair, and a gentle raging fire in his eyes. He recognized Ben Shine. The teacher, Mister Shine, who had been training the little boy before that sorcerer had taken his life. Ben had been living in the shadow of the god murderer for his entire adult life, forced to hide day and night. He looked like he had been waiting a long time for this day.

He stretched his arms out to either side. The air swelled and waved like a mirage. Three of Wauska's men shrieked, as first their clothes, and then their skin burst into flames. They collapsed screaming, and they kept screaming as the fires consumed them.

In the time it took Jathan to blink, massive invisible objects flew through the air, smashing holes through two more of the gangers. Then another two. Then two more. Jathan could not see the objects, but he knew their size by how wide were the holes that smashed perfectly through each man.

It was terrifying to behold. Every bit as terrifying as Seber Geddakur. But this time it was killing to throw off a yoke, not to keep one on. That made it beautiful.

Ben finally stopped when there were no more gangers around the door. He stared down those that remained. His fists glowed like a raging fire, and shimmering golden beams extended from his hands like swords made of sunset. He bent his knees and held them up in a fighting stance, ready to greet whoever was willing to try.

"You will pay for this," Wauska said. "That much I know."

Lanhamer smiled down at him from the rooftop. He pointed one finger back down the street. "The way out is over there. Good luck."

His own enforcers fled two, three at a time down the street without bothering to wait for a command. Three quarters bolted immediately. Half of those remaining waited long enough to eye each other before doing the same. That left only Vorlo Wauska and his personal bodyguards.

Wauska clearly didn't believe what was happening. That was the only possible thing that explained his actions. He charged toward the building, threatening to climb its sheer walls. His own lieutenants had to drag him away. He screamed at them all the way down the street and for a while longer still after they were out of sight, until finally the winding streets of Tenement Lane swallowed the sounds altogether.

The people of Tenement Lane cheered and crossed the intersection to pump their fists and sing as loud as they could the songs which before they had only been able to hum in hushed whispers. They had a long road to travel, and many challenges along it before they made change in this city, but it was a beginning.

Jathan looked up at Jansi. She seemed dazed. He knew that look. He has seen it in his own reflection before. It was the look of someone who had fought a war with every part of their soul for all their life, and now it was over, their duty done, with no way to know what to do with the rest of their life. He was curious to find out what path she would choose to follow from here.

He didn't shed a tear for her for that. It was a good problem to have.

Jansi noticed him looking up at her. She winked.

He nodded to her. *It's yours now.*

She knew.

She smiled wide. It was the first time he remembered seeing her do that.

He smiled to her as well.

He heard her voice in his head. *If I ever see you here again, I'll be just as likely to kill you as to taste your lips, stupid boy.* No words more perfectly summed up who she was. He would cherish hearing those words for the rest of his life.

"What are you looking at?" Lyra asked him. He heard worry in her voice.

"It's up to her now," Jathan said.

"Up to who? Jathan, stay with me." She seemed upset.

He realized he had never told her about Jansi. "Now that the gangers are gone, I mean."

"Who? Jathan, please." His sister sounded frantic. She was pulling his shoulders.

"Are we safe? Are they coming after us? Where are we?"

"Stay calm. Stay with me. We are the only ones here. No one is coming. It's just us. Please stay with me."

"Okay."

He just smiled up at Jansi and she smiled back.

She seemed suddenly far away, a speck on a distant mountain. He was floating down a river away from it.

He looked down. It was not a river, only a street beneath him, seated up on it, pulled away, his legs trailing after him.

Lyra was dragging him away. He forgot why. He left a trail of blood on the ground behind him. That was odd. It made him think that something was wrong. Lyra's arms were under his shoulders. He felt the scrape of the street beneath him, but it didn't hurt. Nothing did. It was strange. He usually walked beside his sister wherever they went. Odd that he wasn't this time.

Jansi Wake was gone away behind him with her people. It felt strange to be seeing her in the daytime, when she wasn't wrapped in shadows. He liked seeing her under the sunlight. He wondered what she would do without the darkness.

He looked up at the sky, hemmed in between the high grey stone walls on either side. It looked the way Tenement Lane always did. He wondered if he would ever see those streets again. It had been ages since he had been there.

He wanted to see Nessa. He was sure she was waiting for him for some reason. He knew he had to get back to her to tell her something. He just couldn't remember what. But it was important. She was waiting. He knew she was.

He felt very tired. So tired he couldn't remember the last time he had felt so tired. His eyes refused to stay open. He wanted to keep looking. He wanted to keep seeing. But they just kept closing.

He glanced up at Lyra. "Where are we going?" he asked.

She had tears in her eyes. He patted her on the arm with one hand. She was always in such a hurry. Going some place more important than any he would ever see.

His eyes kept closing and closing and closing. His head sagged down until his chin sat on his chest. She was pulling him along and he wondered why. His eyes closed. And then they wouldn't open anymore.

21

Now And From Now On

THE SHIP WAS READY to sail by daybreak, the first morning after Jathan could take steps on his own again.

Jathan and Lyra sat side by side on the deck, watching the sea splashing and whorling around the bay, listening to the chirping gulls and distant waves.

"I can't believe we are finally doing this," Lyra said.

Jathan folded his arms, a sleek new black cane sitting across his lap. "I still don't know what *this* even is."

"Looking ahead," she said. "Taking the first step into the future."

Thinking about the future hurt. Every part of him in the present hurt already, and he knew there was only more of the same in store.

He was infinitely aware of the aching bloody cavities in his flesh, still suppurating into the wads of bandaging over them, his reminders of the moment when he had been a dead man. Memorials to that one instant of terror when the sorcerer had blasted holes through him.

I should be dead. And maybe he was dead. *Am I even the same person?*

Jathan had been so sure he was going to die, but somehow he lived. He laughed at the absurd impossibility of it. Seber missed just wide enough, and Lyra dragged him just fast enough, and Trabius had been just skilled enough to see that at least one more sunrise would splash across his face.

One more became fifty more. And then he lost count. And now here they were.

He spat over the edge into the sea. He watched it vanish into the immensity of the water, the wide world swallowing what would have left a mark on any street in his city. "Do you regret living here? With me? All these years?"

"No," Lyra said. "Never. I cherish every moment we had here. Every moment. Being in that house brought us back together and kept us together when the powers that be wanted to shuffle us off alone to the spots they picked for us. I love that house, Jathan. It is the reason we are who we are."

Jathan shrugged. "Makes you think. If our aunt hadn't been so generous..."

"Or if our uncle hadn't had so much money to leave her when he went to everwonder..."

Jathan laughed.

Lyra sighed, but still she smiled at the distant place where the sky met the sea. "If I ever do find someone to have a life with, to have children with, and if we have a child, I will name him for our sweet aunt or uncle."

"So Dresa or Aren, eh? Neither seem particularly noteworthy."

She elbowed him. "That is my child whose name you are disparaging."

"Hypothetical child," Jathan said. "I'll believe it when I see the proof of the existence of a man who could possibly deserve you."

She leaned over and bumped her shoulder against his. "I'm glad you found someone you deserve. While you had the chance." She nodded at Nessifer, clambering up the gangplank with another set of carry-bags and rucksacks full of whatever old tomes, scrolls, maps, quills, ink, she convinced the Historian to part with.

"I don't think I deserve her," Jathan said. "And I am definitely *not* the man she deserves. Not yet. But I hope to be one day."

Lyra made a little frown at him, but her eyes were still smiling. She put a hand to his shoulders and squeezed, one then the other, back and forth, back and forth. "When you say things like that, I have hope for you yet, sweet brother."

He turned to her. "No more lies. Right?"

She squinted, a confused smile spreading on her face. "No more lies, Jathan."

"Do you remember the night after the Chal's Day festival?"

She nodded.

"The one where we all went to the Rusty Salvage?"

Lyra's face turned suspicious. "Yes."

"And I had just won that show-four contest in the goldcards tournament?"

She blinked.

"And I spent a lot of it on wine for our table. But especially a lot for me..."

"Jathan." She was angry now. Very angry.

"And for Nessa..."

"You shitty little rat!" She punched him. Numerous times. In his wounded shoulder. He lost count quickly. "You rotten messy shit garbage waste eating dung face!"

He held up his hands in surrender. "Why are you hitting me?"

She stopped. "I don't know. Probably because you are a rat who keeps fraternizing with my friends."

"Just the one. Now and from now on."

That seemed to set her at ease. "I'm happy you are coming with me. To see the world."

"The world is a big place. I doubt we have time to see the whole world. We will be able to see maybe three places."

She jabbed him. "We will see the world. We will do great things. Things that would have made our parents proud. Now and from now on."

"I want you to tell me about them, Lyra. I want to know about the part of them that I couldn't see."

"I will tell you everything, sweet brother. Now and from now on."

"I hope I can be as good as our parents. When I have a child, I mean."

"You will be. I have no doubt." She laughed. "I hope your future children are just like you, Jathan. I hope they never ever pick up a sword."

"I have never touched a sword my whole life. If they are going to be anything at all like me, then they will have no interest in a blade."

Nessa sat down behind them. "What are you two whispering about?"

"Jathan was just telling me how beautiful he thinks you are," Lyra said.

"No, he wasn't," Nessa said. "He doesn't talk like that, and you were making far too serious faces for it to be about me."

"We were trying to decide where to go next," Lyra said.

Nessifer rolled her eyes. "We haven't even seen Samartania yet. We haven't even left the damn port in Kolchin. I forbid the both of you from talking about where next until we've been to at least *one* place first."

"Fine," Lyra said, hopping to her feet as the leaving bell rang out. "Off we go. Now and from now on."

As the ship edged away from the wharf, Lyra turned to him. "Don't you want to look back once more, Jathan? To see our city one last time?"

He kept his eyes fixed firmly on the sea. He made a sour face. She couldn't see it and he didn't want her to. "No," he said. "I've seen enough."

The ship coasted out over the open water. The water was a promise. A promise of things to come. Things he didn't yet know. Things he couldn't control. Things he would soon find out.

I will not look back any longer. I lived my whole life that way and look where it got me. I was so busy looking back I couldn't see what was right here before me. I was a fool. I spent half a lifetime only looking at where I'd been.

For once in my life, I am going to look where I'm going.

Now and from now on.

He reached into his pocket and let his fingers brush over the familiar shape of the Jecker monocle. It brought a calm to him to know it was there. To know it would always be by his side if he needed it.

His hand already wanted to draw it out and hold it to his eye.

There was no reason why.

There was nothing to look at.

There was nothing to see.

There would be nothing to find here.

Nothing but wide open sea.

But he wanted to look through it again anyway.

The monster needed to be fed.

THE

END

Appendix: Magick

MAGICK - the creation of any unnatural result in reality by drawing out (pulling) streams of altered reality (also referred to as streams of possibility) from the source of infinite possibility (the Slipstream). It is a means by which those who are born with such a skill may temporarily and locally rewrite the laws that govern reality itself, such as making physical shapes out of nothing, changing temperatures, altering the buoyancy of a ship, increasing pressure, changing the way light bends, altering the heat conductivity of metal, multiplying gravitation, swapping the inertia of two object, generating friction between objects that are not in contact, etc.

General Terminology:

AFTERGLOW - the residual patterns of colored particles that occur when any streams have been brought together into reality. The quantity, color, and brightness of the afterglow is determined by the types of renders created, their magnitude, and how much time has elapsed since the render was created. They are most often invisible to the naked eye, but can sometimes be visible when fresh. All afterglow decays over time (both true visible afterglow, and that which can only be seen through a Jecker monocle) and eventually disappears completely.

BLANK IMPULSE - the most common form of render, composed of a specific two- or three-dimensional shape with a certain mass and velocity placed inside it, set to start at a specific location, and either remain still or travel in a certain direction for a certain duration.

BLUESHIFT - a tinge of blueness to the core color particles specific to any individual magus. Indicates the magus is moving closer to the location of the residuals.

CAPTURE - the act of neutralizing and apprehending a rogue magus, the culmination of any Trace.

CORE COLOR - the color of the residual particles given off by the vibration of the *Introduction-of-Change* key pattern. This color never changes. They are the equivalent of eye color or hair color, and cannot by themselves positively identify a specific magus, but are commonly used to rule out afterglow with obviously incorrect core colors.

DECAY TIME - the time required for different forms and magnitudes of afterglow to become completely dispersed. The decay time can be affected by how confined a space they reside in, the altitude, the temperature, the presence of wind or water, or the presence of certain forms of smoke.

INTERDICTION - the act of using Stoppers in close proximity to a magus in order to take advantage of precedence effect, so that the magus would be cut off from access to the streams of magick he employs to render into magick.

JEBEL DEDDER MANUAL - the text that is still used as the primary source for the understanding of techniques and applications of magick, and how to recognize it. It is the textbook of all Render Tracers.

JECKER MONOCLE - an oval lens of ranum crystal, a mineral that is highly reactive to residual afterglow of magick. Attached to the primary lens are four filters: white, rose, green, and blue. Each filter is made of a different mineral, and can be slid into place over the primary lens. Each filter can be used individually, and the white, rose, and green can also be used in combination to expose different aspects of the afterglow.

Use of the Jecker monocle:

PRIMARY LENS - The primary lens of the Jecker monocle displays any ambient afterglow or sensitized fluorescence that has not decayed completely. However, the nature of the transposition of streams from the Slipstream into reality will also result in spatial warping, time arching, and quantum peaks, all of which can obscure subtle details of the afterglow.

BLUE FILTER - used only individually, and filters out most of the layers of afterglow caused by specific forces and specific renders, and thereby exposes the *Introduction-of-Change* pattern, as well as the core color of the introductory wave pattern particles. By studying the core color through the blue filter, it can be determined if the residuals are redshifting or blueshifting.

GREEN FILTER - filters out the quantum peaks caused by the altered reality and displays the Spectral Lines - the temporary scars left in reality after a render has existed, whether stationary or in motion. Any stationary force would leave faint lines in the air where the force was located, indicating its shape. Any force in motion would leave a haze of lines indicating the shape of the force and the direction of its motion through the air. The greater the strength of the force, the thicker and brighter the lines would be. This indicates the vectors of force, which can aid in determining the size, strength, direction, and position of forces used at a given scene. Streak lines decay at a slower rate than the colors of other afterglow, and can allow a Render Tracer to make some inferences about what occurred at a scene that is otherwise cold.

ROSE FILTER - filters out spatial warping caused by the altered reality and displays the Glow Curve - the bleeding of different afterglow colors into one another. This is an indicator of merging residuals, showing how the streams were used in combination to create each effect and how well they merged with reality. Knowing how magi combine streams allows a Render Tracer to identify common streams for Stoppers to look for during a capture.

WHITE FILTER - filters out time-arching caused by the altered reality and allows a Render Tracer to see how the residuals react to the warping of the afterglow alone, displaying the Prismatic Dispersion - the magnitude or power behind the forces used. This aids in determining magi strength and mastery of each render.

ROSE AND WHITE AND GREEN FILTER IN COMBINATION - filters out all side-effects of the altered reality and displays the Variants - these are the interruptions in the Resonance Spectrum. The breaks in the pattern show the separations that delineate each individual stream so that their patterns can be analyzed one at a time.

MAGI - anyone with the ability to both pull streams and combine them into renders.

PRECEDENCE EFFECT - a phenomena of the Slipstream in which a specific stream specific to a particular magus cannot be used by more than one magus or Stopper within a certain proximity (or even used twice by the same magus at the same time).

REDSHIFT - a tinge of redness to the core color particles specific to any individual magus. Indicates when magi are moving farther away from the location of their afterglow.

RENDER - a separate a distinct magick result generated by the combination and binding of multiple streams. A unified fabric of possibility translated into reality.

RENDER TRACER- anyone trained in the arts of detecting, tracing, and apprehending rogue magi. Often armed with tools that are reactive to the presence of the afterglow of magick. Commonly and derisively referred to as Glasseyes.

SENSITIZED FLUORESCENCE - the attaching of afterglow to people, clothes, or other physical objects that it comes into contact with, resulting in stains that can be seen through a Jecker monocle. These decay over time just as the afterglow itself. The decay time of sensitized fluorescence can be affected by washing with water, the use of certain herbs, and the smoke of certain plants.

SLIPSTREAM - the source of all streams, the realm of pure possibility that any magi must reach into with their minds in order to create magick.

STOPPERS - men trained to reach their minds into the Slipstream and hold the streams of a particular magus in order to prevent that magus from employing them to create magick.

STREAMS - the building blocks of magick that magi must match together and combine in a specific fashion in order to achieve a coherent result. A different stream is required for each aspect of the desired result.

TINWOOD LEAF - a plant with sedative properties that make concentration extremely difficult, and as concentration is critical to the pulling and binding of streams, it can render magi inert for as long as it lasts, and can be administered indefinitely. It is the most common method of sedating magi.

THE FIRES - the general term used to refer to the most common method of ensuring magi ares destroyed.

VECTORIC MAGICK - streams that are applied to any force to give it properties that allow it to interact with reality, and common to all magi. Examples: streams of direction, location, size, shape, velocity, etc.

Greetings from the Wasteland Metropolis.
My name is frequently Thomas Howard Riley.
I sincerely hope you enjoyed your time in Luminaworld.
Luminaworld always enjoys those who tumble down the rabbit hole.
But whether you did or not, please consider leaving an
honest review of your experience. It is the best way to help
others know whether this journey is right (or wrong) for them.
Your actions could help someone who needs to find this story.
Or spare someone time to find a different one entirely.
Please help your fellow reader.
Change someone's life.
Leave a review.

Thomas Howard Riley currently resides in a secluded grotto in the wasteland metropolis, where he reads ancient books, plays ancient games, watches ancient movies, jams on ancient guitars, and writes furiously day and night. He sometimes appears on clear nights when the moon is gibbous, and he has often been seen in the presence of cats.

He can be found digitally at
THOMASHOWARDRILEY.COM
where you may subscribe to his
luminous newsletter,
or as **@ornithopteryx** on Twitter.

CPSIA information can be obtained
at www.ICGtesting.com
Printed in the USA
LVHW100502161222
735278LV00008B/224